OTTO PENZLER PRESENTS
AMERICAN MYSTERY CLASSICS

THE PLAGUE COURT MURDERS

JOHN DICKSON CARR (1906-1977) was one of the greatest wii
ers of the American Golden Age mystery, and the only American
author to be included in England's legendary Detection Club
during his lifetime. Though he was born and died in the United
States, Carr began his writing career while living in England,
where he remained for nearly twenty years. Under his own name
and various pseudonyms, he wrote more than seventy novels and
numerous short stories, and is best known today for his locked-
room mysteries.

MICHAEL DIRDA is a Pulitzer Prize-winning critic and essay-
ist for *The Washington Post*, where he writes frequently about
neglected classics of genre fiction. His own books include four
collections of essays, the memoir *An Open Book*, and the 2012
Edgar Award-winning *On Conan Doyle*.

THE PLAGUE COURT MURDERS

JOHN DICKSON CARR

Introduction by
MICHAEL DIRDA

**AMERICAN
MYSTERY
CLASSICS**

Penzler Publishers
New York

Published in 2020 by Penzler Publishers
58 Warren Street, New York, NY 10007
penzlerpublishers.com

Distributed by W. W. Norton

Cover image: Andy Ross
Cover design: Mauricio Diaz

Paperback ISBN 9781613161975
Hardcover ISBN 9781613161968
eBook ISBN 9781613161982

Library of Congress Control Number: 2020923066

Printed in the United States of America

9 8 7 6 5 4 3 2 1

THE PLAGUE
COURT MURDERS

INTRODUCTION

FIRST PUBLISHED in 1934, *The Plague Court Murders* introduced Sir Henry Merrivale, the third of four great detectives created by John Dickson Carr (1906-1977). Initially based on Sherlock Holmes's smarter but sedentary elder brother Mycroft, with traits borrowed from Carr's own father and, later, from Winston Churchill, H.M., as he is sometimes called, would soon become one of the mystery genre's most beloved curmudgeons.

Carr's earliest books featured the sardonic and suave *juge d'instruction* Henri Bencolin, whose macabre cases often carried a whiff of brimstone about them, as their very titles tended to suggest: *It Walks By Night* (1930) *Castle Skull* (1931), *The Corpse in the Waxworks* (1932). Yet while still in his twenties, Carr devised a second sleuth extraordinaire, the larger-than-life, rumbustious Dr. Gideon Fell, whose girth, personality and mannerisms paid homage to that master of the impossible crime story, G.K. Chesterton. Fell first appeared in 1933's *Hag's Nook* and would go on to solve at least a half dozen of the most imaginative locked-room mysteries of all time, most notably *The Three Coffins* (1935), closely followed in chutzpah and ingenuity by *The Arabian Nights Murders* (1936) and *The Crooked Hinge* (1938).

Throughout the 1930s, the young Carr regularly produced four novels a year, never spending more than two months on any of them. After first working out a plot in his head, he would type at white-hot speed for hours on end, while sipping tea and smoking one cigarette after another. Such Georges Simenon-like intensity and focus led to compact, rapid-action books, often reminiscent of stage plays in that they typically preserved the classical unities of time, place and action.

Because Carr relied on his fiction to pay the bills, he needed to be prolific. However, his American publisher, Harper & Brothers, didn't want to bring out more than two of his mysteries each year. Thus was born Carter Dickson. Using this pen name, which fooled almost no one (and which the American Mysteries Classics series has decided to ignore), Carr created a new sleuth for William Morrow and Company, Sir Henry Merrivale. The latter's most celebrated case, 1938's *The Judas Window*, dazzles both as a howdunit and a narrative tour-de-force, being presented almost entirely as a courtroom drama. Robert Adey, compiler of the standard bibliography, *Locked Room Murders*, thought it "the best locked-room novel ever written."

By the end of the 1930s, Carr's glory years, he would write eleven books about Gideon Fell and ten featuring Merrivale. Yet that wasn't all. In 1936 he brought out a work of true-crime nonfiction, *The Murder of Sir Edmund Godfrey*, which examines a dozen possible solutions to a baffling seventeenth-century whodunit. Even the hypercritical Jacques Barzun and Wendell Hertig Taylor conclude—in *A Catalogue of Crime*—that it is "a classic in the best sense—i.e., rereadable indefinitely." Then in 1937, Carr produced what many people regard as his most jaw-droppingly brilliant novel, *The Burning Court*, a *sui generis* mind-boggler about which I will say nothing more except that it concerns witchcraft and was once as controversial as Agatha Christie's *The Murder of Roger Ackroyd*. In that same busy year, 1937, Carr would also launch his last important detective, Colonel March of Scotland Yard, who stars in a series of short stories published by *The Strand Magazine*. These were eventually collected in 1940 under the title *The Department of Queer Complaints*.

But to return to H.M. While Fell is essentially a scholar and historian (of England's drinking customs, among other subjects), Merrivale oversaw Britain's espionage operations during World War I and continues to keep an office in Whitehall. There, nearing age sixty when we first meet him in *The Plague Court Murders*, the peacetime spymaster naps when not improving his mind through the regular perusal of sensational literature. His door flaunts a sign reading "Busy!!! No Admittance!!! Keep Out!!!" and he hides his liquor in an office safe labeled "Important State Documents! Do Not Touch!!" The man himself is bald, corpulent and ornery, wears tortoise-shell glasses that slip down his nose, calls distinguished colleagues "fatheads," employs the terms "son" and "wench" as endearments, and sometimes acts like a naughty little boy or a comic buffoon. Nonetheless, he possesses a cold and deadly brain.

Douglas G. Greene—our leading authority on the life and work of John Dickson Carr—points out that the opening half of *The Plague Court Murders* is soaked in the lurid, Grand Guignol atmosphere characteristic of the Bencolin novels. Carr's narrator, Ken Blake, certainly piles on the Gothicky flourishes, describing the reputedly accursed London mansion of Plague Court as shadowy, suffocating, oozing, purulent, almost disease-ridden and contagious. Picture the House of Usher crossed with a *Tales from the Crypt* dungeon or a Hammer Films torture chamber. Reviewing Carr's novel when it first appeared, Dorothy L. Sayers shrewdly recognized that "it is the kind of thing to which you must willingly abandon yourself if you are to enjoy it." That's still good advice. She quickly added that this is well worth doing, especially "if you like being deliciously frightened into fits."

Carr's opening setup is this: On a wet and sinister night a spiritualist named Darworth plans to exorcise the evil that haunts Plague Court. To this end, he securely locks himself in a little house in its courtyard, while various followers and skeptics keep vigil nearby in the main residence. Ostensibly, the padlock and bolted door will confirm that Darworth's psychic powers are genuine. Instead, he is found dead inside his sealed chamber, stabbed multiple times, apparently by a killer who left no tracks and could pass through walls. Is Darworth, then, the latest victim of an ancient curse? Was the entrance to his refuge locked to keep him in—or to keep something out? Only a week earlier the spiritualist grew deeply agitated at a séance when his own automatic writing generated the ominous message: "Only seven more days." Most puzzling of all, exactly how was the murder committed? And by whom—or what?

Besides fostering an atmosphere of foreboding and intense eeriness, the first half of *The Plague Court Murders* emphasizes the mesmeric influence that Darworth has been exerting over his disciples, among them old Lady Benning, still mourning a beloved nephew who committed suicide, and Marion Latimer, a beautiful young heiress. Inspector Masters, an amateur ghostbuster in his spare time, conducts the murder investigation, along with the assistance of the energetic Sergeant McDonnell. There are tantalizing elements galore in these opening chapters, among them a dead cat, a peculiar awl-like knife, and a superb pastiche of a seventeenth-century diary relating the grisly activities of the hangman's assistant, the diabolical Louis Playge.

As one might expect, the police are utterly bewildered by the brutal crime and come the dawn, as Victorian novelettes used to say, they turn in desperation to Sir Henry Merrivale.

Carr once described his kind of mystery fiction as "the grandest game in the world," calling it "a hoodwinking contest, a duel between author and reader." The details upon which the detective builds his deductions must be fairly presented, yet before the final revelations we almost never properly grasp their significance. As Carr frequently maintained, "The fine detective story . . . is a ladder of clues, a pattern of evidence, joined together with such cunning that even the experienced reader may be deceived . . . until, in the blaze of the surprise-ending, he suddenly sees the whole design." The last thirty pages of *The Plague Court Murders* actually deliver a double or even triple whammy, as one shocking disclosure succeeds another.

John Dickson Carr excelled at almost every aspect of the fair-play mystery story. He aimed to entertain and he does. His narrative pace seldom flags. To quote Sayers again, he can swiftly "lead us away from the small artificial, brightly-lit stage of the ordinary detective plot into the menace of outer darkness. He can create atmosphere with an adjective." Certainly, no night-club conjuror was ever more adept at misdirection and hocus-pocus. Yet even when Carr's characters seem as conventional as those of Agatha Christie, he often keys his plots to unsettling, psycho-sexual secrets.

Moreover, in his best novels Carr almost effortlessly conveys a feeling of unease and wrongness, of mental vertigo. What is real? What is mere smoke and mirrors? Some people complain that the solutions to most locked-room mysteries are overly elaborate and improbable. Certainly, Carr's own favorite, Gaston Leroux's 1907 *The Mystery of the Yellow Room*, requires considerable suspension of disbelief. No matter. "The whole test," argues Carr, "is, *can* the thing be done? If so, the question of whether it *would* be done does not enter into it." To see what a master magician can do, and John Dickson Carr at his best is nothing less than a Houdini, you have only to start reading *The Plague Court Murders*. Enjoy the show!

—MICHAEL DIRDA

THE PLAGUE
COURT MURDERS

I
THE HOUSE IN PLAGUE COURT

OLD MERRIVALE, that astute and garrulous lump who sits with his feet on the desk at the War Office, has been growling again for somebody to write the story of the Plague Court murders; chiefly, it is believed, to glorify himself. He does not have so much glory nowadays. His department has ceased to be called the Counter-Espionage Service; it has become merely the M.I.D., and its work is somewhat less dangerous than taking photographs of the Nelson Monument.

I have pointed out to him that neither of us has any connection with the police, and that, since I left his service some years ago, I have not even his excuse. Besides, our friend Masters—now Chief Inspector of the Criminal Investigation Department—might not like it. I was, therefore, inveigled into playing a cold poker-hand to determine whether I should write it, or somebody else. I forget who the other person was to be, but it was not Sir Henry Merrivale.

My own connection with the case began on the night of September 6, 1930: the rainy night when Dean Halliday walked into the smoking-room of the Noughts-and-Crosses Club and made his startling statements. And one fact must be emphasized. Had it not been for the streak of morbidity that ran through his whole family—as witness James—or possibly for Dean's fits of hard drinking during the years he was in Canada, he would never have reached a dangerous state of nerves. You saw him at the club, wiry and vital in his movements, with his sandy mustache, his young-old face and reddish hair, his heavy forehead above sardonic eyes. Yet you invariably felt there was a shadow there— some snag out of the past. Once, in one of those casual shifting discussions, somebody was haranguing us about the newest scientific terms for madness; and Halliday said suddenly, blasting the talk with the personal, "You never know, do you? My brother James, now—" Then he laughed.

I had known him for some time before we became at all friendly. We used to fall into casual conversation in the smoking-room at the club. What I knew of Halliday—for we never talked of personal matters—was fired at me by my sister, who happened to be well acquainted with Lady Benning, Halliday's aunt.

He was, it appeared, the younger son of a tea-importer who had got so rich that he could refuse a title, and say that his firm was too old for that sort of thing. The old man, Dean's father, had side-whiskers and a turkeycock nose. He was sour enough to his associates, but fairly indulgent toward his sons. The real head of the family, however, was Lady Benning, his sister.

Dean went through a number of phases. Before the war, as an undergraduate, he was one of the customary down-from-Cambridge bloods. Then the war came along. Like a number of others, the drawler suddenly became an amazingly good soldier. He left the army with a D. S. O. and a lot of shrapnel inside, and then started raising hell in earnest. There was trouble; a dubious nymph sued for breach of promise; family portraits wriggled with horror; and, with that happy British optimism which decides that bad ways always change if they are practiced somewhere else, Dean was packed off to Canada.

Meantime, his brother had inherited Halliday and Son at the death of the old man. Brother James was Lady Benning's favorite and darling; James was this, James was that, James was a model of soft-spoken rectitude and precision. . . . The truth of the matter lay in the fact that James was a decayed little prig. He used to go on ostensible business-trips and lie speechlessly fuddled in bawdy houses for two-week periods, then slip back quietly to Lancaster Gate, with his hair brushed straight again, complaining resignedly of his health. I knew him slightly—a smiling man always in a mild sweat, who couldn't sit still in a chair. All this mightn't have hurt him, if it hadn't been for what he called his conscience. His conscience got him, presently. He went home one night and shot himself.

Lady Benning was distracted. She had never liked Dean—I think it probable that, in some obscure way, she held him responsible for James's death—but now it was necessary to recall him as head of the family from his nine year exile.

He had sobered down, but he still had enough of the old humorous devil to make him good (sometimes dangerous) company. He had seen men and places. He had acquired a tolerant droop of the eyelid. Also, there was about him a certain fresh vitality and frankness which must have disturbed the somnolent air round Lancaster Gate. You liked his grin. He was very fond of beer, detective stories, and poker. Anyhow, things seemed to be going well for the returned prodigal; but I think he was lonely.

Then something happened. It was more than unexpected, because I had heard from my sister, a short time before, that he was "understood" to be engaged to be married. After mentioning the girl's name as Marion Latimer, my sister had enlivened the afternoon with a rapid and Tarzan-like inspection of her family tree. When the branches were all tested, my sister had smiled grimly over her folded hands, looked in a sinister fashion at the canary, and said she hoped it would turn out all right.

But something had happened. Halliday was one of those people who carry their own atmospheres about with them. We felt it at the club, though he spoke to us as usual. Nobody said anything; Halliday would glance at us sharply, and try to be the jolly good fellow; and afterwards he would look confused. There was something wrong with his laugh. He used it too often, and spilled cards on the table when he shuffled sometimes, because he had not been looking at them. This went on for a week or two, not very pleasantly. Then, after a time, he stopped coming altogether.

One night I was sitting in the smoking-room after dinner. I had just ordered coffee, and I was in one of those thick sloughs of boredom where every face looks vapid; where you wonder why the whole rushing, solemn routine of a city doesn't get sick of its own nonsense and stop. It was a wet night, and the big, brown-leather smoking-room was deserted. I was sitting idly near the fire making nothing of a newspaper, when Dean Halliday walked in.

I sat up a little—there was something in the way he walked. He hesitated, looked around, and stopped again. He said, "Hullo, Blake," and sat down some distance away.

The silence was doubly uncomfortable. What he thought was in the air, was all about, was as palpable as the fire at which he was staring. He wanted to ask me something, and couldn't. I noticed that his shoes and the edges of his trousers were muddy, as though he had been walking far; he seemed unconscious of the damp-extinguished cigarette between his fingers. There was no humor now in the low chin, the high forehead, the high-muscled jaws.

I crackled my newspaper. Remembering it afterwards, I think it was then my eye caught a small headline towards the foot of the first page: "STRANGE THEFT AT—" but I did not read it at the time, or notice any more.

Halliday inflated his chest. Quite suddenly he looked up.

"Look here, Blake," he said in a sort of rush. "I regard you as a pretty level-headed fellow. . . ."

"Why don't you tell me about it?" I suggested.

"Ah," he said, and sat back in his chair; and looked at me steadily. "If you won't think I'm a jabbering ass. Or an old woman. Or—" As I shook my head he interposed: "Wait, Blake. Wait a bit. Before I tell you about it, let me ask you whether you're willing to give me a hand in what you'll probably call an idiotic business. I want you to . . ."

"Go on."

"To spend the night in a haunted house," said Halliday.

"What's idiotic about that?" I asked, trying to conceal the fact that my boredom had begun to disappear; I felt an anticipatory pleasure, and my companion seemed to notice it.

He laughed a little, now. "Right. I say, this is better than I'd hoped for!—I didn't want you to think I was crazy, that's all. You see, *I'm* not interested in the blasted business; or I wasn't. They may return, or they may not. I don't know. All I do know is that, if matters keep on in the present way, then—I'm not exaggerating—two lives are going to be ruined."

He was very quiet now, staring at the fire, speaking in an absent voice.

"Six months ago, you see, the whole thing would have seemed wildly absurd. I knew Aunt Anne was going to a medium—or mediums. I knew she had persuaded Marion to go along with her. Well, damn it—I couldn't see any harm in that." He shifted. "I suppose I thought of it, if I thought about it at all, as a fad like bagatelle or jigsaw puzzles. I certainly supposed that Marion at least would keep her sense of humor. . . ." He looked up. "I'm forgetting something. Tell me, Blake. Do *you* believe?"

I said I would always be prepared to accept satisfactory evidence, but that I had never come on it as yet.

"I wonder," he mused. " 'Satisfactory evidence'. Ha. What the devil is it, anyhow?" His short brown hair had tumbled partly across his forehead; his eyes were full of a hot, baffled anger; and muscles tightened down his jaws. "I think the man's a charlatan. Well and good. But I went myself to a God-forsaken house—alone—nobody else there—nobody knew I was going. . . .

"Listen, Blake. I could tell you the whole story, if you insist on knowing. I don't want you to walk in blindfold. But I'd rather you didn't ask *anything*. I want you to go with me, tonight, to a certain house in London; to tell me whether you see or hear anything; and, if you do, whether you can explain it on natural grounds. There'll be no difficulty about getting into the house. It belongs to our family, as a matter of fact. . . . Will you go?"

"Yes. You expect a trick, then?"

Halliday shook his head. "I don't know. But I can't tell you how grateful I'd be. I don't suppose you've had any experience in these matters? Old empty house—things. . . . Good God, if I only knew more people! If we could get somebody to go with us who knew all about fake. . . . What are you laughing at?"

"You need a good stiff drink. I wasn't laughing. I was only thinking that I knew our man, provided you don't object——"

"Object?"

"To a Detective-Inspector from Scotland Yard."

Halliday stiffened. "Don't talk rot. Above everything else, I don't want the police in on this. Forget it, I tell you! Marion would never forgive me."

"Oh, not in an official capacity, you understand. Masters makes rather a hobby of this." I smiled again, thinking of Masters the unruffled, Masters the ghost-breaker; the big, stout, urbane man who was as pleasant as a cardsharper and as cynical as Houdini. During the spiritualistic craze that took England after the war, he was a detective-sergeant whose chief business was the exposing of bogus mediums. Since then his interest had increased (apologetically) into a hobby. In the workshop of his little house at Hampstead, surrounded by his approving children, he tinkered with ingenious devices of parlor magic; and was altogether highly pleased with himself.

I explained all this to Halliday. First he brooded, ruffling the hair at his temples. Then he turned a flushed, grim, rather eager face.

"By Jove, Blake, if you can get him—! You understand, we're not investigating mediums now: we're only going to a supposedly haunted house...."

"Who says it's haunted?"

There was a pause. You could hear tangled motor-horns shrilling and squawking outside the windows.

"I do," he said quietly. "Can you get in touch with this detective-fellow at once?"

"I'll 'phone him." I got up, stuffing the newspaper into my pocket. "I shall have to tell him something of where we're going, you know."

"Tell him anything. Tell him—stop a bit! If he knows anything about London ghosts," said Halliday grimly, "just tell him 'the house in Plague Court'. That'll fetch him."

The house in Plague Court! As I went out to the lobby and the telephone, some dubious memory stirred, but I could not place it.

Masters' slow, deep voice was a pleasant sanity over the telephone.

"Ah!" said he. "Ah, sir? And how are *you?* Haven't seen you in a dog's age. Well, and is anything on your mind?"

"A good deal," I told him, after the amenities. "I want you to go ghost-hunting. Tonight, if you can manage it."

"Hum!" remarked the unsurprised Masters, as though I had asked him to go to the theater. "You've hit my weakness, you know. Now, if I can manage it. . . . What's it all about, then? Where are we to go?"

"I've been instructed to tell you 'the house in Plague Court'. Whatever that means."

After a pause, there came over the phone a distinct whistle.

"Plague Court! Have you got anything?" Masters inquired, rather sharply. He sounded startlingly professional now. "Has it anything to do with that business at the London Museum?"

"I don't know what the devil you're talking about, Masters. What's the London Museum got to do with it? All I know is that a friend of mine wants me to investigate a haunted house, tonight, if possible, and bring an experienced ghost-layer along. If you'll come here as soon as you can, I'll tell you all I know. But 'London Museum'——"

Another hesitation, while Masters clucked his tongue. "Have you seen today's paper, then? No? Well, have a look at it. Find the account of the London Museum business, and see what you make of it. We thought that 'lean man with his back turned' might have been somebody's imagination. But maybe it wasn't. . . . Yes, I'll catch the tube—you're at the 'Noughts-and-Crosses', you say?—right! I'll meet you there in an hour. I don't like this business, Mr. Blake. I don't like it at all. Good-by."

My pennies clinked in the telephone, and were gone.

II

WE HEAR OF A LEAN MAN,
AND GO ON AN ERRAND

An hour afterwards, when the porter came in to tell us that
Masters was waiting in the Visitors' Room, Halliday and I were
still talking over that notice we had missed in the morning paper.
It was one of a series of feature articles headed: "*Today's Strange
Story—No. 12.*"

STRANGE THEFT AT LONDON MUSEUM

Weapon Missing From
"Condemned Cell"

Who Was the "Lean Man with His Back Turned"?

At the London Museum, Lancaster House, Stable Yard, St.
James's, there occurred yesterday afternoon one of those thefts
of relics sometimes committed by souvenir-hunters; but in this
case the circumstances were unusual, puzzling, and the cause of
some apprehension.

A history of blood and villainy surrounds many of the exhibits in the basement of this famous museum, where are displayed Thorp's Models of Old London.

In one large room, used mostly for the display of prison relics, is a life-size model of a condemned cell at old Newgate Prison, made of the bars and timbers from the original cell. On the wall—unticketed—hung what is described as a crudely fashioned steel dagger about eight inches long, with a clumsy hilt and a bone handle on which were cut the letters L. P. It disappeared yesterday afternoon between 3 and 4 o'clock. Nobody knows the thief.

Your correspondent visited the place, and confesses he received a start at the realism of the condemned cell. The whole room is grim enough—low and duskily lighted. There is the original grated door of Newgate, ponderous in rusty bolts, salvaged in 1903. There are manacles, legirons, huge, corroded keys and locks, cages, torture-instruments. Occupying one wall, in neat frames, are bills and popular broadsides of old executions from several centuries—all bordered in black, printed in smeary type, with a grisly woodcut showing the butchery, and the pious conclusion, "*God Save the King.*"

The condemned cell, built into one corner, is not for children. I say nothing of a real "prison smell" which seems to cling to it; of the real terror and despair conveyed by this rotting hole. But I want to congratulate the artist who made that shrunken-faced wax effigy in its rags of clothes, which seems to start up off the bed as you look inside.

Still, it is all one to ex-Segt. Parker, who has served as attendant here for eleven years. And this is what he says:

"It was about three o'clock in the afternoon. Yesterday was a 'free day' and there were lots of children. I could hear a party of them going through the next rooms, making a good deal of noise.

"I was sitting near the window, some distance away from the cell, looking at a newspaper. It was a dull day, foggy, and the light bad. So far as I thought, there was nobody else in that room."

Then Sergeant Parker had what he can only describe as a "queer feeling." He looked up. And, though he had thought there was nobody else in the room:

"There was a gentleman standing at the door of the cell over there, with his back to me, looking in.

"I can't describe him, except that he was very lean, and had darkish clothes on. He seemed to be moving his head slowly, and sort of jerkily, as though he wanted to take a good look at the cell but had trouble with his neck. I wondered how he had got there without my hearing and supposed he had come through the other door. I went back to my paper again. But I kept getting that queer feeling; so, to satisfy myself, just before all the children came in, I went over and looked into the cell.

"First I couldn't tell what was wrong, and then it struck me: that knife, hanging up over the effigy, was missing. Of course, the man was gone, and I knew he had got it, and I reported it."

Sir Richard Meade-Browne, curator of the museum, commented later:

"I trust you will broadcast, through the columns of your newspaper, an appeal for public cooperation to stop this vandalism of valuable relics."

The dagger, Sir Richard stated, was listed as the gift of J. G. Halliday, Esq., and was dug up in 1904 on the grounds of a property belonging to him. It is conjectured to have been the property of one Louis Playge, Common Hangman of the Borough of Tyburn in the years 1663-65. Being of doubtful authenticity, however, it was never exhibited as such.

No trace of the thief has been found. Detective-Sergeant McDonnell, of Vine Street, is in charge.

Now all this was, if you will, a journalist's stunt; a penny-a-liner's way of making copy on a dull day. I read it first standing in the lobby of the club, after I had telephoned to Masters, and then I wondered whether I ought to show it to Halliday.

But I put it into his hands when I returned to the smoking-room, and watched his face while he read it.

"Steady!" I said. For the freckles began to start out against his changing face as he read it; then he got up uncertainly, looked at me for a moment, and threw the paper into the fire.

"Oh, that's all right," he said. "You needn't worry. This only relieves my mind. After all—this is *human,* isn't it? I was worrying about something else. This man Darworth, this medium, is behind it; and the plan, whatever it is, is at least human. The suggestion in that blasted article is absurd. What's the man trying to say?—that Louis Playge came back after his own knife?"

"Masters is coming," I said. "Don't you think it would be better if you told us something about it?"

He shut his jaws hard. "No. You made a promise, and I'll hold you to it. I won't tell you—yet. When we start out for the infernal place, I'll stop by at my flat and get you something which will explain a good deal; but I don't want you to see it now. . . . Tell me something. They say that a soul on the lower plane, a malevolent one, is always watchful and always cunning. That this one mass of dead evil is always waiting for the opportunity to take possession of a living body, and change the weak brain for its own, just as it infests a house. Do you think, then, that the clot could take possession . . . ?"

He hesitated. I can still see him standing in the firelight, a curious deprecating smile on his face, but a fierce stare in his red-brown eyes.

"You're talking rot now," I said sharply. "And you've confused your facts. Take possession! Of what?"

"Of me," said Halliday quietly.

I said what he needed was not a ghost-breaker, but a nerve-specialist. Then I dragged him off to the bar and saw that he swallowed a couple of whiskies. He was submissive; he even achieved a sort of satirical jollity. When we returned to the newspaper article, as we did again and again, he seemed again his old, lazy, amused self.

Still, it was a relief to see Masters. We found Masters standing in the Visitors' Room: large and rather portly, with his bland shrewd face, his sedate dark overcoat, and his bowler held against his breast as though he were watching a flag-procession go by. His grizzled hair was brushed carefully to hide the bald spot, his jaw looked heavier and his expression older since I had last seen him—but his eyes were young. Masters suggests the Force, though only slightly: something in the clump of his walk, the way his eyes go sharply from face to face, but there is none of the peering sourness we associate with Public Protectors. I could see that Halliday immediately unbent and felt at ease before his practical solidity.

"Ah, sir," he said to Halliday, after the introductions; "and you're the one who wants a ghost laid?" This time he spoke as though he had been asked to install a radio. He smiled. "Mr. Blake'll tell you I'm interested. Always have been. Now, about this house in Plague Court."

"You know all about it, I see," said Halliday.

"We-ell," said Masters, putting his head on one side, "I know a little. Let me see. It came into possession of your family a hundred-odd years ago. Your grandfather lived there until the eighteen-seventies; then he moved out, quite suddenly, and refused to go back. . . . *And* it's been a white elephant ever since, which none of your people have ever been able to let or sell. Taxes, sir, taxes! Bad." Masters' mood seemed to change—smoothly, but with a compelling persuasion. "Now, Mr. Halliday, come! You're good enough to say I can give you a little help. So I know you won't mind returning the favor. Strictly unofficially, of course. Eh?"

"Depends. But I think I can promise that much."

"Just so, just so. I take it you've seen the paper today?"

"Ah!" murmured Halliday, grinning. "The return of Louis Playge; is that what you mean?"

Inspector Masters returned the smile, blandly. He lowered his voice. "Well, as man to man, now, can you think of anybody—anybody you know, perhaps—any real flesh-and-blood person—who might be interested in lifting that dagger? That's my question, Mr. Halliday. Eh?"

"It's an idea," Halliday admitted. Perching himself on the edge of a table, he seemed to debate something in his mind. Then he looked at Masters with shrewd inspiration. "First off, I'll give you a counter-question, Inspector. Do you know one Roger Darworth?"

Not a muscle moved in the other's face, but he seemed pleased.

"Possibly *you* know him, Mr. Halliday?"

"Yes. But not so well as my aunt, Lady Benning. Or Miss Marion Latimer, my fiancée, or her brother, or old Featherton. Quite a circle. Personally, I am definitely anti-Darworth. But what can I do? You can't argue; they only smile on you gently and say you don't understand." He lit a cigarette and twitched out the match; his face looked sardonic and ugly. "I was only wondering whether Scotland Yard happened to know something of him? Or that red-headed kid of his?"

Those two exchanged a glance, and spoke without uttering a word. In words Masters only answered, carefully: "We know nothing whatever against Mr. Darworth. Nothing *whatever*. I have met him; a very amiable gentleman. Very amiable, nothing ostentatious. Nothing claptrap, if you know what I mean. . . ."

"I know what you mean," agreed Halliday. "In fact, during her more ecstatic moments, Aunt Anne describes the old charlatan as 'saint-like'."

"Just so," said Masters, nodding. "Tell me, though. Hum! Excusing delicate questions and all, should you describe either of the ladies as at all . . . *hurrum?*"

"Gullible?" Halliday interpreted the strange noise Masters had produced from some obscure depth in his throat. "Good Lord, no! Quite the contrary. Aunt Anne is one of those little old ladies who look soft, and actually are honey and steel-wire. And Marion—well, she is Marion, you see."

"Exactly so," agreed Masters, nodding again.

Big Ben was striking the half hour as the porter got us a taxi, and Halliday told the man to drive to an address in Park Lane; he said he wanted to get something from his flat. It was chilly, and still raining. The black streets were a-dazzle with split reflections of lights.

Presently we pulled up outside one of those new, white-stone, green-and-nickel apartment houses (which look somehow like modernistic book-cases) sprouting up amid the sedateness of Park Lane. I got out and paced up and down under the brightly lit canopy while Halliday hurried inside. The rain was blowing over out of the dark Park; and—I don't know how to describe it—faces looked unreal. I was tormented by that sharp, bald image that had been described in the newspaper: a lean man with his back turned, peering into the model of the condemned cell, and moving his head slowly. It seemed all the more horrible because the attendant had referred to him as a "gentleman". When Halliday tapped my shoulder from behind, I almost jumped. He was carrying a flat package wrapped in brown paper and tied with twine, which he put into my hands.

"Don't open it now. It's some facts or fancies concerning one Louis Playge," he said. He was buttoned up in the thin waterproof he affected in all weathers, with his hat pulled over one eye. Also, he was smiling. He gave me a powerful flashlight, Masters being already provided with one; and, when he climbed into the cab beside me, I could feel the pressure of what I thought was another in his side-pocket. I was wrong: it was a revolver.

It is not difficult to talk lightly of horrors when you are in the West End, but I give you my word I was uneasy when we got out among the scattered lights. The tires were singing drowsily on wet streets; and I felt that I had to talk.

"You won't tell me," I said, "anything about Louis Playge. But I imagine it wouldn't be difficult to reconstruct his story, from the account in the newspaper."

Masters only grunted, and Halliday prompted: "Well?"

"The conventional one," I said. "Louis was the hangman, and dreaded as such. The knife, let's say, was the one he used for cutting down his—guests. . . . How's that for a beginning?"

Halliday answered, flatly: "As it happens, you're wrong on both points. I wish it were as simple and conventional as that. What *is* terror, anyway? What is the thing that you come on all of a sudden, as though you'd opened a door; that turns you tipsy-cold in the stomach and makes you want to run blind somewhere, anywhere, to escape the touch of it?—but you can't, because you're limp as pulp, and——"

"Come!" Masters said gruffly, out of his corner. "You talk as though you'd seen something."

"I have."

"Ah! Just so. And what was it doing, Mr. Halliday?"

"Nothing. It was just standing at the window, looking in at me. . . . But you were talking about Louis Playge, Blake. He wasn't a hangman. He didn't have the courage to be—although I believe he did seize their legs sometimes, at the hangman's command, when they'd been twirling too long on the rope. He was a sort of hangman's toady; and held the—the instruments when there was a drawing-and-quartering case; and washed up the refuse afterwards."

My throat felt a little dry. Halliday turned to me.

"You were wrong about the dagger. It wasn't exactly a dagger, you see; at least, it wasn't used for that purpose until the last. Louis invented it for the hangman's labors. The newspaper account didn't describe the blade: the blade is round, about the thickness of a lead pencil, and coming to a sharp point. In short, like an awl. Well, can you imagine what he used it for?"

"No."

The cab slowed down and stopped, and Halliday laughed. Pushing back the glass slide, the driver said: "'Ere's the corner o' Newgate Street, guv'nor. Now what?"

We paid him off and stood for a moment or two looking about us. The buildings all looked lofty and distorted, as they do in dreams. Far behind us there was a hazy glow from Holborn Viaduct; we could hear only a thin piping of night-traffic, and the lonely noise of the rain. Leading the way, Halliday struck up Giltspur Street. Almost before I was aware we had left the street,

I found myself going down a narrow and sticky passage between brick walls.

They call it "claustrophobia", or some such fancy name; but a man likes to be pressed down into a narrow space only when he is sure what he is shut up *with*. Sometimes you imagine you hear somebody talking, which is what happened then. Halliday stopped short in that high tunnel—he was ahead, I followed him, and Masters came last—and we all stopped, in our own echoes.

Then Halliday switched on his electric torch, and we moved on. The beam found only the dingy walls, the puddles in the pavement, one of which gave a sudden *plop* as a stray raindrop struck it from the overhanging eaves. Ahead I could see an elaborate iron gate standing wide open. We all moved softly; I don't know why. Possibly because there seemed such an absolute hush in the desolation of the house before us. Something seemed to be impelling us to move faster; to get inside those high brick walls; something drawing us on and playing with us. The house—or what I could see of it—was made of heavy, whitish blocks of stone, now blackened with the weather. It had almost a senile appearance, as of a brain gone, but its heavy cornices were carven with horrible gayety in Cupids and roses and grapes: a wreath on the head of an idiot. Some of its windows were shuttered, some patched with boards.

At the rear, the wall rose and broadened round a vast back court. It was a desolation of mud, into which refuse had been thrown. Far at the rear of the yard, the moonlight showed a detached structure: a small, oblong house of heavy stone, like a dilapidated smokehouse. The little windows were heavily grated; it stood out among the ruins of the yard, and there was a crooked tree growing near it.

Following Halliday, we went to a weedy brick path to the

carven porch over the front door. The door itself was more than ten feet high, and had a corroded knocker still hanging drunkenly from one bolt. Our guide's light played over the door; it winked back the damp, the swellings in the oak, the cuts where people had hacked their initials in the senility and ruin of Plague Court. . . .

"The door is open," said Halliday.

Inside, somebody screamed.

We met many horrors in this mad business, but none, I think, that took us so off-balance. It was a real voice, a human voice; yet it was as though the old house itself had screamed, like a doddering hag, at Halliday's touch. Masters, breathing hard, started to lunge past me. But it was Halliday who flung the door open.

In the big musty hall inside, light was coming out of a door to the left. I could see Halliday's face in that light; damp and set, and absolutely steady, as he stared into that room. He did not raise his voice.

"What the devil is going on here?" he demanded.

III
THE FOUR ACOLYTES

WHAT ANY of us expected to see, I do not know. Something diabolic; possibly the lean man with his face turned. But that was not to occur just yet.

Masters and I came round on either side of Halliday, so that we must have seemed absurdly like a guard. We saw a large, rather lofty room; a ruin of past splendor, that smelt like a cellar. Its wall-paneling had been ripped away, exposing the stone; above it rotted what might once have been white satin, sagging in black peelings, and puffy with spiders'-webs. The mantelpiece alone remained: stained and chipped, a thin height of stone scrollwork. In the vast fireplace burnt a very small and smoky fire. Strung along the hood of the mantelpiece were half-a-dozen candles burning in tall brass holders. They flickered in the damp, showing above the mantelpiece, decaying fragments of wallpaper that had once been purple and gold.

There were two occupants of the room—both women. It added a sort of witchlike eeriness to the place. One of them sat near the fire, half risen out of the chair. The other, a young woman in her middle twenties, had turned round sharply to look at us; her hand was on the sill of one of the tall shuttered windows towards the front.

Halliday said: "Good God! Marion——"

And then she spoke in a strained voice, very clear and pleasant, but only a note removed from hysteria. She said:

"So it's—it *is* you, Dean? I mean, it's *really* you?"

It struck me as a strange way of wording an obvious question, if that was what she really meant to imply. It meant something else to Halliday.

"Of course it is," he said, in a sort of bark. "What did you expect? I'm still—me. I'm not Louis Playge. Not just yet."

He stepped into the room, and we followed him. Now, it was a curious thing, but the moment we crossed that threshold I felt the lightening of a pressing, crowding, almost suffocating, feeling which was present in the air of the entrance-hall. We all went in quickly, and looked at the girl.

Marion Latimer stayed motionless, a tense figure in the candlelight; and the shadow seemed to tremble at her feet. She had that thin, classic, rather cold type of beauty which makes face and body seem almost angular. Her hair was set in dark-gold waves close to the somewhat long head; her eyes were dark blue, glazed now with a preoccupied and somehow disturbing quality; the nose short, the mouth sensitive and determined. . . . She stood there crookedly, almost as though she were lame. One hand was thrust deep into the pocket of the brown tweed coat wrapped about her thin body; as she watched us, the other hand left the window-sill and pulled the collar close round her neck. They were fine, thin, wiry hands.

"Yes. Yes, of course . . ." she muttered. She essayed a smile. She raised a hand to brush her forehead, and then caught her coat close again. "I—I thought I heard a noise in the yard. So I looked out through the shutter. There was a light on your face, just for a second. Absurd of me. But how did you come to be—how . . . ?"

Some influence was about the woman: an emotional repression, a straining after the immaterial, a baffled and baffling quality that sometimes makes spinsters and sometimes hellions. It was a quality of vividness, of the eyes or the body or the square line of the jaw. She disturbed you; that is the only word I can think of.

"But you shouldn't have come here," she said. "It is dangerous—tonight."

A voice from the fireside spoke softly, without emotion.

"Yes. It is dangerous."

We turned. . . . She was smiling, the little old lady who sat near the dull and smoky fire. She was very modish. Bond Street had coiffed her elaborate white hair; there was a black velvet band round her throat, where the flesh had begun to darken and sag. But the small face, which suggested wax flowers, was unwrinkled except round the eyes, and it was highly painted. The eyes were gentle—and hard. Though she smiled at us, her foot was tapping the floor slowly. She had obviously been shaken at our entrance; her jeweled hands, lying limp along the arms of the chair, were twisting and upturning as though to begin a gesture; and she was trying to control her breathing. You have read, doubtless, of people who are supposed to resemble eighteenth-century French marquises by Watteau. Lady Anne Benning looked like a thoroughly modern, sharp-witted old lady got up to resemble one. Besides, her nose was too large.

Again she spoke softly, without emotion.

"Why have you come here, Dean? And who are these men with you?"

The voice was thin. It seemed to explore and probe, despite its professional sweetness, and I almost shuddered. Her black eyes never left his face, and she retained that mechanical smile. There was a sickliness about her.

Halliday straightened up. He made an effort.

"I don't know whether you are aware of it," he said, "but this is my house." (She had put him on the defensive, as, I imagined, she always had. At his remark she only smiled, dreamily). "I hardly think, Aunt Anne, that I need your permission to come here. These gentlemen are my friends."

"Present us."

He did so, first to Lady Benning and then to Miss Latimer. It was a mad business, those formal introductions in the damp-smelling vault of a room, among the candle-flames and the spiders. Both of them—the cold, lovely girl standing against the mantelpiece, the reptilian pseudo-marquise nodding against her red silk cloak—were hostile. We were intruders in more senses than one. About them both was a kind of exaltation, which some might call self-hypnosis; a repressed and waiting eagerness, as at some tremendous spiritual experience they had once undergone and hoped to undergo again. I stole a sideways glance at Masters, but his face was as bland as ever. Lady Benning opened her eyes.

"Dear, dear," she murmured to me, "of course you are Agatha Blake's brother. Dear Agatha. And her canaries." Her voice changed. "The other gentleman I fear I have not the pleasure of recognizing. . . . Now, dear boy, perhaps you will tell me why you are here?"

"Why?" repeated Halliday. His voice cracked. He struggled with a baffled anger, and put out his hand towards Marion Latimer. "Why? Look at you—look at both of you! I can't stand this fog. I'm a normal, sane human being, and you ask me what I want here and why I'm trying to stop this nonsense! I'll tell you why we came. We came to investigate your blasted haunted house. We came here to get hold of your blasted turnip-ghost and smash it in little bits for good and all; and, by God——!"

The voice echoed and rang blatantly, and we all knew it. Marion Latimer's face was white. Everything was very quiet again.

"Don't challenge them, Dean," she said. "Oh, my dear, don't challenge them."

But the little old lady only twitched up her fingers again, from palms flat on the chair-arm, and half shut her eyes, and nodded.

"Do you mean that something impelled you to come here, dear boy?"

"I mean that I came here because I damned well chose."

"And you want to exorcise this thing, dear boy?"

"If you want to call it that," he said grimly; "yes. Look here, don't tell me—don't tell me that's why *you're* all here?"

"We love you, dear boy."

There was a silence, while the fire sputtered in small blue flames, and the rain ran soft-footed through the house; splashing and echoing in its mysterious places. Lady Benning went on in a voice of ineffable sweetness:

"You need not be afraid here, dear boy. They cannot come into this room. But elsewhere, what then? They can take possession. They took possession of your brother James. That was why he shot himself."

Halliday spoke in nothing more than a low, calm, serious voice. He said: "Aunt Anne, are you trying to drive me mad?"

"We are trying to save you, dear boy."

"Thanks," said Halliday. "That's jolly good of you."

His hoarse tones had struck the wrong note again. He looked round at stony faces.

"I loved James," said Lady Benning, and her face was suddenly pitted with wrinkles. "He was strong, but he could not stand them. So they will come for you, because you are James's brother and you are alive. James told me so, and he cannot . . . you see, it is to give *him* peace. Not you. James. And until this thing is exorcised, not you nor James will sleep.

"You came here tonight. Perhaps it is best. There is safety in the circle. But this is the anniversary, and there is danger. Mr. Darworth is resting now. At midnight he will go alone to the little stone house in the yard, and before daylight he will have cleansed it. Not even the boy Joseph will go with him. Joseph has great powers, but they are receptive. He has not the knowledge to exorcise. We shall wait here. Perhaps we shall form a circle, although that may only hinder him. That is all, I think."

Halliday glanced at his fiancée.

"You two," he said harshly, "came here alone with Darworth?"

She smiled faintly. His presence seemed to comfort her, though she was a little afraid of him. She came close, and took his arm.

"Dear old boy," she said—and it was the first human tone of voice we had heard in that literally damned house—"you *are* rather a tonic, you know. When I hear you talking like that, in just that particular way, it seems to change everything. If we're not afraid, there's nothing to fear. . . ."

"But this medium——"

She shook his arm. "Dean, a thousand times, I've told you Mr. Darworth is not a medium! He is a psychic, yes. But he concerns himself with causes rather than effects." She turned to Masters and me. Marion Latimer looked tired, but she was making an effort to be light and easy in an almost teasing fashion. "I suppose *you* know something about it, if Dean doesn't. Tell him the difference between a medium and a psychical researcher. Like Joseph and Mr. Darworth."

Masters shifted heavily from one foot to the other. He was impassive, he did not even look pleased, standing there turning his bowler round in his hands; but I, who knew him well, could detect a curious ring in the slow, patient, reflective tones.

"Why, yes, miss," he said. "I think I can tell you from my certain knowledge that I have never known Mr. Darworth to lend himself to—demonstrations. Of himself, that is."

"You know Mr. Darworth?" she asked quickly.

"Ah! No, miss. Not exactly, that is. But I don't want to interrupt; you were saying—eh?"

She looked at Masters again, rather puzzled. I was uneasy; the words "police officer" were to me as patent as though he had worn a placard, and I wondered if she had spotted him. Her cool, quick eyes searched his face; but she dismissed whatever notion she had.

"But I was telling you, Dean. We're certainly not alone here with Mr. Darworth and Joseph. Not that we should have minded. . . ." (Now what was this? Halliday had muttered something and jerked his head; while she was trying to look him out of countenance with a thin, bright imperiousness). "Not that we should have minded," she repeated, straightening her shoulders, "but, as a matter of fact, Ted and the major are here too."

"Eh? Your brother," he said, "*and* old Featherton? Oh, my Lord!"

"Ted—believes. Be careful, my dear."

"Because you do. Oh, I don't doubt it. I went through the same phase at Cambridge, at his age. The soundest beef-eater isn't immune. Mystical—incense-swinging—love and glory of God wrapping you round. I believe they get it worse at Oxford."

He stopped. "But where the devil are they, then? Not out daring the emanations?"

"As a matter of fact, they're out in the little stone house. Lighting a fire for Mr. Darworth when he goes to watch." She attempted to speak lightly. "Ted made this fire. It's not very good, is it? Oh, my dear, what *is* the matter with you?"

He had begun to pace to and fro, so that the candle flames swung with his passage. Now he said: "Good! That reminds me; you gentlemen will want to see over the house, and that little fountainhead of iniquity out in the yard. . . ."

"You're not going out there?"

The sandy eyebrows went up. "Certainly, Marion. I was out there last night."

"He will be a fool," Lady Benning said gently and sweetly, with closed eyes. "But we will protect him in spite of himself. Let him go. Mr. Darworth, dear Mr. Darworth, can protect him."

"Come along, Blake," said Halliday, and nodded curtly.

The girl made as if to stop him, with an uncertain gesture. I could hear a curious scraping, ticking sound; it was the rings on Lady Benning's fingers brushing the arm of the chair, but it sounded horribly like rats in a wall. The small dainty face was turned dreamily towards Halliday—and I saw how much she hated him.

"Don't disturb Mr. Darworth," she said. "It is nearly time."

Halliday got out his flashlight and we followed him into the hall. There was a tall creaky door, which he scraped shut by putting his finger into the empty knobhole. Then we stood in the damp, heavy darkness, and there were three electric torches switched on now. Halliday flashed his light first into my face and then into Masters'.

" 'Aroint ye, witch,' " he said, as mockingly as he could. "Well?

What do you think, now, about what I've been through for the last six months?"

Blinking in the light, Masters put on his hat again. He picked his words with care. "Why, Mr. Halliday, if you'll take us somewhere else—where we couldn't be overheard—why, maybe I can tell you. A little, at least. I'm even more grateful at being brought here, now."

I saw him smile as the light moved away. From what we could see of it, the hall was even more desolate than the room behind. Its floor was of stone flags, over which patterned wood had been at one time laid; but this was long carried away, like the paneling. It remained a bleak, square vault, with a heavy staircase at the far end, and three tall doors on either side. A rat scuttled across the light; we could hear the scrape of its feet as it vanished near the staircase. Masters went along ahead, his light probing. Halliday and I followed as quietly as we could; Halliday whispered to me, "Can you feel it again?" and I nodded. I knew what he meant. It had gathered round again, tightening and closing. If you have ever done any swimming underwater, and stayed down too long, and been suddenly terrorized that you will never get to the surface again, you will understand a very similar sensation.

"Don't," said Halliday, "don't let's get separated." For Masters was some distance ahead, prowling near the staircase. It was with a sense of shock that we saw him stop beside the paneling that enclosed its side; stop dead, and stare down. The light before him silhouetted his prim bowler hat and his big shoulders. Stooping, he went down on one knee. We heard him grunt.

There were some darkish stains on the flagstones near the side of the stair. The little space thereabouts was clean of dust. Masters reached out and touched the panel. It was a little door to a low closet under the steps; as Masters pushed it, there was a wild stirring and rushing of rats inside. A few of the creatures darted out—one of them over Masters' foot—but he did not move from his kneeling position. I could see the reflection on the high gloss of one shoe as he poked the flashlight into the foul little space beyond.

He stared; the damp, musty air turned suffocating in my lungs; then he spoke, gruffly.

"It's all right, sir," said Masters. "All right. It ain't nice, though. It's only a cat."

"A cat?"

"Yes, sir. A cat. It's got its throat cut."

Halliday jerked back. I leaned over Masters' shoulder and turned my light inside. Somebody or something had thrust it in there to be out of sight. It had not been dead long, and lay on its back, so I could see that the neck had been slit through. It was a black cat, stiffened out with agony; now turning shrunken and wiry and dusty, and the half-open eyes looked like shoe-buttons. There were things moving about it.

"I'm beginning to think, Mr. Blake," said Masters, rubbing his chin, "that maybe there's a kind of devil in this house after all."

With a stolid disgust he pulled the door shut again, and got up.

"But," said Halliday, "who would—?" He peered over his shoulder.

"Ah! That's it. Who would? And why? Would you call it a piece of deliberate cruelty, now, or was there a reason? Eh, Mr. Blake?"

"I was thinking," I said, "of the enigmatic Mr. Darworth. You were going to tell us something about him, you know. By the way, where is he?"

"Steady—!" Masters struck in quietly, and raised his hand.

We could hear voices and the sound of footsteps coming through the house. They were palpably human voices; yet such was the trick of echoes in this stone labyrinth that they seemed to sheer off the wall and echo softly in your ear just behind you. First there was a gruff mumble in which we could catch scattered words:

"—don't hold with the mumbo-jumbo . . . all the same . . . look a damned fool . . . something . . . ."

"That's it, that's just it!" The other voice was lower, lighter, more excited. "*Why* do you feel like that? Look here, do I look like any namby-pamby aesthete who could be gulled and hypnotized by my own nerves? That's the ridicule you're afraid of. Trust yourself! We've accepted modern psychology. . . ."

The steps were coming from beyond a low archway at the rear of the hall. I saw the light of a candle shielded in somebody's hand; there was a glimpse of a whitewashed passage with a brick floor; then a figure stepped into the hall, and saw us. It jerked back, bumping into another figure. Across that space you could almost feel its shock and stiffening. I saw a mouth suddenly pulled back, and the teeth, over the candle it held. It muttered, "Oh, Christ. . . ." And Halliday threw back in a matter-of-fact tone, faintly edged with spite: "Don't get the wind up, Ted. It's only us."

The other peered, straightening his candle. He was very young. Over the candle-flame hung first a careful Etonian tie, then an uncertain chin, the sproutings of a fair mustache, the faint outline of a square face. His coat and hat were sodden. He said, querulously:

"You ought to have better sense than to try to scare a fellow like that, Dean! I mean, hang it all, you can't go crawling about the place, and—and—" We heard the whistle of his breath.

"Who the devil are these people?" rasped his companion, who had come out from behind him. We threw up our lights mechanically to see the newcomer; he cursed and winked, and we lowered them. Besides these two, there was a thin little red-headed figure behind them.

"Good evening, Major Featherton," Halliday greeted. "As I say, you needn't be alarmed. I seem to have the unenviable quality of making everybody I meet jump like a rabbit." His voice kept rising. "Is it my face, or what? Nobody ever used to think it was so frightful as all that, but as soon as they begin talking to Darworth——"

"Confound you, sir, who says I'm alarmed?" said the other. "I like your infernal, blasted cheek. Who says I'm alarmed, sir? Furthermore, I will repeat to you, as I will repeat to everybody I meet, that I hope I am a fair-minded man, whose motives will not be misunderstood or made a subject for ridicule because I preserve—because, in short, I am here." He coughed.

The voice in the gloom sounded like a disembodied letter to *The Times*. The paunchy figure tilted slightly backwards. From the brief glimpse I had had of him, of the map-veined cheeks and cadaverous eyes, I could fill out the bigness of an outworn buck and gallant of the eighties, tightened into his evening clothes like a corset. "I shall have rheumatism for this," he protested, weakly and almost cajolingly. "Besides, Lady Benning asked my assistance, and what could a man of honor do?"

"Not at all," said Halliday, without particular relevancy. He drew a deep breath. "Well, we've seen Lady Benning too. My friends and I are going to watch and wait for the ghost-laying with you. Now we're going to have a look at the little house out there."

"You can't," said Ted Latimer.

The boy looked fanatical. A smile twitched round his lips, as though he had lost control of the facial muscles. "You can't, I tell you!" he repeated. "We've just put Mr. Darworth in there. He asked to go. He's begun his vigil. Besides, you daren't, even if you could. It's too dangerous, now. They'll be out. And it must be"— his thin, angular eager face, very much like his sister's, bent over his wrist-watch—"yes. Yes, it *is* five minutes past twelve."

"Damn," said Masters. It was unexpected, as though the word had been shaken out of him. He took a step forward, his foot-fall squeaking on the rotting boards towards the rear of the hall, where the floor had not been lifted from the flagstones. I remember thinking, with that dull focus of mind which fastens on trivial details at such moments, that the rest of the flooring had probably been fine hardwood. I remember Ted Latimer's grimy hand, with its grease-covered knuckles, thrust far out of his sleeve. I remember that colorless figure of the red-headed youngster—in the background, vague by candlelight—touching its hair, brushing its face, in inexplicable and rather horrible pantomime. . . .

It was to him that Ted Latimer turned. The candle-flame swung, fluttering with thin noise. His motions abruptly stopped.

"We'd better go into the front room, hadn't we?" Ted demanded. "In the front room, where it's safe, and they can't come. Hadn't we?"

"Yes, I suppose so," replied a colorless voice. "Anyway, that's what I'm given to understand. I never see them, you know."

So this was Joseph, saving the fantastic incongruity of names, whose dull freckled countenance appeared incurious. The candle fluttered round again, and the shadows took him.

"You see?" inquired Ted.

"Monstrous!" said Major Featherton suddenly, for no reason at all.

Halliday strode forward, with Masters after him. "Come along, Blake," he said to me; "we're going to have a look at that place."

"They're out now, I tell you!" cried Ted. "They won't like it. They're gathering, and they're dangerous."

Major Featherton said that as a gentleman and a sportsman he considered it his duty to go along and give us safe conduct. Stopping short, Halliday gave him a kind of satirical salute, and laughed. But Ted Latimer touched his arm, grimly, and the major allowed himself to be led towards the front of the hall. They were all moving now, the major with a rolling stateliness, Ted hurriedly, Joseph in obedient and unperturbed slowness. Our lights followed the footsteps of that little procession, and the high darkness pushed round us like water, and I turned towards that little whitewashed passage that led out to where the rain was splashing. . . .

"*Look out, man!*" said Masters, and dived to yank Halliday aside.

Something fell out of the darkness. I heard a crash; somebody's flashlight jumped and vanished; and, while the vibrations beat and whirled round my ears, I saw Ted Latimer turn round with staring eyeballs, his candle held high.

IV
TERROR OF A HIGH PRIEST

FULL IN the beam of my electric torch, Halliday sat on the floor, supporting himself with his hands behind him, and looking dazed. Another beam—Masters'—after flickering on him momentarily, had gone straight up into the vault like a searchlight; it was playing over the staircase, the stair-rail, the landing immediately above. They were empty.

Then Masters faced round on the group of three. "Nobody is hurt," he said heavily. "You'd better go into the front room, all of you. And hurry. If they are alarmed, tell them—in there—we will join them in five minutes." They did not argue, but turned into the room and the door scraped shut.

Then Masters began to chuckle.

"That's torn it, sir. They're cool, *they* are. Why, sir," said the inspector, with a sort of broad tolerance, "that's one of the oldest, stalest, childishest tricks in the whole bag. Talk about whiskers. . . . Lummy! You can rest easy now, Mr. Halliday. I've got him. I always thought he was a fake. And I've got him now."

"Look here," said Halliday, pushing back his hat, "what the

devil happened anyway?" His voice was under control, but a muscle jerked in his shoulder, and his eyes wandered round the floor. "I was standing there. And then something hit the flashlight out of my hand; I was holding it loose. I think"—he experimented, without rising—"I think my wrist is numb. Something hit the floor, something came flying down; *bang!* Ha. Ha ha. Funny, maybe, but damned if I see it. I need a drink. Ho ho."

Masters, still chuckling, turned the beam on the floor. Lying a few feet in front of Halliday were the smashed fragments of a vessel so heavy that the shards had scattered very little, and a third of it was still intact. It was of grayish stonework, now black with age: a sort of trough some three feet long and ten inches high, which must once have held flowers. Masters' chuckle died, and he stared.

"That thing—" he said, "my God, that thing would've crushed your head like an orange. . . . You don't know how lucky you are, sir. It wasn't meant to hit you, of course. *They* didn't mean it; not them! That wasn't on the cards. But a foot or two to the left. . . ."

"They?" repeated Halliday, starting to get up. "You don't mean——?"

"I mean Darworth and young Joseph, that's who. They only meant to show that the powers, the evil powers, were getting out of control; that they were fighting us, and firing that stone thing at you because you insisted on coming here. It was for somebody, anyhow. . . . That's right. Look *up*. Higher. Yes, it came from the top of the staircase; from the landing. . . ."

Halliday's knee-muscles were not as steady as he had thought. He knelt there, absurdly, until his own rage helped him to his feet.

"Darworth? Man, are you telling me—that—that swine," he pointed, "stood up there—on the landing, and dropped——?"

"Steady, Mr. Halliday. Don't raise your voice, if you please— not at all. I don't doubt Mr. Darworth is out there where they left him. Just so. There's nobody on the landing. It was that kid Joseph."

"Masters, I'll swear it wasn't," I said. "I happened to have my light on him the whole time. Besides, he couldn't have——"

The inspector nodded. He seemed possessed of an endless patience. "Ah? You see? That's part of the trick. I'm not exactly what you'd call an educated man, gentlemen," he explained, with a rather judicial air and broad gesture, "but this trick, now . . . well, it's old. Giles Sharp, Woodstock Palace, sixteen forty-nine. Anne Robinson, Vauxhall, seventeen seventy-two. It's all in my files. A gentleman at the British Museum has been very helpful. I'll tell you how they worked it in just a minute. Excuse me."

From his hip-pocket, solicitous as a steward, he whipped out a cheap gunmetal flask, which had been carefully polished. "Try some of this, Mr. Halliday. I'm not a drinking man myself, but I always take it along when I tackle matters of this kind. I find it useful—eh? For others, I mean. There was a friend of my wife, who used to go and visit a medium at Kensington——"

Halliday leaned against the stairs and grinned. He was still pale; but, somehow, a great weight seemed lifted from him.

"Go on, you swine," he said abruptly, peering up at the landing. "Go on, damn you. Chuck another." He shook his fist. "Now that I know the thing's a trick, I don't care what you do. That's what I was afraid of: that it wasn't. Thanks, Masters. I'm not quite so bad as your wife's friend, but that thing was a jolly close call. I *will* have one. . . . The question is, what do we do now?"

Masters motioned us to follow, and we went over the creaking boards and out into the moldy gloom of the passage beyond.

Halliday's flashlight was smashed, and I offered him mine; but he refused it.

"Look sharp for more traps," the inspector growled in a whisper. "They may have the whole house flummoxed. . . . The point's just this. Darworth and Company are up to some game. They mean to put on a show of some sort, and for some more than ordinary reason. I want to find out why, but I don't want to crash in on Darworth," he nodded, "out there. If I could make sure he doesn't leave his post, and at the same time keep an eye on that kid. . . . Hum. Hay-em——"

All this time his light had been taking in details. The passage was narrow, but of great length, and reënforced by heavy beams; on either side were half-a-dozen doors, set beside barred windows apparently giving on interior rooms. I tried to conceive their purpose, in the middle seventeenth century when this house had been built, and then I remembered. Merchant's warehouse rooms, of course.

Peering through one set of bars (it might have been a counting-house), I saw a tank-like desolation strewn with forgotten firewood. I had hazy remembrances of speckled porcelain, Mecca muslin, canes and snuff-bottles, which was curious, because I could not remember having read of these things. The images came suddenly, mixed with the stifling uneasy air. There were no forms or faces—if you can except the suggestion of somebody pacing up and down, up and down, endlessly, on the brick floor—but only the *things* of finery. I cursed myself for growing light-headed in the bad air; yet the blight of this house grew and grew in my brain. Staring at the dropsical walls, I wondered why they called it Plague Court.

"Hullo!" said Masters, and I pulled up short behind Halliday. He had reached a door at the end of the passage, and had been peering outside. The rain fell very lightly now. On our right, a smaller passage wandered off into a black rabbit-warren of kitchens which looked like burnt-out furnaces. The other door led into the yard. Turning his light upwards, Masters pointed.

It was a bell. A rusty bell set into an iron framework, about the size of a top-hat, and it hung in the low roof just over the door to the yard. Since it seemed only a means of communication from the old days of the house, I saw nothing odd about it until Masters shifted his lamp a little, and pointed again. Down the side of the bell ran a length of fine wire, new wire, gleaming faintly.

"More tricks?" said Halliday, after a pause. "Yes. It's wire right enough. It goes . . . here, down the side, out through the boards of this window, into the yard. Is this another stunt?"

"Don't touch it!" said Masters, as the other stretched up his hand. He peered out into the dark. The cool wind brought a smell of mud, and other odors less pleasant. "Don't want to call the attention of our friend out there, but I shall have to risk a flash. . . . Yes. The wire comes out, down, and runs across the ground towards the little stone house. Hurrum. Well . . ."

With him we stared out. The rain had died to a mutter of splashings, to stirrings along the gutters and a sullen *drip-drip* close beside us, but it still made prankish noises in the yard. I could see very little, for the sky was overcast, and shapes of buildings blocked it out round the wall which enclosed the big piece of ground at the rear. The little stone house was about forty yards away from us. Its only light was a flickering gleam that showed, slyly, at the gratings of little embrasures—they were too small to be called windows—set close under the roof. It stood lonely, with a crooked tree growing near it.

The light flickered again, curled eerily, with a sort of invitation, and shrank back. That faint spatter and stir of the rain made the muddy yard sound as though it were infested with rats.

Halliday made a movement like one who is cold.

"Excuse my ignorance," he said. "This may seem excellent fun, but it isn't sense. Cats with their throats cut. Bells with wire attached to them. Thirty-odd pounds of stone flower-box chucked at you by somebody who isn't there. I'm like the chap at the Circumlocution Office; I want to *know*. Besides, there was something in that passage—I could have sworn. . . ."

I said: "The wire on the bell probably doesn't mean anything. It's too obvious. Darworth may have arranged it with the rest of them as a sort of alarm-bell, in case——"

"Ah! Just so. In case of what?" Masters muttered. He glanced sharply to the right, as though he had heard something. "Ah, ah, but I wish I'd known this! I wish I'd been prepared. They both need watching, and (excuse me) neither of you gentlemen knows enough of the dodges—Just between ourselves, and confidentially, I'd give a month's pay to lay Darworth by the heels."

"You're dead-set anti-Darworth, aren't you?" asked Halliday, looking at him curiously. Masters' tone had not been pleasant. "Why? You can't do anything to him, you know. I mean to say, you told me yourself he's no Gerrard-Street fortune-teller making the tambourines rattle a guinea at a time. If a man wants to investigate psychical research, or try a séance for his friends in his own home, that's his business. Beyond exposing him——"

"H'm. That," agreed Masters, "is Mr. Darworth's own copper-bottomed cleverness. You heard what Miss Latimer said. *He* don't get embroiled. He's only a psychical researcher. He's careful to be only the patron of a tame medium. Then, if anything happens . . . why, he was deceived by a fraud, and his honesty isn't questioned any more than the dupes he introduced his medium to. And got money from. He could do it all over again. Now, as man to man, Mr. Halliday, come!—Lady Benning is a wealthy woman, isn't she?"

"Yes."

"And Miss Latimer?"

"I believe so. If *that's* what he wants—" Halliday snapped, and then checked himself. He went on, obviously changing what he intended to say, "If that's what he wants, I'd write him a check for five thousand any time he agreed to clear out."

"He wouldn't do business. Not him. But you can see this is a heaven-sent chance. If he tries anything himself, tonight—and, you see, not knowing I'm here—why—*huh!*" Masters grunted expressively. "What's more, the kid don't know me. I never saw friend Joseph before. Excuse me, gentlemen. I won't be a minute; but I want to—um—reconnoiter. Stop there, and don't move till I get back."

Before we could speak he had gone down the two or three steps into the yard and disappeared. Though he was a bulky man, he made no noise. He made no noise, that is, until (about ten seconds later) his footstep squelched in the mud; as though he had stopped dead.

Far over in the right-hand corner of the yard, the beam of a flashlight had appeared. We watched it, silent in the soft-rustling rain: sharp in contrast to the ugly, suggestive reddish glow dancing in the windows of the stone house. It was directed on the ground. It held steady; then it winked off and on three times rapidly, a pause, a longer flash, and disappeared.

I nudged Halliday as he started to speak. After a brief interval, mysterious with rustlings and splashings, there was a reply. From the spot where I judged Masters to be, Masters' flashlight did the same.

Then somebody was moving over there in the dark, and Masters' bulk appeared before us on the steps again, breathing heavily.

"Signal?" I asked.

"It's one of our people. Yes. I answered him. That's the code; there couldn't be a mistake. Now what," Masters said in a flat voice, "one of our people. . . ."

"Evening, sir," somebody whispered, from the foot of the steps. "I thought it was your voice."

Masters got him up and into the passage. He was, as the light showed, a thin, wiry, nervous young man, with an intelligent face which caught you with its student-like earnestness. His soaked hat hung down grotesquely, and he wiped his face with a soaked handkerchief.

"Hul-lo," grunted Masters, "so it's you, Bert? Ha. Gentlemen, this is Detective-Sergeant McDonnell." He became indulgent. "He does the same sort of work I used to. But Bert here's a university man; one of our new kind, *and* ambitious. You may have seen his name in the paper—he's looking for that lost dagger." He added sharply: "Well, Bert? What is it? You can speak out."

"Hunch of mine, sir," the other answered respectfully. Continuing to wipe his face, he regarded the inspector through narrowed eyes. "I'll tell you about it in a minute. That rain's filthy, and I've been out there for two hours. I—I suppose I don't have to tell you, sir, that your—your *bête noir,* Darworth, is out there?"

"Now, then," Masters said curtly. "Now, then. If you want promotion, my lad, you stick to your superior officers. Eh?" After this somewhat mysterious pronouncement he wheezed a moment, and went on: "Stepley told me you'd been sent to get a line on Darworth months ago, and, when I heard you were looking into that dagger business———"

"You put two and two together. Yes, sir."

Masters peered at him. "Exactly. Exactly. I can use you, my lad. I've got work for you. But first I want facts, and want 'em quick. You've seen the little stone house, eh? What's the lay-out?"

"One good-sized room. Roughly oblong shape; stone walls, brick floor. Inside of the roof makes the ceiling. There are four of those little grated windows in the middle of each side, high up. The door is under the window you can see from here. . . ."

"Any way out except the door?"

"No, sir."

"I mean, any way the man could get out—secretly?"

"Not a chance, sir. That is, I don't think. . . . Besides, he couldn't get out the door, either. They padlocked it. He asked them to padlock it on the outside."

"Doesn't mean anything. Yes; it means hanky-panky. I wish I could have got a look inside. What about the chimney?"

"I looked into all that," McDonnell answered. He tried to keep from giving a jerk with the cold. "There's an iron grating in the chimney just over the fireplace. The gratings in the windows are solid in the stone, and you couldn't get a lead-pencil through the openings. Also, I heard Darworth drop the bar inside the door. . . . Excuse me, sir. Your questions: I suppose your idea is the same as mine?"

"About Darworth trying to get out?"

"No, sir," replied McDonnell quietly. "About something or somebody trying to get in."

Instinctively we all turned in the dark, to look at the ugly little house where the light was changing and writhing and inviting. The cross-barred grating of that little window—scarcely a foot square—was silhouetted in strong outline as the firelight loomed on it inside. And, just for a moment, a head was silhouetted there too. It seemed to be peering out from behind the grating.

There was no reason for the shock of horror that struck me, and made my muscles watery. There was no reason why Darworth, if he were a tall man, should not stand on a chair and look out of the window. But the silhouetted head moved slowly, as though it had trouble with its neck. . . .

I doubt that any of the others saw it, for the fire-glow had died away, and Masters was speaking harshly. I did not hear all of it, but he was giving McDonnell a dressing-down as a weak-kneed something'd something who had got himself impressed by the damned tomfoolery of——

"Excuse me, sir." McDonnell was still respectful, but I think the tone of his voice had some effect. "Would you like to hear my story? About why I'm here?"

"Come along," said Masters curtly. "Away from here. I'll take your word for it that he's padlocked in. That is, I'll go and see for myself in a minute. Um, don't misunderstand, now, lad——!"

He took us a little way down the passage, threw his light into a door at random, and motioned us in. It was part of an ancient kitchen. McDonnell had taken off his shapeless hat and was lighting a cigarette. His sharp greenish eyes glanced at Halliday and me over the matchflame.

"They're all right," said Masters; he did not mention our names.

"It happened," McDonnell went on, rather jerkily, "just a week ago tonight, and it was the first real progress I'd made. You see, I was sent to get a line on Darworth last July; but I didn't get anything. He might be an impostor, but——"

"We know all that."

"Yes, sir." McDonnell stopped a moment. "But the business fascinated me. Especially Darworth. I think you know how it is, Inspector. I spent a good deal of time collecting Darworth information, looking over the house, and even asking for leads from people—people I used to know. But they couldn't help me. Darworth would open his mouth about psychical research only to a small, closed circle. They were all filthily rich people, by the way. And several friends of mine, who knew him and said he was a poisonous blighter, didn't even know he was interested in spiritualism. Well, you can see how it was. . . .

"I'd almost forgotten the business when I accidentally ran into a fellow I used to know at school; quite a good friend of mine. I hadn't seen him in a long time. We went to lunch, and he immediately began babbling about spiritualism. Latimer, his name is: Ted Latimer.

"Even at school Ted had been inclined in that direction, though there was nothing much dreamy about him: he was as neat a center-forward as I ever saw. But when he was fifteen he got hold of one of the wrong kind of Conan Doyle books, and used to try to put himself into trances. My hobby was parlor magic, like yours, so maybe that's how. . . . Excuse me. When I met him last week, he pounced on me.

"He went on telling me about an amazing medium a friend of his had discovered, and Darworth was the friend. Now, I didn't tell him I was in the force. I felt pretty rotten about it afterwards; it was a dirty trick, in a way; but I wanted to see Darworth in action. So I argued with him, and asked whether I could meet this paragon. He said Darworth didn't meet people, ordinarily—didn't like them to know his interests—all that. But Darworth was going to be at a little dinner, next night, given by a friend of Ted's aunt, named Featherton. He thought he might be able to get me invited. So a week ago tonight I went . . ."

McDonnell's cigarette glowed and darkened. He seemed oddly hesitant. Masters said:

"Get on with it. You mean for a demonstration?"

"Oh, no. Nothing of the kind. The medium wasn't there. Which reminds me, sir. In my opinion, that idiot 'Joseph' is only Darworth's—what do they call it?—*front*. The little devil gets on my nerves, but I don't believe he knows what goes on. I think his trances are drug-trances, induced by Darworth; that maybe the moron believes he *is* a medium. He's a sort of dummy to take any blame, while Darworth produces his own phenomena. . . ."

Masters nodded heavily. "Ah! That's good, my lad. If that's true, it's something tangible to fasten our man with. I don't believe it, except maybe about the drugs, but if so. . . . Good! Go on."

"Just a moment, Sergeant," I put in. "A few minutes ago, out there, anybody would have gathered from what you said that you were convinced there really was something in all this. Something supernatural. At least, the inspector assumed as much."

McDonnell's cigarette stopped in the gloom. It moved up, pulsed and darkened strongly, and then the sergeant said:

"That's what I wanted to explain, sir. I didn't say it was supernatural. But I do say that *something or somebody is after Darworth*. That's as definite as I'd care to make it. And also as vague.

"Let me tell you.

"This Major Featherton—I suppose you know he's here to-night—has a flat in Piccadilly. Certainly there's nothing ghostly about it; he prides himself on his modernism, but all the time he keeps telling anecdotes about how different, and how much better, it was in King Edward's time. There were six of us present: Darworth, Ted Latimer, Ted's sister Marion, a glucose old party named Lady Benning, the major, and myself. I got the impression——"

"See here, Bert," interrupted Masters, who seemed outraged;

"what kind of reports do you make out, I'd like to know? That's not facts. We don't want your blasted impressions; don't stand there and take up our time in the cold with gibbering away——!"

"Oh, yes, we do," Halliday said suddenly. (I could hear him breathing). "That's exactly what we do want. Please go on gibbering, Mr. McDonnell."

After a silence McDonnell bowed slightly in the gloom. I do not know why it struck me as fantastic, as fantastic as that conference with our flashlights turned on the floor. But McDonnell seemed on his guard.

"Yes, sir. I got the impression that Darworth was more than a little interested in Miss Latimer, and that everybody else, including Miss Latimer herself, was completely unconscious of it. He never did anything you could call outspoken; it was his *air*— and there's something about him that can convey an impression better than anyone I ever knew. But the others were too rapt to notice." Here Masters coughed, coughed with a long "Urrrr!" but the young man paid no attention. "They were all polite to me, but they conveyed definitely that I was out of the charmed circle, and Lady Benning kept looking at Ted in a funny way that was worse than merely unpleasant. Then Ted kept blurting things out, sometimes: that's how I put together a lot of hints, piecemeal, that there might be a party here tonight. They shut him up, and afterwards we all went into the drawing-room feeling pretty uncomfortable. Darworth . . ."

But the memory of a silhouette on a red-lit window kept coming at me, so that I could see it all around in the dark; I could not keep it away, and I said:

"Is Darworth a tall man? What does he look like?"

"Like—like a swank psychiatrist," McDonnell replied. "Looks and talks like one. . . . God, how I disliked that man!—Excuse me, sir." He checked himself. "You see, he's a positive quantity. Either you fall under his spell, or he puts your back up so much that you want to land one on his jaw. Maybe it's his possessive air towards all the women, the way he touches their hands or leans towards them; and they tell me he's had plenty. . . . Yes, sir, he's tall. He's got a little brown silky beard, and a sort of aloof smile, and he's pudgy. . . ."

"I know," said Halliday.

"But I was telling you. . . . We went into the other room, and tried to talk, particularly about some Godawful new-school paintings that Lady Benning had persuaded the major to buy. You could see he detested 'em, and was embarrassed; but I gather he's as completely under Lady Benning's thumb as she is under Darworth's. Well, presently they couldn't keep away from spiritualism, despite my presence, and the upshot of all the talk was that they persuaded Darworth to try automatic writing.

"Now, there's one fake you *can't* prove a fake; I suppose Darworth wouldn't have touched it otherwise. First he gave them a little lecture to make their minds receptive, and I am willing to admit that if I hadn't kept myself well in hand I should have been almost afraid to have the lights out. No, sir, I'm not joking!" His head turned towards Masters. "It was all so quiet, so reasonable and persuasive, so deftly tied up in real and sham science. . . .

"The only light in the room was the fire. We made a circle, and Darworth sat some distance away, at a little round table, with pencil and paper. Miss Latimer played the piano for a while, and then joined the circle. I don't wonder the others were shaken. Darworth had got them into that state; he seemed to take pleasure in it, and the last thing I noticed before the lights went out was his complacent little smirk.

"I had a seat so that I was facing in his direction. What with only the firelight, our shadows cut him off. All I could see was the top of his head, resting easily against the back of a tall thin chair, and the firelight rising on the wall just behind him. Above him—I could see it well—was a big painting of a nude sprawled out in ghastly sharp angles, and painted green. That was all, wavering by the firelight.

"We were nervous in the circle. The old lady was moaning, and muttering about somebody named James. Presently it seemed to get colder in the room. I had a wild impulse to get up and shout, for I have attended a good many séances, but never one that made me feel like this. Then I saw Darworth's head shaking over the top of the chair.

"His pencil began to scratch, and still his head kept shaking. Everything was very quiet; only that horrible motion of his head, and the sound of the pencil now traveling in circles on the paper.

"It was twenty minutes—thirty—I don't know how long afterwards that Ted got up and put the lights on. It had got unbearable, and somebody had cried out. We looked over at Darworth; and when my eyes had got accustomed to the light I jumped towards him. . . ."

"The little table had been knocked over. Darworth sat back stiffly against the chair, with a paper in his hand; and his face was green.

"I tell you, sir, that charlatan's face was exactly the soupy color of the damned picture hung over his head. He had himself in hand in a second; but he was shaking. Both Featherton and I had come up to him, to see if we could give any assistance. When he saw us over him he crumpled up the paper in his hand. He got up, walked over stiffly, and threw the paper in the fire. You had to admire him for the way he controlled his voice. He said, 'Absolutely nothing, I regret to say. Only some nonsense on the Louis Playge matter. We shall have to try it again some other time.'

"He was lying. There were distinct words on that paper; I saw them, and I think Featherton did too. It was only a glance, and I couldn't catch the first part; but the last line read——"

"Well?" Halliday demanded harshly.

"The last line read, '*Only seven more days are allowed.*'"

After a pause, McDonnell dropped his glowing cigarette on the floor and ground it under his heel. Sharp through the house behind us, rising in a kind of sob, we heard a woman's voice crying, "Dean—*Dean*——!"

V
THE PLAGUE-JOURNAL

Every flashlight snapped on; Masters was alert, and seized his subordinate's arm.

"That's Miss Latimer. They're all here——"

"I know," said McDonnell quickly; "Ted told me all about it. I watched them tonight."

"And she mustn't find you here. Stay in this room, and keep out of sight till I call you. No, wait! Mr. Halliday!"

Halliday was already stumbling out the door in the dark, but he turned round. I heard McDonnell give a faint start and a snap of his fingers as the name was pronounced. "We promised to be back in five minutes, damn it," snarled Halliday. "And here we are still. She must be nearly dead with fright. Give me a light, somebody. . . ."

"Hold on a bit," urged Masters, as I handed Halliday my own electric torch; "hold on, sir, and listen. You'd better go into the front room and stay with her; for a while, anyhow. Reassure her. But tell them I want that kid Joseph sent out to us, right here, immediately. If necessary, tell them I'm a police officer. This has got too serious for fooling."

Halliday nodded and bolted down the passage.

"I'm a practical man," Masters said to me, heavily, "but I trust my instinct. And instinct said there was something wrong. I'm glad I heard this, Bert. . . . You understand, don't you? That wasn't any ghost-writing. One of those people in that room worked it on Darworth just as he was going to work it on them."

"Yes, I'd thought of that too," agreed McDonnell soberly. "And yet there's one great big thundering hole in it. Can you in any realm of sanity imagine *Darworth* being frightened by faked ghost-writing? It's incredible, sir. And, whatever else might have been a fake, that scare of his wasn't, I'll swear."

Masters grunted. He took a few steps up and down, bumped into something, and cursed. "Some light," he growled; "we want some light—I'm bound to tell you I don't like this. And this talking in the dark——"

"Just a moment," said McDonnell. He was gone a few seconds, his light flickering up the passage, and returned with a cardboard box containing three or four big candles. "Darworth was sitting in one of these rooms," he went on, " 'resting' before he went out there. He called out to Ted and Major Featherton when they were coming back from lighting his fire—naturally he wouldn't light a fire—and they took him out there. . . ." He handed me a flashlight. "This is evidently Darworth's, sir. It was in the candle-box. You'd better take it."

It was still gloomy when the candles were lighted, but at least we could see each other's faces, and the load of darkness was less terrifying. We heard the rats then. McDonnell found a long, battered table, rather like a carpenter's work-bench, and set the candles up on it. The only seat he could find was a decrepit packing-case, which he shoved towards Masters. We stood on a gritty brick floor, blinking at each other in a dreary furnace of a kitchen whose walls had once been whitewashed. McDonnell was fully revealed as a lean, gawky young man going slightly bald. He had a long nose, and a habit of pinching out his underlip between thumb and forefinger. His intensely serious expression was lightened by a somewhat satirical droop of the lids over the greenish eyes. It was a face of whiplash intelligence.

I still did not like the atmosphere, and twice I looked over my shoulder. It was this damnable *waiting.* . . .

Masters appeared ruffled, but he proceeded methodically. He picked up the packing-case, shook it, and crushed with his foot a spider that scuttled out. Then he sat down at the work-bench with his notebook.

"Now, then, Bert. We'll assemble, and we'll consider. Eh? We'll take the business of this faked ghost-writing."

"Very good, sir."

"Well!" said Masters, and rapped a pencil on the table as though he expected to conjure up something. "And what de we have? We have a group of four neurotic people." He seemed to relish the word, like a slight surprise. "Four neurotic people, Bert; or let's except the old major, and say three. We have young Latimer, Miss Latimer, and old Lady Benning. Queer cases, Bert. Now, the trick could have been worked in a number of ways. The paper with the writing could have been prepared beforehand, and shuffled into Darworth's papers when they were handed him before the lights went out. Who gave him the papers?"

"As a matter of fact, it was old Featherton," McDonnell answered with great gravity. "He just ripped 'em out of a tablet and handed 'em over. Besides, sir (excuse me) Darworth would have known all about an ancient dodge like that. He'd have jolly well known *he* didn't write it."

"It was dark," pursued Masters. "No difficulty for one of those people to have left the circle, with a prepared paper; tipped over the little table—you said it was tipped over—shoved the writing on top, and come back."

"Ye-es," said McDonnell, pinching his under-lip and shifting; "yes, possible, sir. But the same objection holds. If Darworth is a fake, he'd know this is a fake; and why in God's name, I repeat, should it scare the living wits out of him?"

"Can you," I put in, "can you remember anything else that was on that paper besides 'Only seven more days are allowed'?"

"That's what I've been trying to think for a week," McDonnell answered, a sort of spasm going over his face. "I could swear I did, and yet—no. I only saw it in a flash, and it was because the last line was rather larger than the rest, in a big sprawly sort of writing, that I caught it. All I can hazard is this: that there was a name written on the paper, because I seem to remember the capital letters. Also, somewhere, the word *buried*. But I couldn't swear to it. I should question Major Featherton, if I were you."

"A name," I repeated, "and the word *buried*." There were rather horrible ideas in my mind, because I was wondering what one of those four, or three, neurotic devotees would do if he suddenly discovered Darworth to be an impostor and a charlatan....

"And Darworth," I also said, without mentioning that shapeless notion, "Darworth, considerably knocked endways, said it was something to do with the Louis Playge matter. By which we assume he blurted out something that was in his mind. Is anything or anybody buried hereabouts, by the way?"

Masters' big jowls shook with quiet mirth. He glanced at me out of a bland eye. "Only Louis Playge himself, sir."

I think I was rightly exasperated, and explained in somewhat heated terms that everybody seemed to know all about what had gone on here; everybody made leering hints, but nobody had given any information.

"Why, there's a chapter about it," Masters said, "in a book at the British Museum. H'm. Didn't Mr. Halliday give you some books, or a parcel, or the like?" He saw my hand go to my pocket, where was the brown-paper package I had forgotten. "H'm. Just so. You'll have time enough to read it tonight, sir, I dare say. You'll've guessed that 'Plague Court' is only a corruption of the name 'Playge'; it was the popular name for it, and it stuck, after all the lad's antics. Eh, he was a *spanker*, he was!" said Masters with some admiration, and no whit impressed. "But let's get to facts, Bert. What happened here tonight?"

McDonnell spoke rapidly and concisely while I drew out the brown-paper parcel and weighed it in my hand. Following out the information he had gained from Ted Latimer, McDonnell had posted himself in the yard—the gate was open—on what he guiltily thought might be the most erratic of wild goose chases. At ten-thirty the six of them: Darworth, Joseph, Lady Benning, Ted Latimer, his sister, and the major, had come in. After being some time in the house (McDonnell had not been able to get a look inside), Ted and Major Featherton opened the back door and set about preparations for making the stone house habitable.

"That bell?" suggested Masters. "The one hung in the passage?"

"Right! Sorry, sir—Yes, I was a good deal puzzled when I saw them working on it. Ted attached a wire to the bell, under Darworth's directions, then unreeled it across the yard, and climbed on a box and shoved one end through the window. Darworth went back to one of the rooms along here, to rest or something; and the others fussed about in the stone house, lighting fires and candles, and moving furniture or something—I couldn't see inside—and swearing generally. I gathered that the bell is for an alarm, in case Darworth thinks he needs help." McDonnell smiled sourly. "Presently they came in again, and Darworth told them he was ready. He didn't seem nervous at all. Whatever he's afraid of, it's not *that*. The rest you know."

Masters considered a moment. Then he got up. "Come along. Our Halliday seems to be having a bit of trouble. *I'll* get that medium away from 'em. Yes. And ask a few discreet questions; eh, Bert? You come with me, but I'll keep you back out of sight. . . ." He glanced at me.

I said: "If you don't mind, Masters, I'll stay right here for a few minutes and see what's inside this parcel. Give me a call if you need me." I got out my knife and cut the string, while Masters watched curiously.

"What," he said, sharply, "what's on your mind, if I may ask? The last time you got a hunch like this, we were able to arrest——"

I denied, not quite truthfully, that I had any idea to play with. Masters said nothing, since he didn't believe me, and jerked his head to McDonnell. When they had gone I turned up the collar of my coat, sat down on the packing-case Masters had vacated, and put the parcel before me. Instead of opening it, I lit my pipe.

There were two ideas; both obvious, and they conflicted. If Darworth had not been terrified by any faked ghostwriting, it followed that he had been terrified by some genuine, everyday, human thing, say a threat or a revelation of knowledge. This might have been supernatural (although I was not, as yet, prepared to accept it as that), or it might have been managed in some such sleight-of-hand fashion as Masters described. In any event, it was something of devastating power and import; and derived added force from having been presented in that manner. On the other hand, it probably had no connection with this house or the events that were now going on here.

This was sheer theorizing, yet it seemed to me that, if Darworth were so panic-stricken by a threat having to do with this house, he would scarcely have acted in the way he did tonight. He alone was calm and sure. He alone enjoyed working his marionettes, and sitting by himself in dark places. Had the writing on that paper really concerned Plague Court, he would in all likelihood have shown it to the others. He mentioned Plague Court because it was a bogey to the others, but not to him.

In that supposition, you perceive, lay the conflict. All the nebulous terrors of Darworth's acolytes centered round this house. They believed that here existed a deadly earth-bound which must be exorcised, lest it take possession of a human soul. Now there had been so much nonsense in what Lady Benning had told us, that spiritualism seemed to violate its own rules; and presumably Darworth had only confused them with vague, Delphic hints. He could make vagueness even more terrifying. Yet, though it did not at all alarm Darworth the mystic, it had struck with ill-controlled panic *Halliday the hard-headed and practical man.*

I watched the pipe-smoke slide round the candle flames, and the whole room whispered with unpleasant suggestions. After glancing sharply over my shoulder, I pulled the wrapping paper off the parcel. It was a heavy cardboard letter-file opening like a book, and it rattled with papers.

Inside were three things: a large folded sheet, flimsy and brownish-mottled with age; a short newspaper-cutting; and a bundle of foolscap letter pages, as old as the first. On the last, the writing was so faded as to be indecipherable under the yellow blotches, but there was a newer copy in longhand folded and wedged under the tape.

The large sheet—which I did not entirely open because I feared to tear it—was a deed. At the commencement the spidery script was so large that I could make out the parties to the sale: Thomas Frederick Halliday, Gent., had bought this house from Lionel Richard Maulden, Lord Seagrave of Seagrave, as attested on March 23, 1711.

From the newspaper-cutting, the headline leapt up: "PROMINENT CITY MAN A SUICIDE," accompanied by a pale photograph showing a rather goggle-eyed man in a high collar, who seemed afraid of the camera. In the picture of James Halliday, Esq., there was a horrible resemblance to Doctor Crippen. There were the same double-lensed spectacles, the same drooping mustaches, the same rabbit-like stare. The cutting told briefly of his connections; that he had shot himself at the home of his aunt, Lady Anne Benning; that he had been worried and depressed for some weeks, "seeming always to search for something about the house"; that it was all very mysterious, and that Lady Benning twice broke down at the inquest.

I pushed it away, untied the tape, and drew out the other documents. The copy of those creased, faded, decaying sheets was headed: "*Letters. Lord Seagrave to George Playge, the Steward and Manager of his Estates, Together with Reply. Transcribed. J. G. Halliday, Nov. 7, 1878.*"

I began to read, under the uncertain candles in that bleak room, now and then referring to the original. There was no noise but the stirrings that are always in an old house; but on two occasions it seemed to me that someone had come in, and was reading over my shoulder:

Villa della Trebbia,
Roma,
13th October, 1710.

PLAYGE:

Your master (and friend) is too ill and distracted to write as befits him, yet I would pray you and charge you, as you love your God, to tell me the truth of this horrible thing. Yesterday comes a letter from Sir J. Tollfer, that my brother Charles is dead at home, and this by his own hand. He said no more, but hinted at some foul business, and when I brought to mind all the things that are said about our House, I was driven near mad; since also my Lady L. is in worse failing health, and troubleth my mind exceedingly, and I cannot travel home; though a learned doctor of physick says she may be cured. So I charge you to tell me everything, Playge, as one who hath been in our family since a boy, and your father before, and pray God Sir J. Tollfer was mistaken.

Believe me, Playge, now more your friend than your master,

SEAGRAVE.

London,
21st November, 1710.

MY LORD:

If it had pleased GOD to avert this misfortune which is upon your Lordship, and indeed on all of us, I should never have been constrained to speak. For indeed I thought it was but a passing calamity, but now I know it was not; and it is a sore task which is laid upon me now, since GOD knows I feel the weight of my guilt. I must tell your Lordship more than you have asked, and of events during my father's stewardship during the Great Plague; but of that I shall speak hereinafter.

Of my Master Charles's death I must tell you this: your Lordship knows him to have been a boy of quiet and studious habits, sweet of disposition and beloved by all. During the month preceding his death (which took place on Thursday, the 6th September) I had indeed noticed him pale and restless, but this I laid to overstudy. G. Beaton, his bodyservant, had told me that he would break into sweats at night; and on one occasion Beaton, waked and roused from the truckle-bed by a cry, found him clutching back the bed-curtains and grasping at his neck as though in dreadful pain. But of this Master Charles remembered nothing next morning.

Nor would he wear a sword, but seemed always restless and seeking for something else at the side of his longcoat, and yet more pale and weary. Moreover, he took to sitting at the window of his bedchamber—which, as well your Lordship knows, looks over the court or yard behind our House—and this he would do especially at twilight, or when the moon was up. Once, he suddenly cried out from this window, and, pointing to a dairy-maid who was returning to the house, he cried to me for Christ's sake to lock this girl up, and that he could see great sores on her hands and body.

Now I must ask your Lordship to call to mind a certain stone house which stands in the yard, and is connected with it by a covered arbor.

This house has been vacant of use for above fifty years. The reason given by your Lordship's father, and *his* father, is this: *viz.,* That the house was built by mischance above a cesspool, and that all things sicken there. To maintain this which is untrue, they had not perforce to pull it down, lest the cesspool should poison us all; and nothing of provisions could be stored there save straw, grain, oats, or the like.

We had then in our service a young man, Wilbert Hawks by name, an ill-faced fellow employed as porter, who got on so ill with the other servants that he would not sleep with them, and cast about him for another bed. (All this, you may be sure, I did not know then). He vowed he believed in no cesspool, since never was there an ill savor about the place; but that the ruling was of mine, to keep honest servants out of a good bed of clean straw. They told him it was forbidden. Says he, then—'Why, I'll take the key of the padlock from Master Snoopnose Playge's ring, when he hangs it up at night, and be up each morning and put it back before him.'

And this he did, this being the wet season and full of high winds. And when they asked him how he had slept, and if the bed was good, 'Aye,' says he, 'good enough. But which of ye thinks to cozen me by trying the door at night, and knocking on it lightly, and pawing round the house, and peering in at the windows? For you'll not befool me to think 'tis Master Snoop-nose, and open.'

Whereat they jeered at him, and said he lied, forasmuch as none in the house was by some feet tall enough to look in at the windows. They noticed that he seemed pale, and had no liking to go on errands after dark; but he kept his bed, lest they should taunt him.

And then began the first week of September, which was wet and windy, and it began to befall as I shall tell you: Master Charles kept to his bed, being ailing, and was attended by Dr. Hans Sloane himself.

On the night of the 3rd September, the servants complained of somebody in the house, who seemed to brush them in the dark hallways. Moreover, they said the air was hard to breathe, and sickened them; but they saw nothing.

On the night of the 5th September, one Mary Hill, a maid-servant, was sent out after dark into the passage which runneth past the storerooms and counting house to water some stone boxes of geraniums which stand on the window-ledges inside the passage. So goes she out—this part of the house being now deserted—with her candle and watering-pot, though afeard to do so. And when she did not return after many minutes, they grew sore alarmed and began to shriek, whereat I myself went out after her, and found her lying in a swound there, her face a blackish color.

She did not speak until morning (it being necessary for two women to sit up with her) she finally told us that this was true: *viz.,* that, as she was watering the geraniums a hand appeared between the bars of the window before her. That this hand was of a grayish hue, very wasted, and covered with large bursting sores. That this hand twitched weakly in the flowers, and tried to seize her candle. That there was another hand, holding something like an awl or a knife, with which it picked at the window; but this she was not sure of, because she remembered no more.

I pray that your Lordship will excuse me of writing fully what occurred the succeeding night, 6th September. I will say that towards one of the clock, in the morning, we were roused by a screaming which came from outside. And when I went out with pistol and lanthorn, and others behind me, we found that the door of the little stone house was barred on the inside. Hawks, who had been sleeping there, presently opened it, but we could not persuade him to talk in a befitting manner. But he told us, most piteously, Not to let it in—not to let it in, for God's sake. And then he said, It was hacking at the bars with its awl, seeking to get in, and he could see its face.

This was the night (or it was rather towards morning, as G. Beaton told the constables) that Master Charles expired of cutting his throat, in his bed. I will say, with obedient circumspection, and in the hope that your Lordship will understand me, that certain swellings which I observed upon his face and body were altogether disappeared by the time the laying-out women——

I found my heart beating heavily, and I was warm despite the damp air. These people lived before me: the pale lad sitting at the window, the steward painfully writing his account, the shadows of that cramped and greasy time come back upon a damned house. I began to have a hideous notion of what haunted Dean Halliday now.

Then I got up, with a muscle of fear jerking in my leg, because I could have sworn somebody had walked down the passage, and past my door. It was only a flash out of the tail of the eye; I went over to reassure myself. Stone window-boxes? They were not here now, although I could remember one, and the passage was empty.

Returning, and wiping my hands aimlessly on my overcoat, I wondered whether I ought to call Masters and show him. But the spell took me.

. . . And now it behooves me, though with a sick and doubtful heart, to throw what light I can upon this Visitation which GOD in his inscrutable ways hath wrought. Some part of it I observed myself, but most I learned in later time from my father; for I was bare ten years old then, which was in the year of the Great Plague, or 1665.

Doubtless your Lordship has heard men talk of this time, since there are many now alive who did not flee the city, yet survived.

My father, who was a good and pious man, used to gather us his children and in his great voice he would read the text which says, 'Thou shalt not be afraid for the terror by night; nor for the arrow that flieth by day; nor for the pestilence that walketh in darkness: nor for the destruction that wasteth at noon day. A thousand shall fall at thy side, and ten thousand at thy right hand, but it shall not come nigh thee.' This was in August and September, the worst months because the hottest. Even shut into our room I can remember hearing from the upper windows of neighboring houses the shrieks of the women that broke the great silence that was on the city. Once my sister and I crept out on the roof-tiles, at a giddy height, and saw the hot murky sky, and no smoke going up from the chimneys, and such people as were abroad hurrying in the middle of the streets, and the watchmen with their red wands before houses that were marked in a red cross on the doors below the words, 'Lord, have mercy upon us.' I only saw a plague-cart once, which was when I crept to a window at night: it was stopped near by, and the bellman was clanging his bell and bawling towards an upstairs window, and so was the watchman, and the linkman was holding up his light so that I saw the cart full of bodies that were covered with sores. I heard these carts every night.

However, this was later, as I shall speak of hereinafter, and the Plague (which broke out in the parish of St. Giles) took so long a time to reach us that people said it would not come at all; and it was mayhap to my father's forethought that we owed our lives. For my father took thought to GOD's signs and omens, like others less fortunate. When the great comet appeared, and burned dull and sluggish in the sky, he went to Sir Richard—as he was then, your Lordship's grandfather—and told him what it was. (This was in the month of April).

Now Sir Richard's own room of business, set apart from his counting-room and warehouses, was the stone house before mentioned. Here he entertained the great people who came to buy of him: which is to say, inside by the fire in cool weather, and outside under the trees in fine. Sir Richard was a vasty awesome figure in his great periwig and grave fur gown, with the gold chain round his neck; but he did not take amiss what my father said to him.

My father urged on him the precaution he had heard was taken by a Dutch family in Aldersgate Street: *viz.*, that the house should be well provisioned and shut up of itself, suffering none to go in or out until the scourge abated. Sir Richard heard him out, and pinched his chin and was mighty thoughtful. For he had a dear wife, who was soon to be brought to bed of child;

likewise a beloved daughter Margaret, and a son Owen, your Lordship's own father. Whereat he said—Ay, there was reason in the plan, and if the plague showed no abatement in a fortnight, they would do it. For they dared not leave the town, because of his wife.

Your Lordship well knows that it did *not* abate; nay, that it breathed fiercer as the warm weather came with the flies (although all birds had gone from the town). It smote northwards to Holbourne, down the Strand and Fleet Street, and was upon us, and everywhere were people fleeing mad from the stricken town with their goods piled into carts and waggons. These stormed at the gates of the Mansion House, beseeching of my Lord Mayor passes and certificates of health, without which no other town would suffer them to enter, or no inn allow them to lie there. To some it came slowly, first the pains and vomit, then the swelling sores, and mayhap lingered a week ere dying in convulsions; to others it came in the vitals, without outward sign, until they fell in the street and died there.

Whereupon Sir Richard ordered the house to be shut up, dismissing his clerks and keeping only such servants as were of necessity. He desired his son and daughter to leave and join the Court (which had fled to Hampton), but they would not. So none were suffered to go out into the air, save only within the enclosure of our wall; and these with myrrh and zedory in their mouths. I except only my father, who manfully offered to carry abroad such messages as Sir Richard should wish. But indeed he would have thought himself fortunate, had it not been for one thing: that is to say, his half-brother, Louis Playge.

Now in truth I turn sick when I write of this man, who hath affrighted my dreams. I saw him only twice or thrice. Once was when he came boldly to the house, demanding to see the steward his brother; but the servants knew who he was, and ran from him. He caught my little sister, so that when my father came upon him he was twisting her arm horribly, and laughing, and telling her how they cut up a man at Tyburn yesterday. (For your Lordship must know he was assistant to the Hangman, a thing of horror and shame to my father, and which he strove to conceal from Sir Richard). Nor had he the courage or skill for the Hangman's office, but could only stand beside and . . .

Some things I shall not include; it is not well that I should.

. . . But my father said—That if once he could gain the stomach for all he desired to do, then, Louis Playge must be so evil that he could not die like other men. In appearance he was a short man, with a face something bloated. He wore his own lank hair, and had a greasy flopping hat pinned up at one side; and instead of a sword he wore at his side a curious dagger with a blade like a thick awl, which he was very proud of because he had made it himself, and which he called *Jenny*. He used it at Tyburn for . . .

But when the noisome pestilence blew upon us, we did not see him, and I know my father hoped him dead. Then one day (it was August) my father went abroad with a message, and when he returned he sat down by my mother in the kitchen—and put his head in his hands. For he had seen his brother Louis in an alley off Basinghall Street, and his brother was kneeling and stabbing at something with his weapon. Beside him there was a handcart full of small furry bodies, the which were cats. (For your Lordship must know that by an ORDER conceived by the Lord Mayor and Aldermen, no hogs, dogs, cats or tame pigeons, being bearers of contagion, were suffered to be kept; but all must be made way with, and killers appointed for that purpose). . . .

Somehow, as my eyes fell on this sentence, I found myself nodding as though in confirmation, and saying, "Yes!" and being positive that I remembered seeing the Order—which was bordered in black, and posted outside a tavern with people muttering about it.

And, seeing this, my father would have hastened on, but that Louis called to him, and he was laughing and saying—How now, brother, but are ye afeard of me? And the cat was still writhing, so that he trod on its neck, and came stepping through the filth of the alley, all lean and bespattered, with his hat flopping against the muddy yellow sky behind. When my father asked him if he did not fear, he replied that he had a philtre, gained of a potent necromancer at Southwark, which kept him immune.

Though indeed there were many with philtres, and plague-waters, and amulets (so that quacks grew rich), yet it did not save them, and they were put into the deadcart with the amulets still round their necks. But it seemeth that *his* charm was of the Devil, forasmuch as through all those crazed days he had his safety, and grew crazed with what he dared do among the dead and dying. These things I will not repeat, save only to tell your Lordship that he grew to a thing shunned like the plague itself, nor would any tippling-house take him in.

Him, however, my father forgot, for on the 21st August Master Owen—your Lordship's father—fell ill as he was rising from dinner.

Nor was Sir Richard behind-hand with taking action. He desired Master Owen to be conveyed to the stone house, that others might not be infected. Here a bed was caused to be made of Sir Richard's finest tapestries, and he lay moaning among the lacquer cabinets, and the hard gold and silver, and Sir Richard was as one demented. It was agreed (though this against the ORDER) that no report should be made to the council; that Sir Richard and my father should attend him, and a chirurgeon sent for under oath of secrecy.

Throughout that month, I say, they watched. (It was a few days afterwards, I think, that Sir Richard's wife was delivered of a stillborn son). Dr. Hodges waited daily on Master Owen, as he lay there with his shaven head, and let blood and administered clysters; and held him up in his bed to prevent choking, an hour at a time. And it was in the most terrible time of the Visitation, the week of the 1st September, that Dr. Hodges told us the turn was past, and he would grow well.

That night Sir Richard, and his lady near death herself, and their daughter, wept for joy. We knelt and gave thanks to GOD.

On the night of the 6th September my father roused himself at midnight, and went out to take night watch at Master Owen's side. He carried a flaring link in his hand, and when he did start across the yard, then he saw a man on his knees before the house, who was pawing at the door.

And Sir Richard, who was inside, thought it to be my father, so that he came to open the door. But the man staggered up and turned round, and my father saw that it was Louis Playge. And he saw that Louis Playge was moving his neck curiously He held up the light, and perceived that this was because a great plague-sore had blossomed on his throat; and even as he watched, other sores began to swell on his face. Whereat Louis Playge began to scream and cry.

'Twas then that Sir Richard opened the door, asking what the matter was. Nor did Louis Playge speak, but only made a dart to go in at the door; but my father thrust the flaming link into his face as I have seen done with wild animals. Whereupon he tumbled down and rolled, crying—*For Christ's sake, brother, will ye turn me out to die?* Sir Richard stood horror-struck, not being able to shut the door. And cries my father—*Get to the pesthouse,* or he would set fire to his clothes and burn the plague out of him. But Louis Playge said they would not have him, that they cursed and reviled him, and no man would look on his face, and he must die in a gutter. When my father would not let him, of a sudden he gathers himself together, and drawing his dagger leaps at the door a-slashing; the which Sir Richard closed in bare time.

Then my father's brother ran about the yard, so that my father was compelled to bespeak aid; and half-a-dozen fellows with torches pursued him to drive him out, a-jabbing the torches while he ran screaming before them. Presently they heard him no more, and came on him fallen dead under a tree.

There they buried him, seven full feet beneath the tree, because had they given him to the dead-cart, then they would have acknowledged the plague in their house and been guarded by watchmen; nor did they dare cast him into the street, because of who might see and report. Yet my father heard him say before he died, crying out in the yard, that he would come back, and find a way in, and butcher who should be in the house as he butchered cats; and, if he were not strong enough, he would take the body of an inmate or him who owned the house. . . .

Master Owen heard him (or his shape) even that same night, clinging to the door like a great flattened bat, and trying to force the door with his awl.

Therefore, my lord, since it hath pleased you to ask me for this account of horror and suffering. . . .

Something drew my eyes off the page, and to this day I do not know what it was. The evil images were so entangled with this room that I felt not here, but in the seventeenth century. Yet I found myself standing up, staring about the place. . . .

There were footsteps in the yard. There was a creak and scrape outside in the passage.

And then, harsh and sudden as though at a dying jerk, the bell in the passage began to ring.

VI
DEATH OF A HIGH PRIEST

THAT INTRODUCED it. And, since the ringing of that bell began one of the most astounding and baffling murder cases of modern times, it is as well to be very careful of what I say; not to exaggerate or mislead—at least, any more than *we* were misled—so that you may have a fair opportunity to put your wits to work on a puzzle apparently impossible of solution.

First, then, the bell did not clang out strongly. In the stiffness of its rust and disuse, that would have been impossible even with a heavy hand pulling the wire. It creaked, and jarred down with a low reverberation; creaked again more weakly, and the clapper fell in little more than a whisper. But to me it was more horrible than though it had banged a sharp alarm through the house. I got up, with a faint sickishness in the pit of my stomach, and hurried to the door into the passage.

A light flashed in my face, and the beam of my own lamp crossed that of Masters. He was standing in the door to the yard, looking back over his shoulder at me, and he was pale. He said hoarsely:

"Follow me out, and close behind. . . . *Wait!*" The voice grew to a bellow as hurrying steps and the gleam of candles plunged towards us from the throat of the passage behind. First came stalking Major Featherton, paunchy and rather wild-eyed, with Halliday and Marion Latimer behind him. McDonnell elbowed past them, holding firmly to the arm of the red-headed Joseph.

"I demand to know—" roared the major.

"Stand back," said Masters. "Stand back, all of you. Stay where you are, and don't move till I give the word. No, I don't know what's happened! Round 'em all up, Bert. . . . Come along," he said to me.

We slipped down the three steps into the yard and cast our lights out across it. The rain had stopped some time ago; the yard was a thick sea of mud, undulating in places, but sloping a trifle towards where we stood, so that it was almost drained of puddles.

"There isn't a footmark," snapped Masters, "going near that stone house on this side. Look at it! Besides, I've been here. Come on, and keep in my tracks. . . ."

Slogging out across the yard, we examined the unbroken mud in front of us. Masters cried, "You in there! Darworth! Open the *door*, will you?" and there was no reply. The light flickered much lower against the windows. The last few steps we ran at the door. It was a low door, but immensely heavy: built of thick oak boards bound in rusty iron, with a broken handle. And it was fastened now by a new hasp and padlock.

"I'd forgotten that damned padlock," Masters breathed, wrenching it. He threw his shoulder on the door, to no effect. "Bert! Ahoy there, *Bert!* Get the key to this lock from whoever's got it and bring it out! . . . Come on, sir. The windows. . . . There we are, where the bell-wire runs in: ought to be that box, or whatever it was, that young Latimer stood on when he ran the wire in.—No? By God, it isn't here! Let's see . . ." We had hurried round to the side of the house, keeping close in against the wall, and making sure that there were no footprints ahead of us. There was the window to which the wire ran, a foot square and about twelve feet above the ground. The roof, which was low-pitched and built of heavy rounded tiles, did not overhang the wall.

"No way to climb," snarled Masters. The man was upset, and breathing hard; also, he was dangerous. "That must have been a devil of a big box young Latimer stood on, to climb up there. Give me a leg up, will you? I'm pretty heavy, but I'll not be long. . . ."

It took a strain to support that weight. I braced my back against the stone wall, knitting my fingers to give him a stirrup. My shoulder-bones seemed to go out of joint as the weight pulled them; we staggered and grunted a moment, and then Masters steadied us with his fingers on the window-ledge.

There was a silence. . . .

With that muddy boot cutting into my fingers, I bucked and braced on the wall for what seemed like five minutes. By craning my neck I could see a part of Masters' face from below; the flickering light was on it, and touched his staring eyeballs. . . .

"All right," Masters grunted, vaguely.

I gasped and let him slide down. He stumbled in the mud; and, when he spoke, after gripping my arm and rubbing his sleeve insistently across his face, it was in a gruff, steady, unhurried voice.

"Well . . . that's done it, sir. I don't think I ever saw so much blood."

"You mean he's——?"

"Oh, yes, he's dead. Stretched out in there. He looks—pretty well cut and hacked. Not pretty. Louis Playge's dagger is there, too. But there's nobody else in the place; I could see all of it."

"But, man," I said, "nobody could have——"

"Ah, just so. Just so. Nobody could have." He nodded, dully. "I don't think the key to that padlock will be of much use now. I could see the inside of the door. It's bolted, and there's a big bar across it too. . . . It's a trick, I tell you! It's *got* to be a trick, somehow! *Bert!* Where the hell are you, Bert?"

Lights crossed again as McDonnell stumbled round the side of the house. And McDonnell was afraid: I saw that in the glaze of his greenish eyes, shutting up as the light struck them, and the twitch of his narrow face. There was a wild contrast in the rakishness of his hat, which was pulled over one eye with a sort of sodden jauntiness. He said: "Here, sir. Young Latimer had the key. Here it is Has anything—?" He swept out his hand.

"Give it to me. We'll try. . . . What the devil have you got in your other hand?"

McDonnell blinked, stared, and then looked down. "Why—Nothing, sir. They're cards—playing cards, you know." He exposed a handful, in one of those movements of conscious grotesqueness suited to what he carried in that place. "It was the medium. You said to keep an eye on him when you were out. And he wanted to play Rummy——"

"To play Rummy?"

"Yes, sir. I think he's dotty, sir; clean off his head. But he got out the cards, and——"

"Did you let him get out of your sight?"

"No, sir; I did not." McDonnell thrust out his jaw; his eyes were level and positive for the first time. "I'll swear I didn't."

Masters snapped something and took the key out of his hand; but it did no good to open the padlock on the door. The three of us hurled our shoulders at the door together without even shaking it.

"No good," Masters panted. "Axes: that's what we need. Only thing'll do it. Yes, yes, he's dead, Bert!—don't keep asking fool questions! I know a corpse when I see one. But we've got to get in there. Nip back to the house, and look in that room where there's some wood piled; see if you can find a fair-sized log. We'll use it for a battering-ram, and maybe the wood's rotten enough to smash. Hop it, now." Masters was sharp and practical now, though a trifle short of breath. He played his light round the yard. "No footprints anywhere near this door— no footprints anywhere. That's what sticks me. Besides, I was here, I was watching. . . ."

"What happened?" I demanded. "I was reading that manuscript. . . ."

"Eh, ah. Just so. Do you know how long you were at it—a-mooning, sir?" He did not sound pleasant. Then he hauled out a notebook. "Reminds me. I'd better put that down. Noted the time when I heard the bell. Time: 1:15 exactly. 'Heard bell, one-fifteen.' Ha. Now, sir, you were sitting there a-mooning that long, maybe you found something out. That's near on three quarters of an hour."

"Masters," I said, "I didn't see or hear anything. Unless . . . you say you were out at the back. Did you pass the door of the room where I was sitting when you went out?"

He was twisted round, his torch propped under one arm with its beam focused on the notebook. His muddy fingers stopped writing.

"Ah! Passed your door, eh? When was that?"

"I don't know. While I was reading. I had such a strong feeling of it that I got up and looked out the door, but I didn't see anybody."

"Haaa—!" said the inspector, rather ghoulishly. "Wait a bit, though. Is that facts—you know what I mean: hard, absolute, really 'appened *facts,* that no counsel could shake—or is it only more impressions? You'll admit you've had a lot of those impressions, you know."

I told him it was a hard, absolute, really 'appened fact, and he smeared the notebook again.

"Because, Mr. Blake, it wasn't me. I came out the front door, and round the side of the house: as you'll hear. Now, can you give any description of those steps, say. Man or woman, eh? Kind of walk—fast or slow; something that'd be helpful?"

This was impossible. It was a brick floor, and the sounds had been only half-heard in the midst of cryings and shadows built up from George Playge's manuscript. That they were quick footsteps, as of one anxious to escape being seen, was all I could tell him.

"Well, sir, then here's what happened after Bert and I left you. . . . I'd better get it down on paper. They'll be asking . . . and I shall catch hell for all this. Down on paper. . . . Do you know what that crowd was doing, what they've been doing for the last half-hour?" Masters demanded bitterly. "Yes, you've guessed it. Round a circle in the dark. Exactly as they were a week ago tonight, when somebody slipped that fake message among the papers and scared Darworth. How could I prevent 'em?"

"A séance—" I said. "Yes, but what about Joseph?"

"It wasn't a séance. They were praying. And there, if you look at it, is the fishy part of the whole thing. They didn't *want* Joseph there. The old lady was a bit heated about it. She said Darworth had given specific instructions that Joseph was not to be present: some sort of bosh about his being a strong psychic, which would only tend to gather bad influences rather than . . . I don't know. But McDonnell and I took him in hand instead. Ha. Little enough we got out of him, or them either, for that matter. They wouldn't talk."

"Did you tell them you were a police officer?"

Masters made a sound through his nostrils. "Yes. And it only made a mug of me. What right had I to do anything?" He brooded. "The old lady only opened and shut her hands, and said, 'I thought so.' I thought the young fellow—Latimer—was going to come after me with a poker. Only one who tried pacifying me was the old gentleman. Ah, and they ordered me out of their prayer-meeting, too. If it hadn't been for Mr. Halliday I should have been chucked out altogether. . . . Here we come. Bert!" he shouted towards the house. "Get Mr. Halliday with you on that log, and keep the rest back. Make 'em get back, d'ye hear?"

There was a shrilling of protest, mingled with the sound of argument, at the back door. Trundling a heavy log, McDonnell bumped it down the steps against the uncertain gleam of candles that others were holding high. Halliday picked up the other end of the log, and they stumbled out towards us.

"Well?" Halliday demanded. "Well? McDonnell says——"

Masters interrupted: "He says nothing, sir. Catch hold here; two of us each side. Aim for the center of the door, and we'll try to split it in half. Torches in your pockets; use both hands. Ready, when I give the word . . . *now!*"

The noise of the separate crashes blasted in that enclosed space, and seemed to make windows tingle roundabout. Four times we drove that ram at the door, slipping in the muck, drawing back, and plunging again at Masters' word. You could feel it cracking, but the old iron snapped before the wood. A fifth time, and Masters' light was playing on two halves splintered cleanly down.

Breathing hard, Masters drew on a pair of gloves, lifted one sagging flap, and slid through it on his knees. I followed him. Across the center of the door, a large iron bar was still wedged into its socket. As I ducked under it, Masters turned his light round to the back of the door. Not only was the bar still in place, but a long and rusty iron bolt, of the type common in seventeenth-century houses, was shot into place. When Masters tested it with his gloved hand, a stiff wrench of the wrist was required to draw it out. The door had no lock or keyhole: only a dummy handle of the type nailed on outside. So closely did it fit the doorframe all around that the brittle iron binding had been crushed and ripped out.

"Take note," said Masters, gruffly; "and now stand where you are—turn round—be sure there's nobody here. . . ."

I whirled round quickly; for I had glimpsed fragments of the sight as I crawled inside, and it was not one for a weak stomach. The air was foul, for the chimney could not have drawn well, and Darworth had evidently been burning spices in the immense fire. Then, too, there was an odor of singeing hair.

In the wall towards our left (the same narrow side of the oblong through whose window Masters had seen the body), in this wall was the fireplace. The fire had sunk lower now, but it was heaped into a red-glowing mass that threw out fierce heat. It still winked invitingly, and it looked demoniac. A man was lying in front of it, his head almost among the embers.

He was a tall man, with a sort of shattered elegance about him. He lay partly on his right side, hunched and shrunken as though with pain. His cheek was against the floor, head twisted round towards the door in what might have been a last effort to look up. But he never could have looked up, even had he been alive. Evidently in the fall forward, his eyeglasses—with a little gold chain going round to his ear—had been smashed in his eyes. From this ruin the blood had run down over his face, past the teeth of the wide-open mouth now wrenched back in agony, and into his silky brown beard. The heavy brown hair had been worn long; it had tumbled out grotesquely over his ears, and was streaked with gray. He seemed almost to be imploring us, over the limp left arm that was stretched out towards the side of the fireplace.

Except for the red-pulsing fire, there was no light in the room. It looked smaller here than from the outside: about twenty feet by fifteen, with stone walls crusted in green slime, a brick floor, and a groined ceiling of solid oak. Though there had been a recent attempt to clean it—a broom and mop were propped against one wall—this had done little against—the corruption of years. And now the place was sticky and sickly with something you could smell through the damp fog of heat. . . .

Masters' footfalls echoed on the brick floor as he walked towards the body. Insane words came back to me, and reverberated in my mind as they reverberated here when I spoke them aloud.

"'*Who would have thought the old man to have had so much blood in him . . . ?*'"

Masters wheeled. It may have been in the way I repeated what the Scottish thane's wife had said. He started to say something, but checked himself. The echoes still came back. "There's the weapon," said Masters, pointing. "See it?—lying over there the other side of him? It's Louis Playge's dagger, right enough. Table and chair, knocked over. Nobody hiding here. . . . You know a bit about medicine. Look at him, will you? But be careful of your boots. Muddy . . ."

It was, of course, impossible to avoid the blood. The floor, the walls, the hearthstone had been splashed before that twisted figure (hacked like a dummy at bayonet practice) had writhed forward with its hair in the fire. He seemed to have run from something—wildly, blindly, banging round in circles like a bat trying to get out of the room—while *it* set upon him. Through the hacking of his clothes I could see that his left arm, side, and thigh had been slashed. But the worst damage was to his back. Following the direction of his outflung hand, I saw hanging beside the chimney-piece a part of a brick that had been tied as make weight to the wire of the bell.

I stooped down over him. The fire stirred and fell a trifle. It made a changing play of expressions on the blind face, as though he were opening and shutting his mouth; and his dabbled cuff-link was fine gold. So far as I could ascertain, there were four stabs into the back. Most of them were high up and rather shallow, but the fourth was straight through the heart, driven down under the left shoulder-blade, and it had finished him. A small air-bubble, assuming blackish tints through the mess, had formed on the last wound.

"He's not been dead five minutes," I said. (This, we later learned, was a correct estimate). "Though," I was bound to add, "it might have been difficult for a police surgeon's diagnosis later. He's lying directly in front of a blaze that would keep the body at a much hotter temperature than blood-heat for some little time. . . ."

The fire, in fact, was scorching, and I moved back on the slippery bricks. The man's right arm was doubled up behind him; his fingers were gripping an iron blade about eight inches long, with a crudely fashioned hilt and a bone handle on which were visible the letters L. P.—faintly visible through the stains. It was as though he had plucked it out before he died. I stared round the room.

"Masters," I said, "this thing is impossible——"

He swung round savagely. "Ah! Now we have it. I know what you're going to say. Nothing could have come through windows or door, and got out again. I tell you it did happen, and by ordinary means, and, so help me, I'm going to find out—!" His big shoulders relaxed. The bland face looked suddenly dull and old. "There must be a way, sir," he repeated doggedly. "Through the floor or ceiling or something. We'll go over every inch of it. Maybe one of the window-gratings can be removed. Maybe—I don't know. But there must be. . . . Keep out, *if* you please!" He broke off and waved towards the door. Halliday's face had appeared in the aperture. His eyes slid momentarily to the thing on the floor; he winced with a startled spasm, as though somebody had prodded a wound; then he looked straight at Masters, his face a muddy pallor, and spoke rapidly:

"There's a copper out here, Inspector. You know, a—" he was having trouble with his words, "a policeman. We—we made a row with that log, and he heard it, and—" Suddenly he pointed. "Darworth there. He's——?"

"Yes," said Masters. "Keep out of here, sir, but don't go up to the house yet. Tell Sergeant McDonnell to bring the constable in. He'll have to make a station report. Steady, now!"

"I'm all right," said Halliday, and put his hand over his mouth. "Funny. It—it looks like bayonet practice."

That unholy image had occurred to me also. I peered round in the gloom again. The only touch of past splendor in this ruin, of a time when it had been lined with Sir Richard Seagrave's Bayeux tapestries and cabinets of Japanese lacquer, remained in the solid oak ceiling. I saw Masters carefully putting down an inventory in his notebook, and as I followed his eyes I noted also the only other things in the room: (1) a plain deal table, overturned about six feet out from the fireplace, (2) a kitchen chair, also overturned, with Darworth's overcoat across it, (3) a fountain-pen and some sheets of paper, lying in the blood behind Darworth's body, (4) an extinguished candle in a brass holder, which had rolled to the middle of the floor, (5-6) the brick attached to the bell-wire, already indicated, and the mop and broom leaning on the wall beside the door.

And, as a final touch of horror, the spice burned in the fire was a sort of wistaria incense, which clogged the air in a sickly-sweet fog. . . . The whole case, the whole atmosphere, the whole tangle of contradictions, cried that there was something *wrong* in these facts.

"—Masters," I said, as though in the middle of a conversation, "there's another thing, too. Why didn't he cry out, when he was attacked like that? Why didn't he scream or make some noise, in addition to trying to get at that bell?"

Masters looked up from the notebook.

"He did," said the inspector unsteadily. "That's just it. He did. I heard him."

VII
PLAYING CARDS AND MORPHINE

"You see," Masters went on, clearing his throat, "that's the worst part of it. It wasn't a good healthy yell or scream, that'd 'uv brought me out fast and ready for trouble. It wasn't very loud at all; but it got faster and faster—I could hear him talking—and then as though he were begging and imploring somebody, and then as though he'd begun to moan and cry. You wouldn't have heard it at all, in where you were. I only heard it because I was outside, coming round the side of the house before then. . . ."

He stopped, stared round, and wiped his forehead with a gray cotton glove much too large for him.

"I admit it scared me. But I thought it was only a part of this man's game, whatever it was. The voice got quicker and quicker, and more shrill. I could see some shadows chasing round on the window; it looked—it looked hellish, in that red light. And I wondered what to do. Did you ever have the sure and certain instinct that something's really wrong, though you think it's only a game?—and yet you hesitate, and stand there without doing anything, and afterwards it turns you sick to think what you should have done." He opened and shut his hands: big and grizzled, a solid man in a mad world, peering round with dull blue eyes. "I shall be—lucky not to be demoted for this, sir. Well, I heard that; and all I did was stand there. Then I heard the bell."

"How long afterwards?"

"Well, say a minute and a half after the noises had stopped. I've bungled," he said bitterly, "I've bungled everything."

"And how long did these noises last?"

"A little over two minutes, I should think." He remembered something, and entered it in his notebook; the furrows were deepening in his big face. "But I only stood there at the back door to the passage. Like a mug! Like——never mind, sir. As though something was holding me, eh? Ha! You see, I was exploring. I'd gone out the front door of the house. . . ."

The shattered door creaked then. McDonnell slid through, accompanied by a policeman whose helmet and great black waterproof seemed to take up the whole room. He saluted Masters, seemed unsurprised, and said in one of those crisp Force voices of indeterminate accent: "Yes, sir? District station-house report, sir. Very necessary." His waterproof made a big surge and swish as he whipped out a notebook, and under cover of it I got out at the door.

Even the yard smelled fresh after the foul air of the little room. The sky had cleared, and there were stars out. A short distance away, Halliday stood smoking a cigarette.

"So the swine's done in," he observed in a matter-of-fact tone. I was startled to see that there was neither nervousness nor affected ease about him. The glow of his cigarette caught crinkled, rather mocking eyes. "And with Louis Playge's dagger, all according to schedule, eh? Blake, this is a great night for me. I mean it."

"Because Darworth's dead?"

"No-o. Because the whole game has been queered." He hunched his shoulders under the raincoat. "Look here, Blake. I suppose you've read the dark history? Masters said you were hard at it. Let's be rational. I never really believed in all that nonsense about 'possession', or the prowling spook either. I'll admit it upset me. But now the whole air is cleared—Lord, and *how* it's cleared! By three things."

"Well?"

He meditated, drawing deeply on his cigarette. Behind us we could hear Masters and McDonnell arguing, and heavy footsteps clumping about.

"The first, old boy, is that this bogus ghost has definitely destroyed his ghostliness by killing Darworth. So long as it only prowled and rattled windows, it could alarm us. But here's the funny thing: the moment it takes an extremely ordinary lethal weapon and punches holes in somebody, we get skeptical. Maybe if it had only come in and slashed at Darworth a couple of times, then killed him *with fright*, it would have been effective. A stabbing ghost may be good spiritualism, but it isn't good sense. It's absurd. It's as though the ghost of Nelson had stalked up from the crypt of St. Paul's, only to bean a tourist with its telescope. . . . Oh, I know. It's horrible, if you like. It's inhuman murder, and somebody ought to hang. But as for the ghostliness . . ."

"I see the point. And what's the second thing?"

His head was cocked on one side, as though he were staring at the roof of the little house. He made a sound as though he had started a chuckle, and cut it off in the presence of death.

"Very simple. I know perfectly damned well, my boy, that nothing 'possessed' me. While all this was going on I was sitting in the dark, on an uncomfortably hard chair, and pretending to pray. . . . To pray, mind you!" He spoke with a sort of surprised pleasure, as at a discovery. "For Darworth. Then was when my sense of humor got started. . . .

"And that brings me to my final point. I want you to talk to those people in there: Marion and Aunt Anne in particular. I want you to see what's happened to the atmosphere, and you may get a shock. How do you think they're acting?"

"Acting?"

"Yes." He turned round excitedly and flung his cigarette away before he faced me again. "How do you think they've taken Darworth's cropper? Is he a martyr? Are they prostrated? NO!— They're relieved, I tell you! Relieved! All, maybe, except Ted, who'll go on believing Darworth was done in by a spook to the end of his days. . . . But it's as though some hypnotic influence had got off them at last. Blake, what's the insane, upended psychology of the whole business? What's——?"

Masters thrust his head out of the door at this juncture, and hissed mysteriously. He looked even more worried. He said:

"We've a lot to do. Police surgeon—photographers—reports. And now we're testing. Look here, sir, will you go back to the house and just *chat* with those people? Don't examine them, exactly. Let 'em talk, if they like. Hold them there until I come. And no information, beyond he's dead. None of the things we can't explain; eh? Eh?"

"How's it going, Inspector?" Halliday inquired, somewhat genially.

Masters turned his head. The words had jarred.

"It's murder, you know," he answered heavily, and with a faint inflection that might have been suspicion. "You ever see a trial, sir? Ah, just so. I shouldn't call it funny. . . ."

Halliday, as though on a sudden resolution, walked up to the door and faced him. He hunched up his shoulders, in that old gesture of his, and fixed Masters with his rather bovine brown eyes.

"Inspector," he said, and hesitated—as though he were rehearsing a set speech. Then he went on with a rush: "Inspector, I hope everybody will understand everybody else before we start this thing. I know it's murder. I've thought it all over; I know the notoriety, the unpleasantness, the sticky nastiness that we'll have to go through; oh, yes, and what a lot of soft-headed dupes we shall look at a coroner's inquest. . . . Can't you let us off *anything*? I'm not blind. I know the implication will be that somebody up there stabbed Darworth. But you know better, don't you? You know it wasn't one of his own disciples. Good God, who would kill him? Except, of course"—his finger moved up slowly and touched his own chest, and his eyes opened wide.

"Ah!" said Masters in a colorless voice. "Possibly, possibly. Why, I shall have to do my duty, Mr. Halliday. I'm afraid I can't spare anybody. Unless—you're not meaning to give yourself up for murder, are you?"

"Not at all. All I meant . . ."

"Why, then," said Masters, with a deprecating motion of his head. "Why, then—! Excuse me, sir. I've got to get back to work."

The muscles tightened down Halliday's jaws. He was smiling. Taking me by the arm, he strode off towards the house. "Yes. Yes, the inspector's got his eye on one of us, very definitely. And do

I care, my son? I do not!" He threw back his head, as though he were laughing to heaven, and I could feel him shaking with that silent and rather terrible mirth. "And now I'll tell you why I don't. I told you we were sitting in the dark: the lot of us. Now if Masters can't fix the slashing on young Joseph—which is what he'll try to do, first off—then he'll pitch on one of us. You see? He'll say that during twenty-odd minutes of darkness, one of us got up and went out. . . ."

"And did anybody?"

"I don't know," he answered very coolly. "There was undoubtedly somebody who got up from a chair; I heard it creak. Also, the door of the room opened and closed. But that's all I could swear to."

Apparently he did not yet know the impossible (or difficult, if you prefer the word) circumstances surrounding Darworth's murder. But it struck me that the picture he had been presenting had elements rather worse than the supernatural.

"Well?" I demanded. "Nothing very laughable about that, you know. It's not altogether reasonable, on the face of it. Nobody but a lunatic would risk a chance like that, in a room full of people. But as for being uproariously funny——"

"Oh, yes, it is." His face was pale, almost inhuman in the starlight, and split by that fantastic jollity. But his head jerked down. He grew serious. "Because, you see, Marion and I were sitting in the dark *holding hands*. By God, won't it sound amusing in a coroner's court? Clapham Common on parade. I think I hear the giggles. . . . But it will have to be told; because that, my boy, is what is known as an alibi. You see, it doesn't seem to have occurred to the rest of them that they may be suspected of murder. I can tell you it's jolly well occurred to *me*. However, that doesn't matter. So long as my own light-o'-life can present a brow of radiant innocence . . . why, they may lock up old Featherton, or Aunt Anne, or anybody they like."

There was a hail from ahead of us, and Halliday hurried forward. From the old kitchen where I had read the letters, the light of the candles was still shining out into the passage. And silhouetted against it in the back door was the figure of a tall girl in a long coat. She stumbled down the steps, and Halliday had her in his arms.

I heard little dry sobs of breathing. The girl said: "He's dead, Dean. He's *dead!* And I ought to feel sorry, but I don't."

Her trembling shook the words. The flickers of light made dazzling her yellow hair, against the gaunt doorway and the gray time-bitten house. When Halliday began to say something, all he could do was shake her shoulders; and what he actually stammered out, gruffly, was:

"Look here, you can't come down in this mud! Your shoes——"

"It's all right. I've got galoshes; I found some. I—what am I saying? Oh, my dear, come in and talk to them. . . ." Raising her head, she saw me, and looked at me steadily. All the scenes in this puzzle had seemed fragments in half-light: a face shadowed, a gleam on teeth, a gesture indicated, as Marion Latimer was now. She pushed herself away from Halliday.

"You're a policeman, aren't you, Mr. Blake?" she asked quietly. "Or a sort of one, anyway, Dean says. Please come with us. I'd rather have you than that awful man who was here a while ago. . . ."

We went up the steps, the girl stumbling in heavy galoshes much too large for her; but at the door to the kitchen I gestured the others to stop. I was interested in that kitchen. Joseph was sitting there.

He sat on the packing-case, as I had done when I read the manuscript; his elbows on the work-bench and fingers propped under his ears. His eyes were half shut, and he breathed thinly. The light of the four candles brought his face strongly out of the gloom; his face, his thin, grimy hands and meager neck.

It was an immature face, immature and small-featured, with freckles staining the muddy skin across the flattish nose and round the large, loose mouth. The red hair—of a light shade, and cut short—was plastered against his forehead. He might have been nineteen or twenty years old, and looked thirteen. On the work-bench before him were spread out the papers I had been reading, but he was not reading them. A soiled pack of playing-cards had been spread out fanwise across them. He was peering dully at one candle, swaying a little; the loose mouth moved, slobbering, but he did not speak. His clothes, of a violent reddish check pattern, made him look even more weird.

"Joseph!" I said, not loudly. "Joseph!"

One hand fell with a flat smack on the table. He rolled his body round slowly, and peered up. . . . It was not that the face was witless; once upon a time it might have been highly intelligent. A film was over his eyes, whose pupils were contracted nearly to invisibility, and yellowish round the iris. When they came to focus on me, he cringed away. A smile was parodied on his big mouth. When I had seen him a few hours before, by the beam of a flashlight, he had seemed quiet and dull and incurious enough. But not like this.

I repeated his name, and went slowly towards him. "It's all right, Joseph. It's all right. I'm a doctor, Joseph. . . ."

"Don't you touch me!" he said. He did not speak at all loudly, but he gave such a jerk backwards that I thought he meant to duck down under the bench. "Don't you touch me, now. . . ."

I got my fingers on his wrist, by dint of keeping his eye (an excellent hypnotic subject); he trembled, and kept jerking back. To judge by the pulse, whoever had given him that dose of morphine had gone a little too far. He was not in danger, however, for he was obviously accustomed to it.

"Of course. You're ill, Joseph. You're often ill, aren't you? And so you get medicine, of course. . . ."

"Please, sir." He shrank again, with a ducking motion, and an ingratiating look. "Please, sir, I feel quite well now, thank you, sir. Will you let me go?" Suddenly he became voluble. It was the voice of a young schoolboy blurting out a confession to a master. "I know now! You want to find out. Please, *I didn't mean any harm!* I know he told me I shouldn't ought to have any medicine tonight, but I took it anyway, because I know where he keeps the case. So I took the case . . . but I only took the medicine a *very* little while ago, sir! Only a *very* little while ago. . . ."

"Medicine you put in your arm, Joseph?"

"Yes, sir!" His hand moved towards his inside pocket, with the child's hurry to show you everything once he has confessed, and lighten the blame. "I'll show you. Here——"

"Mr. Darworth gives you this medicine, Joseph?"

"Yes, sir. When there is to be a séance, and then I go into a trance. That's what makes the forces gather; but of course I don't know that, because *I* never see anything. . . ." Joseph burst out laughing. "I say, I shouldn't be telling you this. I was told never to tell. Who are you? Besides, I thought it would be better if I took twice as big a dose tonight, because I liked the medicine, and I'd like it twice as well if I took twice as big a dose. Wouldn't I?" His smeary eyes came round at me with a sort of pounce, eagerly.

I wanted to look round and see how Halliday and the girl were taking this, but I was afraid to lose his eye. That extra grain had fuddled him into speech. It was a blunder that might bring us on the truth.

"Of course you would, Joseph" (he looked gratified), "and I don't blame you. Tell me, what's your whole name: all of it, you know?"

"You don't know that? Then you can't be a doctor—!" He moved back a little, changed his mind, and said: "You know it. Joseph Dennis."

"Where do you live?"

"I know! You're a *new* doctor. That's it. I live at 401B Lough-borough Road, Brixton."

"Do you have any parents, Joseph?"

"There's Mrs. Sweeney—" he said doubtfully. "Parents? I don't think so. I don't remember, except I never had enough to eat, much. All I remember is a little girl I was going to get married to, that lived in a house and had yellow hair, but I don't what happened to her, sir. There's Mrs. Sweeney. We were each of us only eight years old, though, so of course we couldn't."

"How did you come to know Mr. Darworth?"

This question took more time. I gathered that Mrs. Sweeney was a guardian of his, who had known Mr. Darworth once. It was Mrs. Sweeney who told him he had great psychic powers. She went out one day and came back with Mr. Darworth "in a coat with a fur collar on, and a shiny hat, and rode in a long car that had a stork on the bonnet." They had talked about him, and somebody had said, "*He'll never blackmail.*" Joseph thought this was three years ago.

Again—while Joseph was giving an involved description of

the parlor at 401B Loughborough Road, with special reference to the bead curtains at the door and the giltclasped Bible on the table—I wanted to look round at my companions. How the acolytes would take this tolerably clear evidence about Darworth was uncertain: the difficulty might be in persuading him to repeat it afterwards. Besides, I could tell that he was nearly at the limit of his volubility. A few minutes more, and he would turn sullen and fearful, possibly savage. I pressed him on gently, thus:

"No, of course you needn't worry about what Mr. Darworth says, Joseph. The doctor'll tell him you took that medicine because you had to——"

"Ah-h!"

"—and the doctor'll tell him, naturally, you couldn't be expected to do what Mr. Darworth told you to do. . . . Let's see, old man: what was it he told you to do, now?"

Joseph put a grubby thumb-nail in his mouth and nibbled at it. He lowered his voice portentously, almost as though he were imitating Darworth. "To listen, sir. To listen. That's what he said, please, sir." Then Joseph nodded several times, and looked triumphant.

"Listen?"

"To listen to *them*. The people here. He said not to stay with them at all, and if they wanted a sitting to refuse it, but to keep listening. Please, sir, that's true. He said he wasn't sure, but that somebody might want to hurt him, and come creeping out. . . ." The boy's eyes grew more hazy; evidently Darworth had described that process of "creeping out" with sharp and hideous detail. Also evidently, Darworth was no stranger to the medical use of hypnotic suggestion. "Creeping out. . . . And I was to see who it was. . . ."

"What then, Joseph?"

"He told me how good he had been to me, and the money he had given Mrs. Sweeney for me; and that my mind would know it, and if anybody did I should know who it was. . . . But I took my medicine, you see, sir, and then all I wanted to do was play cards. I *don't* understand the games, much, but I like to play cards. After a while the cards with the pictures on them all seem to come alive, especially the two red queens. You hold them to the light and turn them round, and then you can see new colors on them you didn't see before. . . ."

"Did he expect anybody to come creeping out, Joseph?"

"He said—" The weak mind groped obscurely within itself. He had already turned round, and was picking up the cards and sorting them over in eager haste. A thin hand plucked out the queen of diamonds. As he looked up again, his eyes wandered past me.

"Please, sir, I won't talk any more," he said in a sort of whine. He got up and backed away. "You can beat me, if you like, the way they used to, but I won't talk any more."

With a jerk he had slid past the packing case, holding the card jealously, and retreated into the shadows.

I turned round sharply. Marion Latimer and Halliday were standing close together, her hand on his arm: both of them staring at Joseph's white face writhing and retreating towards the wall. Halliday's eyes were heavy-lidded; his mouth showed either pity or contempt, and he held the girl closer. I thought that she shuddered, that relief had weakened her, that it was as though her eyes were growing accustomed to the light in here; even that her angular beauty had grown softer like the loosening in the sharp waves of her blonde hair. But, looking past them, I saw that the audience had been augmented.

There was a figure in the doorway.

"Indeed!" said Lady Benning harshly.

Her upper lip was pulled up. In contrast to the primness of the waved white hair and the black velvet band round her throat, her face was full of darkish wrinkles. The black eyes were on mine. She was leaning, incongruously, on an umbrella, and with this she abruptly made a gesture and struck the wall of the passage behind. "Come into the front room, you," she cried shrilly, "and ask which one of us killed Roger Darworth. . . . Oh, my God, James! *James!*" said Lady Benning, and suddenly began to cry.

VIII
WHICH ONE OF FIVE?

IN THE front room I faced five people. For the moment the most curious study was the self assured old lady breaking to pieces like the wax-flower placidness of her face. It was as though she had tumbled down and could not get up: and there existed a very real physical cause behind the mental. Either slightly lame, or afflicted as I judged with some slight paralytic weakness of the legs, Lady Benning remained a stately little figure (got up deftly into her Watteau marquise's role, as though to have her portrait painted) while she only sat in the chimney corner and nodded against her red cloak. But once she got up, and moved uncertainly, you saw only a decaying, spiteful, very bewildered, elderly woman, who had lost a beloved nephew. Such at least was my impression, though you sensed in her a more baffling quality than in any of the others.

She sat in the same chair as before, beside the smoky fire that had long ago gone out, under the six candles in the ruined room. Nor would she use a handkerchief; she sat with a hand pressed to her pouched and smeary eyes, her breast heaving, and would not speak. Major Featherton stood over her, glaring at me. Ted Latimer was on the other side of the fireplace, and he had a poker in his hand.

Yet to face these people down was so easy that you felt uncomfortable, for the most palpable thing in that room—standing behind each person's shoulder—was fear.

"Now, sir!" boomed Major Featherton, as though he would get down to business at once. But he stopped.

A rather imposing figure, the major, when seen at last in full light. He had that look of being tilted slightly backwards, compressed into a correct overcoat whose tailoring almost hid his paunch. His shiny, bald head (much at variance with the port-wine-colored flabby face, big nose, and jowls swelling over the collar as he spoke) was inclined on one side. One hand was oratorically bent behind his back; with the other he pulled at his white mustache. Pale blue eyes studied me from under grizzled brows that needed combing. He coughed. A curious, pacifying expression spread over his face, as though he were about to say, "Ahem!" At the back of all this hesitancy you perceived sheer bewilderment; and also something fundamentally nervous, honest, and solidly British. I expected him to burst out with: "Oh, dammit, let somebody else do the talking!"

Lady Benning drew a sobbing breath, and he put a hand gently on his shoulder.

"They tell us, sir, that Darworth's—dead," he said, with an attempt at a growl. "Well, it's a bad business. A confoundedly bad business, I don't mind telling you. How did it happen?"

"He was stabbed," I said. "Out there in the stone house, as you know."

"With what?" Ted Latimer asked swiftly. "With Louis Playge's dagger?"

Ted had pulled out a chair with a quick gesture, and sat down with his legs straddling the back of it. He was trying to be very cool. His tie was disarranged, and there were smears of dirt at the edges of his carefully brushed, wiry, yellowish hair.

I nodded.

"Well, damn it, say something!" rasped the major. He brought his hand up from Lady Benning's shoulder, and put it down again more softly. "Come, now. None of us feel too pleasant about this. When the friend that Dean introduced, that fellow Masters, turned out to be nothing else than a police officer——"

Ted glared at Halliday, who was unconcernedly lighting a cigarette; but Ted met his sister's eye, and jerked his hand before his face as though he were brushing away a fly.

"—that," said the major, "was bad enough. It wasn't like you, Dean. It was rank violation. It was——"

"I should call it foresight, sir," Halliday interrupted. "Don't you think I was justified?"

Featherton opened and shut his mouth. "Oh, look here! I'm not up to all these tricks, confound it! I'm a plain man, and I like to know where I am. If the ladies will pardon me for saying so, that's the truth. I haven't approved of these goings-on, never did approve of 'em, and, by Gad, I never will!" He was considerably on edge, but he seemed to grow penitent as he glanced down at Lady Benning, and turned his tirade at me. "Now, come, sir. After all! I hope we all speak the same language here. Lady Benning knows your sister." (He spoke with a sort of accusation). "What's more, Dean tells me you were connected with Department 3. You know, M.I.D. Why, confound it, I know your Chief there; the one you call Mycroft. Know him well. Surely you don't want us tangled up in any of the rotten mess that's bound to follow this?"

There was only one way to get these people to speak frankly.

When I had finished explaining, the major cleared his throat.

"Good. Ah, good. Not bad, I mean. What you mean's this: You're not a policeman. You won't press any inquiries you think are absurd—about us. Hey? You'll try to help if that police officer, humph, gets gay . . ."

I nodded. Marion Latimer was staring at me with a curious expression in her dark-blue eyes, as though she had remembered something.

She said in a clear voice: "And also you think the key to this affair lies in—in—what did you say?—some associate or association of Darworth aside from us. Say in the past . . ."

"Rot!" said Ted, and let out a high laugh such as urchins give when they have smashed a window and run.

"That's what I meant. But before we can go on, one question must be answered by all of you, and answered frankly. . . ."

"Ask, by all means," said the major.

I looked round the group. "Then can any of you honestly say now that he still believes Darworth was killed by a supernatural agency?"

There is, or used to be, a game called Truth. It is popular among adolescents, with an end towards drawing out all the giggling secrets; but a grown-up with a curious turn of mind will do well to encourage it sometimes among his own associates, and observe closely the result. Watch their eyes and hands, the way they form their sentences, the devious turn of their lies or else their shattering frankness; and much is to be learned of their natures. . . . After asking that question, I was reminded of nothing so much as a group of adolescents playing with an uneasy question in a game of Truth.

They looked at each other. Even Lady Benning had stiffened. Her jewel-gaudy hands were still pressed over her eyes, but she might have been peering out between the fingers; she began to tremble, then uttered what might have been a moan or a sob, and slid back against the gaudier red-lined cloak.

"NO!" said Major Featherton explosively.

It broke the tension. Halliday murmured, "Good man! Speak up, old girl. Banish the hobgoblins. Tell 'em all about it."

"I—I don't know," said Marion, with a dull and incredulous half-smile at the fireplace. She looked up. "I don't honestly know, but I don't think so. You see, Mr. Blake, you've got us into such a position that we shall look most awful fools if we say, 'No.'—Wait! I'll put it another way. I don't know whether or not I believe *in the supernatural.* I rather fancy I do. There's something in this house—" her eyes moved round quickly. "I—I haven't been myself, and there may be something terrible and unnatural here. But if you ask me whether I think Mr. Darworth is an impostor, the answer is YES! After hearing what that Dennis boy had to say. . . ." She shuddered.

"Then, my dear Miss Latimer," boomed the major, massaging his jaw, "why, in the name of heaven——"

"You see?" she said quietly, and smiled. "That's what I meant. I didn't like that man. I think I hated him. It was the way he talked, the manner he had; oh, I can't explain it, except that I've heard of people getting in the power of—of doctors before. He was a kind of super-doctor who poisoned you so that—" her eyes slid quickly to Halliday, and as quickly darted away, "so that: well, it's horrible to talk of, but you could almost see maggots crawling on people you knew—and loved! And the odd thing is that it's like a spell in the story-books. He's dead. And we're all free, as I wanted to be free."

Her cheeks were flushed, and her speech rapid to incoherence. Ted let out a whinny of laughter.

He said: "I say, angel, I shouldn't go on like that, you know. You're only providing motives for murder."

"Well, well," said Halliday, and took the cigarette out of his mouth. "Want your face knocked off, do you?"

Ted studied him. Ted was very much the young intellectual then, drawn back a little, supercilious, touching his sprouting mustache. He would have been ludicrous had it not been for the fighting fanaticism of his eyes.

"Oh, if it comes to that, old son, motives for all of us. With the possible exception of myself. And that's unfortunate, because I haven't much objection to being accused. . . ." It was the very familiar aloof Chelsea strain, and I think he caught Halliday's slight grimace, for his face hardened; he went on rapidly: "Especially as they'll never be able to arrest anybody. Yes, I believed in Darworth, and I still do! It seems to me you're all doing a hell of a lot of shuffling and sliding, the moment someone says, 'Coppers!' Let 'em come! I'm glad of this, in a way. It'll throw a demonstration of the truth at the whole world, and the morons who've always tried to block every bit of real scientific progress—" He swallowed hard. "All right, all right! Say I'm potty, but this will have demonstrated it to the world. Now isn't it worth a man's life—and what's a man's life compared to scientific——"

"Yes," said Halliday. "You only seem to be interested in man's life after he's dead. As for the rest of it, I've heard all that poisonous nonsense before." He looked at the other sharply. "By the way, what are you getting at, anyhow?"

Ted thrust out his neck. He tapped his finger slowly on the back of the chair. His head was wagging, and his face screwed up into a probably unintentional sneer.

"Only this, my boy. Simply this. We're not altogether without brains. We heard your policemen smashing down that door; we heard a good deal of what was said, and what's thought. . . . And until your Scotland Yard can tell us how Darworth was killed, I'll keep my own ideas."

He glanced across the hearth, as though carelessly, and his eyes narrowed. Inexplicably, we must all have experienced a sense of shock to see that Lady Benning was sitting up.

She was dry-eyed now, but so dull of face that the blacklace gown, all the elaborate deckings-out of a shell, became harsh travesty. On God knows what impulse—but I remembered it afterwards—Major Featherton bent over and settled the cape about her shoulders. With the red lining gone, she became a somber part of the gloom. Only the bracelets on her arm glittered as she put her elbow on the arm of the chair, her flabby chin against her knuckles, and stared down as though at flames in the dead fire. She hunched her shoulders, drearily.

"Thank you, William," she said. "These courtesies—! Yes. Yes, I am better now."

Featherton said gruffly: "If anything's upset you, Anne, I'll——"

"No, you won't, William." Her hand slid up as his big shoulder lifted. It was comedy, or tragedy, or whatever you like. "Ask Mr. Blake, or Dean, or Marion," she went on without lifting her eyes. "*They* know."

"You mean, Lady Benning," I said, "what Joseph told us?"

"In a way. Yes."

"Seriously, then: had you never suspected Darworth of being an impostor?"

We heard voices begin calling outside the house; a hail, somebody's answer, the clumping of footsteps coming nearer. A muffled voice at the front said: "Carry y'r own ruddy tripod, can'tcher? W'ere the 'ell? . . ." Somebody replied, there was a mutter of mirth, and the footsteps clumped on round the side of the house. Lady Benning spoke.

"Suspected? We do not know Mr. Darworth was an impostor. If so, I am sure of one thing. . . . *They* are not impostors. They are real. He tampered with them, and they killed him."

There was a pause. She felt the atmosphere.

"I am an old woman, Mr. Blake," she said, looking up suddenly. "I had very little to make me happy. I never asked you into my life. But you came into it, with your—your great boots, and your bullyings of half-witted children like Joseph—and you trampled that little garden down. For the love of God, my friend, in the name of His mercy, do nothing more!"

She pressed her hands together, and turned away.

"Part of it, Lady Benning," I said, "would seem a very terrible gospel. Were you made happy to think, or did you really think, that your nephew could be possessed, and go amuck like a devil?"

For answer she regarded Halliday.

"You! Oh, my dear boy, I don't doubt *you're* happy. You're young, you're rich, you have a beautiful girl. . . ." Lady Benning spoke with soft malevolence, turning out her wrist as she uttered each phrase, so that she sounded horribly like a burlesque Shylock. "You have health, and friends, and a quiet bed at night. Not like poor James, out there in the cold. Why shouldn't you worry and squirm a little? Why shouldn't that pretty doll, with her lips and her fine body, why shouldn't she sicken and worry her heart out? Do her good, instead of so much kissing. Why shouldn't I encourage it? . . . It wasn't *you* I worried about. It wasn't for you I wanted this house cleansed. It was for James. James must stay there in the cold until the foul thing is gone out of this house. Perhaps James *is* the foul thing——"

"Anne, my dear old friend!" said Major Featherton. "Good God, this won't do. . . ."

"And now," Lady Benning went on, in a sharp but very matter-of-fact tone, "Roger Darworth has cheated me. Very well. I only wish I had known it sooner."

I restrained Halliday, who was regarding his aunt with incredulous eyes, and he had started to say, "You encouraged—" I said quickly:

"Cheated you, Lady Benning?"

She hesitated, seeming to come to herself. "If he was an impostor, he cheated me. If not, he still failed to exorcise what is in this house. In either case, it slew him. He failed. And therefore he cheated me." Lady Benning lay back in her chair and commenced to laugh, in shuddering convulsions, as though she had made a hilariously witty reply. Then she wiped her eyes. "Ah, ah. I mustn't forget. Was there anything else you wanted to ask me, Mr. Blake?"

"Yes. Something I should like to ask everybody. . . . A week ago tonight, I am given to understand, there was an informal gathering at Major Featherton's flat. At this gathering, Mr. Darworth was persuaded to try automatic writing. Is that correct?"

The old lady turned and prodded at Featherton's coat.

"Didn't I tell you?" she demanded, in malevolent triumph. "Didn't I tell you, William? . . . I knew it. When that police-officer came in here a while ago, and tried to bully us, he had a younger man with him. Another policeman, the one who took charge of Joseph. He didn't show his face to us, but I knew who it was. It was the police spy they sent to us, and we received as a friend."

Ted Latimer jumped up. "Oh, I say! That's utter rot! Bert Mc-

Donnell—oh, yes, I know!—I thought I recognized him, in the dark, when he came in after that log, and didn't answer when I spoke to him . . . but, damn it, that's impossible! Bert McDonnell's no more on the police force than I am. The idea's absurd. Fantastic. . . . Look here, it isn't true, is it?"

I evaded as well as I could, by referring them to Masters, for I wished no more digressions. Halliday, I could see, was preventing Marion from speaking; and I kept my eyes on Major Featherton while I sketched out what we knew of the evening. The major seemed uneasy.

"And we are informed that Darworth was terrified, apparently by what he saw on that paper. . . ." I glanced round.

"Yes, by Gad, he was!" Featherton blurted, and drove one gloved fist into his palm. "Funk. Sheer funk. Never saw it worse."

Ted said blankly: "Yes. Yes, it *must* have been Bert. . . ."

"And, of course, if anybody saw what was on that paper——"

The silence held for so long a time that it appeared I had drawn a blank. Lady Benning was disinterested, but she had a contemptuous eye on Ted, who was blankly muttering something to himself.

"A pack of foolery, of course," the major announced. He cleared his throat several times. "But—aaah—for what it's worth, I think I can tell you the first line. Don't look at me like that, Anne! Confound it, I never did approve of your nonsense, and I'll tell you this besides . . . those pictures I was dragooned into buying . . . H'm, yes. Now that I think of it. They go into the fire tomorrow. . . . What was I saying? Ah! The first line. Remember it distinctly. It said, '*I know where Elsie Fenwick is buried.*'"

There was another silence, while the major stood back, wheezing and stroking at his mustache in a sort of swaggering defiance.

You could hear no sound but his asthmatic breathing. Repeating the words aloud, I looked round the group. Either one person in that group of five was a magnificent actor, or else the words meant absolutely nothing to anybody. Only two remarks were made in the space of possibly three minutes: which can seem a very long time. Ted Latimer said, "Who's Elsie Fenwick?" in a querulous tone, as though irrelevant matters were being dragged in; and later Halliday observed thoughtfully: "Never heard of her." Then they all stood and looked at the major, whose port-wine cheeks were growing more mottled, and his puffings louder, as at some slur on his veracity.

And I was becoming morally certain that one of the five people before me was the murderer of Roger Darworth.

"Well?" Featherton demanded explosively. "Say something, one of you!"

"You didn't tell us of this before, William," said Lady Benning.

Featherton made a vague and irritated gesture. "But it was a *woman's* name, confound it," he protested, as though he were not certain of the issues himself. "Don't you see? It was a woman's name."

Ted looked round in a sort of wild amusement, as though he had seen a caricature he could not believe. Halliday muttered something about the Medes and the Persians; Marion's face wore a bright and interested expression, and she said, "Oh!" Only Lady Benning studied him grimly, catching her cloak about her neck. . . .

Heavy footfalls clumped along the hall outside, and we all turned. The tension went back to chill hostility as Masters strode into the room.

Masters returned the hostility. I have never seen him look more disheveled, more worried, or more sinister. His coat was muddy, like the bowler jammed on the back of his head. He stood in the doorway, surveying the group slowly.

"Well?" asked Ted Latimer. The way he pitched his voice, in those circumstances, was less like defiance than childish impertinence. "Are we free to go home? How long do you intend keeping us here?"

Masters kept looking round. As though on an impulse, he let himself smile. He said, nodding:

"Why, I'll tell you, ladies and gentlemen." Carefully drawing off his muddy gloves, he reached inside his overcoat and drew out a watch. "It's now just twenty-five minutes past three. To be frank, we may be here until daylight. You may go as soon as I have had a statement from each of you—needn't be on oath, of course, but I should suggest frankness. . . .

"We shall want these statements separately. My men are making one of the rooms as comfortable as possible, and we shall want you in one at a time. Meantime, I'll send a constable in here to keep you company, and see that no harm comes to anybody. We regard you all as valuable witnesses, ladies and gentlemen."

The smile grew tighter. "And now, um, excuse me. Mr. Blake! Will you step out here a moment, please? I should like a word in private."

IX
"LOCKED IN A STONE BOX"

MASTERS TOOK me down to the kitchen before he spoke. Joseph was not there now. The work-bench had been slewed round so that it faced the door; with the candles burning in a line across it, and a chair drawn up a few feet out for witnesses, the background made it resemble pictures of the Inquisition's tribunal-room.

The yard behind was noisy and full of darting lights. Somebody was climbing up on the roof of the little stone house; the puff of a flashlight-powder glared out momentarily, so that the house, the wall, the crooked tree, looked as wild as a scene from Doré. Close at hand, a muffled voice said in an awed tone, "Lummy, but 'e *got* it, didn't 'e?" Another voice muttered, "Uh!" and somebody scratched a match.

Masters jabbed his finger out towards the scene of activity.

"I'm beaten, sir," he said. "Right now, at least, I'm beaten, and I don't mind admitting it. This thing can't have happened, but it did. We've got the evidence—clear evidence, plain evidence— that nobody in God's world could have got into that house or out of it. But Darworth's dead. Let me tell you how bad it is. . . . Wait! Have *you* learned anything?"

I started to sketch out what I had learned, and he stopped me when I was telling about Joseph. "Ah! Ah, yes. I'm glad you saw him; so did I." He was still smiling grimly. "I sent the boy home in a cab, under guard of a constable. He may not be in any danger, but on the other hand——"

"Danger?"

"Yes. Oh, the first part of it hangs together, sir. Neat; very neat. Darworth didn't fear this house because of its ghosts. He was very, very easy about the ghosts. What he did fear was physical harm from somebody—eh? *Why else, d'ye think, did he bolt and bar his door out there?* He wasn't trying to keep out a ghost with an iron bolt. But he thought somebody in his little spiritualist circle had designs on him, and didn't know which one. That was why he wanted to keep Joseph away from them tonight: to watch, and to find out. He knew it was one of this group, from the bogus message that'd been stuck among his automatic-writing drivel when only one of them could've done it. D'ye see, sir? There was something, or somebody, he was deadly afraid of; and this was a good time to get a line on who it might have been. He thought he was safe out there. . . ."

Then I told Masters about Major Featherton's evidence.

"'I know where Elsie Fenwick is buried—'" he repeated. His big shoulders grew rigid, and his eyes narrowed. "That name's familiar. By George, that name's familiar! And it's associated with Darworth. I could swear to it. But it's been a long time since I've seen the man's dossier, so I'm not sure. Bert will know. Elsie Fenwick! We've got something; I'm positive of it."

He was silent a long time, biting at the joint of his thumb, muttering to himself. Then he turned.

"Now, then, let me tell you the mess we're into. Do you realize it won't do us an ounce of good even to fasten on somebody we think is the murderer, if we can't show how the murderer did it? We shouldn't dare go to court, even. Eh? Listen.

"First, the house. The walls are solid stone; not a crack or rat-hole in 'em. One of my men has been going over the ceiling inch by inch, and it's as solid and unbroken as the day it was put in. We've been over every inch of the floor also——"

"You don't," I said, "waste any time."

"Aaa-h!" grunted Masters, with a sort of battered pride, as though that were all he had left. "Yes. 'Tisn't every Force could get the police surgeon out of bed at three o'clock in the morning. Well! We've been over floor, ceiling, and walls. Any idea of hinges or trap-doors or funny entrances you can get out of your mind. Statement to that effect is signed and initialed by my men.

"Next, the windows, and they're out. Those gratings are solid in the stone; no question of that. The gratings are so small that you can't even get the blade of that dagger through 'em, for instance; we tried it. The chimney isn't big enough to admit anybody, even if you could drop down into a blazing fire; and, finally, there's a heavy iron mesh across it only a little way up. That's out. The door . . . " He paused, stared out at the yard, and bellowed: "GET OFF THAT ROOF! WHO'S ON THAT ROOF? Didn't I tell you we'd wait till morning for all that? You can't see anything——"

"*Daily Express,* Inspector," replied a voice out of the gloom. "The sergeant said——"

Masters charged down the steps and disappeared. There was a flurry of high-colored language, and presently he came back breathing hard.

"It don't much matter, I daresay," he said gloomily. "According to what we know. I was telling you. The door—well, you know about the door. Bolted, and barred; and not one of those bolts you could do tricks with, either. It's hard enough to pull back even when you're inside the place . . .

"Finally, here's the incredible thing. We shall have to wait until daylight for full confirmation, but I can tell you I know now. With the exception of the tracks you and I made—and those who came out afterwards all carefully kept in our tracks, so there'd be one line and no confusion—*there isn't a footprint anywhere within twenty feet of that house*. And you and I know, *don't* we, that when we first walked out there we saw no footprints at all along the direction we went?"

That was unquestionably true. I cast my mind back along that thin and glue-like sheet of mud: unbroken anywhere in the direction we walked. But I said:

"Still, look here, Masters. . . . Plenty of people had been walking about the yard earlier in the evening, and in and out of the house, while it was raining. Why is the mud unbroken, then? How did there come to be no footprints when we went out?"

Masters got out his notebook, pinched his nose, and frowned. "It's something to do with the soil. Something about stratum-deposits, or physics or the like; I don't know, but I've got it here," he said. "McDonnell and Dr. Blaine were talking about it. The house out there is on a kind of plateau. When the rain stops, it runs down and carries a fine sandy silt away from the place—like a mason spreading out mortar with a trowel, Bert said. The yard smells badly, you noticed. And you could hear a sort of wash out there when the rain had stopped. Bert thinks there's probably a drain somewhere, running underground to the cellar. . . . Anyhow, the rain had stopped a good three quarters of an hour before Darworth was killed, and the mud had thickened over like a jelly."

He went back into the kitchen, rubbing his face dully. Then he sat down dully on the packing-case behind the work-bench; a weird and muddy-looking Inquisitor for this bleak room.

"But there it is—solid. Unbreakable. Impossible. Ur! What am I talking about?" the Inspector muttered. "I must be getting old, and I'm sleepy. No footprints approaching the house; none! Doors and windows, floor, ceiling and walls, tight as a stone box! Yet there's got to be some way out. I won't believe——"

He was looking down at the papers on the work-bench: at George Playge's manuscript, the deed, and the newspaper cutting. He turned them over with dull curiosity, and then put them into the file-book.

"I won't believe," he went on, holding up the file and rattling it savagely, "*this.*"

"You've left few enough tatters of the supernatural, Masters. Once the police come trampling in, poor old Louis. . . ." I remembered Lady Benning twisting round to glare at me, and the words she had said. "Never mind. Anything in the nature of a definite clew?"

"Fingerprint men working now. I've got a cursory report from the doctor, but we can't get the full P-M until tomorrow. The van's here, and they'll move *him* as soon as Bailey gets finished with the interior photographs. . . . Aaa-h!" he snapped, and clenched his hands. "I wish it 'ud get daylight. Between ourselves, I never wanted daylight so much. There's an indication somewhere— somewhere—if I could see it. And I've bungled this, too. The assistant commissioner'll say I shouldn't have let *any* footprints get out there; that we should have put down boards, or some like foolishness. As though you could! I begin to see, ah, ah! I begin to see how hard it is to be methodical, and think of everything, when you're mixed up in a case yourself. Clews? No. We didn't find anything more than you saw—except a handkerchief. It's Darworth's; had his initials on it, and it was lying under him."

"There were some sheets of paper and a fountain-pen on the floor," I suggested. "Anything written?"

"No such luck. Blank. Empty. Swept clean. And that's all."

"So—now what?"

"Now," said Masters vigorously, "we interview our little tea-party. Bert's taking charge outside, and we shan't be inter-rupted. . . . Now, let's get this straight, from my notebook. It was, h'm, I judge it was roughly half-past twelve when Bert and Mr. Halliday and I left you here reading this—this bosh, and went out front there. Miss Latimer thought something had happened to Halliday, and grabbed him when we got to the front hall. Then we went into the room where the rest of 'em were, Bert stopping outside, and I had a talk which was—" he scowled.

"Abortive?"

"Ah! I suppose so. Yes, I daresay. Anyhow, the old lady (as cool as you please) ordered me to hunt over the house for some chairs so's they could all sit down. And I did. Blast her. . . . Besides, it was a good chance for a look round. The place is full of broken furniture. Then they slammed the door in my face; but we'd got young Joseph. Bert and I took him to a room across the hall from theirs, which is full of old junk, and we lit a candle and had a talk with Joseph. . . ."

"Was he full of morphine then?"

"No. But he needed it. He would sit quiet for a while, and then he'd jerk. He wouldn't admit anything. But then, I can re-member now, was when he got the morphine. He kept complaining about it being too warm, and rushed over to where it was dark and pretended to be trying to push the boards off a window. He wasn't doing that, because when I went over after him I caught him putting something back in his inside pocket. . . . Oh, there was no rough stuff!" Masters added suspiciously. "Just a little, um, polite firmness. Ha. Well, I thought if it *was* dope, I'd give it a chance to work before I tackled him again. So I left him with Bert—who," snapped Masters, "who's too bloody polite to be in the Force anyway, and I went out to have a thorough look round the house. That would have been about ten minutes to one, maybe more; but we hadn't been much time.

"I went out in the hall. The other room, where the five of 'em were, was quiet, and I thought it was dark. . . . But the front door was partly open. The big door, you know. The one we came in by."

His face was so portentous as he looked at me that I said:

"Masters, this is nonsense! Surely nobody would dare, when there was a police officer just across the hall. . . . Besides, that big door was open when we arrived. Maybe the wind. . . ."

"Ah!" growled the inspector. He tapped his chest. "That's what I thought, too. I wasn't paying any attention to these people inside; I had my eye on Darworth, you see. I wanted to queer a game of his, and so. . . . Well! I shut the door: firmly. Then I went upstairs to prowl. We'd thought, before, that you might get a better view of the house from a back upstairs window, but you couldn't. And when I came downstairs, *the front door was partly open again.* I'd only a flashlight, but it was the first thing I spotted."

He knocked his fist on the work-bench. "I tell you, sir, alone in that place . . . I damned well got the wind up myself. If I'd only thought that somebody had designs on *Darworth* . . . I went out the front door. . . ."

"The place is muddy all around," I suggested. "Footprints?"

"There were no footprints whatever," Masters returned quietly.

We looked at each other. Even with the police in possession, with flash-powders exploding and reporters fighting for news, this house had become full of more monstrous and terrible things than existed in the letters I had read.

"I went round the side of the house," the inspector continued, "and I've told you what I saw and heard. Shadows inside. Darworth moaning or imploring. Then—the bell."

He paused, and let out a sound resembling, "Haa-ah!" as of a man finishing off a deep drink that has almost choked him. "Now, sir! Now! And here's what I wanted to ask you. You tell me you heard somebody walking past your door, when you were sitting in this room reading? Yes. Well, then: which direction was it going? Was it going out towards the back yard, or returning from there?"

The only answer was, or could be, "I don't know."

He wheezed. "Because, if it was coming back to the house—I mean this house; the big one here—after, say, 'visiting' Darworth. . . . You see, I came round the side of the house into the back yard. I could see the back door, with the candlelight shining from here, I could even see the part of the yard towards me. . . . Then what kind of hell-bound thing is it that can walk out a front door, round through a muddy yard without leaving footprints; can kill Darworth in a stone jug of a house, and return here by the back door, and pass through candlelight without being seen?"

During the ensuing silence he nodded curtly and went to the door. I could hear him addressing the constable he had sent up to the front room as a guard against the five suspects' comparing notes. Vaguely I heard him giving instructions that Lady Benning was to be sent back here to our "council-room"; vaguely I wondered what my old Chief at the M.I.D., that rather great figure whom Featherton's remark had put into my mind, would have thought of this muddle. "What kind of hell-bound thing is it that can . . . ?" I looked up, to see Masters striding back.

"If," he said uncertainly, "the old lady goes to pieces again, the way you say she did before——"

He hesitated. His hand went slowly to his hip-pocket, and he took out that gunmetal flask, which in his own placid thoroughness he kept for the convenience of nervous believers at spiritist sétances. He juggled it in his hand. His eyes wore a curiously blank look. Along the passage we could hear someone limping towards the council-room, and the booming tones of a constable urging caution.

"You drink it, Masters," I said.

X
THE TESTIMONY IN THE CASE

IT IS to Masters' thoroughness that I am indebted for the actual word-for-word record of the testimony we received. Masters does not trust to brief notes. Into his fat notebooks you will find entered in shorthand every word spoken by the person he has questioned: except, of course, things obviously irrelevant. This is later deciphered, rearranged, and typed into a statement which he submits for the witness to initial. With his permission, I have got copies of these notes, filled in also with the questions he asked but did not write down at the time.

These, then, constitute mere extracts from that vast jumble of talk: they are designedly incomplete, but they are submitted because they may be of interest to the puzzle-analyst, and for the significance of certain statements among them.

The first is headed *"Lady Anne Benning, widow; wife of the late Sir Alexander Benning, O.B.E."* It does not convey the atmosphere of that bleak room, where the spurious Watteau marquise faced Masters across the candles; with the clock-hands crawling towards four, and the stolid constable looming in the shadows behind, and outside the noise of Darworth's body being dumped into a black van.

She was even more hostile than before. They had given her a chair; the red cloak-lining gleamed again, and she sat upright with her jeweled hands clenched tightly in her lap. About her there was a sort of evil jauntiness. She moved her head as though she were looking for a place to touch Masters on the raw; the pouched eyes were half shut, and you could see wrinkles along the lids; and she still smiled. They went through the formalities without clashing, though Major Featherton—who insisted on accompanying her—had to be rather forcibly urged from the room. I can see her yet, lifting an eyebrow or hand slightly, and hear the thin chill metal of her voice.

Q. Lady Benning, how long have you known Mr. Darworth?

A. I really can't say. Does it matter? Eight months, possibly a year.

Q. How did you come to make his acquaintance?

A. Through Mr. Theodore Latimer, if it matters. He told me of Mr. Darworth's interest in the occult, and brought him to see me at my home.

Q. Yes. And we understand that you'd been in what we'll call a receptive state for that sort of thing. Is that correct, Lady Benning?

A. My dear man, I am not going to answer mere impertinences.

Q. Just so. Did you know anything about Darworth?

A. I knew, for instance, that he was a gentleman, and well-bred.

Q. I mean, anything about his past life?

A. No.

Q. Did he tell you, in fact, something like this: That, though he was not a medium himself, he was intensely psychic; that he felt you had suffered a great bereavement, and influences were trying to get in touch with you; that he was the patron of a medium who he thought could help you? Did he, Lady Benning?

A. (A long hesitation) Yes. But not at first, not for a long time. He was very sympathetic about James.

Q. And a meeting with the medium was arranged?

A. Yes.

Q. Where?

A. At Mr. Darworth's house in Charles Street.

Q. Were there many such meetings afterwards?

A. Many. (Here the witness began to show discomposure).

Q. Where, Lady Benning, you 'got through'—so to speak—to Mr. James Halliday?

A. For God's sake, will you stop torturing me!

Q. Sorry. You understand, ma'am, I have to do this. Did Mr. Darworth join the circle?

A. Rarely. He said it disturbed him.

Q. So that he was not in the room at all?

A. No.

Q. Did you know anything about the medium?

A. No. (Hesitation). Except that he was not altogether of sound mind. Mr. Darworth had discussed his case with the doctor in charge of the London League of Mercy for the mentally deficient. He told me how highly the doctor had praised James, and how much they thought of him. James used to send £50 yearly to the League. Mr. Darworth said it was only a small piece of thoughtfulness, but it was wonderful.

Q. Just so. You made no inquiries about Mr. Darworth?

A. No.

Q. Ever give him money?

No reply.

Q. Was it a great deal of money, Lady Benning?

A. My dear man, surely even you must have the intelligence to see that it is none of your business.

Q. Who first suggested that Plague Court should be exorcised?

A. (The witness spoke very strongly). My nephew James.

Q. I mean, who—Let's say, among people who can be called more easily as witnesses, who first put the suggestion into audible English?

A. Thank you so much for the correction. It was I.

Q. What did Mr. Darworth think of it?

A. He did not wish to do it at first.

Q. But you convinced him?

A. (The witness made no reply, but used the words '*or said he didn't,*' as though to herself).

Q. Does the name 'Elsie Fenwick' mean anything to you, Lady Benning?

A. No.

This dialogue, as I remember it, contained nothing more than is set down in Masters' notes. She had not rambled or digressed, even when she faltered; and she had definitely had the better of the exchange. Masters, I think, was coolly angry. When he said, "*Now we come to tonight*—" I expected on her part a quick watchfulness or tension. Nothing of the sort happened.

Q. In this room a while ago, Lady Benning, after Mr. Blake had been speaking to Joseph Dennis, you made use of the expression, 'Come into the front room, you, and ask which one of us killed Roger Darworth?'

A. Yes.

Q. What did you mean by it?

A. Did you ever hear of sarcasm, sergeant? I simply supposed the police would be fools enough to think so.

Q. But *you* don't think so?

A. Think what?

Q. Frankly, that one of the five people in the front room murdered Mr. Darworth?

A. No.

Q. Will you please tell us, Lady Benning, what happened after the five of you closed the door and retired for your (a word erased and substituted in the notes) prayers?

A. Nothing happened, in a psychic sense. We did not form a circle. We sat round the fireplace, and sat or knelt as we chose.

Q. Was it too dark for you to see anybody?

A. I dare say. The fire had gone out. I really did not notice.

Q. Not notice?

A. Oh, go away, you fool. My mind was on other things. Do you know what prayer is? Real prayer? If you did, you wouldn't ask stupid questions.

Q. Just so. You didn't *hear* anything at all, then—a chair creaking—a door opening—somebody getting up—for example?

A. No.

Q. You are sure?

No reply.

Q. Did anyone speak between the time this, this vigil began and the time you heard the bell ringing?

A. I heard nothing at all.

Q. But you are not prepared to swear there was nothing of the kind?

A. I am not prepared to swear anything, sergeant. Not just yet.

Q. Very well, Lady Benning. Then at least you will tell us this: How were you sitting? I mean, what was the order of chairs in which you sat?

A. (Here were some protestations and denials). Well, I was

on the extreme right of the fireplace. My nephew Dean was next to me, and then I think Miss Latimer. The others I am not sure of.

Q. Do you know of anybody, any living person, who wished to do Mr. Darworth harm?

A. No.

Q. Do you think he was a fake?

A. Possibly. It in no way affects the truth of—the Truth.

Q. Do you still deny that you gave him money?

A. I don't think I've denied anything of the sort. (Very bitterly and suddenly). If I had, do you think I should be such a fool as to admit it?

She seemed to feel triumphant as Masters let her go; Major Featherton was summoned to give her his arm back to the front room. Masters made no comment, and his face was inscrutable. He asked next for Ted Latimer.

Ted made a different sort of witness. He sauntered in with a defiant superciliousness, and tried to rattle Masters with a scrutiny of this sort: which only succeeded in making Ted look slightly drunk. Masters let him look, pretending to be mulling over his notes. During the silence, Ted scraped his chair noisily before sitting down; frowned, and appeared to grow conscious of his grimy face. Though he tried to keep his aloof disdain, he grew rather verbose in his testimony, wherein deleted parts are indicated with dots.

Q. How long have you known Mr. Darworth?

A. Oh, a year, more or less. It was through our mutual interest in modern art. D'you know the Cadroc galleries in Bond Street, Inspector? Well, it was there. Leon Dufour had been exhibiting some rather fine things in soap——

Q. In what?

A. (The witness showed amusement, and grew more at ease). That's right, Inspector; I said soap. Sculpture, you know. Mr. Darworth preferred and bought some more massive library-pieces in rock-salt. I admit they had life, but they lacked Dufour's delicacy of line. . . .

Q. Now, come, Mr. Latimer; I'm afraid we're not interested in all that kind of thing. Lady Benning's told us about making Mr. Darworth's acquaintance, and what happened then. I suppose you got to be pretty good friends?

A. I found him very interesting. A cultured man of the world, Inspector, such as we rarely find in England. He had studied under Dr. Adler, of Vienna—you know of him, of course?—and was himself a proficient psychiatrist. Of course, as one man of the world to another, we had many interesting talks.

Q. Know anything about his past life?

A. Not much that I remember. (Hesitation). At one time, though, I was very much in love with a young lady in Chelsea, and, ah, certain inhibitions were preventing me from making her my mistress. Mr. Darworth straightened out my difficulties, explaining that this was a fear complex due to her resemblance to a governess I had once had in childhood . . . which adjusted my mind, and for some months afterward she and I were successfully adjusted. . . . But I remember Mr. Darworth mentioned he had once had a wife, now dead, with whom he had experienced a similar difficulty. . . .

There was much more piffle of this description, in which Ted enjoyed himself and Masters was obviously shocked. No further facts were elicited. The whole affair, however, tended to make Ted more and more kindly disposed towards Masters; growing, in fact, almost paternal.

Q. You introduced Mr. Darworth to your sister?

A. Oh, yes. Right away.

Q. Did she like him?

A. (Hesitation). Yes, she seemed to. Quite a lot. Of course, Inspector, Marion's a strange kid; not quite developed, if you understand me. I thought he would do her good, explaining her own emotions to her.

Q. Um, just so. Did you introduce him to Mr. Halliday?

A. You mean Dean? Oh, Marion did; or Lady Benning. I forget which.

Q. Did they get on well together?

A. Well, no. You see, Dean's a very good fellow, but he's a little pre-war and (N. B. I think the word here is *bourgeois,* although it is strangely spelled in Masters' account).

Q. But was there any definite trouble?

A. I don't know whether you'd call it trouble exactly. Dean told him one night that he had a mind to smash his face and hang him on the chandelier for luck. You see, it was hard to quarrel with old Darworth. He wouldn't take fire. Sometimes, confound him——!

Pauses and mutterings; witness pressed to go on.

A. Well, all I can say is that I should like to have seen that fight. Dean's the fastest amateur middleweight I ever watched. I saw him flatten Tom Rutger. . . .

This sudden splash of honesty, I could see, brought the young man up in Masters' estimation. The questioning went on rapidly. Darworth, it seemed, had plunged almost at once into occult matters. At Joseph's first séance there was mention of the uneasy ghost at Plague Court, and the spiritual agonies of James Halliday. When this was mentioned to Darworth, he had grown more interested and disturbed; had many long conferences with Marion Latimer and Lady Benning, "especially Marion"; had borrowed Halliday's account in the form of the Playge letters; and, at the insistence of Lady Benning, the experiment was to be tried. Perhaps Masters made a mistake in dwelling too long on this. In any event, Ted had time to work himself into his old state of fanaticism. What loomed always larger, and swelled and assumed monstrous shapes, was the smiling figure of Darworth. It mocked us after death. We felt and fought, but could not break, the uncanny power he had exercised over these people: the grim old woman with her spites and dreams, the unstable young man sitting in the chair and glaring back at Masters.

The struggle grew as question after question was flung at him. On one point, that boy was definitely mad. He rubbed his grimy face, he struck the arm of the chair; sometimes he laughed and sometimes he almost sobbed; as though it were Darworth who was the true ghost, standing at his elbow and prodding him to hysteria, in those chill hours before dawn. Masters was calling for full stage-thunder now.

Q. Very well! If you don't believe Darworth was killed by a human being, what have you to say to Joseph Dennis' statement that Darworth *did* fear somebody here—in this house—feared harm?

A. I say it's a damned lie. Are you going to take the word of a damned drug-addict?

Q. So you knew he was a drug-addict, did you?

A. I thought he might be.

Q. And you still believed in him?

A. What difference does that make? It didn't affect his psychic powers. Can't you see anything? A painter or composer doesn't lose his genius because of drugs or alcohol. God damn it, are you blind? It's just the opposite.

Q. Steady, sir. Do you deny that one of the people in that

front room might have got up and gone out while you were all in the dark. Do you deny it?

A. Yes!

Q. You will swear that nobody did?

A. Yes!

Q. What if I told you that a chair was heard to creak in there, and the door open or close?

A. (Slight hesitation). Whoever says that is lying.

Q. Careful, now. Are you sure?

A. Yes. We might have shifted round in our chairs. Creakings! What's that, anyway? You sit in any dark room, and you'll hear plenty of creakings.

Q. How close were you sitting together?

A. I don't know. Two or three feet apart, maybe.

Q. But you did hear noises of some kind? So that one person might have got up, on a stone floor, and gone out without attracting attention?

A. I've just told you that nobody did.

Q. You were praying?

A. Rot! Absolute rot, like everything else. Praying! Of course not. Do I look like a pious Methodist? I was trying to establish communication to give power to a mind exorcising the earthbound. I was focusing, as powerfully as I could. I—I could feel my brain almost bursting. Praying!

Q. In what order were you sitting; how arranged?

A. I'm not positive. Dean blew out the candles, and we were all standing up then. Then we started groping after the chairs that were already there. I was on the extreme left of the fireplace, that's all I know. We were all—flurried.

Q. But didn't you notice when you heard the bell, and you all got up again?

A. No. There was a lot of milling about in the dark. It was old Featherton who lit the candles, and he was swearing. The next thing I knew we were all going towards the door. I don't know who was where, or anything about it.

Masters let him go then. Masters offered to let him go home; but, although he was patently exhausted and on the verge of breaking-down, he refused to go until the others had gone.

The inspector brooded, his head in his hands. "It's a worse muddle yet," he said. "They were all exalted or hysterical, or something. If we can't get any clearer evidence than that. . . ." He wriggled his fingers, cramped from the note-taking, and then wearily told the constable to send in Major Featherton.

The examination of Major William Featherton, retired, 4th Royal Lancashire Foot, was very brief, and not till the end did it seem to grow informative. The major's earlier pompous manners were gone, and his rolling diction subdued into sharp, concise replies. He sat straight in his chair, as though at a court-martial; the eyes under the downpulled, grizzled brows fixed Masters bluntly, and his words were interrupted only when he cleared his throat, or leaned his head on one side to brush his neck with a handkerchief. I noticed that, aside from Lady Benning, he was the only person there with clean hands.

He explained that he had known Darworth only slightly; that he was drawn into the affair only through his friendship for Lady Benning; that he saw and knew little of the man. He knew of nobody who had a definite animus against Darworth, though he understood the man had not been generally liked, and had been blackballed from several clubs.

Q. Now, about tonight, sir

A. Ask anything you like, Inspector Masters. I'm bound to tell you that your suspicions are nonsense, but I know your duty and mine.

Q. Thank you, sir. Exactly so. Now, how long should you say you were sitting in the dark?

A. Twenty to twenty-five minutes. I several times looked at my watch. It has a luminous dial. I wondered how long the foolery would go on.

Q. Then you were not concentrating, or anything?

A. No.

Q. Then didn't your eyes get accustomed to the dark, so you could see?

A. It was confoundedly dark there, Inspector. And my eyes— not strong these days, confound it. No, I couldn't see much. Shapes, maybe.

Q. Did you see anybody get up?

A. No.

Q. Did you hear anybody?

A. Yes.

Q. Ah, just so. Please describe what you heard.

A. (Slight hesitation). Hard to do. Naturally, at first, there was a lot of settling round and creaking in chairs. It wasn't that. It was more like somebody pushing back a chair a little, a scraping. Didn't notice it much, I'm bound to tell you. Later I thought I heard somebody's footstep somewhere. Hard to judge sounds in the dark.

Q. How much later?

A. I don't know. Fact is, d'ye see, I was going to call out and say 'Hey!' But Anne—Lady Benning—had driven it into us that nobody was to speak or move no matter what happened. We'd all to promise that. First off, I thought 'Somebody sneaking out for a cigarette.' Damned rummy thing to do, though, I thought. Then I heard a squeak out of the door, and felt a draft.

Q. As though the door had been opened?

A. (The witness here had a fit of coughing, and paused). Look here, say more as though the big door—the front door, d'ye see—opened. Not much draft in that hall to begin with. Wouldn't like to say, though. Now, see here, Inspector, I'm bound to tell you the truth. But, as a sensible man, come! You know yourself that it don't mean a tinker's curse, a thing like that. Somebody went out, and now is afraid to admit. . . .

The major here for the first time was definitely perturbed, as though he had given the wrong impression or said more than he intended. He attempted to cover it up by pointing out that there were any number of noises in the dark; that he might have been mistaken on some of them. After some sharp wrangling, Masters dropped the point. I think he felt a shrewd suspicion that Featherton, in a coroner's court, could easily be made to swear to this again. He went on swiftly to the question about the arrangement of chairs.

A. Lady Benning sat where she's been sitting: right hand side of the fireplace. Funny, too. I wanted to sit beside her, to—well, I wanted to sit there, but she pushed me away. Young Halliday sat down there. I know, because I almost tumbled in his lap. Ha. They'd blown out the candles, then, d'ye see, and I had to grope along. Miss Latimer was sitting beside him. I got the next chair. I'm pretty certain young Latimer was just the other side of me. He hadn't got up.

Q. When you heard this noise, which direction did it come from; the noise of the chair being scraped back?

A. Confound it, I told you you can't place noises in the dark! Might have been anywhere. Mightn't have been at all.

Q. Did you feel anybody brush past you?

A. No.

Q. How far were the chairs apart?

A. Don't remember.

The candles were almost burnt out by now. One of them leaped into a broad sheet of flame, wabbled, and puffed out just as the major rose from his chair. "All right," Masters said dully. "You're free to go home if you like, major. I should suggest that you take Lady Benning. Of course, you must hold yourself in readiness for further questioning. . . . Yes. And please ask Miss Latimer and Mr. Halliday to come in. Oh, I won't detain them five minutes unless something turns up, um, important. Thanks, ah, thanks. Most helpful."

Featherton stopped in the doorway; and the constable stepped forward and handed him his hat, rather as though the major had just finished a victorious street-fight. It was a silk hat, which he brushed with his sleeve while he peered about the room. For the first time he seemed to observe me; I was sitting on a window-sill over in the gloom. Major Featherton puffed out his blue-veined cheeks. Fitting on the hat somewhat rakishly, he gave it a pat on top, and said: "Ah, Mr. Blake! Yes, of course . . . Mr. Blake, would you mind telling me your home address?"

I told him, subduing curiosity.

"Ah, yes, the Edwardian House, yes. If it's convenient, I'll call on you there tomorrow. Good night, gentlemen, good night."

Settling his coat on his shoulders with an air of mystery, he stalked out, and almost bumped into Sergeant McDonnell coming in.

XI
THE HANDLE OF A DAGGER

McDonnell looked harassed, and there were sharp lines of fatigue drawn slantwise under his eyes. In one hand he carried a bundle of penciled notes, and in the other a big lantern which he set down on the floor.

For the first time I realized how chill it was in the room, how sleep was stiffening my eyelids and joints, how for the last half hour sounds had been dwindling in the yard outside until it was now silent. Voices and footsteps had passed; the gears of a car ground far away. It was the dead, misty hour when you could smell dawn in the air. The street-lamps still burned, but there were already faint stirrings from the city.

McDonnell's lantern made a cartwheel of light on the brick floor. It wove a little before my eyes; and above it was the sergeant's ugly, sharp-nosed, whimsical face. His greenish eyes contemplated Masters, who was sitting with knuckles pressed against forehead. McDonnell's hat was plastered on the back of his head, and one strand of hair waved out grotesquely over his eye. He clinked his foot against the lantern to rouse Masters.

He said: "How much longer do you want me to carry on, sir. They've all gone now. Bailey said he'd be back for those pictures as soon as it was light."

"Bert," said the inspector dully, without looking up, "you had a line on Darworth. Who's Elsie Fenwick?"

McDonnell jumped a little. "Elsie——?"

"For God's sake don't tell me *you* don't know! I know the name; I know it's connected with Darworth, and also with funny business; but I can't remember how. You were right; we got it from Featherton. The first line on that paper was, 'I know where Elsie Fenwick is buried.'"

"What ho!" said McDonnell, and opened his eyes. He remained staring at the candles for so long that Masters slapped the work-bench. "Sorry, sir. But it's pretty significant, you see. It's a confirmation of funny business right enough. Elsie Fenwick," he said grimly, "is the reason why our people became interested in Darworth to begin with. That was sixteen years ago, and long before my time; but I got it out of the files when I was digging back on Darworth. It's been pretty well forgotten, but it was the bad odor of it that stirred up Number 8 Office when they heard Darworth was playing about with the occult. . . . Elsie Fenwick was Darworth's first wife."

"Got it!" said Masters abruptly. "Ha. Yes, certainly. I've got a notion I remember that case. Elsie Fenwick was the old woman, the very wealthy one, eh? She died, or something like that——"

"No, sir. At least, they tried to prove she was dead, and it would have been rather rough on Darworth if they had. She disappeared."

"Facts," said Masters. "Out with it. Story briefly. Come, now!"

McDonnell got out his notebook and leafed through it. "H'm. Dar—oh, yes. Elsie Fenwick was a romantic old girl, tied up with spiritualism, filthy rich, and no relations. She had a splay foot or shoulder, something to do with the deformity of the bones. At the tender age of sixty-five she married young Darworth. That was before the Married Woman's Property Act, so you can see what happened. Then the war came along. Darworth ducked out to avoid military service; he took his blushing bride, and a maid of hers, to Switzerland.

"One night about a year later, distracted husband phones doctor—ten miles away. Wife taken with a seizure; afraid she's dying; explains carefully she has been troubled with gastric ulcers. Mrs. Darworth was tough, apparently, and was still alive when the doctor got there. By a stroke of luck, this chap was as shrewd as they make 'em, and also knew his business better than the distracted husband had hoped. He pulled her through, then had a talk with Darworth. Darworth said: 'Horrible. Gastric ulcers.' The doctor said, 'Tut, tut.' He looked Darworth in the eye and said, 'Arsenic poisoning.'"

McDonnell lifted a sardonic eyebrow.

"Not as smooth," grunted Masters, "as he became afterwards, eh? Go on."

"There was trouble. A nasty scandal was only averted by the maid—Elsie Darworth's maid—swearing the old woman had swallowed arsenic herself."

"Ah! The maid. Good-looking girl?"

"I don't know, sir, but I rather doubt it. Darworth was too clever to play about when there was no cash in it."

"What did the wife say?"

"Nothing. She stood by Darworth; or forgave him, anyhow. That's the last we hear of them until the end of the war. They returned to England and settled down. One day Darworth, distracted again, walks in to our people and informs them that his wife has disappeared. They had a country place out Croydon way; the wife, according to Darworth, had simply taken a train to town to do some shopping, and never come back. He had a doctor's report to prove she had been suffering from fits of melancholia, depression, and possible amnesia—he was learning. At first the Yard let it go at that, and instituted the customary missing-person inquiries. But somebody had a suspicious mind; dug into the past, found the arsenic-episode; and then there was trouble. . . . I'll send you up the full report, sir; it's too long to go into now. The only result was that they never proved anything. . . ."

Masters hammered his fist slowly on the desk. He peered round at me.

"Yes. That's the part I do remember, though I'd have to refresh my memory. Old Burton was working on that business in '19. He told me about it. Ah, Darworth was the very living picture of outraged innocence, he was! Threatened to sue. Yes, I remember. H'm. Well, we'll look it up. What'd he do, Bert, apply for a court-order to presume her dead?"

"I believe so, but he didn't get it. He had to wait his seven years before it became automatic. Didn't much matter; he had the money."

"Yes," said Masters. He rubbed his chin. "I was only thinking—You said 'first wife.' Has he got another?"

"Yes, but they don't seem to get on. She lives on the Riviera somewhere . . . he keeps her out of the way, anyhow."

"Money?"

"I should suppose so—" McDonnell broke off. There was a shuffling of footsteps at the door, evidently to attract our attention, and somebody coughed.

Halliday and Marion Latimer were standing in the doorway. I became conscious, with that instinct we all have, that they had overheard a good deal of what McDonnell had been saying. The girl's face looked hard and contemptuous. Halliday seemed embarrassed; he glanced quickly at his companion, and then saunteerd into the room.

Halliday said: "This, Inspector, is what you really call making a night of it. It's nearly five o'clock. I tried to bribe your constable into hopping out after some coffee and sandwiches from an all-night stall, but he wouldn't do it. . . . Look here," he frowned, "I hope you'll let us off quickly. We're at your service any time, and this place isn't exactly conducive——"

Whether deliberately or unintentionally, Masters then did something which destroyed the police-court atmosphere and gave to everybody a sense of intimacy and ease. With his hand over his mouth, he brought up one of the most prodigious yawns I have ever seen; smiled at them, and blinked his eyes.

"Ah-aha-h!" said Masters, waving the girl towards the chair. "No, by George! I shan't detain you. I thought I'd see you both at once; saves time. Besides, it's like this." He grew heavily confidential. "I'm bound to tell you that I've got to ask some questions you'll probably consider pretty impertinent. Funny, though; I thought if you both heard 'em, you'd both prefer it—eh?"

Marion had a severe brown hat pulled down on her yellow hair now; the collar of the coat was turned up, and she sat down with her shoulders hunched. The dark-blue eyes regarded Masters coolly. Halliday stood behind her, and lit a cigarette.

"Yes?" she said in a clear voice, with barely perceptible nervousness. "Ask anything you like, of course." Halliday grinned.

Masters briefly reviewed the evidence about everyone's acquaintance with Darworth. "So you knew him fairly well, Miss Latimer?"

"Yes."

"Did he tell you anything about himself?"

Her gaze did not waver. "Only that he had been married, a long time ago, to a woman he'd been very unhappy with. And that she was now—I don't know; dead, I gathered." Some faint mockery tinged the voice. "He grew quite sad-eyed and Byronic about it, really."

Now, Masters has his failings, but he is quick to turn every possible situation, even a bad one, to his advantage.

"Did you know he had a wife living, Miss Latimer?"

"No. Not that it was of great interest to me. I certainly never inquired."

"Just so." He switched, instantly. "Was it Mr. Darworth who suggested to you, miss, that—we'll say, that Mr. Dean Halliday's mind and future were—well, tied up at Plague Court?"

"Yes!"

"He talked about it a lot?"

"Always," she replied, jerking the word out. "Always! I—I've tried to explain to Mr. Blake how I felt about Mr. Darworth."

"I see. Did you ever suffer from headaches, miss, or nervous disturbances?"

Her eyes opened slightly. "I don't quite see. . . . Yes, that's true."

"Which he suggested he could cure through the proper medical use of hypnotic suggestion?" She nodded. Halliday twitched his head round, and seemed about to speak, but Masters caught his eye. "Thank you, Miss Latimer. Did he ever tell you, now, why he didn't exploit his psychic talents, say? You all believed he had great powers, for instance. But nobody ever inquired whether he was a member of the Psychical Research Society, or connected with any genuine scientific body of that nature; even whether he had any genuine associations. . . . I mean, miss, didn't he ever say why he—hid his light under a bushel, or whatnot?"

"He said he was interested in savings souls and giving peace. . . ."

She hesitated, and Masters lifted his hand inquiringly.

"He said that sometime his powers might be demonstrated to the world, but that he wasn't interested in that. . . . He said he was more interested, if you want the truth, in setting *my* mind at rest about Plague Court." She spoke vacantly, but in a rapid tone. "Ugh! I say, when I remember—! He told me it would be horribly dangerous. But. that he wanted my gratitude. You see I'm frank, Inspector. I—I couldn't have said all this a week ago."

She raised her eyes. Halliday's face was ugly and satirical; with an effort, he kept himself from speaking, and mouthed his cigarette as though he would jab it against his teeth like a pipe-stem.

Masters got up heavily. The room was very quiet while he drew out the end of his watch-chain, to which was attached a small, brightly polished object. He said, smiling: "It's only a new latch-key, Miss Latimer. One of those flat ones. I happened to remember it. If you don't mind, I'd like to try a sort of experiment. . . ."

He went round the work-bench and picked up McDonnell's lantern. The girl flinched as he came towards her; she gripped the sides of the chair, and her eyes strained up at him. Close to her, he held the lantern high and steady over her head—a weird scene, with the shadow-barred glow streaming down over her upturned face, and Masters' bulk silhouetted against it. The key glittered a dazzling silver as he held it about three inches above the line of her eyes.

"I want you, Miss Latimer," he growled softly, "to look steadily at this key. . . ."

She started to get up, scraping back her chair. "No! I won't! I won't do it, I tell you, and you can't make me! Every time I look at that——"

"Ah!" said Masters, and lowered the lantern. "It's quite all right, miss. Please sit down again. I only wanted to test something." As Halliday strode forward the inspector lumbered back to his work-bench, turned, and regarded him with a sour smile. "Steady, sir. You ought to be grateful to me. I've broken at least one ghost. That there's a part of Darworth's trick of making people believe him. If the patient's a good hypnotic subject. . . ."

Wheezing, he sat down. "Did he try to cure your headaches, Miss Latimer?"

"Yes."

"*Did he ever make love to you?*"

The question was shot out so quickly after the lazy tone of the preceding one that the girl had said, "Yes," before she seemed to realize it. Masters nodded.

"Ever ask you to marry him, Miss Latimer?"

"Not—not exactly. He said that if he succeeded in cleansing this house of evil spirits, he would ask . . . I say! It—it sounds so crazy, and absurd, and—" She swallowed hard, and her eyes were hysterically amused. "I mean, when I think of it. He was like a Monte Cristo and Manfred rolled into one; gloomy and apart; like a cheap film, like—But you didn't know him, you see. That's the point."

"A rare sort of fellow, that gentleman," the inspector said dryly. "He had a different mood and character for everyone he approached. . . . But after all, you see, he was murdered. That's what we want to talk about now. It wasn't hypnotism or suggestion that let somebody walk through a stone wall or a bolted door and hack him to pieces. Now, Mr. Halliday!—I want to hear everything that went on in that front room from the time the lights were put out. Tell your story, and I'll ask Miss Latimer to confirm it."

"Right you are. I'll tell it exactly," nodded Halliday; "because I've been thinking of nothing else all night." He drew a deep breath, and then glanced sharply at Masters. "You spoke to the others. Did *they* admit hearing somebody moving around in there?"

"You're telling the story, sir," Masters reminded him, lifting his shoulders blandly. "But, um, didn't you have a conference among yourselves? All that time between witnesses, up there?"

"I don't know about the conference. We jolly well nearly had a fight. Nobody would admit what they'd told you, and Ted was a bit loony. Nobody would go home with anybody else . . . they all left in separate cars. Aunt Anne wouldn't even let Featherton help her out to the street. Fine, sweet gathering. Never mind. . . .

"This is what happened.

"Aunt Anne insisted on sitting round and concentrating, trying to help Darworth out. I didn't want to do it; but Marion begged me not to make a fuss, so I said all right. Also, I wanted to make up the fire—it had gone out. I didn't see any sense in sitting around in a cold room when it wasn't necessary. But Ted said the wood was green and damp, and wouldn't burn anyway, and was I a pampered little duckling to be afraid of the cold? Ha! Well! We got our chairs——"

The inevitable question followed. Both he and Marion verified the order of which he had been informed: Lady Benning on the right of the fireplace, then Halliday, Marion, Major Featherton, and Ted at the other end.

"How far were the chairs apart?"

The other hesitated. "A good distance. That's an immense fireplace in there, you know. I had to stand on tiptoe to blow out the candles on the ledge over it. I don't think any of us could have touched anyone else by stretching out a hand . . . except"—he looked Masters in the eye—"except Marion and myself."

The girl was staring at the floor. Halliday put his hand on her shoulder. He went on: "I'd taken good care to get my chair only a little way from hers; couldn't get too close, because Aunt Anne was watching like a hawk; and I didn't want to seem—oh, damn it, you know!

"I got hold of her hand, and we sat there. I don't know how long; and what was worse—I'll admit it—that darkness was beginning to get on my nerves. I don't care how matter-of-fact a man is—" He looked at us defiantly, and Masters nodded. "Besides, somebody was whispering or mumbling, very low. The same words, over and over again, with a sort of rustling sound, and there was a noise like somebody swaying backwards and forwards in a chair. God, it was enough to make your hair stand on end!

"I don't know how long afterwards it was, but I had a feeling that somebody had got up. . . ."

"You heard something?" demanded Masters.

"Well, it's hard to explain, but if you've ever sat at a séance you'll understand. You can *feel* movement; a breath, or a rustle, a sense of something moving in the dark. You can only call it a feeling of nearness. I did hear a chair scrape, a little before that; but I'm not prepared to swear it was—whoever it was that got up."

"Go on."

"Then I did definitely hear two footsteps directly behind me; but I've got pretty good ears, and nobody else seemed to notice it until—well, all of a sudden I felt Marion go stiff, and she pressed my hand. I admit I nearly jumped out of my skin. I felt her other hand come out towards me, and she was trembling all over. . . .

It wasn't till afterwards that I found out what had gone past and touched her. . . . You'd better tell him, Marion."

Though she tried to keep her former self-control, the old terrors were coming back. The lantern was at her feet, throwing spangles of light up across the white, lovely, tortured face as she slowly looked up.

"It was the handle of a knife," she said, "touching the back of my neck."

XII
WHAT WAS MISSING AT DAWN

THE LAST candle on the work-bench had puffed out in a welter of grease. A faint, grayish light was stealing into the passage beyond; but the shadows in the kitchen were still thick, and the lantern burned at their core below Marion Latimer's dull face. It was the climax of the night's horrors, the last voice of them before they paled at cockcrow. I looked round at Masters, and at McDonnell, almost invisible back in a corner. But I thought, curiously enough, of a room situated high over Whitehall; and, in the midst of the sedate government upholstery, a fat man sitting with his feet on the long desk reading a cheap novelette. I had not seen that room since 1922. . . .

"You see," Marion told us carefully, after a pause, "the idea of some one of us prowling like that was—was rather more ghastly than the other."

Masters expelled his breath. "How did you know it was the handle of a knife, miss?"

"It was feeling—it was the handle, you know, and then the

crosspiece, the hilt, together: brushing past. I'd swear to it. Who-ever had it must have been holding it by the blade, you see."

"As though the person holding it had tried to touch you?"

"Oh, no. No, I don't think so. It jumped back at once, if you understand what I mean. It was as though somebody had gone in the wrong direction in the dark, and accidentally brushed me. . . . Anyway, it was after that—maybe a minute afterwards, though it's awfully hard to be certain—I heard the only footstep I could be sure of. It seemed to come from the middle of the room some-where."

"You heard this too?" Masters asked Halliday.

"Yes."

"And then——?"

"And then the door squeaked. There was a draft along the floor, too. Hang it all," said Halliday uneasily, "surely everybody must have felt it! You couldn't miss."

"It 'ud seem so, wouldn't it? Now, sir, how long after all this did you hear the bell ringing?"

"Marion and I have compared notes on that. She estimates something over ten minutes, but I say nearer twenty."

"Did you hear anybody coming *back?*"

Halliday's cigarette was burning his fingers; he glanced at it as though he had never seen it before, and dropped the stump. His eyes were vacant. "Shouldn't like to swear to more than that, Inspector. But I should say there was a pretty definite noise of somebody sitting down. That was before we heard the bell, but I don't remember how long. It's all a matter of guess-work, anyhow. . . ."

"When the bell rang, was everybody sitting down?"

"I can't tell you, Inspector. There was a rush for the door, and either Marion or Aunt Anne screamed——"

"It wasn't I," said the girl.

Masters glanced slowly from one to the other of them. "The door to that room," he said, "was closed while you were having your—meeting. I saw that myself. When you rushed out as the bell rang, was it open or closed?"

"I don't know. Ted was first at the door, because he was the only one with a flashlight. Marion and I crowded after him—anywhere we could see a light we'd have gone, and he switched his on then. The whole affair was so confused that I don't remember. Except that Featherton got a match struck to light the candles, and shouted, 'Wait for me!' or something like that. Then I think we all realized the futility of dashing out that door—I don't know who started the rush in the first place; it was like sheep following a leader. So—" He waved his hand. "Look here, Inspector, haven't we told you enough for one night? Marion is dead exhausted. . . ."

"Yes," said Masters, "yes. You may go." Suddenly he looked up. "Young Latimer—wait a bit!—young Latimer was the only one with a flashlight? Yours was broken; then Mr. Blake gave you his when we heard Miss Latimer calling in the passage . . . ?"

Halliday looked at him a moment, and then laughed. "Still suspicious of me, Inspector? Well, you're quite right to be. But, as it happens, I'm strictly innocent in the flashlight business. I gave that one to Ted, at his request. You should ask him, you know. . . . Well, good night." He hesitated, and walked over to me, putting out his hand. "Good night, Mr. Blake. I'm only sorry I dragged you into this mess. But I didn't know, you see. By God, we *did* start a hare, didn't we?"

. . . They went out the back door, and we remained in our separate and foolish positions; conscious of a city waking to daylight all around, and only the ashes of a haunted house. Presently

McDonnell came over to the work-bench, beginning to sort out the penciled notes he had brought in.

"Well, sir?" Masters addressed me. "What about it? Brain working?"

I said that it wasn't, and added: "Of itself, the conflicting testimony may not be so inexplicable. That is, three people said there was somebody moving about in the room, and two people said there wasn't. But the two people who denied it, Lady Benning and Ted Latimer, were the ones who might be so rapt in concentration or prayer, or whatever it was, that they wouldn't hear it. . . ."

"Yet they all heard the bell fast enough," said Masters. "And it didn't ring at all loudly, I'll swear."

"Yes. That's the part that sticks. . . . Oh, admittedly somebody was lying. And it was as expert lying as we'll probably ever listen to."

Masters got up. "I'm not going to hash the thing over now," he snapped. "Not with a dead brain. I'll forget even the great big snag in the business that's worse than people who can walk over soft mud without leaving footprints. I'll put it out of my mind. And yet I've a hunch—a hunch—I don't know—what *is* a hunch, anyway?"

"Well, sir," said McDonnell, "I've generally discovered that a hunch is what you call an idea that you're afraid is wrong. I've been having them all evening. For instance, it struck me——"

"I don't want to hear it. Lummy, I'm sick of the business! I want a cup of strong coffee. And some sleep. And—wait a minute, Bert. What about those reports you've got? If there's anything interesting, let's have it now. Otherwise let it wait."

"Right you are, sir. Surgeon's report: 'Death of a stab wound, made by the sharp instrument submitted for inspection—that's the L. P. dagger—penetrating through. . . .'"

"Where is the blasted thing, by the way?" interrupted Masters, struck with an idea. "I shall have to take it along. Did you pick it up?"

"No. Bailey was photographing it on the table; they set up the table after we'd taken the measurements and shot the scene as it was. It's probably still out on the table. By the way, its blade had been ground to a needle-point sharpness. Doesn't sound like a ghost there."

"Right. We'll pick it up. I don't want our man with his back turned, messing about with it again. Never mind the doctor's report. What about fingerprints?"

McDonnell scowled. "Not a print on the dagger of any kind, Williams says. He says it had been wiped clean, or the chap used gloves; that was only to be expected. . . . Otherwise, the whole place is alive with 'em. He counted two separate sets of prints aside from Darworth's. The photos will be around this morning. Also a lot of footprints. The place was dusty. No marks in the blood, though, except half a footprint that probably belongs to Mr. Blake."

"Yes. We shall want to go over this house here, and try to match up the prints; take care of it. Whatj'you get out of his pockets?"

"Usual lot. Nothing enlightening. No papers of any kind, in fact." McDonnell took from his pocket a folded sheet of newspaper, wrapped round a small collection of articles. "Here it is. Bunch of keys, notecase, watch and chain, some loose silver: that's the lot. . . . There was just one other funny thing. . . ."

Masters caught sharply at the other's uncertainty. "*Well?*"

"The constable noticed it when we were raking out the fire, to see whether somebody might have got down the chimney. It was glass, sir. In the fire. Big fragments like a jar or bottle, maybe; but they were so splintered and burnt and softened out of shape that you couldn't tell. . . . Besides, it might have been there some time."

"Glass?" repeated Masters, and stared. "But wouldn't it melt?"

"No. It bursts and splinters, that's all. I thought perhaps——"

The inspector grunted. "Whisky-bottle, maybe. Dutchcourage for Darworth. I shouldn't worry about it."

"Might have been, of course," admitted McDonnell. But he was not satisfied. His fingers tapped his pointed chin, and his eyes roved about the room. "Still, it's dashed funny, though, isn't it? I mean, chucking a bottle in the fire when you've finished with it: hardly a natural action, is it, sir? Did you ever see anybody do it? It struck me that——"

"Stow it, Bert," said Masters, dragging out his words and making a wry face. "We've had plenty. Come along. We'll have a last look at the place in daylight, and then we'll clear out."

A cool wind blew drowsily on our eyelids as we went down into the yard. The gray light was uncertain and murky as though we saw the whole place under water; it looked larger than I had imagined it last night, and must have covered a good half-acre. Set down in the midst of decaying brick buildings, gaunt and crooked against the dawn, with their blind windows staring into it, this yard was uncanny in its desolation. You felt that no churchbells, or street-organs, or any homely, human sound, could ever penetrate it.

A brick wall perhaps eighteen feet high closed it round on three sides of a rough oblong. There was a few dying plane trees straggling beside it, with an ugly coquettish appearance like the wreaths and Cupids on the cornice of the big house, as though they were dying in the mopping, mincing postures of the seventeenth century. In one corner was a disused well, and the crooked foundations of what might once have been a dairy. But it was the little stone house, standing out in the center and alone towards the rear wall, that carried the most evil suggestion.

It was blackish gray and secret, gaping with its smashed door. On the pitch of the roof were heavy curved tiles that might once have been red; the chimney was squat black, with a toppling chimney-pot like a rakish hat. Not far away grew the dead, crooked tree.

That was all. The stiff sea of mud about it, and only the broad squashy lines of tracks where many people had tramped up to the door in the same path. From this path, just two sets of prints—Masters' and mine—straggled close to the wall of the house towards the window at which I had held Masters up for his first sight of Darworth dead.

In silence we walked all around the house, keeping to the margin of the yard. The puzzle grew more monstrous and incredible as we stared at every blank side. Yet I have not overlooked, omitted, or misstated anything, and all was exactly as it seemed to be: a stone box, with door and windows solidly inaccessible, no tricks of secret entrances, and no footprints near it anywhere before Masters and I had gone out. That is literal truth.

It remained, to complete it, only for Masters to snatch at the only remaining lead, and to have that swept away also. We had got round to the other side of the house—the left side, looking towards it from the back door—and Masters stopped. He stared at the blighted tree, then back at the wall.

"Look here—" he said. The voice sounded strange and hoarse in that dead-silent place. "That tree. I know it won't explain the rest, but it might explain the absence of footprints . . . a very agile man who got on to that wall might swing from the wall to the tree, and then from the tree to the house. It could be done, you know; they're not very far apart. . . ."

McDonnell nodded. He said grimly: "Yes, sir. Bailey and I thought of that too. It was one of the first things we did think of, until somebody got a ladder round at the side, and I climbed up on the wall and walked round and tried to test it." He pointed up. "You see that broken branch? That's where I damned near broke my neck. The tree's dead, sir. It's as rotten as pulp. I'm fairly light myself, and I didn't do much more than touch it. It wouldn't support any weight. Try it for yourself. . . . You see, the tree has a different connotation."

Masters turned round. "Oh, for Lord's sake quit being superior!" he said raspingly. "What do you mean, 'connotation'?"

"Well, I was wondering why they'd cut down the rest of 'em, and left this one here. . . ." Pressing a hand over his eyes, the other looked puzzled and disturbed. His bleary gaze was turned on the ground at the foot of the tree: that slight plateau of which the house was the center. "Then I tumbled to it. That tree is where our good friend Louis Playge rests six feet under. I suppose they didn't want to disturb him. Funny, about superstitions. . . ."

Masters had strode out over the unmarked ground and reached up to test the tree. He was so irritated that his yank splintered off a branch altogether.

"Yes. It's funny, right enough. Ah, bloody lot of good *you* are, Bert!" He ripped off the branch and flung it on the ground; then his voice rose querulously: "Stow it, will you, or I'll heave this thing at you! This chap's been murdered. We've got to find out how, and if you keep on gibbering about superstitions——"

"I admit it isn't much good for telling us how the murderer reached the house. But, on the other hand, I thought maybe——"

Masters said, "Bah," and turned to me. "There's got to be some way, you know," he insisted with a sort of dull persuasiveness. "Look here, can we be sure there weren't any footprints going out towards the place before *we* came? There's a terrible mess, you know, now, going up to the door. . . ."

"We can," I said with conviction.

He nodded. In silence we came round again to the front. The house kept its secret. In that drugged hour of the morning, it was as though we were not three practical men out of a sharp-eyed age; but that the old house had been recreated again, and that, if we looked over the boundary wall, we should see the doors of houses painted with a red cross below the words, "Lord, have mercy upon us." When Masters wormed his way through the shattered doorway into the gloom of the place, my thick head could only picture what he *might* see inside.

I tried to shake off these fancies as McDonnell and I stood outside, the smoke of our breath going up in the still air.

McDonnell said: "I don't think I shall get a look-in on this business. I'm district, you know; Vine Street; and the Yard will probably handle it. Still. . . ." He whirled round. "Hullo! I say, sir, what's up?"

There had been a sound of thrashing about inside. It so fitted in with my distorted fancies that for a moment I did not look. Masters was breathing hard, and the beam of his flashlight darted about. The next instant he was in the doorway, very quiet.

He said: "It's a rum thing, but you know how you get a verse or a jingle or something stuck in your head, so that you can't get it out?—and you keep on repeating it all day, and try to stop yourself, but a little while later you forget, and you find yourself saying it again? Eh? Just so. Well——"

I said: "Stop babbling, and tell us——"

"Ah. Yes." His head moved round heavily. "What I've been repeating to myself—don't know why; sort of consolation, maybe; repeating all night to myself—'Last straw that broke the camel's back.' Just like that. Over and over. 'Last straw that broke the camel's back.' By God, somebody'll pay for this!" he snapped, and brought his fist down on the iron bar. "Yes, you've guessed it. Wait for the newspapers, now. 'Spare man with his back turned. . . .' Somebody's got that dagger again, that's what! It's not here. It's pinched—gone. . . . D'you think they want to use it again?"

He looked rather wildly from one to the other of us.

Nobody said anything for a full minute. Suddenly McDonnell started to laugh, but it was a sort of laughter exactly like Masters' mood.

"There goes my job," said McDonnell.

Then he walked away in silence, away from the place that had the look of a ballroom the morning after a party. There were pinkish hints in the sky now, and the dome of St. Paul's was looming out purple-gray against thin shreds of light. Masters kicked a tin can out of his way. A motor horn hooted raucously in Newgate Street, and the milkcarts were already bumping down below the gilt figure of Justice on the cupola of the Old Bailey.

XIII
MEMORIES IN WHITEHALL

It was past six o'clock when I got back to my flat, and two o'clock in the afternoon before I was roused out of loggish slumber by somebody drawing the curtains and talking about breakfast.

That I had become in some measure a celebrity was evident from the presence of Popkins, autocrat of the Edwardian House's domestic staff. He stood at the foot of my bed, all chin and buttons like a Prussian junior-officer, with several newspapers under his arm. He did not comment on these newspapers, seeming to imply that they were not there at all when he insinuated them into my hands; but he was very careful about how I wanted my eggs, bacon, and bath.

Anybody who was in England at the time will remember the terrific, the enormous and ghoulish splash that was caused by "The Plague Court Horror." At the Press Club I have been informed that from a newspaper point of view this compound of murder, mystery, the supernatural, and a strong dash of sex, missed not a single element in Fleet Street's recipe for the ideal dish. More, it promised bitter controversy for some time to come. Tabloid newspapers, in the American style, were not then so common as they are now, but a tabloid was first on the sheaf of papers Popkins gave me. Although the story had broken too late for the early editions, beyond brief glare in Stop-Press, the noon editions broke their front pages open with a double column of leaded type.

Sitting up in bed, on a gray drizzly morning with the electric light turned on, I read all the papers and tried to realize that this was real. And it was difficult. There was the prosaic sound of water running for my bath; watch, keys, and money laid out on the bureau as usual; the noise of cars bumping down the narrow hill of Bury Street, and the rain.

Pictures occupied the entire first page, which was headed: PHANTOM KILLER STILL HAUNTS PLAGUE COURT! In an oval round the center-piece were ranged photographs of everybody (obviously old ones from the Morgue). One of those faces, which was set in a murderous leer, I recognized as my own. Lady Benning looked shy and virginal in a whalebone collar and cartwheel hat; Major Featherton's, in full army regalia, was a curious half-picture which made him look as though he were holding up and admiring a bottle of beer; Halliday was pictured as incautiously descending some steps with his head turned sideways and his foot poised in the air; Marion's alone was a passable likeness. There was no picture of Darworth, but inside the oval the artist had spread himself on a lively sketch intended to represent his murder at the hand of a hooded phantom with a knife.

Somebody had obviously been indiscreet. Scotland Yard can muzzle the press tolerably well; and there had been an error somewhere, unless—it suddenly occurred to me—Masters wanted to accentuate the supernatural side of the business for reasons of his own. The stories were all reasonably accurate so far as they went, though there was no hint of suspicion towards any of our group.

Curiously enough, these wild speculations about the supernatural tended to diminish rather than accentuate in my own mind the very suggestions they made. In the clear-headed morning after, away from the echoes and dampness of Plague Court, one fact became apparent. Whatever others might believe, nobody who had been in the house at the time could doubt that we faced nothing more than either a very lucky or a very brilliant murderer, who could be hanged like anybody else. But that in itself might be problem enough.

When I was still mulling it over after breakfast, the house-phone rang and they told me that Major Featherton was downstairs. Then I remembered his promise of last night.

Major Featherton was annoyed. Despite the rain, he was tightened into morning-dress, with a silk hat and a rather startling tie; his shaven jowls were waxy with grooming, but his eyes looked puffy. The aroma of shaving-soap was strong. On my writing-table, as he planked down his hat, he caught sight of the tabloid with his bottle-of-beer picture; and he exploded. Evidently it was familiar. He said things about lawsuits; he drew comparisons between reporters and hyenas, stressing the more exalted moral character of the latter; and he was full of wild references to something that had just happened "at the Rag." I gathered that there had been certain observations at the Army and Navy Club, together with some talk of presenting him with a tambourine for his next séance. It also appeared that a facetious brigadier had come up behind him and hissed, "Guinness is *good* for you."

I offered him a cup of coffee, which he refused, and a brandy and soda, which he accepted.

"I was salutin' the flag, dammit!" snorted Major Featherton, when he had been pushed into a chair with a consoling cigar lighted. "Now, confound it, I won't be able to show my face anywhere; all because I tried to oblige Anne. A mess. Devil of a mess, that's what it is. Now I don't even know whether I ought to—go through with what I came to ask you about. Be in for a confounding ragging from. . . ." He paused, and sipped his drink. He brooded. "I phoned Anne this morning. She was snappish last night; wouldn't let me take her home. But she didn't take my head off this morning, because the poor old girl's upset. I gather Marion Latimer had phoned her before I did; called her an old trouble-maker; and practically said straight out, both for herself and young Halliday, that the less they saw of her in the future the better they'd both like it. However——!"

I waited. . . .

"Look here, Blake," he continued, after another pause. The old cough was racking him again, at intervals of minutes. "I said a lot of things last night that I shouldn't have; eh?"

"You mean about hearing noises in the room?"

"Yes."

"Well, if they were true. . . ."

He scowled, and grew confidential. "Certainly they were true. But that ain't the point, my lad. Surely you can see it? Point is this. We can't have them thinking what they're bound to think, sooner or later, and that's plain downright tommyrot. That one of us—eh? H'mf. Tommyrot! And it ought to be stopped."

"What's your own notion of a solution, Major?"

"Confound it, *I'm* not a detective. But I'm a plain man, and I do know this. The idea that one of us—baah!" He leaned back, made a heavy gesture, and almost sneered. "I tell you it's somebody who sneaked in unknown to us, or it's that medium. Why, see here! Suppose one of us did want to do that blighter in: which we wouldn't, mind you. Fancy anybody taking risks like that, with a whole room full of people all around! It's all nonsense. Besides, how could anybody do a thing like that without getting all smeared up with blood? I've seen the niggers trying to knife our sentries too often; and anybody who cut old Darworth up like that would've been soaked—couldn't help it. Bah."

Some cigar-smoke got into his eye, and he rubbed it blearily. Then he leaned forward with great intentness, his hands on his knees.

"So what I suggest, sir, is this. Put it in the proper hands. Then it'll be all right. I know him well, and so do you. I know he's devilish lazy; but we'll put it up to him as a matter of—of *caste*, dammit! We'll say, 'Look here, old boy. . . .'"

Then there occurred to me what should have occurred long before. I sat up. "You mean," I said, "H.M.? The old Chief? Mycroft?"

"I mean Henry Merrivale. Exactly. Eh?"

H.M. on a Scotland Yard case. . . . I thought again of that room high over Whitehall, which I had not seen since 1922. I thought of the extremely lazy, extremely garrulous and slipshod figure who sat grinning with sleepy eyes; his hands folded over his big stomach and his feet propped up on the desk. His chief taste was for lurid reading-matter; his chief complaint that people would not treat him seriously. He was a qualified barrister and a qualified physician, and he spoke atrocious grammar. He was Sir Henry Merrivale, Baronet, and had been a fighting Socialist all his life. He was vastly conceited, and had an inexhaustible fund of bawdy stories. . . .

Looking past Featherton, I remembered the old days. They began calling him Mycroft when he was head of the British

Counter-Espionage Department. The notion of even the rawest junior calling him Sir Henry would have been fantastic. It was Johnny Ireton, in a letter from Constantinople, who started the nickname; but it failed to stick. "The most interesting figure in the stories about the hawk-faced gentleman from Baker Street," Johnny wrote, "isn't Sherlock at all; it's his brother Mycroft. Do you remember him? He's the one with as big or bigger a deductive-hat than S.H., but is too lazy to use it; he's big and sluggish and won't move out of his chair; he's a big pot in some mysterious department of the government, with a card-index memory, and moves only in his orbit of lodgings-club-Whitehall. I think he only comes into two stories, but there's a magnificent scene in which Sherlock and Mycroft stand in the window of the Diogenes Club rattling out an exchange of deductions about a man passing by in the street—both of them very casual, and poor Watson getting dizzier than he's ever been before. . . . I tell you, if our H.M. had a little more dignity, and would always remember to put on a necktie, and would refrain from humming the words to questionable songs when he lumbers through rooms full of lady typists, he wouldn't make a bad Mycroft. He's got the brain, my lad; he's got the *brain*. . . ."

But H.M. discouraged the use of the nickname. In fact, he was roused to ire. He said he was not an imitation of anybody, and roared about it. Since I left the service in 1922, I had seen him only three times. Twice in the smoking-room of the Diogenes Club, when I was a guest; and on both occasions he was asleep. The last was at one of Mayfair crushes, where his wife had dragged him. He had slunk away from the dancing to see whether he could get a drink of whisky; I found him prowling near the butler's pantry, and he said he was suffering. So we waylaid Colonel Lendinn and got up a poker-game at which the colonel and I lost eleven pounds sixteen shillings between us. . . . There had been some talk of the old days. I gathered that he was tinkering with the Military Intelligence Department. But he said—sourly, flicking the cards with a sharp *crrr-ick* under his big thumb—that the glamour was gone; that these were dull times for anybody with a brain; and that, because the thus-and-so's were too parsimonious to install a lift, he still had to walk up five thus-and-so'd flights of stairs to his little office overlooking the gardens along Horse Guards Avenue.

Featherton was talking again. I only half-heard him, for I was remembering the days when we were a very young crowd, and juggled with our lives twenty-four hours in a day under the impression that we were having a fine time, and thought it great sport to pull a tail-feather or two from the double-eagle that was Imperial Germany. The rain still slashed monotonously, and Featherton's voice rose:

"—tell you what we'll do, Blake. We'll pick up a cab and go straight round there. If we phone to say we're coming, he'll swear he's busy, eh? And go back to reading his confounded shockers. What say? Shall we go?"

The temptation was too much.

"Immediately," I said.

It was raining hard. Our cab skidded down into Pall Mall; and five minutes later we had swung left off the stolid, barrack-windowed dignity of the Be-British Street, down a little, sylvan-looking thoroughfare which connects Whitehall with the Embankment. The War Office seemed depressed, like the dripping gardens that enclosed it behind. Away from the bustle at the front, there is a little side door close to the garden wall, which you are not supposed to know about.

Inside, I could have found my way blindfolded through the little dark entry, and up two flights of stairs past doors that showed rooms full of typists, filing-cabinets, and harsh electric lights. It was surprisingly modern in this ancient stone rookery, whose halls smelt of stone, damp, and dead cigarettes. (This, by the way, is a part of old Whitehall Palace). Nothing had changed. There was still a peeling war-poster stuck on the wall, where it had been for twelve years. The past came back with a shock, of men grown older but time stood still; of young fledglings clumping up these stairs a-whistling, with officers' swagger-stick cocked under one arm; and outside on the Embankment a barrelorgan grinding out a tune to which our feet still tap. That flattened cigarette-stump on the stairs might just have been tossed away by Johnny Ireton or Captain Bunky Knapp, if one hadn't been dead of fever in Mesopotamia and the other long disposed of by a pot-helmeted firing party outside Metz. I never realized until then how damned lucky I had been. . . .

On the fourth flight you must pass a barrier in the person of old Carstairs. The sergeant-major looked exactly the same, leaning out of his cubicle and smoking a forbidden pipe. Our greetings were affable, though it was strange to be saluted again; I told him glibly that I had an appointment with H.M.—which he knew was a lie—and trusted to old times. He looked dubious. He said:

"Why, I dunno, sir. I daresay it's all right. Though there's a sort of bloke just gone up." His boiled eye was contemptuous. "A bloke from down the way, 'e said. From Scotland Yard. Ayagh!"

Featherton and I looked at each other. After thanking Carstairs, we hurried up the remaining and darkest flight of stairs. We caught sight of the bloke on the landing, just raising his hand to knock at H.M.'s door.

I said: "Shame on you, Masters. What would the assistant commissioner say?"

Masters looked first angry, and then amused. He was back in his old stolid placidity again, where he could feel the brick walls of Whitehall: well-brushed, and heavy of motion. Any reference to his unheard-of behavior last night would probably startle him as much as it startled me to think of it.

"Ah! So it's you?" he said. "Um. *And* Major Featherton, I see. Why, that's all right. I've got the assistant commissioner's permission. Now——"

In the dingy light of the landing, I could see the familiar door. It bore a severe plate which said, "Sir Henry Merrivale." Above this plate H.M. had long ago taken white paint and inscribed in enormous staggering letters: "*BUSY!!! NO ADMITTANCE!!! KEEP OUT!!!*" and below the plate, as though with a pointed afterthought, "This means *YOU!*" Masters, like everybody else, merely turned the knob and walked in.

It was still unchanged. The low-ceilinged room, with its two big windows overlooking the gardens and the Embankment, was as untidy as ever; as full of papers, pipes, pictures, and junk. Behind a broad flat desk, also littered, H.M.'s great bulk was sprawled in a leather chair. His big feet were on the desk, entangled with the telephone and he wore white socks. A goose-neck reading-lamp was switched on, but bent down so far that its light fell flat on the desk. Back in shadow, H.M.'s big baldish dusty head was bent forward, and his big tortoise-shell spectacles had slid down his nose.

"Hullo!" grumbled Major Featherton, rapping on the inside of the door. "I say, Henry! Look here——"

H.M. opened one eye.

"Go 'way!" he rumbled, and made a gesture. Some papers

spilled out of his lap to the floor, and he went on querulously: "Go 'way, will you? Can't you see I'm busy? . . . Go 'way!"

"You were asleep," said Featherton.

"I wasn't asleep, damn you," said H.M. "I was cogitatin'. That's the way I cogitate. Ain't there ever goin' to be any peace around here, so a man can fix his mind on the coruscations of the infinite? I ask you!" Laboriously he rolled up his big, wrinkled, impassive face, which rarely changed its expression no matter what his mood was. The corners of his broad mouth were turned down; he looked as though he were smelling a bad breakfast-egg. He peered at us through the spectacles, a great, stolid lump with his hands folded over his stomach, and went on testily: "Well, well, who is it? Who's there? . . . Oh, it's you, Masters? Yes, I've been readin' your reports. Humph. If you'd only let a man alone for a while, I might'a been able to tell you something. Humph. Well, since you're here, I s'pose you might as well come in." He peered, suspiciously. "Who's that with you? I'm busy! BUSY! Get out! If it's that Goncharev business again, tell him to go jump in the Volga. I got all I want now."

Featherton and I both started to explain at once. H.M. grunted, but looked a little less severe.

"Oh, it's you two. Yes, it would be. Come in, then, and find a chair. . . . I s'pose you ought to have a drink. You know where the stuff is, Ken. Same place. Go get it."

I did know. A few more pictures and trophies were added to the walls, but everything was in its old place. Over the white marble fireplace, where a dull heap of embers glowed was the tall Mephistophelian portrait of Fouche. Incongruously, on either side of it was a smaller picture of the only two writers H.M. would ever admit had ever possessed the least ability: Charles Dickens and Mark Twain. The walls on either side the fireplace were disorderly with crammed bookshelves. Over against one of those stood a large iron safe, on the door of which (H.M. has a very primitive sense of humor) was painted in the same sprawling white letters, "IMPORTANT STATE DOCUMENTS! DO NOT TOUCH!!!" The same legend was added beneath in German, French, Italian and—I think—Russian. H.M. has a habit of ticketing, according to his fancy, most of the exhibits in this room; Johnny Ireton used to say it was like going through Alice in Wonderland.

The safe door was open, and I took out the whiskybottle, the siphon, and five rather dusty glasses. While I was doing the proper offices, H.M.'s voice kept on in its same rumbling strain: never raising or lowering, always talking. . . . But he sounded even more querulous.

"I ain't got any cigars, you know. My nephew Horace—you know, Featherton, Letty's kid; the fourteen-year-old 'un with the feet—gave me a box of Henry Clays for my birthday. (Sit down, dammit, can't you? And mind that hole in the rug; everybody who comes in here kicks it and makes it bigger). But I haven't smoked 'em. I haven't even tried 'em. Because why?" inquired H.M. He lifted one hand and pointed it at Masters with a sinister expression. "*Eh?* I'll tell you. Because I've got a dark suspicion that they explode, that's why. Anyway, you have to make sure. Fancy any right kind of nephew givin' his uncle explodin' cigars!—I tell you, they won't take me seriously, they won't. . . . So, d'ye see, I gave the box to the Home Secretary. If I don't hear anything about it by tonight, I'll ask for 'em back. I got some good pipe-tobacco, though . . . over there. . . ."

"Look here, Henry," interposed the major, who had been wheezing and glaring for some time, "we've come to you about a dashed serious matter——"

"No!" said H.M., holding up his hand. "Not yet! Not for a minute! Drink first."

This was a rite. I brought the glasses, and we went through it, though Featherton was fuming with impatience. Masters remained stolid, holding his glass steadily as though he were afraid it might fall; but there was some new development on his mind. H.M. said, "Honk-honk!" with the utmost solemnity, and drained his glass at a gulp. He relaxed. He adjusted his feet on the desk, wheezing. He picked up a black pipe. When he settled back in the chair, it was with an air of gentle benevolence wrapping him round. His expression did not change, but at least he looked like a Chinese image after a good dinner.

"Humph. I'm feelin' better. . . . Yes, I know what you came for. And it's a confounded nuisance. Still—" His small eyes blinked, and moved slowly from one to the other of us. "If you've got the assistant commissioner's permission. . . ."

"Here it is, sir," said Masters. "In writing."

"Eh? Oh, yes. Put it down, put it down. He'd always got pretty good sense, Follett had," H.M. admitted grudgingly. He grunted. "More than most of your people, anyhow." The small eyes fixed on Masters with that disconcerting stare which the old boy knew best how to employ. "That was why you got me, eh? Because Follett backed you up. Because Follett thought you'd tossed 'em a loose pack of dynamite, and at last you'd got a real up-and-at-em Sizzler of a case?"

"I don't mind admitting that," said Masters, "or, as you say, that Sir George thought——"

"Well, he was quite right, son," said H.M., and nodded somberly. "You have."

During a long silence the rain splashed on the windows. I

looked at the spot of yellow light made on the desk by H.M.'s goose-neck lamp. Among a litter of typewritten reports, spattered over with tobacco-ash, lay a sheet of foolscap sprawled over with notes in thick blue penciling. H.M. had headed it, "Plague Court." I was fairly certain that, if Masters had furnished him with all the reports, he knew as much as we did.

"Any ideas?" I inquired.

With painful effort H.M. moved his heel on the desk and struck the foolscap sheet. "Plenty of ideas. Only, d'ye see, they don't altogether make sense—just yet. I shall want to hear a lot of talkin' from you three. Humph, yes. What's more, and it's a blasted nuisance, I'm afraid I've got to go and have a look at the house. . . ."

"Well, sir," Masters said briskly, "I can have a car at the door in three minutes, if you'll let me use your phone. We'll be at Plague Court within fifteen minutes. . . ."

"Don't interrupt me, dammit," said H.M. with dignity. "Plague Court? Nonsense! Who said anything about Plague Court? I mean Darworth's house. Think I mean to get out of a comfortable chair to mess about in the other place? Bah. But I'm glad they appreciate me." He spread his spatulate fingers and examined them with the same sour expression. The voice grew querulous again. "Trouble with the English people is, they won't take serious things seriously. And I'm gettin' tired of it, I am. One of these days I'm goin' over to France, where they'll give me the Legion of Honor or something, and shout about me with bated breath. But what do my own flesh-and-blood countrymen do, I ask you?" he demanded. "The minute they learn what department I'm in, they think it's funny. They sneak up to me, and look round mysterious-like, and ask whether I have discovered the identity of the sinister stranger in the pink velours hat, and if I have sent K-14 into Beloochistan disguised as a Veiled Touareg to find out what 2XY is doing about PR2.

"Grr-rr!" said H.M., waving his flippers and glaring. "And what's more, their idea of sending me messages, and bribing Chinamen to call, and the cards that're sent up here. . . . Why, only last week they phoned up from the downstairs office and said an Asiatic gent wanted to see me, and gave his name. I was so bloomin' mad I chewed the phone, and I yelled down and told Carstairs to chuck the feller down all four flights of stairs. And he did. And then it turned out that the poor feller's name really *was* Dr. Fu-Manchu after all, and he come from the Chinese Legation. Well, sir, the Chink Ambassador was wild, and we hadda cable an apology to Pekin. And what's more——"

Featherton hammered the desk. He was still coughing heavily, but he contrived to get out: "I tell you, Henry, and I've been telling you, this is a dashed serious business! And I want you to get down to it. Why, I said to young Blake only this afternoon, I said, 'We'll put this thing up to Henry as a matter of—*caste*, dammit. Won't be any aspersions cast on the ruling classes of England, by Gad, if old Henry Merrivale——'"

H.M. stared, and literally began to swell. As an appeal to a fanatical Socialist, this was not precisely the way to draw a man out.

"He's ragging you, H.M.," I said quickly, before the storm broke. "He knows your views. What we did say was this. We agreed to try you as a last resort, but I pointed out that this was utterly beyond you—not in your line—foolish to think you could see through it——"

"NO?" said H.M., and leered. "You want to bet? Hey?"

"Well, for instance," I continued persuasively, "you've read all the testimony, I suppose?"

"Uh. Masters here sent it over this morning, along with a pretty first-class report of his own. Oh, yes."

"Find anything interesting, suggestive, in what anybody said?"

"Sure I did."

"In whose testimony, for example?"

Again H.M. inspected his fingers. Again the corners of his mouth were turned down, and again he blinked. He grunted:

"Humph. For a starter, I'll call your attention to what was said by the two Latimers: Marion and Ted. Eh?"

"You mean—suspicious?"

Major Featherton snorted. H.M.'s expressionless eyes moved to him; H.M. was locked up at last, in the cage of his own brain. Once enticed into the cage, you could let him alone to pad up and down noiselessly, until the door was opened and he pounced.

"Oh, I dunno as I'd call it suspicious, Ken. What do *you* think? . . . Point is, I'd rather like to talk to 'em. I'm not going to stir out of this room, mind you. I'm not wastin' good shoe-leather just to give Scotland Yard a bouquet. Too much trouble. All the same——"

"You can't, sir," Masters said heavily.

There was something in the tone of his voice that made us all look at him. What had been on his mind, some new development that was worrying him, all seemed packed into those few words.

"Can't what?"

"See Ted Latimer." Masters leaned forward, and his placid tones got a little out of control. "He's bolted, Sir Henry. Done a bunk. Packed a bag and cleared out. That's what!"

XIV
CONCERNING DEAD CATS
AND DEAD WIVES

NOBODY SPOKE. Featherton made a movement as though to protest, but that was all. The patter of the rain grew loud in the quiet room. Masters, drawing a deep breath as though he had at last got a weight off his chest, took out his notebook and an envelope stuffed with papers. He began to sort over the papers.

"Has he, now?" inquired H.M., blinking. "That's—interesting. Might mean something, might not. All depends. I shouldn't jump at it, if I was you. Humph. What have you done?"

"What *can* I do? Swear out a warrant for murder without even being able to tell a coroner's jury how it was done? . . . No, thanks," Masters said curtly. His face showed that he had not been to bed for twenty-four hours. He looked straight at H.M. "This is my official head, Sir Henry, if I make any more mistakes, and if I don't pull it off. The papers are saying, 'While an inspector of the C.I.D. was amusing himself with the occult, it seems rum that a brutal murder should be pulled off under his nose; very rum indeed.' To top that, the dagger was pinched under

my nose. To top *that*, the story got into the papers in spite of me.
. . . Sir George gave it pretty straight to me this morning. So, if
you've got any ideas, I'd appreciate them."

"Oh, hell," said H.M. gruffly. He looked down his nose. "Well,
what the devil are you waiting for? Get started! Give me facts!
Get down to business.—Tell me what you've done today."

"Thanks." Masters spread out his papers. "I've got a few
things, anyhow, that may be leads. As soon as I got back to the
Yard, I began rummaging the files about Darworth. Part of the
information I've already sent you, but not *this*. You read about
that scandal over his first wife, Elsie Fenwick's disappearance,
following the alleged attempt to poison her while they were in
Switzerland?" H.M. grunted.

"Just so. Now, there was a woman mixed up in that business
who might or might not've been important. That was the maid;
the maid who swore old Elsie had swallowed the arsenic herself, and pretty well saved Darworth's bacon. I was curious about
that maid, so I looked her up. And now," said Masters, lifting his
dull eyes, "here are some names and figures. The alleged poisoning attempt took place at Berne some time in January, 1916, and
the maid's name was Glenda Watson. She was still with the old
woman when Elsie disappeared from their new home in Surrey
on April 12th, 1919. Afterwards the maid left England. . . ."

"Well?"

"At eight o'clock this morning I cabled the French police for
any information about Darworth's *second* wife. They keep tabs
on everybody in the country, harmless or otherwise. This was the
reply."

He shoved a cable-form at H.M., who scarcely glanced at it,
grunted, and passed it to me. It said:

"MAIDEN NAME GLENDA WATSON. MARRIED ROGER GORDON DARWORTH, HOTEL DE VILLE, 2ND ARRONDISSEMENT, PARIS, JUNE 1, 1926. WIFE'S LAST ADDRESS VILLA D'IVRY, AVENUE EDWARD VII, NICE. WILL INVESTIGATE AND COMMUNICATE.

DURRAND, SURETE."

"Well?" inquired H.M., blinking placidly at me. "Make anything of it, son?—Y'know, Masters, I got a suspicion you're on a blinking awful wild-goose chase. I got an even darker suspicion that it ain't Glenda Watson who's going to figure in this; but somebody in nice high-up places that knew what Glenda knew. But you're right to keep kickin' the ball. . . . Well, Ken?"

I said: "The first of June, 1926. Seven years and a month-odd. They're devilish law-abiding people. They wait exactly the length of time until old Elsie is legally dead, and then rush into each other's arms. . . ."

"But I don't see—!" protested Featherton, rumbling and drawing himself up. "I'm dashed if I can understand——"

"Shut up," said H.M. austerely. "And quite right they are too, son. Got to have it legal. And this raises the interesting point: was it worth it for the Watson woman? Darworth got any money, by the way?"

Masters smiled heavily. He was growing more assured now.

"Has he got any money? Ha! Listen, sir. Immediately after the splash in the papers, we got a phone call from Darworth's solicitor. Now it happens (and this I'll admit is a piece of luck) that I know old Stiller pretty well. So I hopped round to him straightway. He hemmed and hawed and looked out the window; but it boils down to the fact that Darworth leaves an estate of about two hundred and fifty thousand pounds. Eh?"

The major whistled, and Masters peered round the desk as though well satisfied. But this information acted on H.M. in a rather different way than I had expected. He opened his fishy eyes wide. He pulled off his spectacles and shook them in the air. For a second I thought his feet were going to slide off the desk or his chair tip backwards.

"*So it wasn't the money!*" said H.M. "Burn me, it wasn't the money after all! Of course not. Humph." He rumbled with un-smiling satisfaction, and looked at his black pipe. But he was too lazy to light it, so he settled back again dully with his hands folded over his stomach. "Carry on, Masters. Carry on. I like it."

"What's on your mind, sir?" the Inspector asked. "I got it straight from Stiller. Darworth's got no other relations, made no will, and his wife will inherit. Stiller describes her as a—what-is-it—'statuesque brunette, not at all a servant-type. . . .'"

"Chuck it," said H.M. "What're you insinuatin', son? That the woman came over and murdered Darworth for his money? Tut, tut. That's not fair detective-fiction, to go and dump down a mere name, somebody we haven't seen and that ain't connected with the business. Don't growl, now. Because why?" He pointed his pipe at Masters. "Because the person who planned this crime planned it exactly like a detective-story. It's skillful; even I'll admit that. But that locked-room situation is too rounded and complete, too thoroughly worked out and smacked down as a deliberate puzzle for us. It was staged for months. Everything led slowly up to just that situation, when just that crowd would be assembled under just those emotional circumstances. . . . They even provided themselves with a scapegoat. If something went wrong, we should fasten directly on good old Joseph. That was why he was there at all; he wasn't needed otherwise. Man, d'ye think he could really have pinched a needleful of morphine from Darworth without Darworth knowing all about it but pretendin' not to?"

"But—" Masters protested.

"Humph. It's time to pry off a few layers of wrappin' in this thing. Joseph doped himself and slid out of the package; all right; but he was always there, and the British public always knows what to think when it finds a Dope-Fiend, especially if he can't give a coherent account of what he's been doing. When the Dope-Fiend is also that other figure of suspicion, a Medium— arragh! That's why you can stop lookin' for a mythical outsider, son, who dived into the pool after the water'd been all colored up nice and proper."

He was gabbling on as though sleepily addressing the telephone; a little more rapidly than usual, but with no change of voice.

"Hold on, sir!" said Masters. "Stop the bus! I've got to get this straight. You said, '*They* provided themselves with a scapegoat.' Then you said something about *Darworth*. And all this time you were talking about somebody who planned things to happen along the line of a detective-story. . . ."

"Right-ho. So I did."

"And have you any idea who it was that planned it?"

H.M.'s little eyes roved. They seemed amused, though he preserved his sour expression, and kept on twiddling his thumbs across his waistcoat. He blinked.

"Well, I'll tell you," he said, as though suddenly determined to impart a confidence. "It was Roger Darworth."

Masters stared at him. Masters opened and shut his mouth. In the silence we could hear a door bang shut downstairs the honking of taxis outside on the Embankment. Then Masters bent his head a little, raised it, and said with the quiet air of one who is determined to hold to reason:

"Are you trying to tell me, sir, that Darworth killed himself?"

"No. A man can't give himself three good hearty stabs through the back and then finish himself with a fourth. Not possible. . . . You see, something went wrong. . . ."

"You mean there was an accident?"

"Dammit, man," said H.M., "what sort of accident'll slosh a man about like that, hey? You think the dagger was workin' like a Ouija-Board or something? The answer is, NO. I said something went wrong. Which it did. . . . Can't anybody give me a *match?* . . . Humph. Thanks."

"This," said Major Featherton, "is outrageous!" He coughed again.

H.M. looked at him blankly.

"I can tell you a little, Masters," he went on, "without being able (I mean *yet*, you understand; I'll get it presently)—what was I sayin'?—without being able to solve the thundering riddle of the no-footprints and the locked room. It's rather uncanny, by God, it is! And there're going to be a lot of people believe it was spooks after all. . . .

"Look here, son. You thought Darworth was going to put on a spiritualistic show last night. You were right. He was. If it had gone as he planned it, it would still have splashed him into terrific prominence in the world. *It would also have got him Marion Latimer,* awed, tied, and delivered for life; and that was what he wanted. Eh? I don't have to stress that to you, do I? Read the testimony, if you don't recall it. . . .

"Well, Darworth had a confederate. One of those five people sitting in the dark was to help him put on his show. But the confederate didn't play fair. Instead of doing what he or she was supposed to do, the confederate went out to that house and murdered him . . . after Darworth had worked out the play and set the stage so that it could be done. . . ."

Masters leaned forward, his hands clenched on the desk.

He said: "I think I'm beginning to get this, sir. You mean that Darworth *intended* there to be a locked room?"

"Sure he did, Masters," H.M. replied somewhat querulously. He struck his match for the pipe, but it went out immediately. As though he were acting automatically, Masters struck another match and held it across the table. His eyes did not leave H.M.'s face as the Chief went on: "How else could he prove to the world that spooks had done—what he intended to have done?"

"And what," demanded Masters, "what did he intend to have done?"

Laboriously H.M. heaved his feet down from the desk. He took the light from Masters' match when it had nearly burnt the Inspector's fingers. The pipe went out, but he kept on puffing as though he did not notice. Putting his elbows on the desk and his big head in his hands, he brooded over the notes that lay before him. Outside it was nearly dark now, and the rain whispered faintly. Against grayish mist you could see the necklace of street-lamps winking out along the curve of the Embankment below, and the lights on the bridges making gleams in black water. Under pale trees—taller than the buses that shouldered past in shadows and sullen red flickers—traffic crawled with a firefly glitter. Startlingly near, the voice of Big Ben commenced to bang and vibrate high above us. It had struck five before H.M. spoke. . . .

He said: "I was sittin' here this afternoon, thinking about those reports. And the key to the whole isn't difficult to find.

"It's this, d'ye see? Darworth's intentions towards that Latimer girl were what they call strictly honorable. That's the hellish part of it! They were strictly honorable. If he'd only a-wanted to seduce her, he could've done it long ago, and then there wouldn't be this mess. Bah! Then, after a while, he'd have got tired of his game with the Benning-Latimer circle, or got all the money he wanted from the old lady, and moved on to better game. Burn me, why couldn't it have been like that?"

H.M. spoke plaintively. He ruffled his hands across his head in an angry manner; he did not look up.

"It don't take much brains to see his course. First off, he was after the old lady to work on her bereavement. But it was pretty fair generalship; he learns how she's tied up with the Latimer-Halliday crowd, and goes after Ted—you know it all. I dunno whether he knew about the Plague Court legend at the beginning or not; but he finds that a perfect ghost-story situation has dropped into his lap for him to twist any way he likes through the spirit of poor weak-headed James. Then he meets the Latimer girl. *Bang.* The big hunt's started. . . .

"He means to get a wife out of this, d'ye see? He combs his whiskers, assumes his Byronic air, paralyzes her with every psychological trick in the bag—and watch him work. Son, he damn near did it! If it hadn't been for this chap Halliday, he'd have succeeded. As it was, he got round her with that 'possession' nonsense. It took a long build-up, of course. He filled her head with ideas she'd never thought of before; he danced in front of her; bewildered, soothed, cajoled her; even tried hypnosis, and scared her nearly out of her wits. All the time, for one reason or another, the old lady was helping him. . . ."

Again H.M. knocked his hands against his head. Masters said:

"Ah! Bit of jealousy there, I should think.—But this business of 'exorcising' Plague Court was in the nature of his last big——"

"Knockout!" said H.M. "A stinger. Have the girl exactly where he wanted her, if he'd pulled it off. Oh, yes."

"Go on, sir," prompted the Inspector, after a pause.

"Well, I was only sittin' and thinkin', you understand. It was probably a pretty dangerous stunt he was going to try. Had to be, you see. It had to be a stinger, or the whole scheme would fall through. It had to be a jolly sight more spectacular than makin' passes at a pretended ghost nobody else could see. The bell, for example. It might have been for effect—or it might have been because there was a real, grim, deadly danger. Eh? In any event, it indicated he *expected* 'em to be called out. He was locked in there with a padlock on the outside of the door. That smelled more like trickery, but when he also bolted and barred the door in the inside. . . . Why, he was going to stage a fake 'attack' from Louis Playge, in a room where nobody but a ghost could have entered.

"As I say, I was sittin' and thinkin'. . . .

"So I asked myself, 'Here! First, how was he goin' to do it; and, second, was he goin' to do it alone?'

"I read your report. It said how you were outside yourself, and how you'd come round the side of the house a few minutes before you heard the bell. And you heard funny noises from the house. You said you heard his voice, '*as though he were beggin' or implorin' somebody, and as though he'd started to moan or cry?*' Man, that don't sound like a violent attack. No sounds of a fight, mind you, though he was cut up with rather tolerable thoroughness. No yells or blows or curses, such as any ordinary person would make. It was pain, Masters. *Pain!* And he was simply standing there takin' it. . . ."

Masters ran his hand savagely through his hair. But he spoke in a low voice. "Do you mean, sir, that he deliberately allowed himself to be mutilated——"

"We'll come to the mutilation in a minute. Now, that might or might not argue the presence of a confederate. But it looked a good deal like it. Because what good were mere wounds in his locked-room scheme unless they were in a place where he couldn't have inflicted 'em himself?"

"Go on."

"Then I read all about that room, and I kept askin' questions. First, why was there so *infernally* much blood about? There was too much blood, Masters. Darworth might have been one of your Messianic neurotics; might 'a' been willing to undergo more than usual jabs to make this piece of trickery ring in the world—to snare the Latimer girl—to feed his ego—I dunno what. Mind you, he was wealthy himself; it was partly the incense-drunk prophet, not able to resist the sound of his own voice, who let himself. . . . But I repeat, son, there was too much blood."

H.M. lifted his head. He spoke for the first time with a curious smile on his ponderous face; his little eyes fixed Masters. You felt the power of the man, growing steadily. . . .

"And then I remembered two things," he said softly. "I remembered that in the fire, where they had no business to be, were the smashed fragments of a big glass bottle. And in the big house, under the stairs, lay the body of a cat with its throat cut."

Masters whistled. The major, who had started to get up, sat down again.

"Humph," said H.M. "Humph, yes. I phoned through to your analyst, Masters. I shall be a good deal surprised if most of that blood didn't come from a cat. It was part of the spectacular element. And you'll see now why there was so infernally much blood—without any marks or imprints in it, as there'd bound to be if the murderer had really chased round after Darworth cutting at him.

"And I also kept askin' myself, 'Was that why there was such a *very* hot fire?' Darworth could have carried the blood under his coat in a flattish bottle, and it wouldn't be long till he could splash it round artistically on himself and on the floor: making a very effective picture. But it had to be kept warm in the meantime, so it wouldn't coagulate.... Maybe it was the reason for the very hot fire, or maybe not.

"Anyway, thinkin' about that mess, I said to myself, 'Look here,' I said, 'the man's clothes were torn scandalous, he was saturated with blood, and he'd accidentally smashed his glasses in his eyes when he tumbled over on the floor. But disregard the splendor and vividness of the stage-setting,' I said——"

"Hold on a bit, H.M.!" I interrupted. "You say Darworth killed the cat?"

"Uh," snorted H.M., glowering round near-sightedly to see who had made the interruption. "Oh, it's you, is it? Yes, that's what I said."

"When did he do it?"

"Why, when he'd sent young Latimer and poor old Feath-erton here out to set his house in order; they took enough time about it. He was only resting, d'ye see. Now shut up and——"

"But wouldn't he get blood on him?"

"Sure he would, Ken. A bloomin' good thing, too. He in-tended to splash himself later on, d'ye see, and the more ev-idence the better. Simply put on his overcoat and gloves to conceal it *then* (you'll notice he didn't go back in the front room where anybody could see him in a decent light, or ex-amine him; oh, no. He rushed out and had 'em lock him in that house awful abrupt. Remember? That blood hadda be kept fresh). What was I saying . . . ?"

H.M. paused, his little eyes fixed. He said, slowly, "Oh—my—God," and put his fists down on the desk.

"I say, you chaps stimulate me, you do. I just thought of somethin'. Oh, this is bad. Very bad. Never mind. Let me go on. Where was I?"

"Keep to the point," rasped the major, knocking his stick on the floor. "This is all damned nonsense, but go on. You were talking about Darworth's wounds——?"

"So I was. Yes. Humph. 'Well,' I said to myself, 'disregard the stage-setting.' Everybody talked a lot about how terribly slashed up he was, after a good look at all the blood and slit clothes. But, leavin' out the good straight stab that killed him, just how serious were his injuries? Eh?

"Y'see, the point about that dagger is that it ain't a slashing weapon in the least. You can't *cut* with a straightbladed awl, no matter how sharp it is. Old Darworth had to use it, to keep up the Louis Playge illusion. But what happened to him, actually? . . . I sent over for the full post-mortem report, I did.

"There were three very superficial wounds in his left arm, thigh, and leg: the sort of thing a nervous person might do to himself, and get scared and not dig more than half an inch in. I think maybe Darworth screwed up his courage and did that himself; then got frightened and wanted to back out of his confederate sticking him from behind. That might account for some of his moanings. The exaltation must 'a' been wearing a bit thin by that time.

"Nervous strain. It couldn't have hurt him much. But the confederate had to give him wounds he couldn't have made himself.

Thus: one cut high in the flesh over the shoulder blade. One that stabbed sideways, straight across his back and very shallow. And that was *all* the confederate WAS *supposed to do to him. . . .*"

H.M.'s desk-telephone rang stridently, and I think we all started. He cursed and shook his fist at it, talking to it for some time before he took down the receiver. Then he immediately said he was busy, protesting querulously about the fate of the British empire depending on it, and was interrupted by a strident voice. The voice went on speaking. A dour expression of satisfaction overspread H.M.'s face. Once he said, "Ehocaine Hydrochloride!" as though he were gloating over a delicacy.

"That settles it, lads," he said, replacing the receiver. His eye twinkled. "Doc Blaine on the wire. I might have guessed it. A section of Darworth's back was shot full of ehocaine hydrochloride; you know it as novacaine, if you've ever had a dentist sittin' on your chest. . . . Poor old Darworth! Couldn't stick the pain even in a good cause. Damn fool. He might 'a' stopped his heart. Somebody did stop it though. It's interesting to think of that suave, unctuous blighter knowing what he had to do to win everything he wanted, but scared green when the time came for the operation. Ha. Ha-ha-ha. Give me a match."

"The confederate," said Masters, who had been writing busily, "was supposed to give him those light stabs. . . ."

"Yes. And didn't. He cut loose suddenly with two deep ones, before Darworth knew what was happening. He stabbed through the back close to the spine, and then under the shoulder-blade——"

H.M. brought down a big flipper out of the air. There was something ghoulish, rather inhuman, about the expression of his face. His eyes seemed to know exactly what you were thinking, and I looked away from them.

"This is all very well, sir," Masters began doggedly, "but it doesn't get us anywhere! You've still got to explain the locked-room. If it was a confederate, I can understand how Darworth might have drawn the bolt and raised the bar and let him in, but——"

"After," I said, "the confederate walking thirty yards of mud from the big house without leaving a footprint. . . ."

"Don't mix me up, now," growled Masters, making a fierce gesture as though he were balancing a pail of water on his head, "I said I could understand how Darworth let him in——"

"Steady on," interposed H.M. "Remember that there was a padlock on that door that had to be opened from outside. By the way, who had the key to that padlock?"

"Ted Latimer," said Masters.

There was a silence.

"Now, now," urged H.M. soothingly. "Might have been. But I shouldn't jump to conclusions—yet. That reminds me, you said something about his doing a bunk; and you haven't explained it yet. Oh, I want to hear a lot of things yet. Yet, yet, yet. . . ."

Masters squinted up his eyes. "If we could explain how the murderer went in and out of that house without leaving foot-prints——"

"I read a story once," volunteered H.M., like an urchin from the back of a classroom. "It was funnier than watchin' somebody sit on a silk hat. Feller committed a murder in a house with six inches of unmarked snow all around. How'd he get in and out? It appears he walked to and from the place on stilts. The police thought they was rabbit-tracks. Ha ha ha. Burn me, Masters, wouldn't it have given you a turn if you'd seen somebody stagger-in' out of that place on stilts? Reasonable. Bah.

"Y'see, fatheads, the fundamental trouble with the locked-room situation is that it generally ain't reasonable. I don't mean that it can't be worked, any more than you'd deny one of Houdini's escapes; oh, far from it. I mean that, under ordinary circumstances, no real murderer would think of indulging in all the elaborate hocus-pocus we're required to believe at the end of the story. . . . Unfortunately, this case is different. We're up against Darworth: a man whose whole mind was devoted to hocuspocus, and who was admittedly staging an unreasonable show for a very reasonable purpose. It becomes logical—devilish logical, Masters. He didn't intend to be murdered; the murderer simply took advantage of a plan all worked out for him . . . but, burn me, *how?*"

"That's what I was trying to say," retorted Masters. "*If* we could explain no footprints, we might explain the bolted and barred door."

H.M. looked at him.

"Don't gibber, Masters," he said austerely. "I detest gibbering. That's like saying that, after all, if you can only hang the roof of a house in the air first, there won't be any difficulty about putting up the walls. But go on. I want to see the fountains play and the star-shine of your brow. . . . How do you explain it?"

The Inspector remained stolid. But he said:

"It only occurred to me, sir—sittin' and thinkin'—that, after the murderer had gone, Darworth himself might have bolted and barred the door after him. That might have been their scheme, when Darworth only expected to be wounded. He mightn't have realized that he was really dying, and wanted the plan to go through as arranged."

"Man," H.M. replied, putting his head in his hands again, "I'll say nothin' of the fact he couldn't have moved three steps after the murderer stabbed him in earnest; that all he could do was grope for the bell-wire and then tumble down and smash the glasses in his eyes. I'll say nothin' of the fact that there was no blood-trail or marks from him to the door—as there must have been. We won't argue whether a man stabbed through the heart could have lifted a heavy iron bar and shot a bolt that it takes a strong man to move in the first place. All I'll say is, we've got to look for another explanation. . . .

"*Facts!* I want more facts, Masters. Now, about what you've been doing today, and about young Latimer. Let's have it all. Talk!"

"Yes, sir. I'll get it in order. Order's what we want. And it's getting late. . . . After I'd talked to Stiller, the solicitor, we both went round to have a look at Darworth's house. It's funny how houses have a habit of drawing people back. We'd no sooner got inside, than we met——"

Again sharply, almost in H.M.'s ear as he bent forward with a curious expression on his face, the telephone rang.

XV
A SHRINE OF GHOSTS

With the receiver at his ear, H.M. glared. "No!" he said quickly. "No! Wrong number! . . . How do I know what number you want? My good man, I don't give a gore-stained farthing of immoral habits *what* number you want. . . . No, this is *not* Whitehall 0007! This is Museum 7000. The Russell Square Zoo, you fathead. . . . Certainly there's a zoo in Russell Square. Look here. . . ." (A girl's voice, from the switchboard downstairs, cut in audibly). "Hang it, Lollypop," said H.M. to the new voice, "why can't you shut off these blighters and not put 'em through to me . . . ?" His voice became freezingly austere. "No, my good man, I did not call you 'Lollypop'. . . ."

"I expect it's for me, sir," said Masters, rising hurriedly. "Excuse me. I left orders for calls for me to be transferred here. I hope you didn't——"

H.M. left off glaring at the telephone to look at him. The telephone tinkled, "Ha ha." It was still making derisive remarks when Masters dexterously got it out of H.M.'s hands.

"That was not," Masters said to it, "a secretary being funny. That was Sir Henry Merrivale." The voice died in a gurgle. "I can't help what you thought. Get on with it, Banks! What do you want? . . . Oh! . . . When? . . . In a cab, eh? Did you see who the other person was? . . . Get the number of the cab? . . . Well, for reference. No, it probably isn't important. Nothing suspicious? . . . No; I should just keep a sharp eye out. . . . Get into the grounds, if it won't hurt your conscience. . . . Right. . . ."

He seemed uncertain and rather disturbed as he rang off, and his hand almost went back to it. But he was distracted by all the other matters weighing on him; and H.M. was in a mood to lecture.

"There now!" said H.M., in a tone of gloomy satisfaction. He pointed at Masters. "There's a first-class example of the intolerable outrages that are perpetrated on me. And they call me 'eccentric'! Imagine it! People simply walk into my room when they like, or ring me up, and they call me eccentric! . . . Pour me out another drink, Ken. I've tried every way of keepin' people out. I tried puttin' the most complicated Yale lock on my door. And the only person I ever locked out was myself, and Carstairs had to break down the door, and I still got a dark suspicion that somebody deliberately pinched that key out of my pocket. Bah. And even my secretary, even little Lollypop, mind you; as nice a girl as ever mussed up my desk; *she* betrays me. I ask you, what's a man goin' to do?"

Masters, who had his hands crooked as though on the steering-wheel of a wildly skidding car, was trying to divert him. There was one way of doing it, not strictly fair. Thinking of Lollypop, I began to reminisce as though sentimental about old times. I began telling him of the day when Bunky Knapp and I had walked up unannounced, when Lollypop was with him and he was supposed to be dictating letters to her. . . . It was effective. He turned on Masters.

"If I'm not goin' to get any help from you, man, we might as well call this thing off. Go on! You were telling me about visiting Darworth's house. Get on with it."

He paused, peering up. Major Featherton had risen. The major had put on his top-hat with a sort of angry precision. I could only faintly see his face in the gloom round the desk-lamp; but apparently the major had groped his way through all the intricacies of which we had been talking, and he had now adjusted his thoughts to voice a coldly furious conclusion.

"Merrivale!—" he said.

"Eh? Oh! Sit down, my boy, sit down. . . . What's the matter?"

"I came to you, Merrivale," boomed the major, with precise enunciation, "for help. By Gad, I did! And I thought you'd help us. And did you? You did not. You persist in this insufferable tommyrot about one of *us*——"

"I say, my boy," interposed H.M., wrinkling his brow, "how long have you had that cough?"

"Cough?"

"Cough. You know: *whoosh!* Huh-huh-huh! Cough. You've been blastin' up the dust all afternoon. Did you have it last night, for instance?"

Featherton stared. "Certainly I did," he replied, with such dignity that it sounded like pride in the achievement. "But, dammit, I don't see that this is the time for discussing coughs! I don't like to admit it, Henry, but you've betrayed us. I don't think I care to hear much more. Gad! Confound it! I'm due at the Berkeley for a cocktail; past due. And I'll wish you all good afternoon."

"Sure you don't have a drink?" asked H.M. vaguely. "No? Sorry. Well—er—goo'by."

The door slammed, and H.M. winced. He blinked owlishly in that direction. Then he shook his head, curiously as though there were some puzzling thought which he tried to roll into place. H.M. repeated suddenly:

> "'You are old,' said the youth, 'as I mentioned before,
>   And have grown most uncommonly fat;
> Yet you turned a back-somersault in at the door—
>   Pray, what is the reason of that?'"

"What?" said Masters.

"Oh, I was just thinkin'. . . . never mind. Let's see, I was born in '71. Yes, that would make Bill Featherton born in '64 or '65. There's energy for you, hey? He'll be dancin' at a supper-club tonight. 'Si la jeunesse savait, et si—' Bah. Go on, Masters. You went to Darworth's house with the solicitor. Tell me about it."

Masters spoke hurriedly.

"Number 25 Charles Street. Stiller and McDonnell and I went there. Very quiet, dignified place, mostly shuttered. He's had it about four years. Only person there was a kind of butler-manservant; Darworth lived out, I gathered. He used to keep a chauffeur, but for the last few years he's driven his car himself."

"This butler, now—?" suggested H.M.

"N-no. Straight, I should say, sir. Excellent references. In fact, he named somebody he used to work for, also in Mayfair, who'd called him up as soon as Darworth's death was in the papers, and asked him if he wanted his old place back. We verified it. It's true."

"Uh-huh. Sounds like my wife. Watch out for gossip, Masters. Well?"

"I gathered he'd only taken the place because there was so much time off. Get that, sir? I asked him about the visitors and the séances. He said he knew Darworth was interested in the occult. But, whenever there was to be a séance, he was always given the evening off.

"The house is dismal inside; like a museum. No fires, few rooms lived in, full of all those rummy pictures and statuary. We went upstairs to Darworth's bed-and-dressing room, and Stiller opened a wall safe in the dressing-room. There wasn't much that was revealing; Darworth had been very careful about his papers, or else he's got 'em somewhere else.

"Then we went to the séance-room." Masters looked amused and contemptuous. "It was a big room up under the roof. It had a black carpet as soft as feathers, and a curtained alcove for the medium to sit in. Ah, ah! And then, sir—well, I'll admit we had a bit of a shock. Coming on her suddenly like that, sitting in the chair with her neck twisted over the back and moving round like it hurt her, with just that dullish light through the windows—I tell you, I don't mind admitting . . ."

"Coming on *who?*" demanded H.M., and opened his eyes.

"That's what I was going to tell you, sir, when the phone rang. On Lady Benning. And she was moaning."

"Oh, yes. Yes. What was Lady Benning doing there?"

"I don't know, sir. She gabbled some nonsense about this being James's room, and for us to get out. Porter—that's this butler chap—swore he hadn't let her into the house. Then she started to curse us. Lummy, it was awful, sir! That is, her being a lady, and refined and all that—you know—you feel embarrassed—and an old lady, too. That seemed to make it worse. Then I felt a bit sorry for her, because she got up, and was very lame. But she wouldn't let anybody help her, and sat down again. . . . Well, we hadn't time to waste, so we had to go to work on the room. . . ."

"Go to work on the room? How?"

Again the easy, tolerant, contemptuous smile. "I tell you, sir, of all the clumsy stuff I ever saw, this was the worst! How Darworth got away with it I don't know, unless it was his personality that carried him. Lord, *he'd* never court investigation. . . . The whole room was wired. Electric coils and magnet in the table for spirit-raps. Dictograph attachment in the chandelier, so every word spoken could be heard in another room—we found the little place, a sort of trunk-room, on the same floor, where Darworth could sit and control the whole séance. One of those home wireless-sets hidden in a panel behind the medium's alcove: microphone arranged, so Darworth could be all the voices. Gauze ectoplasm in those folding packets; a gauze panel on a sort of magic-lantern projection outfit for floating-faces; tambourines on wires; a rubber glove stuffed with wet tissue paper——"

"Never mind the inventory," H.M. interrupted irritably.

"Well, sir, Bert and I went to work and ripped that room to pieces. And Lady Benning—it's funny how noise must affect some people. She watched us. Every time we'd tear out a wire or something, she'd stiffen up and shut her eyes. When I was pulling that dummy wireless-attachment out from behind the medium's alcove, I carried it over to the table. I saw the tears were running out of her eyes. . . . Not crying like you think of people crying, just those tears and no blinking or anything. Then she got up and started to go out again; and I'll admit I was nervous. I ran after her (she let me take her arm then), and I said I'd take her down and put her in a cab."

The recollection disturbed Masters. He stroked his solid jaw, and he seemed annoyed with himself for giving what he would have called "impressions" instead of facts; for he pulled himself up and abruptly recited in a strange police-court fashion:

"I took the witness downstairs. Er—the witness looked up at me and said, '*Would you like to take the clothes off me, too?*' She emphasized the word 'clothes', so I—er—I didn't know what in lum's name she—er—what the witness was getting at, sir. She was wearing something fancy, not like an old lady at all, and had a lot of paint on. . . ."

At H.M.'s gesture, I had already gone over to pour out our drinks; and both H.M. and I looked at the Inspector. The hiss of the soda-siphon seemed to affect him as a slur on his powers of understanding.

"Just so, sir. I got a cab and put the witness into it. She leaned out of the window and said . . ." He picked up his notebook. "The exact words were, 'I talked to my dear, dear nephew's fiancée this morning, Sergeant. I think you ought to take a little interest in *those* people, you know. Especially since dear Theodore has seen fit to go away so suddenly.'"

H.M. nodded. He did not seem much interested. I said:

"Hullo! Featherton spoke to Lady Benning on the telephone this morning, but she didn't mention to him——"

"Naturally that wasn't pleasant news, sir," Masters continued. "I hurried inside and phoned the Latimers. Miss Latimer answered, very upset. I was pretty sharp with her, but she couldn't tell much. She hadn't got back home (they live in Hyde Park Gardens) until past six this morning. He had got home before her, for she saw his hat and coat in the hall; but she didn't disturb him, and went to bed.

"When she woke up this morning, her maid gave her a note

from her brother. All it said was, 'Investigating. Don't worry.' The maid said he had left the house with a traveling-bag at about ten o'clock. It was eleven when she got the note. I asked her why she hadn't let us know immediately, and she admitted she'd been afraid. She begged me not to take any notice of it; said it was another of his vagaries; and that he'd probably be back by evening. First she thought he might have gone to Lady Benning's, but she phoned the old Lady and he wasn't there. Since then she'd been calling everybody he knew, without result.

"It was close on time for my appointment with you here, sir. So I sent Bert round there to make inquiries. But I warned her that I would issue a writ compelling his presence at the inquest; that's the legally safe way of arresting somebody if he tries to bolt; that his description would go out through the usual police channels as 'wanted,' and over the wireless, and so on." Masters shut up his notebook. He absently took the stiff drink I offered him, put it down on the table, and added savagely: "Personally, sir, I think that kid is either guilty or stark mad. Bolting like that—! Mad, or guilty; maybe both. If I had a scrap of evidence, beyond his having that key to the padlock, I'd hold him for murder. But if I make just one more mistake. . . ."

He gestured. It was graphic enough.

"It could be," said H.M. "Yes. Humph. If he deliberately wanted us to get suspicious of him, now, and frame a charge— why, that's how he'd do it. I wonder. That all you know?" he asked sharply. His little eyes wheeled round.

"I've got a complete record, if there's anything else you want to know."

"Yes. There's something missing, son. It ain't what I want, somehow. Burn me, I've a feeling that. . . . Look here. Darworth's house, now. You sure there wasn't *anything* else you noticed? Let your imagination float. That's it! Quick, what were you thinkin' about?"

"Only Darworth's workshop, sir," answered the Inspector. He seemed taken back by H.M.'s uncomfortable habits of reading the most wooden poker-face. "But you didn't want to hear about the fake spiritist devices, so I thought——"

"Never mind, son. You keep talkin'. If I seem to shut you off, that may be because I've got ideas all of a sudden."

"It was only a room in the basement where he manufactured his boxes of tricks. No magic-supply-house for *him*, sir; too dangerous. He made 'em himself, and he was skillful with his hands. Quite. I—you see, I mess about with that sort of thing myself, just as a hobby, and there was the finest little electric lathe you ever saw; delicate as a razor-blade. I wondered what trick he'd been up to last, for there were little whitish powdery traces on it . . . "

H.M. stopped with his whisky-glass half way to his lips.

" . . . and some calculations on a slip of paper, measurements in millimeters, and a few scribblings; I didn't pay much attention to it. Also, he'd been tinkering with lifemasks, and made a good job of it. It's quite easy; tried it myself. You vaseline the person's face, and then spread the soft plaster on it. It doesn't hurt when it hardens, unless it catches in the eyebrows. Then you remove the cast, and fit over its inner side sheets of moist newspaper. . . ."

I was watching H.M. Now if, at this point, H.M. had dramatically slapped his forehead or uttered a startled exclamation, I should have known that he was off on one of his intolerable digressions. But he didn't. He remained very quiet, except that he was wheezing a little. Taking a deep drink, he removed his feet from the desk, motioned the Inspector to go on talking, and picked up the sheets of Masters' report.

"—and not only that," H.M. suddenly observed, as though he were continuing a discussion with himself, "but a heavy incense, spices of some kind, burned in the fireplace of that little stone room."

"I beg your pardon, sir?" said Masters.

"Oh, I was just sittin' and thinkin'," the other replied, twiddling his thumbs and blinking about him with a heavy lift of his shoulders. "And I've been askin' myself all day why there was heavy incense. And now—white powder. . . . Well, I'm a ring-tailed bastard," he murmured softly and admiringly. "I wonder if it could be? Ha ha ha."

"Just so, sir. You were thinking?" demanded Masters.

"Ho-ho-ho," said H.M. "I know what *you're* thinkin', Masters. And you too, Ken. I read another locked-room story once. I read plenty of 'em. Mysterious fiend invents a deadly gas unknown to science, and stands outside the room and blows it through the keyhole. Feller inside smells it and instantly goes off his onion. Then he strangles himself to death, or something. Ha-ha-ha. Boys, I actually read one of them things where the feller smells it in bed, and is so enlivened that he leaps up and perforates himself by accident on the spike of the chandelier. If that don't take all records for the sittin' high-jump, I hope I never read another. . . .

"No, no, son. Get your mind off *that.* This was something that let our murderer, our X, get in and skewer his man as neat as you please." He scowled, remembering old injuries. "Besides, there ought to be a law against stories about gases unknown to science, or poisons that leave no trace. They give me a pain. If you're allowed to be as staggerin'ly fantastic as all that, you might just as well have the murderer drink something that would allow *him* to slide in and out through the keyhole instead of the gas.

"Now that's interesting!" said H.M., struck with an idea. "Burn me, if I wanted to be poetic and figurative about this business, crawling in and out through the keyhole, I should say that in a matter of speakin' it's exactly what the murderer did."

"But there wasn't any keyhole!" protested Masters.

H.M. looked pleased.

"I know it," he agreed. "That's the interesting thing."

"I've had about enough of this!" said Masters, after a long pause. With controlled wrath, he began stuffing papers back into the long envelope. "This is no joking matter for me, you know. I feel like Major Featherton. I came to you for help——"

"Now, now, don't get your back up," H.M. put in soothingly. "Man, I'm serious too. Word of honor, I am. Here's our problem, the problem we've got to solve before we can do anything else: how was the trick worked? Without that, we can be morally certain who the murderer is and yet be absolutely unable to do anything about it. You want me to sit here and mull over, 'Was *he* guilty, or was *she* guilty, and what was the motive?'—and all the rest of it. . . . Now, don't you?"

"I certainly thought that if you had any ideas——"

"Right. Well, we'll do some chinning, then, if you want to. Before we do, I wish you'd order round that car you were speakin' about; I want a look at Darworth's house."

The Inspector muttered, with obvious relief, that this was more like it. He put through the call; and, as he turned back again, we all felt the new tension that had settled down. It had grown altogether dark now, and there was a bustle and clatter of people leaving the building.

"Now, then, sir!" Masters plunged straightway. "Here's what

I've figured out. We could work up a case against any one of those people——"

"Steady," said H.M., frowning. "Is there something new, or didn't I read it correctly? Accordin' to that testimony, you'd have to narrow it down to three people. Two have definite alibis. Young Halliday and the Latimer girl were sitting in the dark holding hands."

The other regarded him curiously. Masters' dogged alertness seemed to have struck a bump where Masters had least expected it.

"Good Lord, sir! You don't mean to say you necessarily believe that?"

"Son, I'm afraid you got a nasty suspicious mind. Don't you believe it?"

"Maybe, and maybe not. Maybe part of it. I've been trying to look at every side. Um. Just so."

"You mean they were together in a plot to puncture old Darworth's liver and then back each other up with a story like that? Eyewash, my lad; first-class, guaranteed-British eyewash. Besides, it's bad psychology. There are a dozen objections to it."

"I wish you'd try to understand me, sir. I didn't say anything like that. What I mean is this: Miss Latimer, now, is completely gone on Halliday. More so than ever now. She was sitting next to Halliday. Well, if she knew for a fact that he'd actually got up—if it was *he* carrying the dagger that brushed her neck—and he urged her for God's sake to support him with that story; eh? They had a whole lot of time when they could have talked to each other just after the murder was discovered."

He was leaning forward rather fiercely. H.M. blinked.

"So that," he remarked, "is why you're not so eager to pitch on young Latimer? I see. So that's your solution?"

"Ah! Be careful there, sir. I don't swear it's the right one; un-derstand that. As I say, I'm looking at possibilities. . . . But I didn't like that gentleman's manner, and that's a fact! Too flip-pant; much too flippant; and I distrust that. I've had experience, and the man who walks up to you and says, 'Come on, arrest me! It won't do you any good, but have a good time; come on and arrest me,'—well, in most cases he's bluffing."

H.M. growled: "Look here, have you realized one thing? Out of the whole crowd of suspects, you've unerringly fastened on the one against whom it'll be hardest to make out a case?"

"I don't follow that. How?"

"Why, if you accept my analysis of things (and apparently you have) then can you think of anybody on this broad green foot-stool who'd be less likely to be a confederate of Darworth than *Halliday?* . . . Burn me, can you imagine Darworth saying to him, 'Look here, let's us put over a jolly good joke on all of them, what? Then I can prove I'm a genuine medium, and your girl will tumble into my arms.' Masters, the crystal busts with that vision. My murderer crawling through the keyhole is elementary beside it. I grant you Halliday might have pretended to help him put over the joke, in order to give it a whackin' exposure, if Darworth had ever asked his help. But Darworth would no more have asked Halliday's help than he'd have asked—yours."

"Very well, sir, *if* you like. All I say is, there are deeps in this case we *don't* understand. . . . His bringing Mr. Blake and me to that house, just at that time and under those circumstances, looks very fishy. It looks like a put-up job. Besides, his motive. . . ."

H.M. stared disconsolately at his feet.

"Yes. Now we come to motive. I'm not tryin' to be superior at your expense; the motive beats me beyond all. Granted Halliday had a motive, then what becomes of poor old Elsie Fenwick? Dammit, that's the part that sticks me."

"I should say, sir, that the words 'I know where Elsie Fenwick is buried,' and the way Darworth took them, made a threat of some kind."

"Not a doubt, not a doubt. But I'm afraid you don't see all the difficulties. It's like this——"

At this moment the inevitable happened. This time H.M. did not protest at the ringing of the telephone. He said grumpily, "That's the car," and with a series of painful efforts began to hoist himself out of his chair. He is actually only five feet ten inches tall, and stoop-shouldered at that! but his sluggish bulk, without any animation of face, makes him seem to fill a room.

Unfortunately, he insists on wearing a top-hat. In the fact itself there is nothing out of the way: it is the particular hat. He would, of course, scorn the customary glossy silk article, associating it with Toryism and grinding-the-faces-of-the-poor, as well as the comical aspect it provides. But this hat—high and topheavy, worn by many years to a rusty indeterminate hue—is a mascot. So also is his long coat with the moth-eaten fur collar. He guards them jealously, with bitter resentment against slurs, and invents fantastic tales in defense of them. At various times I have heard him describe them as (1) a present from Queen Victoria, (2) the trophy of his winning the first Grand Prix automobile-race in 1903, and (3) the property of the late Sir Henry Irving. Other things he takes without undue seriousness, despite his pretenses; but not, I assure you, this hat or coat.

While Masters answered the phone, he was carefully getting them out of a closet. He saw me looking, and his broad mouth turned down sourly; he put on the hat carefully, and assumed great dignity with the coat. "Come on, come on," he said to Masters; "stop jawing with the chauffeur, and——"

" . . . yes, I admit it's queer," Masters was saying to the telephone rather impatiently, "but . . . What else did you find out? . . . Are you sure? . . . Then look here; we're going over to Darworth's house now. Meet us there, and let's hear all about it. If you can find Miss Latimer, ask her if she'll come along. . . ."

After a long hesitation, Masters hung up the receiver. He looked worried.

"I don't like this, sir," he snapped. "I've got a feeling that—that something's going to happen."

The words sounded more eerie spoken by the practical and unimaginative Inspector. His eyes fixed on the spot of light from the desk-lamp. The rain flicked in little whips against the window-panes, and there were echoes in the old stone building.

"Ever since that damned dagger was stolen again——!" He clenched his hand. "First Banks a while ago, and now McDonnell. That was McDonnell. Somebody's been making queer phone-calls to the Latimers' place, and there was something about a—a 'horrible voice', or the like, talking to Ted early this morning. Look here, you don't think——?"

H.M. stood with his shoulders hunched, a huge silhouette in the top-hat and fur-collared coat. With his little eyes gleaming, his broad mouth and blunt nose, he looked like a caricature of an old actor.

"I don't like it either," he rumbled, with a sudden gesture. "I'm funny like that. Psychic. I can smell trouble. . . .Come on, you two. We're goin'. Now."

XVI
SECOND STROKE OF THE MURDERER

LONDON WAS going home. You could hear the buzz of the liberated, that swelled in a calling from the dazzle of Piccadilly Circus: shadows moving on misty yellow-and-red sketches, cars jerking like the electric-signs, and their horns honking through it with a weary plaintiveness. This we could perceive up the long hill as the policecar nosed past the foot of the Haymarket. Waves of lighted buses rose at us and plunged past down Cockspur Street with a flying hoot; and H.M. leaned out and gave a very tolerable raspberry in reply. He did not like buses. He said they were required to put on extra speed just as they shaved round corners. That was why he gave the raspberry. By accident, at a break in the traffic, he delivered a very malevolent one into the face of a policeman on duty at Waterloo Place; and Masters was not amused. It was a police-car, and he said he did not want it thought that the C.I.D. sent people around doing that sort of thing.

But once up St. James's Street, through the crush in Piccadilly and into the quiet of the shuttered houses northwards, we were

all silent. As we passed the Berkeley, I thought of Major Featherton sitting on a tall bar-stool and smirking in a fatherly way at
a young lady who enjoyed his dancing: very much a contrast to
the queer, bitter face of Lady Benning that would always hover at
the back of any picture in which these characters were concerned.
"Something's going to happen. . . ." It was difficult to fit those
uneasy words even into the rather sinister quiet of Charles Street.
And yet it did. . . .

Somebody was plying the knocker of Number 25, filling in
the intervals by pressing the bell. As our car drew up, the caller
came down the steps under a street-lamp; and we saw that once
more McDonnell was waiting in the rain.

McDonnell said: "I can't make him answer the door, sir. He
thinks it's another reporter. They've been after him all day."

"Where's Miss Latimer?" barked Masters. "What's the matter?—wouldn't she come, or were you too polite to use pressure?"
(It was remarkable how the Inspector's manner underwent a
change when he met a subordinate). "Sir Henry especially wanted to see her. What's happened now?"

"She wasn't at home. She'd gone out calling on people to see
whether she could find Ted, and she hasn't got back yet. I'm *sorry*,
sir . . . but I waited half an hour to see her myself, after I'd got
back from chasing all over Euston Station. I'll tell you about it.
She and I were both mad good and proper over that telephone
call——"

H.M. had been sticking his neck out of the car like a tur-
tle, and somewhat damaging his hat in so doing; he was making remarks, not in an amiable manner. When the situation was
explained, he said, "So?" Painfully he climbed out and waddled
up the steps. He roared, "Open the goddammed door, you!" in a
voice that must have carried as far as Berkeley Square, and then

hurled his full weight against it. This was effective. A rather pale, middleaged man opened it, after turning on some lights. The middle-aged man explained nervously that reporters had been impersonating officers of the law——

"That's all right, son," said H.M. in a voice abruptly turned dull and disinterested. "Chair."

"Sir?"

"Chair. Thing you sit in. Ah! Here."

The hallway inside was high and narrow, with a polished hardwood floor, on which one or two small starved-looking rugs were laid out like hazards on a golf course. I could understand why Masters had said the whole place resembled a museum. It was swept and stiff and unlived-in, and there were too many shadows arranged as precisely as the scanty furniture. Faint concealed lights along the cornices illumined a piece of snaky-looking white sculpture towering up over a black-upholstered chair. Darworth had known the value of atmosphere. As an anteroom to the supernatural, it was uncannily effective. H.M. did not seem impressed. He spread himself out in the black chair, wheezing, and Masters went into action at once.

"Sir Henry, this is Sergeant McDonnell. He's under me in this business. I've taken an interest in Bert, and he's ambitious. Now, tell Sir Henry——"

"Hey!" said H.M., with a powerful contraction of memory. "I know you. Knew your father, of course. Old Grosbeak. He was against me when I stood for Parliament, and I got licked, thank God. I know everybody, y'see. Last time I saw you, son——"

"Report, Sergeant," said Masters curtly.

"Yes, sir," returned McDonnell, bringing himself to attention. "I'll begin at the time you sent me to Miss Latimer's home and went to Whitehall for your appointment.

"They live in a big place in Hyde Park Gardens. It's too big for them, as a matter of fact; but they've lived there since old Commander Latimer died and the mother went to live with her people in Scotland." He hesitated. "Old Mrs. Latimer's not—not quite right in the head, you know. Whether that explains anything of Ted's erratic conduct, I don't know. I'd been in the house before, but, queerly enough, I'd never met Marion until last week."

Masters warned him to keep to the point, and the sergeant went on:

"When I went round this afternoon, she was rather cut up. She as much as told me I was a filthy spy—which," said McDonnell bitterly, "I suppose I was. But she forgot that, and appealed to me as a friend of Ted. It was like this: she'd no sooner got done talking to you, sir, than she got another phone-call. . . ."

"Who from?"

"It purported to be Ted. She said it didn't sound like his voice, but that it might have been; and she didn't know what to think. 'Ted' said he was at Euston Station, and not to worry: that he was after somebody, and might not be home until tomorrow. She started to tell him that the police were looking for him, but he rang off immediately.

"So naturally she wanted me to hop over to Euston Station; find out if he meant to take a train or had taken one; try to trace him, anyhow, and drag him back before he made a fool of himself. That was about twenty minutes past three o'clock. In case it was a hoax, she was going after some friends of his and try to trace him in that way——"

H.M., who was stroking his plowshare chin, with his hat on the back of his head and his eyes half closed, interrupted.

"Hold on, son. Just a minute. Did young Latimer say anything about taking a train?"

"That's more or less the idea she got, sir. You see, he'd taken a bag with him when he went out this morning; and, since he was phoning from a railway station——"

"More jumpin' to conclusions," observed H.M. sourly. "Seems to be a favorite sport. All right. What happened then?"

"I got over to Euston as fast as I could, and spent over an hour combing the place. It was a warm trail, and Marion gave me a good photograph; but no result. Only one remotely possible identification, when a platformguard thought he might have gone through on the 3:45 express for Edinburgh; but I couldn't get any identification at the ticket-window, and the train had gone. I don't know what to think. It might have been a hoax."

"Dj'you wire the police at Edinburgh?" demanded Masters.

"Yes, sir. I also sent a wire to—" he checked himself.

"Well?"

"It was a personal wire. Ted's mother lives in Edinburgh. Hang it, sir, I knew Ted pretty well; I couldn't imagine what would have taken him up there, if he did go, but I thought I'd better warn him for God's sake to get back to London before he found himself in the dock. . . . Then I came back to the Latimer place, and found out the next queer thing."

McDonnell's eyes roved about the dim, harsh-shadowed hall. He said:

"One of the servants heard a voice talking to Ted at just about daylight this morning. They said it was high and queer and talking very rapidly. They said it came either from in his room, or the balcony outside."

There was something in those unadorned words which brought new terrors into the cold place. McDonnell felt it; even Masters felt it; and it conjured up shapeless images without faces. H.M. sat with his arms folded, blinking vacantly; but I felt that at any moment he might get up. Masters said: "Voice? What voice?"

"Couldn't be identified, sir. . . . This is the way it was. When I went to the house first, Marion had mentioned something about the servants' hearing things in the house that morning, and she wanted me to look into it. But I put it off until I returned from Euston. She had gone out, so I got the servants together and put the question.

"You remember, Ted seemed a bit—well, shaky and upset when he left us last night. At about half-past four this morning the butler at Latimers', level-headed fellow named Sark, was awakened by somebody throwing pebbles at his window. I may mention that the house is set back from the street, with gardens around it, and a high wall. Well, Sark looked out the window (it was still pitch dark) and heard Ted calling to him to come down and open the door; he'd lost his key.

"When Sark opened the front door, Ted fell inside on the floor. He was muttering to himself; Sark said it gave him a turn to see him as dirty as a chimney-sweep, spotted with candle-grease and dazed-looking about the eyes—and with a crucifix in his hand."

The last detail was so weird that McDonnell involuntarily stopped, uneasily, as though expecting comment. He got it.

"A crucifix?" repeated H.M., stirring abruptly. "This is news, this is. Very religious turn of mind, was he?"

Masters said in a flat voice: "The boy's mad, sir; that's all. I could have told you. . . . Religious? Just the contrary. Why, when I asked him if he'd been praying, he flared out at me as though I'd insulted him. He said, 'Do I look like a pious Methodist?' or some such bilge. . . . Go on, Bert. What else?"

"That was all. He told Sark he'd walked a good deal of the way back, and was in Oxford Street before he could find a cab. He said not to wait for Marion; she'd be back in good time; then he poured himself a big dose of brandy and went up to bed.

"The rest of it happened about six o'clock. There's a girl who gets up to start the fires, and she was coming down from the third floor past Ted's bedroom. It was very quiet and darkish outside, with a mist in the garden. When she passed the room she heard Ted mumbling something in a low voice; she thought he was talking in his sleep.

"And then the other voice spoke.

"The girl swears she never heard it before. It was a woman's voice, apparently of a quality ugly enough to scare the girl half to death; talking fast. . . . Then she recovered herself, and thought something different. It seems that one night about a year ago Ted had been pretty drunk, and he'd brought a girl-friend, also remarkably tight, back to the house with him; smuggled her up to the bedroom by way of a balcony, with a staircase, that runs all along that side of the house. . . ."

McDonnell gestured.

"It was a simple enough conclusion; but when this girl heard the news about the murder later on, and what time Ted had got in, and all the rest, she got scared. And she told Sark. All she could say was that it didn't sound *'like what I'd thought.'* She said the voice was *'creepy and crazy'.*"

"Did she get any words?" asked Masters.

"She was so frightened when I talked to her that I couldn't get her to make it clear. She made one remark (not to me; to Sark; but I got it second-hand) that's either startlingly imaginative or plain damned ludicrous, according to your conception. She said that, if an ape could talk, it would talk just like that voice. The only words she remembers are, *'You never suspected it, did you?'*"

There was a long silence. Masters discovered that Darworth's butler was listening; and, to cover the things we were all thinking, Masters thunderously ordered him out of the room.

"A woman—" Masters said.

"Doesn't mean a blasted thing, worse luck!" said H.M., opening and shutting his fingers. "You get anybody of nervous type all worked up, man or woman, and the voice will go into falsetto. Humph. That very curious and interestin' remark about an ape suggests something big—something—I dunno. And yet why does Ted rush off like that, with a traveling bag . . . ? Humph." He brooded. His somnolent eyes moved round the hall. "All I can do for the time bein', Masters, is agree with you that I don't like it either. There's a murderer walkin' around this town that I wouldn't want to meet on a dark night. Ever read De Quincey, Masters? Remember that part about the one poor devil hidin' in the house, who'd got overlooked when the murderer butchered all the rest? And he tries to creep downstairs and get out, when he knows the murderer's prowlin' around in the room by the front door. And he's crouchin' on the stairs, scared to a jelly, and all he can hear is the noise of the murderer's squeaking shoes goin' around and around, and up and down, in that front room. Just the shoes. . . .

"That's all we're hearing. Just shoes. . . .

"Now I wonder—Ha." For a moment he leaned his big head on his hand, tapping at his forthead, and then he sat up irritably. "Well, well, this won't do. Work! Got to get to work. Masters!"

"Sir?"

"I'm not navigatin' any stairs, d'ye hear? I got enough stairs to navigate as it is. You and Ken go down to this Darworth's workshop. Get me that slip of paper you were talking about, with the figures on it; also scrape some of that white powder off the lathe and put it in an envelope for me." He stopped. He rubbed his nose thoughtfully. "And by the way, son. In case the idea occurs to you: I shouldn't taste any of that powder, if I were you. Just a precaution."

"You mean, sir, it's——?"

"Go on," the other commanded gruffly. "What was I thinkin' about? Oh, yes. Shoes. Now, who'd know? Pelham? No; he's eye and ear. Horseface! Yes, Horseface might. Where the devil's the telephone around here? Hey? People are always hidin' telephones on me! Where is it?" Darworth's butler, who had magically reappeared, hurried to drag open a cupboard at the back of the hall, and H.M. was consulting his watch. "Um. Won't be at his office now. Probably home. McDonnell! . . . Oh, there you are. Hop to that phone, will you? Ring Mayfair six double-O four, and ask for Horseface; say I want to speak to him."

Fortunately I happened to remember who Horseface was, and passed the word to McDonnell as Masters led the way towards the rear of the hall. No misdirection was intended in the least. It would simply never have occurred to H.M. that there was anything strange about telephoning the home of Doctor Ronald Meldrum-Keith, possibly the most eminent bone-specialist in Harley Street, and inquiring for Horseface: either on his own part or McDonnell's. It is not at all that he dislikes the sometimes stuffed dignities into which the people about him have grown; it is that he is unconscious of them. What he wanted with the Harley Street man I had no idea.

But, as Masters opened a door at the rear of the hall, I got a definite notion that for the moment he wanted everybody else out of the way. He had got up, and was stumping towards a curtained door at the left.

Masters led the way downstairs, and through a cluttered cellar, turning on lights as we went. He very deftly picked the lock on the door of a boarded-off partition at the front; and, as I followed him inside, I could not help jumping a trifle. A dim green-shaded bulb made a sickly glow from the ceiling; the place still smelled of dead heat from an oil stove, of paint, wood, glue, and damp. It resembled a toymaker's workshop, except that all the toys were ghoulish. A number of faces stared at me; they hung drying on the walls above a clutter of workbenches, tool-racks, paintpots, and thin sheets of wood stretched in frames; they were masks, but they were hideously lifelike. One mask—it was of a bluish skim-milk color, one eye partly shut and the other eyebrow lifted, peering down through a parody of thick spectacles—one mask I could not only have sworn was alive, but that I knew it. Somewhere I had seen that moth-eaten drooping mustache, that nervous cringing leer. . . .

"Now, this lathe—" said Masters, laying his hand on it rather enviously. "This lathe—" He picked up a slip of paper from a steel shelf under it, and from the turningblade scooped some whitish grains into an envelope; then he went on discussing the lathe's excellences. It was as though he were wrenching his mind away, with a sense of relief, from the riddles of the case. "Oh, you're admiring the masks, eh? Yes, they're good. Very good. I did a Napoleon once, to see how it looked, but nothing like this chap's stuff. It's—it's genius."

"'Admiring,'" I said, "isn't exactly the word. That one there, for instance. . . ."

"Ah! You'll do well to have a look at that one. That's *James.*" He turned away abruptly, asking me whether I had ever seen any gauze ectoplasm treated with luminous paint. "Can be compressed to a packet the size of a postage stamp, sir, and stuck on the inner side of the medium's groin. A woman in Balham used to do it like that; so that she could be searched beforehand. Wore only two garments, above and below the waist; and manipulated 'em so quickly that they could swear they'd searched her beyond doubt. . . ."

Upstairs, the doorbell was ringing. I stared at that replica of James's face, at Darworth's canvas work-apron carefully folded over the back of a chair; and the presence of Darworth stood as vividly in the room as though I had seen him standing by that workbench, with his silky brown beard, his eyeglasses, and his inscrutable smile. These toys of sham occultism seemed all the more ugly for being shams. And Darworth had left one even more terrible legacy—the murderer.

Sharp in my mind was a picture, as I imagined it, of the servant-girl standing outside the closed door of Ted Latimer's room just before daybreak; and hearing the intruder's voice cry, exultantly, "*You never suspected it, did you?*"

"Masters," I said, still looking at the mask, "who, in the name of God—! Who got into that fellow's room this morning? And why?"

The Inspector said imperturbably: "Did you ever see the slate-trick worked? Look here. Lummy, I wish I dared pinch some of this stuff! It's expensive in the shops, much more than I can afford. . . ." He turned round to face me. His voice grew heavy. "Who? I only wish I knew, sir. I only wish I had. And I'm getting worried, so help me. I only hope the person who called on young Latimer this morning wasn't the same person——"

"Go on. What do you mean?"

He said in a low voice "—the same person who called on Joseph Dennis this afternoon, and was going up the walk leading Joseph to that house in Brixton, and patting him on the back. . . ."

"What the devil are you talking about?"

"It was the phone call; don't you remember? The phone call

from Sergeant Banks, when Sir Henry talked all that nonsense about the Russell Square Zoo. He was making such a row about the call that I didn't have time to tell him then; and, besides, I don't think it's important. It can't be important! Blast it, I'm not going to get the wind up like I did last night!——"

"What was it?"

"Nothing much. I sent Banks, who's a good man, out to get a line on that house, and the Mrs. Sweeney who runs it. I told him to keep a sharp eye out. There's a greengrocer's just across the street, it seems, and he was standing in the door talking to the grocer when a cab drove up. . . . The grocer pointed out Joseph getting out, with somebody else who was patting him on the back and leading him up to the gate in the wall around the house. . . ."

"Who was the other person?"

"They couldn't see. It was foggy and raining, and the body of the cab was in the way. They could only see a hand urging Joseph forward; and by the time the cab had driven off the two were inside the wall round the house. I tell you, it's all bosh! It was only some caller, and what the devil could I do about it?"

He looked at me a moment, and then said that we had better go upstairs. I made no comment on the story; I only hoped he was right. On the stairs we heard a new voice coming from the hall. Marion Latimer was standing in the middle of that cold place, her face rather pale, and holding out a crumpled sheet of paper. She was breathing quickly; she started a little as she saw us emerge from the door at the rear of the hall. From somewhere close at hand we could hear H.M.'s voice booming over the telephone, though we could distinguish no words.

"—they *must* know something about him in Edinburgh," the girl was saying to McDonnell, almost pleadingly. "Or else why should they send this telegram?"

I had realized before that she was beautiful, even at that dark hour in the squalor of Plague Court: but not to the dazzling extent she showed against the background of Darworth's crookedly brilliant hall. She was dressed in some sort of shimmering black effect, with a black hat and a large white-fur collar. It might have been animation, it might have been only more make-up; yet, despite the pale face, her eyes had a softness and appeal as though the woman had found herself again after some blighting influence. She greeted us quickly and warmly.

"I couldn't resist coming over here," she said. "Mr. McDonnell left word he was on his way, and said he wanted to see me. And I wanted all of you to see this. It's from my mother. She's in Edinburgh now . . . staying there. . . ."

We read the telegram, which said:

"MY BOY IS NOT HERE BUT THEY SHAN'T HAVE HIM."

"Ah," said Masters. "From your mother, miss? Any idea what it means?"

"No. That's what I wanted to ask *you*. That is, unless he's gone up to her." She gestured. "But why should he?"

"Excuse me, miss. Has Mr. Latimer the habit," asked Masters with blunt contemptuousness, "of running off to his mother when he's got into trouble?"

She looked at him. "Do you think that's altogether fair?"

"I'm only thinking, miss, that this is a murder case. I'm afraid I've got to ask for your mother's address. The police will have to look into this. As for the telegram—well, we'll see what Sir Henry makes of it?"

"Sir Henry?"

"Merrivale. Gentleman who's handling this. He's using the telephone now; if you'll sit down a minute. . . ."

The door of the telephone-closet creaked, letting out a wave of smoke and H.M. with the old pipe fuming between his teeth. He looked sour and dangerous; he had started to speak before he saw Marion; then his whole expression changed instantly to a sluggish benevolence. He took the pipe out of his mouth, and inspected her in frank admiration.

"You're a nice-lookin' nymph," he announced. "Burn me, but you are!" (This, as heaven is my witness, is H.M.'s idea of a polite social compliment, which has frequently caused consternation). "I saw a girl in a film the other day, looked just like you. About the middle of the picture she took off her clothes. Maybe you saw it? Hey? I forget the name of the picture, but it seems this girl couldn't make up her mind whether to———"

Masters emitted a loud, honking noise. He said: "This is Miss Latimer, sir———"

"Well, I still think she's a dashed nice-lookin' nymph," returned H.M., as though defending a point. "I've heard a lot about you, my dear. I wanted to see you and tell you that we mean to clear up this mess, and get your brother back for you without any fuss. . . . Now, my dear, was there anything you wanted to see me about?"

For a moment she looked at him. But such had been H.M.'s obvious sincerity that it was hardly possible to rap out whatever may be the modern equivalent for "*Sir!*" Suddenly she beamed at him.

"I think," she said, "that you're a nasty old man."

"I am," H.M. agreed composedly. "Only I'm frank about it, d'ye see? Humph. Now, now, what's this——?" Masters had thrust the telegram into his hands, to shut off further discourse. "Telegram. 'My boy is brr-rr brrr—'" he mumbled through it, and then grunted. "To you, hey? When did you get it?"

"Not half an hour ago. It was waiting for me when I got home. *Please*, can't you tell me anything? I hurried over here. . . ."

"Now, now. Don't get excited. Dashed good of you to let us have this. But I'll tell you how it is, my dear." He became confidential. "I want to have a long talk with you and young Halliday——"

"He's outside in the car now," she told him almost eagerly. "He brought me over."

"Yes, yes. But not now, you see. But we got lots of work to do; find the man with the scar, and so on. . . . So look here. Why don't you and Halliday arrange to be at my office tomorrow morning; say, about eleven o'clock? Inspector Masters will call for you, and show you where it is, and everything?" He was very easy and pleasant, but there was a slow dexterity about the way in which he maneuvered her towards the door.

"I'll be there! Oh, I'll be there. And so will Dean. . . ." She bit her lips. Her appealing glance took us all in before the door closed.

For a time H.M. remained staring at that door. We heard the sound of a motor starting in the street. Then H.M. slowly turned round.

"If that girl," he said with a meditative scowl, "if that girl hasn't tumbled off the apple-tree years before this, then somebody's been damned unenterprising. Nature abhors a vacuum. What a waste. Humph. Now, I wonder. . . ." He scratched his chin.

"You shoved her out of here quick enough," said Masters. "Look here, sir, what's up? Did you find out anything from that specialist?"

H.M. looked at him. There was something in his expression. . . .

"I wasn't talking to Horseface," he said, in a voice that seemed to echo in the bleak hall. "Not just then."

There was a silence, and still the words echoed with ugly suggestion. Masters clenched his fists.

"It was at the end of that," continued H.M. in that heavy, unemotional voice. "It was a relay call through from the Yard. . . . *Masters, why didn't you tell me somebody called on Joseph at five o'clock this afternoon?*"

"You don't mean——?"

H.M. nodded. He stumped over and flopped his vast weight into the black chair. "I'm not blamin' you. . . . I wouldn't have known. . . . Yes, you've guessed it. Joseph has been murdered. With Louis Playge's dagger."

XVII
CHOCOLATES AND CHLOROFORM

WITH THE second murder by the person they described in their stereotyped fashion as the "phantom killer"—words which do not in the least convey the horror, or give a proper impression of the circumstances—with the second murder, the Plague Court case had not even yet taken its last and most terrible turn. Remembering the night of the 8th of September, of our sitting in the stone house staring at the dummy on the chair, I can realize that other things were only a prelude. All events seemed to return to Louis Playge. If Louis Playge still watched, he would have seen his own fate reenacted in the solution of the case.

But the second murder was ghoulish enough, especially in the actions of the murderer. As soon as the news came through, H.M., Masters and I piled into the latter's car and drove out that long distance to Brixton. H.M., spread out in the tonneau with the dead pipe between his teeth, snapped out the brief facts that had been given him.

Sergeant Thomas Banks, detailed by Masters to find out what he could about Joseph and the Mrs. Sweeney who owned the house, had spent the day in discreet inquiries about the neighborhood. There was nobody at home that day; Mrs. Sweeney had gone out visiting for the day, and Joseph to the motion pictures. An affable greengrocer, who supplied the little that was known about the house and its occupants, said this was Mrs. Sweeney's weekly day for visits, "in a Queen Mary hat and a coat with black feathers all over it." All he knew of Mrs. Sweeney was that she was suspected of having once been a medium herself; was very genteel; didn't mix with anybody; and discouraged conversation with neighbors. Since she had brought Joseph to live there about four years ago, the house had rather a haunted reputation. People shunned it. Sometimes its occupants were away for long periods, and occasionally "a fine motor-car 'ud come up, with a bunch of toffs in it."

At ten minutes past five that afternoon, Sergeant Banks had seen a taxicab drive up through the mist and drizzle. One of the occupants had been Joseph; the other only a hand that was urging him towards the gate in the brick wall round the house. Phoning this news to Masters, Banks had received instructions to get inside and have a look round, if it didn't strain his conscience. After the two had been inside some little time, Banks crossed the road and found the gate open. Inside everything seemed in order: a squat, two-storied house, a bedraggled lawn and strip of back-garden. A light was burning in a ground-floor room at the side; but the curtains were drawn, and he could neither see nor hear anything. At length Sergeant Banks, a somewhat unenterprising man, had decided to call it a day.

A public-house called the *King William IV,* some little way down from the house, at the corner of Loughborough Road and Hather Street, had opened its doors by this time.

"Banks left the pub," said H.M., chewing at his pipe, "about a quarter past six. It was fortunate he'd stopped for that drink. To get his bus, he had to walk back past that house—it's called, burn me, 'Magnolia Cottage.' When he was about a hundred yards away he saw a man tear open the gate in the wall, come out a-yellin', and rush up Loughborough Road ahead of him. . . ."

Masters kept the siren roaring on the blue car; this time we were flying back along the way we had come. He shouted, "Not——?"

"No! Wait, dammit! Banks chased the fellow and finally caught him. It turned out to be a workman, a sort of general odd-job man in overalls; scared green, and running for a policeman. When he got to talkin' coherently he kept talkin' murder, murder; and wouldn't believe Banks was a police officer until a constable came along and they all went back to Magnolia Cottage.

"It seems he'd got instructions from Mrs. Sweeney to bring a carload of dirt and mortar and make some kind of repairs to the back-garden. Well, he was late from his last job that day; so he thought he'd only dump the stuff in the yard and come back next day to do his work. So he comes in through the back gate, pretty nervous about the house, and thinks he'll go round the front way and tell Mrs. Sweeney it's too dark to go on with the job until tomorrow. And, on the way, he sees a light in the cellar window. . . ."

They had given us a clear right of way through the West End. Masters was hurling the Vauxhall with dangerous swings and skids on the wet turnings. We shot down Whitehall, skidded left at the Clock Tower, and out across Westminster Bridge.

"He saw Joseph lying on the cellar floor, still squirmin' around in a lot of blood, and trying to wriggle his hands. He was on his face, and the handle of the dagger was stickin' out of his back. He died while this fellow outside was watchin'. . . .

"But that wasn't what scared him so much, it appeared, as the other thing. There was somebody else in the cellar."

I had turned round from the front seat, and was trying to decipher the strange, almost wild expression on H.M.'s face as the lamps of the bridge flickered past it.

"Oh, no," he said satirically; "I know what you're thinkin'. . . . Just shoes. Just shoes again, but a worse kind. He didn't get a look at the other person. The other person was stokin' the furnace.

"That's what I said. Banks says it's a big furnace for hot air pipes in the middle of the cellar. This workman was on the other side from the furnace door when he looked through the window, so he couldn't see who our little playmate was. Besides, there was only a candle burnin'. But there was a crack in the glass at the window, and the workman could hear the shovel bump on the furnace door, and then coal being scraped up, and the shovel bump again. . . . That was when he bolted. . . . He must have given a yell, because he just saw somebody start to come round the side of the furnace.

"Shut up, now. Don't ask questions yet. Banks says that when he and the constable and this workman got back to Magnolia Cottage, and smashed a window to get in, there was still one of Joseph's feet stickin' out of the furnace door. But there was such a blaze inside that they had to get buckets of water before they could drag him out. Banks swears he was alive when he was put in, but he'd been soaked in kerosene, so . . ."

The lamps over the dark water faded as we slid into the shadows of the Lambeth side; and it grew even darker when we had penetrated out into the somber streets beyond Kensington Road. It may be a pleasant or even cheerful region by day; I do not know. But those miles of black thoroughfares, too broad and too infrequently lit with gas-lights; those ramparts of squat, double houses showing furtive gleams behind doors checkered in red-and-white glass; all this is enlivened sometimes by the glare of a cinema or pub, or those desolate squares full of small shops, through which trams scrape wearily and everybody in sight seems to be riding bicycles.

Nowadays the sound of a bicycle-bell is associated in my mind with that small house—like all its neighbors, with solid gable and red-and-white glass door, except that it was detached in its own grounds—before which our car presently drew up. The pallor of a street-lamp, blurred with mist, showed us the crowd that had gathered before the wall round Magnolia Cottage. It was a tractable crowd. Its members said nothing and did nothing; they shifted and stared thoughtfully at the pavement, as though they were philosophizing about death. Some bicycle-bells rang insistently beyond them; otherwise the broad dark road was quiet. Frequently a policeman would tower through the crowd, saying, "Now, then; now, then!" with absentminded briskness; the crowd would shift round slightly, and stay the same.

Sighting our car, the policeman made a lane for us. Somebody whispered, "'Oo's the old josser?" In ceremonial quiet the policeman opened an iron gate; we went up a brick path, followed by more whisperings. A stout, nervous-looking young man with a ruddy face—obviously not used to plain clothes—opened the front door and saluted Masters.

"Right, Banks," said the Inspector curtly. "Anything new since you rang up?"

"The old lady's come back, sir," replied Banks. He wiped his forehead rather doubtfully. "Mrs. Sweeney. Bit of a handful. I've got her in the parlor. . . . That corpse's still in the cellar, sir; we had to take it out of the furnace. And the knife's still in its back, though the rest is a mess. It's that—that Plague Court knife right enough."

He led us into a dismal hallway, which smelt strongly of yesterday's cooked mutton. Another smell had got into it, too; but I will not suggest an analogy. A tipsy gasmantle burned on a bracket near the staircase; there was cracked oil-cloth on the floor and the flowered-paper walls had a tendency to sweat. I noticed several closed doors, before which hung bead curtains. Masters asked for the man who had discovered the body; and became sarcastic when informed that the man had been allowed to go home for a time.

"His 'ands were burned bad, sir," Banks replied, rather stiffly. "He did a man's job, and that's a fact. I got one or two burns meself. And he's straight. I've got it from everybody: they all know him. 'E lives just round the next turning; lived there all his life."

Masters grunted. "Right. Find out anything new?"

"Not much time, sir. If you'd like to look at that corp———?"

The Inspector glanced at H.M., who was glumly peering round the hall.

"Me? Oh, no. You go look at it Masters. I got other business. I'm goin' out and talk to that bunch of people on the pavement. Why do you police fellers always want to chase crowds away? They come right up to you, better than if you'd rounded up the whole neighborhood on purpose—which you couldn't do if you wanted—and yet you don't use 'em. Then I'm goin' to look in the yard. See you later."

He sniffed absently, and tottered out. A moment later we heard him saying, "Howdy, boys?" to the obvious stupefaction of the crowd.

Banks took us first to a little dining-room, where everything had that sickly and fish-glazed look of the stuffed trout in a case over the mantelpiece. A decanter of port had been set out on the blotched table-cloth, but only one glass had been used. Opposite it—obviously where Joseph had sat—was a five-pound box of chocolates from which the whole top layer had been greedily eaten. It was that which intensified the evil of the business: Joseph greedily eating chocolates probably brought him by somebody; and across from him, X sipping port and watching. . . . Masters sniffed the air.

"This the room where you saw the light first, Banks?" he asked.

"Right. There's something I can smell——"

"Chloroform, sir. We found the sponge downstairs." Again Banks nervously wiped his forehead with the back of his hand. "Whoever it was got behind him, slipped the sponge on; then dragged him downstairs and killed him easy. No blood up here. . . . I don't think we were expected to find the body, sir. I think whoever it was intended for him just to disappear, shoved in the furnace and gone. But John Watkins happened to see it, and—and whoever it was just cut and ran."

"Maybe. Downstairs now."

We did not linger in the basement. In fact, I came up after one look. The place was splashed with water from their attempts to put out the fire; the furnace still sizzled, winking with angry red gleams, and harsh smoke hung in sheets along the floor. One candle was burning on a box: lying near it was something which at first glance looked as though it had rotted and blackened, now crumbling to pieces with little curls of sparks winking along it. You could not make out much except the legs, whose shoes were only badly scorched; but you could see the handle of the dagger in the back. One fragment of Joseph's gayly checkered clothes hung singeing still on the open furnace door. It was not alone the odor, acrid smoke or human; the sight itself turned my stomach, and I had to get back up to the comparative cleanness of the mutton-greasy air in the hall.

As I did so, one of the doors moved quickly shut again, as though someone had been peering out; and that set the last touch on it. Banks had said Mrs. Sweeney was in one of the rooms; but always the slyness! Always the voice, the soft footfall, the glutinous something just round the corner, never seen until it leaped and struck! What, for instance, had Joseph thought (munching his chocolates under the singing gas-light, in a prosaic dining-room) when somebody smiling at him from the other side of the table had got up, strolled round him, and——?

Masters' footfalls clumped up the stairs. Banks was repeating his story; but there seemed to be nothing new. The Inspector made a few notes, after which we went in to see Mrs. Sweeney.

Mrs. Sweeney was a large woman, with a heavy face which seemed to come sailing at us as she got up from her seat by the small round table in this waxy best-parlor. She was not ill-featured; she resembled one of those old ladies who sit and knit in boarding-houses, but larger, harder, and more archly cunning. Her grayish hair was folded into buns over her ears. She wore the black coat "with black feathers"; and a rimless pince-nez attached by a gold chain. This last she twitched off with a gesture which tried to indicate that she had been improving her time by studying the Bible on the center-table.

"So!" said Mrs. Sweeney. Her dark eyebrows went up. She lifted the pince-nez slightly to one side of her eyes, as though she had been removing a mask, and rasped accusingly: "I suppose you know, my friend, the horror and the awfulness of what has been done in this house?"

"Yes, we know it," replied Masters, wearily, in the tone of one who says, "Chuck it!" He got out his notebook. "Your name, please."

"Melantha Sweeney."

"Occupation?"

"I am an independent widow." She gave a shake of her ample bust, rather as though she were dislodging worldly cares; but it was a gesture curiously like that performed by the chorus in a musical comedy.

"Just so. Any relation to the deceased, Joseph Dennis?"

"No. That is what I wished to explain. I was very fond of poor Joseph, though he resisted all my attempts to know him better. I have been fond of him ever since Mr. Darworth, the gentleman who was the victim of that brutal assault last night, brought him to me and provided a home for him. The boy had genuine—truly genuine—psychic talents," said Mrs. Sweeney, knocking her knuckles on the Bible.

"How long have you lived here?"

"Over four years."

"How long has Joseph Dennis lived here?"

"I believe—I believe it will be three years this quarterday.... I am very worldly-minded, you see." She was trying to strike a note of lightness, for a reason I could not understand. Then she turned a little sideways, and the gaslight showed sweat on her forehead; it brought out suddenly the fact that this woman was nearly frightened out of her wits. We heard her breathing.

"How well did you know Mr. Darworth?"

"Not at all well! I—I used to be interested in psychical research; that was how I met him. But I gave it up. It was much too fatiguing."

These, I could tell, were merely quick routine questions; Masters was not attacking. The real test would come after all evidence had been straightened. He went on:

"Do you know anything about Joseph Dennis? His parents, say?"

"I know absolutely nothing." She added, with a curious inflection: "You would have to ask Mr. Darworth about his parents."

"Come, come!"

"That is all I can tell you. He was a foundling, who had been starved and ill-treated in childhood, I believe."

"Did you have any reason to suspect that he was in danger?"

"No! He—he was upset when he returned last night; naturally. But he had forgotten about it this morning. I gathered they did not tell him Mr. Darworth was dead, and he was eager to go to the cinema this afternoon. . . . I—I suppose he did. I myself left the house at eleven o'clock this morning. . . ."

Mrs. Sweeney faltered. She grasped the edges of the Bible, and began to speak earnestly, partly incoherently. "Listen to me. Please listen. You want to know what I know about this ghastly business this afternoon. And I tell you I can account for every minute I've spent today, after I left here this morning. I went round to see John Watkins, the odd-job man; there is a filled-in well in the back garden that has been cracking its cement and flooding out, and I wanted it repaired. Afterwards I went straight to the home of some friends of mine in Clapham, and stayed there all day. . . ."

She looked from Masters to me, and then at Banks. Yet, despite all this, the woman's main motive was not fear lest she would be suspected; this did not worry her nearly so much as something else. And there was also something about her that did not quite ring true. An overdone gesture, a trick of speech; what was it?

"What time did you return?"

"I took a bus from Clapham—it must have been shortly after six o'clock. You know what I found. Your—your man will tell you when I arrived." She backed away, and sat down in a horsehair chair behind the table. Taking out a small handkerchief, she dabbed at her face as though she were putting on powder. "Inspector—you are an inspector, aren't you?" she corrected herself hastily. "Yes. There's one other thing. In heaven's name, you won't force me to stay the night here, will you? I beg you, I *pray* . . . !" Even to her this seemed to sound a trifle flowery. She went on in an even but a very vehement tone: "You may investigate these friends of mine. They are good, respectable people. Won't you allow me to spend the night with them?"

"Well, well . . . why do you want to do that?"

Mrs. Sweeney looked straight at him.

"*I'm afraid,*" she said.

Masters shut up his notebook. He said to Banks, "See if you can find Sir Henry: the man who came with us. I want him to speak to this witness. . . . Wait! Have you searched the house, upstairs and all about?"

This question was directed at Mrs. Sweeney; I saw her give a slight movement, which she disguised by industrious work with the handkerchief.

"Been a lot of ransacking upstairs, sir. I don't know. The lady here'll have to tell if anything's missing."

I went with Banks out into the hall. Some instinct had begun to warn all of us that this house, and Mrs. Sweeney, might be of more significance in the case than anybody had suspected. There was something wrong about Mrs. Sweeney which did not rest alone in mere lies. She was acting; and, either in fear or guilt or only in nervousness, was overplaying the part. I wanted to see H.M. in action with this witness.

He was not at the gate outside, and the crowd had thinned. But the policeman on duty, who was imbued with a Jovian amusement, informed us. H.M. was over at the *King William,* standing drinks to half the population. Banks went back to tell Masters, whom I could hear cursing in the doorway, while I went out in search of him. I believe the good Inspector was also shaking his fist.

The *King William IV,* a snug public-house exhaling a mist of tobacco-smoke through its lighted doors, was crowded. The chairs along the walls were occupied by the usual red-faced gentlemen with brass-collar-studs, who sit in a line like figures in a shooting-gallery and chuckle at everything. H.M., with a pint tankard in his hand and an admiring crowd about him, was throwing darts at a scarred board. In the intervals he was saying, "Gentlemen, we must not, we will not, as free British subjects, submit to the indignities perpetrated by the present Government in grindin' the faces of the working—" I stuck my head through the doorway of the bar-parlor and whistled. He stopped, disposed of the pint of bitter with a shark-like gulp, shook hands with everybody, and lumbered out pursued by cheers.

In the misty street outside his expression changed. He turned up the collar of his coat; and, if I had not known him so well, I could have sworn the man was nervous.

I said: "The old tricks are still successful. Did you learn anything?"

He growled something that sounded like an affirmative.

He stumped on a few paces, blew his nose violently on a handkerchief, and said: "Yes. About Darworth, and—other things too.

Humph. Get the old residents if you want information, son. Stick to the pubs. There's been a woman seen visitin' that house from time to time. . . .

"Ei, why didn't I guess it? I started to suspect it while we were at Darworth's house, but I don't mind tellin' you that I've very nearly made the biggest mistake of my life. . . . Well. Tisn't irreparable; that's a consolation. If luck's with me, tomorrow night— maybe later, but I hope tomorrow night—I can introduce you to the coolest and quickest-thinking criminal devil that. . . ."

"*A woman?*"

"I didn't say that. Shut up, now. Somebody knows more about that house than we do. Darworth was murdered partly because of it. Joseph was murdered to get him out of the way. And now. . . ."

He had stopped on the pavement across the street from Magnolia Cottage. It looked bleak and sinister, with the constable pacing under the street-lamp, the sagging iron gate and the glimpse of a weedy brick walk. H.M. pointed.

"Darworth owned that house," he said casually.

"Then——?"

"Before the Sweeney woman took it, it stood vacant for I dunno how many years; no notice-board up; nobody could buy. But the old gossip-hands remember somebody of Darworth's description that used to come there. If it hadn't been for a peculiar bone-structure, that could be identified as long as eternity if the body ever got dug up; so Horseface says. . . . Son, I shouldn't be at all surprised if that's not where Elsie Fenwick is buried."

Round the corner of Hather Street whirled the lights of a police-car, its siren crying ahead. On a common impulse H.M. and I started across the road. We came up just as the car scraped in at the curb and three men in plain clothes got out. Masters, hurrying down the brick walk, held open the gate for them. One of the newcomers said, "Inspector Masters, sir!" and there was urgency in his voice.

"Well?"

"They said you'd probably be here, but there isn't a telephone here and we couldn't reach you. You're wanted back at the Yard. . . ."

Masters' hands closed on the spikes of the gate. He seemed to have frozen there, and it was several seconds before he got out:

"Not—anything—another——?"

"Don't know, sir; may be. It's a call from Paris. Everybody in the translation department had gone home. Chap was jabbering French so fast the operator could only get half what he said. He said he'd call again at nine o'clock, and it's nearly half past eight now. It's important, sir, and it's something about murder. . . ."

"Go through the routine, photographs, search and fingerprints," Masters said curtly. He jammed on his hat and hurried out to the car.

XVIII
THE WITCH ACCUSES

THAT WAS the night before the day of the startling accusation made by Lady Benning. During the fifteen hours that intervened, I had by pure accident stumbled on a point that nearly provided a solution to the riddle. . . .

If this were anything but an account of facts, I should describe a breakneck rush back to town to intercept that call; an inquiry until far into the morning, without food or sleep. But a real murder case is not all "Thou-art-the-Man." There are the intervals when you suddenly realize that the business of life must go on as usual; the intervals of torture and wit-puzzling, and of futile breathings on a mirror already beclouded. For instance, I had a dinner engagement that night. It was with my sister, a gentle Gorgon, and it would never have occurred to any of the family to break an engagement with Agatha. In fact, my chief concern was in the realization—when I learned how late it was—that I should be an hour late even if I did not bother to dress. I had forgotten all about it; still, I must be there.

Masters drove us back to Town, and both the Inspector and

I promised to be at H.M.'s office at eleven o'clock next morning. He was driving H.M. home to Brook Street; I dropped off in Piccadilly, caught a Kensington bus, and was pitched off at Agatha's in time to be smuggled in the side door for a brushup before I faced whatever guests might be. Surprisingly, there was only Angela Payne, my sister's less superannuated crony, who is supposed to be my future wife. She was sitting by the fire in Agatha's cutglass drawing-room, wriggling with excitement and chewing that jade cigarette-holder which had nearly poked out so many people's eyes at intimate dinners. Angela is very modern, which I am not; she has her hair shorn and displays a great deal of back.

The moment I walked in, I knew I should be a Personage as a bearer of news about the murder, and pumped by two terrifying experts. That is probably why the dinner was so intimate. Agatha did not even mention my lateness. But, the moment we sat down to one of those clear soups which are about as sustaining as something the conjuror pours out of different jugs on the stage, the attack began. I was puzzling over the problem of Mrs. Sweeney, and kept the defense fairly well. Agatha had said to Angela, as though reprovingly, "Of course he can't tell us anything, but at least, in courtesy to me, he ought to explain his lateness. . . ."

During the fish, Angela tossed her bomb in among the candles. She asked when the inquest would be, and I said tomorrow.

"And," she inquired, "will poor Mr. Darworth's wife be here for it?"

This gave even my sister a surprise. "*Was* Mr. Darworth," she inquired, "a married man?"

"But I know her!" said Angela triumphantly.

At this point I had become so intent that I refused Sauterne. Angela said: "Well—good-looking, possibly, if you like that type.

Thin. Tall. Brunette. They say, Agatha, dear, that she had low beginnings: in a circus or a Wild West show or something. . . . But an actress! Oh, yes, I'll admit——"

"You know her personally?"

"Well, not exactly. . . ." She was talking to Agatha now. "She would probably have run to fat by this time, because that was years ago. Don't you remember, my dear, the winter in Nice—'23 or '24—I think the year dear Lady Bellows had such bad attacks of acute alcoholism, or am I thinking of somebody else that fell over the railing from the dress circle, and all the rude people in the gallery positively laughed?—well, anyway, it was that English Repertory Company, and all the papers said it was so very fine? They were reviving Shakespeare," explained Angela, as though she were talking of movements for resuscitating the drowned, "and those delightful Restoration things by Which—Wycherley——"

"Don't hiccough, Angela," said my sister severely. "Well?"

"They said she was superb in that Twelfth Night thing, or one called 'The Plain Dealer,' was it? But I didn't see those; I saw one where she was a middle-aged, heavy-set frump, something like a schoolmistress, you know, Agatha. . . . Aren't you listening, Ken?"

I was.

"*Mrs. Sweeney*—"The alleged Mrs. Sweeney——

When the duties of the evening were over, and I had got away without wringing anybody's neck, I walked back trying to puzzle the thing out. If Mrs. Sweeney were Glenda Watson Darworth, as seemed likely, then many things could be explained over a trail stretching far back into the past. Glenda Watson's personalities were many and various, but *always profitable.* She had fastened on Darworth, either by accident or design, back in the days when Darworth had bunglingly tried to poison a rich wife. She had been with Elsie Fenwick Darworth when the happy couple returned to England; she could have been, and undoubtedly had been, instrumental in the disappearance of the first wife. Darworth buys the house in Brixton; and what lay buried there—say in that filled-up well—became a deep vein of blackmail. The humble assistant turns on Darworth, saying, "Buy my silence!" Or possibly, "Buy it with marriage." The erstwhile lady's maid sets herself up on the Riviera with Darworth's money, goes in for theatricals, amuses herself, and *waits*. There's the patient strength of mind for you: no marriage, no tightening the noose, until such time as it can become incontestably legal. . . .

Then she reappears, with new plans and fresh notions for the plunder of the gullible. Has she still a hold over him? Yes. Even if Elsie Fenwick's bones were never found, bones that could be identified incontestably—and, on the evidence of a few bones, Eugene Aram was hanged eleven years after he had stabbed Daniel Clark in a cave—still Darworth's own record could not stand her threat to turn King's evidence.

So? I remember I was walking fast past the rails of Hyde Park at this point, mumbling to my pipe and arousing the curiosity of pedestrians. So what? It looked very much as though Glenda Watson constituted the brain behind Darworth's magnetic Front. She sets out to exploit, financially, his talents. All his victimizing of the wealthy credulous had begun—when? Four years ago, just after his marriage to Glenda Watson in Paris, *and* Mrs. Sweeney took up her secluded residence at Brixton. She is after money; quite content never to play actually the part of Darworth's wife . . . *because his appeal is to women, and he will be more valuable as a romantic bachelor.*

But would she have been content to grub along in this minor part? And then I remembered: she didn't. There were those long absences from Brixton, of which we had heard: vacations of months during which Darworth was taking a holiday from his occult frauds, and Mrs. Sweeney became again the talented Mrs. Glenda Darworth at the Villa d'Ivry, Nice. She and Darworth were slowly building up a fortune; they had provided themselves with a half-witted scapegoat in case the police interfered. . . .

But, unfortunately, this did not help us. When I got back to my flat, wet with perspiration from stalking along the streets like a two-miler, I resisted an impulse to get into communication with Masters. All this was probably true enough, but, so far as concerned the identity of the murderer, it only added another suspect to an already bewildering list. Where was the woman's motive for murder?

Besides, there is a fable about the goose and the golden eggs. . . .

I went to bed, and, of course, overslept.

The morning of the 8th of September was fine and clear, with an autumnal tinge in the air. Far from being on time for the appointment at eleven o'clock, I did not wake up until nearly then. Breakfast was a matter of haste and profanity; I tried to scan the papers while hurrying towards Whitehall, and only gathered that the "Plague Court double tragedy" had erupted in one form or another on nearly every page. The gilt clock in the tower of the Horse Guards was striking the half hour as I turned down towards the Embankment. And, close down towards the garden behind the War Office, a purple touring-car was parked. . . .

I should not have noticed it at all, having one eye on the newspaper, if it had not been for an impression that somebody in the tonneau had just jerked back out of sight. The back of the car was towards me, and I could have sworn that an eye was still peering out through the rear-window. Anyhow, I turned back to the little door that leads up to H.M.'s lair, just as the door opened. Marion Latimer came out, laughing, and Halliday behind her.

If there were anything weighing on the mind of either, you would never have known it. The girl was radiant, and Halliday looked better than he had looked for months. He had groomed himself from polished shoes to sandy mustache; the twinkle had come back to his heavy-lidded eyes, and he made a swaggering salute with his umbrella.

After saying, "What ho, what ho!" and uttering a variety of noises to indicate greeting, he added: "Thunder and lightning. Enter third murderer, and you look it. Go up and join the other two. Your friend H.M. is having a fine time, but poor old Masters is on the edge of homicidal mania. Ho ho ho. I will *not* be depressed today."

I said I supposed they had been on the grill. Marion was trying to keep back laughter; she punched Halliday in the ribs and said, "In public! Will you stop it?—I suppose you're invited to Mr. H.M.'s little party tonight, Mr. Blake? Dean's going. It's at Plague Court."

"We are going," he said firmly, "to motor to Hampton Court and have lunch. Who cares about tonight?" He took a swing at the air with his umbrella. "Come along, wench. I'm not likely to be arrested. Come along."

"It's all right," the girl told me, and looked round the street as though every stone in smoky London pleased her. "Mr. H.M. does buck you up, rather. He's a strange old fellow, and he keeps on telling me about the girl in the pictures who took off her clothes; but he—well, you believe in him. He says everything's all right, and he'll tell me where Ted is, and everything. . . . I say, I'm sorry, but I can't control Dean. . . ."

I watched them cross the street, Halliday twirling his umbrella and apparently using it for a pointer in a lecture about the beauties of London; down past the yellowing trees, and towards the smoky river glistening beyond the parapet. They did not see the touring-car, or seemed not to do so. They were both laughing.

Up in H.M.'s office I found a different scene. H.M., who had neglected to put on a necktie that day, was piled into his usual chair with his feet on the desk, sleepily smoking a cigar. Masters was glowering out of the window.

"There's news," I said, "and it may be big news. Look here, through sheer chance last night I discovered who Mrs.——"

H.M. took the cigar out of his mouth.

"Son," he observed, squinting down it through his big spectacles, "if you're about to tell us what I think you are, then I must warn you you're goin' to be murderously assaulted. By Inspector Humphrey Masters. Eh, Masters? The French they are a funny race. Burn me, but it appalls the Anglo-Saxon mind how you can print slap out in a Frog newspaper things that'd get you in a libel-suit if you whispered 'em in this room." He waved a paper. "*Voici 'l'Intransigeant,' mon très cher panier de salade. Ecoutez. 'LE MYSTERE DE PLAGUE COURT. UNE PROBLEME FORMIDABLE! MAIS RIEN N'EST DIFFICILE POUR NOTRE CHEF DE SURETE, M. LAVOISIER GEORGES DURRAND!' Nous avons l'honneur de vous présenter*"—"Want to hear it?" inquired H.M., leering. "Public official has a cut at solving the thing. Y'see, the whole trouble is this. . . ."

A buzzer sounded at his desk. He pressed another, took his feet off the desk, and his whole expression changed.

"To your posts," he said. "Lady Benning is on her way up."

Masters turned round sharply. "Lady Benning? What's she want?"

"I think she wants to accuse somebody of murder," said H.M.

Nobody spoke. Smoky sunlight lay on the frayed rug, and dust motes moved in it. But the mere pronouncing of that name, Lady Benning, had somehow put a chill on us. She was here and everywhere; unseen, but a presence. During what seemed like minutes we waited. Then we heard a tap on the staircase out in the hall; a pause, then another tap. She had condescended at last to use a cane. I remembered the purple touring-car parked in the street, and who must have been watching as those others went past in uproarious happiness. . . . The tapping came on. . . .

Your first impression was pity; not altogether for the infirmity. Masters opened the door for her, and she came in smiling. On the night before last you might have guessed her age as sixty; now you could have added many more years. The Watteau marquise was still there, in her way; yet now she had bedaubed it too much with rouge, lip-salve, and rather unsteady eyebrow-penciling. The eyes were brilliantly alive, and they smiled and roved.

"So you are all here, gentlemen," she said, in a voice that cracked slightly and raised in the scale. She made a delicate attempt at clearing her throat. "That is good. That is very good. And may I sit down? Thank you so much." She nodded her large hat, under which the waves of the white hair curved, and it shadowed the wrinkles. "I have heard my late husband speak of you, Sir Henry. So good of you to allow me to see you."

"Well, ma'am?" said H.M.

He spoke sharply, with the deliberate intent of rousing her; but, as she only smiled and blinked, he prompted:

"You said that you had a communication of some sort you wished to make?"

"Dear Sir Henry. And you—and you—" After a pause she took one hand off her cane and put her fingers gently on his desk. "Are you all blind?"

"Blind, ma'am?"

"Do you mean that clever men like you—and you—haven't seen? Must I tell you? Do you really mean that you don't know why dear Theodore left town and rushed away to his mother in that mad hurry? Either out of fear, or in case he should have to tell what he might not wish to tell? Don't you know what *he* guessed, and now he knows?"

H.M.'s dull eyes flickered open. She leaned abruptly towards him. Her voice was still low, but it was as though another of Darworth's ghoulish toys—say a fantastic, unholy jack-in-the-box—had snapped open.

"That Marion Latimer is mad," said Lady Benning.

Silence. . . .

"Oh, I know!" She spoke more sharply, and peered at us. "I know how you would be deceived. You think that because a girl is young, and pretty, and can laugh at your man's jokes, and goes swimming and diving and playing tennis on two strong legs, that there can't be any maggot—up here. Don't you? Don't you?" she demanded, and her glance flickered round again. "You wouldn't hesitate to believe it of me, though. And why? Because I am old, and because I believe things you are simply too blind to see. That's why; that's the only reason.

"All the Melishes are rotten with insanity. I could have told you that. Sara Melish, that girl's mother, is kept under observation in Edinburgh. . . . But if you won't believe what I tell you, won't you believe plain evidence?"

"Humph. Such as——?"

"The voice in Ted's room that morning!" She apparently caught some expression on H.M.'s face, for she kept smiling and nodding. "Why did you all so easily assume it was an outsider? Was it likely that an outsider should be on the balcony at that hour of the morning? But, you see, the balcony runs all around the house: past dear Marion's bedroom. . . . But was it a wonder that a poor kitchen-maid was deceived in the voice? Dear Sir Henry, she *had* never heard it before—speaking in that manner. That was the dear girl's real voice. What else can one make of the words, 'You never suspected it, did you?'"

I heard hard breathing behind me. Masters lumbered past and up to H.M.'s desk.

"Ma'am," he said, "ma'am——"

"Shut up, Masters," said H.M. softly.

"And that dear gullible police-sergeant of yours, that Mr. Mc-Donnell you sent to spy on us before," continued Lady Benning, lifting and lowering her fingers on the desk. Her painted face moved snakily around. "He called on poor Marion at an inconvenient hour yesterday afternoon. She got rid of him—oh, so easily, the dear clever girl! She had to go out. Oh, yes. She had other work to do."

Lady Benning giggled. Then her head jerked up.

"I believe the inquest is to be held this afternoon, Sir Henry. I shall perform my duty. I shall go into the box and accuse poor Marion of the murder of Roger Darworth and of Joseph Dennis."

The silence after those sharply enunciated words was broken by H.M.'s thoughtful voice: "Now, ma'am, that's most interestin'. You won't be able to do it this afternoon, of course; I forgot to tell you there's been an adjournment——"

She leaned again. It was like a pounce. "Ah! You believe me, don't you? I can see it in your face. Dear Sir Henry. . . ."

"But it's interestin'. It shows rather a change of attitude, don't it? I wasn't there, and all I know is what I read, but didn't you say Darworth had got himself done in by ghosts?"

Her little eye gleamed like a crumb of glass. Say that, and you touch the fanatic. "Make no mistake, my friend. If *they* had chosen to kill Mr. Darworth——"

There was a late and somnolent fly drumming along the edge of H.M.'s desk. Her black-gloved hand shot out. The next moment she brushed the dead thing softly to the carpet; then she dusted her hands together, smiled at H.M., and went on evenly: "That is why I supposed it, you see. But when the unfortunate imbecile was murdered, I knew that *they* had only stood by in their power, and watched a human being commit these murders. In a way, it was their direction. Oh, yes. *They* were instrumental. But they chose a human agent." Slowly she lifted herself across his desk; and, leaning nearly in his face, scrutinized H.M. with a hideous earnestness. "You do believe me? You do believe me, don't you?"

H.M. rubbed his forehead. "It seems to me, now that I remember it, something about Miss Latimer and Halliday holdin' hands. . . ."

She was a wise general. She knew the value of not saying too much; she knew the value of her effects. After carefully watching H.M.'s face—and, in general, cardplayers have found this a highly unprofitable proceeding—she seemed satisfied. There was a thin frosty light of triumph about her. She got to her feet, and so did H.M. and I.

"Good-by, dear Sir Henry," she said softly, at the door. "I shall not take up your time. And—holding hands?" She giggled again, raised her hand and wagged a finger at us. "Surely my dear nephew is chivalrous enough to uphold her if she cares to say that? It is the simple conduct of a gentleman. Besides, you know, he may have been deceived." Her face assumed a sly and coquettish simper. "Who knows? In her absence, he may have been holding mine."

The door closed. We heard the cane slowly tap-tapping down the hall.

"Sit still!" said H.M., as Masters made a movement forward. His command rang in the ugly quiet. "Be still, you fool. Don't go after her."

"My God," said Masters, "do you mean to tell me she's right?"

"I'm only tellin' you we've got to work fast, son. Take a chair. Light a cigar. Be calm." He hoisted his feet on the desk again, and drowsily blew smoke-rings. "Look here, Masters. Did you have any suspicions of the Latimer girl?"

"I'll be honest about it, sir. I never even considered it."

"That's bad. On the other hand, y'see, the mere fact that she was the farthest from suspicion *don't* necessarily mean she's guilty. Things'd be too easy like that. Find the unlikeliest person—call the Black Maria. The trap is that, since it don't seem likely, you'll believe it all the more. Besides, in this case it happens to be the most likely one who's guilty. . . ."

"But who is the most likely one?"

H.M. chuckled. "That's been the trouble with the case; we haven't been able to see it. Still, at my little party tonight . . . by the way, you didn't know about it, did you, Ken? Plague Court at eleven o'clock sharp. This will be strictly stag. I want you, and young Halliday, and Bill Featherton. . . . Masters, you're not to be with us; I'll give you your instructions presently. I'll need some extra men for help, but they'll come from my own department. Shrimp's the man I want, if I can find him."

"All right," the Inspector agreed wearily. "Whatever you say, sir. If you'll agree to introduce me to the murderer, I'll do anything in this nightmare of a business. I'm just about crazy, and that's a fact. After that fiasco of Mrs. Sweeney——"

"You know about it?" I interrupted, and hastened to lay out my information. Masters nodded.

"Every time we *get* a lead," he said, "even a small one, it's cut out almost as soon as it's mentioned. . . . Yes, I know. That was Durrand's brain-wave. That was the reason he dragged me in with a trunk-call from Paris that we had to pay for. He found out about Glenda Darworth; and then that there were long periods when she was not seen in Nice. I'll admit he got me excited about the thing. . . ."

H.M. waved his cigar in the air.

"Burn me," he said admiringly, "Masters was inspired with a real *joie de vivre,* he was. Back he goes to Magnolia Cottage a-flying, with a female searcher in tow. So they leap on Mrs. Sweeney with triumphant shouts, and then they discover that something's wrong. No padding. No wig. . . ."

"But, blast it, the woman isn't young any more," Masters protested; "she mightn't have needed any disguise——"

H.M. pushed over the copy of *l'Intransigeant.* There was a large photograph labeled, "Mme. Darworth." "Full measurements here, son. It was taken eight years ago; but eight years ain't long enough to change brown eyes to black, alter the shape of a nose, mouth, and chin, and add four inches to height. . . . Well, Ken, Masters was wild. Not so much as La Sweeney, I'll admit. More so as good old Durrand put through another call this morning, at the Yard's expense, saying, 'Alas, one is desolated. One fears, my old one, that this handsome small idea will not march. One finds that Madame Darworth has herself telephoned from her other flat, which discovers itself at Paris, to appellate one a species of large imbecile. Truly, it is unfortunate.' Then he rings off, and the exchange says, 'Three pound nineteen and fourpence, please.' Ho, ho."

"All right," said Masters bitterly. "Go on. Have a good time. You yourself said that Elsie Fenwick is buried close to that cottage; you said——"

"She is, son."

"Then——?"

"Tonight," said H.M., "you'll see. All this is a clew, but not the kind you think it is. It leads to London, not Paris or Nice. It leads to somebody you've seen and talked to, and yet never once more than suspected a little bit. Yes, the person's been under suspicion; but not very much. The person who used that dagger, and stoked the furnace, and has been laughing at us behind the best kind of mask all the way through this case. . . .

"Tonight," said H.M., "I'm goin' to have somebody murdered exactly as Darworth was murdered. You'll be there, and the stroke will come straight over your shoulder, and yet you may not see it. Everybody might be there, including Louis Playge."

He rolled up his big head. The pale sun behind him silhouetted a bulk still lazy, but irresistible and deadly.

"And the person ain't goin' to laugh—much longer."

XIX
THE DUMMY THAT WORE A MASK

THERE WAS a bright moon over the little stone house. It was a cold night; so cold that sounds acquired a new sharpness, and breath hung in smoke on the luminous air. The moon probed down into the well of the black buildings round the yard of Plague Court; it etched flat shadows, and the shadow of a crooked tree lay across our path.

A face was looking at us out of the door of the little stone house, which stood open. It was a pallid and rigid face, which yet seemed to be winking one eye.

Halliday, at my elbow, jerked back with an exclamation that he stifled in his throat. Major Featherton muttered something, and for a second we did not move.

Far away and muffled, a City clock began to toll out the hour of eleven. In the door and windows of the house shone a glow of red firelight. And, motionless, its hands crossed in its lap, something was sitting tall on a chair before the fire; and the face was hanging over one shoulder with a witless smirk on the bluish-white features; with a drooping mustache, and one eyebrow raised over goggling spectacles. There seemed to be drops of sweat on its forehead.

I could have sworn the thing grinned. . . .

It was not a nightmare, suddenly coming down on us. It was as real as the night and the moon, which we met after we had come up through the echoing passage to Plague Court, round in the dark yard past the ruined arbor.

"That," said Halliday loudly, and pointed, "that's the damned thing—or something like it—I saw when I came out here alone the night before. . . ."

A big shadow moved across the firelight inside. Somebody peered out and hailed us, blotting away the white-faced thing behind.

"Good," said H.M.'s voice. "I rather thought it might 'a' been, d'ye see, after what you said this morning. That's why I used James's mask in makin' my dummy. It's the dummy we're goin' to use for the experiment. . . . Come on in, come on in!" he added testily. "This place is full of drafts."

H.M.'s elephantine figure, in the fur-collared coat and the ancient top-hat, only enhanced the evil grotesquerie of the room inside. An enormous fire, too big a fire, ran with a roar up the black chimney. A table had been set up before the fire; a table and five kitchen chairs, of which only one had a complete back. Supported on one chair, and propped sideways against the table, sat a life-sized dummy roughly constructed of canvas filled with sand. It was even fitted out with an old coat and trousers, and on its head a rakish felt hat held in place the painted mask where a face should have been. The effect was one of jaunty horror, enhanced by a pair of white cotton gloves sewn to the sleeves in such fashion that the dummy seemed to have its hands placed together as though praying. . . .

"It's good, ain't it?" inquired H.M. with admiring complacency. He had his finger in the pages of a book, and his chair had been drawn up on the opposite side of the table. "When I was a kid, I used to make the best Fifth-of-November Guys in London. There wasn't time to make this one more elaborate. Blasted thing's heavy, too. Weighs as much as a full-grown man."

"Brother James—" said Halliday. He wiped his hand across his forehead, and tried to laugh. "I say, you go in for realism, don't you? What are you going to do with it?"

"Kill it," said H.M. "There's the dagger on the table."

I looked away from the bulging eyes of the dummy, the goggling spectacles and rabbit-like smile under the mustache as the thing sat with its hands together against the firelight. On the table a single candle burned in a brass holder, just as it had been last night. There were some sheets of paper and a fountain-pen. There was also—blackened with fire from bone handle to point—Louis Playge's knife.

"Dash it, Henry," said Major Featherton, clearing his throat. The major looked strange in an ordinary bowler and tweed coat; less imposing, and more like a querulous elderly man with asthma and a face colored by too much tippling. He coughed. "After all, I mean to say, this seems merely damned childish. Dummies and whatnot, eh? Look here, I'm in favor of any reasonable thing——"

"You needn't try to avoid those stains on the floor," said H.M., watching him. "Or on the walls, either. They're dry."

We all glanced at what he indicated, but we all looked back at the smirking dummy. It was the most evil thing there. The fire threw out a fierce heat, moving its shadows on the red-lit walls. . . .

"Somebody bolt the door," said H.M.

"Good God, what *is* this?" demanded Halliday.

"Somebody bolt the door," repeated H.M. with sleepy insistence. "You do it, Ken. Make sure. Oh, you hadn't noticed that the door'd been repaired? Yes. One of my lads did it this afternoon. Clumsy job, but it'll do. Hop to it."

The bolt, after the wrenchings it had got that night, was more stiff then ever. I pulled the door shut and with a fairly powerful jerk got the bolt into place. The iron bar across it had been moved up vertically; I yanked it down and with several fist-poundings got it firmly wedged in the iron nests along the door.

"Now," said H.M., "'now,' as the ghost observed in the story, 'we're locked in for the night.'"

Everybody jumped a little, for one reason or another. H.M. stood by the fire, his hat on the back of his head. The firelight shone on his glasses; but no muscle moved in his big face. His mouth was drawn down sourly, and his little eyes moved from one to the other of us.

"Now, about your chairs. Bill Featherton, I want you sitting on the left hand side of the fireplace. Pull the chair out and a little away from it—that's it. Dammit, don't bother about your trousers; do as I tell you! You sit next in order, Ken . . . about four feet away from Bill; so. The dummy's next, sittin' by the table, but we'll turn him round like a companionable feller, to face the fire. The other side of the table—you there, Mr. Halliday. I'll complete the little semi-circle, thus."

He dragged his own chair over to the far side of Halliday, but set it down sideways to the chimney-corner, so that he could look along the little line we formed.

"Humph. Now, let's see. Conditions are exactly as they were night before last, with one exception. . . ." Fumbling in his pocket, he drew out a gayly colored box and tossed its contents at the fire.

"Here!" roared Major Featherton. "I say——!"

First there were sparks, and a greenish light rolled out of the blaze. Then, in thick clouds, an overpowering wave of sickly smelling incense crept out and curled sluggishly up along the floor. Its odor seemed to get in my very pores.

"Got to do it," said H.M. in a matter-of-fact voice. "It ain't my artistic taste; it's the murderer's."

Wheezing, he sat down and blinked along the line.

There was a silence. I looked over my right shoulder at the dummy, leering at the fire with its black hat jauntily cocked over where the ear should be; and I had a horrible fancy, What if that damned thing should come alive? Beyond it was Halliday, grown quiet and satirical now. The candle burned on the table between him and the dummy, and flickered as the incense rose up. It was the sheer absurdity of the thing which made it come close to the terrible.

"Now that we're all locked in here nice and cozy," said H.M., and his voice echoed in the little stone room, "I'm goin' to tell you what happened night before last."

Halliday scratched a match to light a cigarette; but he broke the head off, and he did not try again.

"You'll imagine," continued H.M. drowsily, "that you're in the positions you occupied then. Think back, now, to where everybody was. But we'll take up Darworth first; the dummy indicates him, and"—H.M. took his watch out of his pocket, leaned across the table, and laid it down—"we got some time to spare before somebody I'm expectin' arrives here tonight. . . .

"I've already told you some of what Darworth's done; I repeated it to Ken and the major yesterday, and to Halliday and Miss Latimer this morning. I told you about the confederate, and what was planned. . . .

"We'll start from where Darworth murders the cat; and that's where I began sittin' and thinkin'."

"Not to interrupt," said Halliday; "but who are you expecting tonight?"

"The police," said H.M.

After a pause he got his pipe out of his pocket and went on:

"Now, we've established that Darworth killed that cat with Louis Playge's dagger, by the punctures and rips in its throat. Very well; afterwards he's got the blood to splash hereabouts, he's got himself smeared up a bit—but that will pass unnoticed in the dark, under coat and gloves, if he doesn't see anybody, but gets Featherton and young Latimer to rush him out and lock him in here immediately. Point really is: What did he do with that dagger? Eh?

"Only two things he could 'a' done: (1) He could have brought it in here with him, or (2) Passed it to his confederate.

"Take the second point first, my lads. If he passed it to a confederate, that'd mean that his confederate had to be either young Latimer or Bill Featherton. . . ." Here H.M. sleepily raised the lids from his eyes, as though expecting a protest.

Nobody spoke. We could hear the watch ticking on the table.

"Because those were the only two with him, to whom he could have passed it. Now, it's not reasonable that he did such a fat-headed thing. Why hand it over to the confederate merely to take into the big house and bring out again?—runnin', meantime, the risk of being seen giving it to the confederate by the other person who's not in the plot, and the even bigger risk entailed by the confederate carryin' around a blood-stained dagger which will give the show away if anybody in the front room happens to spot it. No, no; Darworth took it into this room with him. That's the reasonin'.

"As a matter of fact, I knew from another cause that he did take it in; but we'll pass over that other cause for a minute: I'm showin' you the obvious reasons for things. . . . *Well, speak up, somebody!*" he added with a sudden sharp look. "*What d'ye gather from that?*"

Halliday turned round from gazing blankly at the watch.

"But what about," he said, "what about the dagger that touched the back of Marion's neck?"

"Humph. That's better. Exactly. What about it? Son, that apparently inconsistent point clears up a big difficulty. Somebody was prowlin' in the dark. Was that person holdin' another dagger? If so, the whole point is that he or she was holdin' it in a very odd way; an unnatural way; a way nobody under heaven ever carried a dagger before. Mind you, she wasn't touched by the blade, but by the handle and hilt, so that the person must have been gripping it under the hilt, by the blade. . . . What is it, son, that you *do* naturally hold like that? What is it that is shaped rather like a dagger, so that a mind running on daggers might possibly mistake it for one in the dark . . . ?"

"Well?"

"It was a crucifix," said H.M.

"Then Ted Latimer——?" I said, after a pause that seemed to echo like thunder. "Ted Latimer——?"

"As I say, I was sittin' and thinkin'. And I thought a good deal about the psychological puzzle of Ted Latimer, both before and after we heard how he come home with a little crucifix in his hand. . . .

"Y'know, that half-cracked young feller would have concealed that crucifix from you quicker and deeper than he'd have concealed a crime. He would honestly have considered himself shamed if you had thought that he, the intellectual snipe, carried it because he reverenced it or thought it holy: which he would say he didn't at all. . . . And that's the dancin', topsy-turvy puzzle of people nowadays. They'll sneer at a great thing like the Christian Church, but they'll believe in astrology. They won't believe the clergyman who says there's something in the heavens; but they will believe the rather less mild statement that you can read the future there like an electric sign. They think there's something old-fashioned and provincial about believing too thoroughly in God, but they will concede you any number of deadly earthbound spirits: because the latter can be defended by scientific jargon.

"Never mind. . . . Point's this. Ted Latimer fanatically believed in the earthbound soul Darworth was goin' to exorcise. He'd got himself into a state of ecstasy and exaltation. He believed this house was swarmin' with deadly influences. He wanted to go out among 'em—face 'em—see 'em! He had been forbidden to move, and yet, d'ye see, he felt that he had to go out of the 'safe' room into their midst. . . . And, my lads, when Ted Latimer got up and crept out of that circle, he was carrying the traditional weapon against evil spirits: a crucifix."

Major Featherton asked hoarsely:

"You're saying *he* was the confederate? He was the one who went out?"

"Man, doesn't that crucifix sound like it? He went out, yes. But he was the one you *heard* go out."

"Two—" said Halliday blankly. "Then why didn't he tell us he'd gone out?"

H.M. leaned over and picked up his watch. Something was on the way; some force gathering round with the quick ticking. . . .

"Because something happened," said H.M. quietly. "Because he saw or heard or noticed something that made even him suspect Darworth wasn't murdered by ghosts. . . . Can you account for his wild behavior afterwards in any other way, son? He was done up. He screamed belief at you. How did Lady Benning feel when Masters ripped out all those wires in Darworth's séance room, and tore the bowels out of her beloved phantom James? Ted still believed in Darworth; and yet he didn't. In any case—whatever it was, d'ye see?—he still thought the Truth was bigger than Darworth; better to have everybody believe Darworth was really killed by spooks, *if* the trickery in this case went to support the Truth in the eyes of the world! . . . Didn't somebody tell me how he kept repeating, over and over, that this would bring the truth before the world, and what was one man's mere life compared to that? Didn't he keep hysterically insisting on that? By God, I thought so!"

"Then what was it," said Halliday, choking suddenly, "what was it Ted saw or heard or noticed?"

H.M. slowly got to his feet, immense in the firelit room.

"D'you want me to show you?" he asked. "It's nearly time."

The heat of the fire was suffocating, rather hypnotic. The mist of incense, the distortion of fire and candlelight, made the expression on the dummy's mask one of satirical enjoyment; as though, behind the embodiment of canvas and sand, Roger Darworth were listening to us in the haunted place where he had died.

"Ken," said H.M., "take Louis Playge's dagger off the table. Got a handkerchief? Good. You remember, there was a handkerchief found under Darworth's body. . . . Now take that knife and give the dummy three hard, scratching cuts: use your strength and rip the clothes: on his left arm, hip, and leg. Go on!"

The thing must have weighed fourteen stone. It did not move when I did as I was told, except a hideously lifelike jerk against the table. The face slid a little sideways under the rakish hat, as though the dummy had glanced down. Sand sprayed and spilled out across my hand.

"Now cut his clothes a little, but don't puncture the canvas . . . that's it—anywhere—half a dozen good ones. *Now!* Now you've done what Darworth himself did. So wipe your fingerprints off the handle with that handkerchief and drop the handkerchief on the floor. . . ."

Halliday said very quietly:

"*There's somebody walking round outside this house.*"

"Dagger back on the table, Ken. Now, then, I want all of you to watch the fire. Don't look at me; keep your eyes straight ahead, because the murderer's nearly here. . . .

"There's no blood to distract you now. Only a little sand. If you only knew it, all the ingenuity of this crime lies in Louis Playge's dagger being exactly that kind of dagger; in preparing your mind for it, as Darworth did; and in the splendid window-dressing of cat's blood and slashed clothes. And a very hot fire, and heavy incense in it, so that you couldn't smell. . . . Keep looking at the fire, now; don't look at me or at each other or at the dummy; watch the fire and how it blazes . . . and in just a second you'll solve this thing for yourself. . . ."

From somewhere in the room, or near it, there was a creaking and what sounded like a dull scrape. Always I was conscious of the dummy, so close to me that I could touch it, as though I were standing beside a guillotine. The fire crackled and pulsed; most of all, you heard the steady, sharp ticking of H.M.'s watch. The creaking grew louder. . . .

"My God, I can't stand this!" said Major Featherton hoarsely. I shot a side glance at him; his eyeballs were starting and his face mottled as though it had begun to color in a fit. "I tell you I——"

Then it happened.

H.M.'s hands slapped together sharply; how many times I

could not tell. In the same moment the dummy rose forward in its chair, upsetting the candle on the table. It hesitated, wavered, and thudded forward on its face—a canvas sack outflung, with the rakish black hat almost in the fire. There was a clang and clatter as Louis Playge's dagger struck the floor just beside it.

"What in God's name—!" shouted Halliday. He was on his feet, peering wildly about the firelit room, and so were all the rest of us.

None of us had moved, none of us had touched the dummy; and yet, but for ourselves, the room was empty.

My knees were shaking as I sat down again. I drew a sleeve across my eyes, and yanked one foot back; for the dummy was resting against it, and the floor was gritty with spurted sand from its back. There were wounds in the dummy's back: one that had nipped across the shoulder-blade, one high up on the shoulder, one beside the spine, and one under the left shoulder-blade that would have pierced the canvas heart.

"Steady, son!" said H.M.'s slow, calming, easy voice. He gripped Halliday by the shoulder. "Look for yourself, now, and you'll see. There's no blood and no hocus-pocus. Examine that dummy as though you didn't know anything about what Darworth intended to do; as though you'd never heard of Louis Playge or his dagger; as though no suggestion had been forced on you as to what was to happen. . . ."

Halliday came forward shakily and bent down.

"Well?" he demanded.

"Look, for instance," said H.M., "at the hole that finished him; the one straight through the heart. Pick up Louis Playge's dagger, and fit it into that hole. . . . Fits, don't it? Quite, quite. Why does it fit?"

"Why does it—?" said Halliday wildly.

"Because the hole's round, son; the hole's round. And the dagger is just the same size. . . . But if you'd never seen any dagger, and never had any suggestion of a dagger forced on you, what would you say it looked like? Answer, somebody! Ken?"

"It looks," I said, "like a bullet-hole."

"But, my God, the man wasn't shot!" cried Halliday. "There'd have been bullets found in the wounds. And there weren't any found by the police surgeon."

"It was a very special sort of bullet, my dear fathead," said H.M. softly. "It was made, in fact, of rock-salt. . . . They dissolve, my fathead, between four and six minutes at blood-heat; it takes longer than that for a dead body to cool. And, when a dead body is lying in front of one of the hottest fires in England with its back exposed. . . . Son, it's nothing new. The French police have used 'em for some time; they're antiseptic, and no dangerous extractions of the bullet necessary when used on a burglar; it dissolves. But if it pierces the heart, the man's just as dead as though it had been lead."

He turned, and heaved up an arm to point.

"Was Louis Playge's dagger originally exactly the same circumference as a bullet from a thirty-eight caliber revolver? Eh? Burn me, I dunno. But Darworth ground it down to the same size: not a millimeter difference. Darworth constructed his own rock-salt bullet, fatheads, on his own lathe. He got his material from one of those pieces of rock-salt 'sculpture' that Ted very, very innocently mentioned to Masters and Ken. He left traces of the salt on the lathe. It might have been fired, there bein' no noise, either from an air-pistol—which is the method I should have chosen myself—or from an ordinary pistol with a silencer. When thick incense is burned in a small room, notwithstandin', I conclude that it was an ordinary pistol with powder-smoke that might be smelled. . . . Finally, it could have been fired through a big keyhole; but, as a matter of fact, the muzzle of a .38 exactly fits one of the nice grating-spaces of any of the four windows round this room. The windows, somebody may have told you, are up against the roof. If—I say *if*—somebody could get on that roof. . . ."

From outside, in the yard, there was a shout, and then a scream. Masters' voice yelled, "*Look out!*" and two heavy shots exploded just as H.M. pushed aside the table and heaved himself towards the door.

"That was Darworth's scheme," snarled H.M. "But the little joker firin' them shots now is the murderer. Get that door open, Ken. I'm afraid the murderer's loose. . . ."

I wrenched the bolt back, pushed up the bar, and dragged the door open. The yard was a nightmare of darting lights. Something ducked past us, a low shape in the moonlight, started to run for our door, and then whirled as we stumbled out. There was a needle-spit flash, and a flat bang almost in our faces. Through a wake of powder smoke, we could see Masters—a bull's-eye lantern in his hand—charging after that running figure which zigzagged about the yard. H.M.'s bellow rose above the din of shouts:

"You goddamned fool, didn't you search——"

"Didn't say anything," Masters yelled back chokingly, "about being under arrest. . . . You said not to. . . . Head off, boys! Close in! Can't—get—out of the yard now. . . . Penned in. . . ."

Other shapes, flickering long flashlight beams, darted round the side of the house. . . .

"Got the devil!" somebody shouted out of the dark. "Penned in a corner——"

"No," said a clear thin voice out of the dark; "no, you haven't."

I will swear to this day that I saw the revolver flash lighting up a face, a mouth split in triumphant defiance, as that woman fired a last bullet into her own forehead. Something went down in a sodden heap, over against the wall near Louis Playge's crooked tree. . . . Then there was a great silence in the yard, smoke white against the moon, and dragging footsteps as men closed in.

"Let's have your lamp," H.M. said in a heavy voice to Masters. "Gentlemen," he said with a sort of bitter flourish, "go over and take a look at the most brilliant she-devil who ever gave an old veteran the nightmare. Take the lamp, Halliday—don't be afraid, man!"

The bright light shook in his hand. It caught a white face turned sideways in the mud by the wall, the mouth open still sardonically. . . .

Halliday started, and peered. "But—but who is it?" he demanded. "I'll swear I never saw that woman before. She's——"

"Oh, yes you have, son," said H.M.

I remembered a picture in a newspaper; a fleeting one, cloudy and uncertain, and I hardly heard myself saying:

"That's . . . that's Glenda Darworth, H.M. That's his second wife. But you said—Halliday's right—we never saw. . . ."

"Oh, yes, you did," repeated H.M. Then his big voice raised: *"But you never recognized her all the time she was masquerading as Joseph', did you?"*

XX
THE MURDERER

WHAT ANNOYS me most," growled H.M., who was heating water on a forbidden gas-ring in the lavatory connecting with his office, "what annoys me most is that I should've spotted this whole business a day earlier—naturally, fatheads—if I'd only known everything that *you* knew. It wasn't until last night and this morning (or yesterday morning) that I got a chance to go over everything with Masters; and then I could 'a' kicked myself. Humph. Comes o' tryin' to be godlike."

It was close on two o'clock in the morning. We had come back to H.M.'s office, roused the night watchman, and stumbled up the four flights of stairs to the Owl's Nest. The watchman built us a fire, and H.M. insisted on brewing a bowl of whisky punch to celebrate. Halliday, Featherton, and I sat in the decrepit leather chairs about H.M.'s desk while he came back with the boiling water.

"Once you'd got the essential clew, that Joseph was Glenda Darworth all the time, the rest is easy. Trouble is, there was so much wool and padding round the business that it was last night before I tumbled to it. Another thing got in the way, too; I can see that now. . . ."

"But, look here!" grumbled the major, who was struggling to light a cigar. "It can't be! What I want to know is——"

"You're goin' to hear it," said H.M., "as soon as we get comfortable. This water should be what the Irish call 'screeching hot'—just a minute—that sugar, now! . . ."

"And also," said Halliday, "how she happened to be in that yard a couple of hours ago, and who fired those shots through the window tonight; and how the devil the murderer reached the roof in the first place——"

H.M. said, "Drink first!" After the punch had been tasted, and H.M. flattered on its quality, he grew more expansive. He settled down so that the light of the desklamp did not get in his eyes, stretched his feet on the desk with an expiring sigh, and began talking to his glass.

"The funny part was, Ken and old Durrand in Paris stumbled slap on the whole explanation, even to the dead give-away of the business, if they'd only had the sense to apply it to the right person. But they picked on poor Mrs. Sweeney; naturally, I suppose, becoz Joseph was apparently lyin' burned to a cinder on a morgue-slab with the dagger in his back.

"Son, in essentials that theory was absolutely right. Glenda Darworth *was* the strong-minded, bleed-their-purses lady; the brain behind Darworth's personality; and she'd have played the part of a Cherokee Indian if it had helped their game. Trouble is, you had to look farther than Mrs. Sweeney. Because why? Because Mrs. Sweeney was never in the thick of things; she was never in a position where she could keep an eye on the people and make strategic moves unobserved; all she did was sit at home and be a respectable housekeeper for a weak-minded boy. But

Joseph—well, if you're considerin' a suspect to occupy that position, Joseph jumps out at you. He was never out of the middle of things, because he was the medium. They had to have him; he was indispensable; and not one thing could occur without his knowing it. And you had the complete answer, Ken, when that lady friend of yours deliberately told you the names of the plays in which Glenda Darworth had made her big hits. . . . Remember 'em?"

"One," I said, "was Shakespeare's 'Twelfth Night', and the other was Wycherley's 'The Plain Dealer'."

Halliday whistled. "Viola!" he said. "Hold on a bit! Isn't Viola the heroine who dresses in boy's clothes to follow the hero——"

"Uh. And I was glancin' over the other one, 'The Plain Dealer'," vouchsafed H.M., chuckling, "while I was waitin' for you in the stone house tonight. What did I do with that book?" He fished in his pocket. "And Fidelia, the heroine there, does exactly the same thing. It's a rare good play for entertainment. Burn me, did you know they were crackin' Scotch jokes in 1675? The Widow Blackacre refers to a wench as a Scotch Warming Pan. Heh-heh-heh. Never mind. . . . But those two plays, with exactly the same kind of part, stretch the thing a bit too far to be coincidence. If you fatheads only had a little more erudition, you'd 'a' spotted Glenda much sooner. However——"

"Get down to cases," growled the major.

"Right. Now, I'll admit we learned all that a little too late. So I'm goin' to start at the beginning and follow out the story, with what could have been deduced from it even if I had first tumbled to Joseph. We'll assume we don't know Glenda Darworth is Joseph; we don't know anything; we're only sittin' and thinkin' about the facts. . . .

"We've decided that Darworth had a confederate, who was

goin' to help him stage a fake attack by Louis Playge's ghost. That confederate was to go to the museum and take the dagger. The little trick of moving the neck in the manner of Louis Playge was meant to catch the attendant's eye; Darworth knew that the papers would play it up, and it was fine publicity for his scheme. We've even decided how the real murder was committed; with rock-salt bullets fired by somebody on the roof through one of those grated windows. If Darworth had cleaned up his lathe, and if Ted hadn't so casually mentioned those pieces of sculpture, it might have been a snag. Lord!" grunted H.M., taking a hasty drink of his punch, "Burn me, but I was afraid you'd find it out for yourselves, I was!" He glared at us. "If one of you had spoiled my effect, hanged if I wouldn't have backed out of the case altogether. I don't mind helpin' you, but you got to let the old veteran have his way, or he won't play. Humph. I even hadda tell Masters not to taste the stuff, or he'd have found out it was salt, and even *his* brain might 'a' been started workin'. Purpf. Bah. Well!

"Now, that's all we know, you understand. There's where we begin lookin' for a murderer.

"We look around. And what do we see but the obvious one starin' us in the face—the person who *would* be a confederate, and was more likely to be than anybody else: namely, Joseph. So why don't we suspect him and drag him under the spotlight straight-away?

"First, because the apparent boy is a weak-minded drug-addict, under Darworth's domination, and certainly full of morphine after the murder was committed.

"Second, because we've been told Darworth keeps him as a dummy or front for his activities, and Joseph knows nothing.

"Third, because apparently he has a perfect alibi; and was sitting playing cards with McDonnell the whole time."

H.M. chuckled. He got his pipe lit after a herculean effort; inhaled soothing smoke; and his stare became vacant again.

"Boys, it was rather an ingenious set-up, d'ye see. First the obvious thing, then smeared over with a number of hints or facts which would make people say, 'Poor old Joseph! Framed; not a doubt of it.' Oh, I know. I fell for it myself, for a few hours. And then I began thinkin'. It was a funny thing, but, when I read over all that testimony again, not one of the people in that circle— who'd known Joseph for nearly a year—had ever suspected him of being a drug-addict before that night. In fact, it came as a shock to everybody. Now, throughout all that time, it might have been possible for Joseph and Darworth to have concealed this; though it would have been difficult; but, most of all, that constant doping of Joseph would have seemed *unnecessary*. Why keep shooting him full of morphine before a séance—ain't that a highly expensive, dangerous, and complex way of puttin' a person to sleep, when it could have been done as well with cheap legitimate drops from the chemist's, and leave no dangerous after-effects? What's to be gained by it? All you do is create a drug-addict who may babble and tilt the beans all over the floor at any minute! Why not even ordinary hypnosis, if Joseph were such an easy subject? It struck me as a fishy, roundabout way of attaining a very ordinary object: that is, to keep the boy quiet in the medium's cabinet while Darworth was manipulating strings. You wouldn't even need to put a weak mind to sleep in order to do that.

"So I asked myself, 'Look here,' I said, 'where did that suggestion of his being a drug-addict first come from?' It was first mentioned by Sergeant McDonnell, who'd been investigating the case; but by nobody else until it was backed by Joseph's obviously showing himself under the influence, and babbling.

"Then it struck me, lads, that of all the inconsistent, dubious, and suspicious things we had heard in this case, that story of Joseph's was the worst. First, he said that he had pinched the hypodermic needle and morphine from Darworth, and given himself a dose. Now, that's wildly unlikely, as you'll admit. . . ."

Major Featherton, stroking his white mustache, interrupted:

"But dammit, Henry, you yourself said, in this office, it was because—look here, what was it?—that he'd done it with Darworth's connivance. . . ."

"And don't the flaw of that belief immediately strike you?" demanded H.M., who hates to be reminded of his mistakes. "All right, all right; I admit it didn't strike me for a minute, but don't it shout aloud in the universe? *Darworth, according to Joseph, wants Joseph to keep on the watch for somebody who may do him harm.* That's what Joseph said to Ken and Masters; that was his story. Well, can you think of anything more unreasonable than allowing somebody to shoot himself full of morphine in order to keep on the watch? Either way you looked at it, the thing was fishy. It didn't ring true. . . . But there was another explanation, so obvious and simple that it was a long time before it occurred to me. Suppose old Joseph wasn't a drug-addict at all; suppose all the others had been right, and all we had was his own word, which we accepted too easily? Suppose that whole tale was spun up to avert suspicion? Granted that he'd taken a dose of morphine *then*— he couldn't counterfeit the actual physical symptoms—still, the symptoms of the *addict*, the twitching hand, the wandering eye, the jerks and babblings, could have been put forward by a good actor and corroborated by our own instinctive belief that a person won't admit he's a drug-addict unless he actually is. Neat psychology, son; not at all bad.

"As I say, I was sittin' and thinkin'. . . .

"So I asked myself, 'Here,' I said, 'let's take that as a workin' hypothesis; is there anything to support it?' It'd prove, for instance, that Joseph was very far from being the idiot he pretended, and assumin' the colors of a dangerous character, if we could prove it.

"Look at his story again. He said that Darworth was nervous about being attacked by somebody in that circle. We had it from everybody's testimony that Darworth wasn't nervous at all about goin' out to keep a vigil in that house; that whatever it was he feared didn't seem to come from *here;* but let that pass.... What I knew, as I told you, was Darworth's plan: the confederate who was to stage a fake attack on him. Therefore, if the confederate were a member of that circle in the front room, was it likely that he'd deliberately have asked Joseph to keep on the watch? God love us, gents, Joseph might 'a' seen the confederate, raised a row, and the beans upset again! On whichever side you looked at Joseph's story, it was equally dubious. But it was precisely the story he might have told, to protect himself, if *he* had been that confederate; if *he* had murdered Darworth instead of assisting him; and *he* had shot morphine into himself after the murder to provide an alibi.

"Keep starin' at that rather sinister-lookin' person now, and examine the second reason why we didn't suspect him—the statement that he was only Darworth's Front, to take the blame in case of mishaps. Again, who suggested that to us? Only McDonnell, who'd been investigatin', and Joseph who admitted it. And we accepted it ... my hat, how meekly we accepted it! We believed Joseph simply walked about in a daze, while Darworth did all the work and the lad knew nothin'.

"But then I remembered—the stone flower-box."

The smoke of our pipes and cigars mingled in a haze with the steam of the punch-bowl. Beyond the glow of the desk-lamp, H.M.'s face was sardonic in gloom. A late taxi honked on the

Embankment, sharp in the silence of the morning. Halliday leaned forward.

"That's what I want to know about!" Halliday said. "That flower-box that dropped out of the ceiling or somewhere, and damn near smashed my head. Masters talked very easily and grandly about what a stale trick it was. Right-ho. But the stale trick nearly finished me, and if it was that swine Joseph—or Glenda Darworth—if *she* did it——"

"Sure she did, son," said H.M., with a heavy gesture. "Ladle me out some more of Father Flaherty's medicine, will you? Umph. Ha. Thanks. . . . Now, cast your mind back to that time. You and Ken and Masters were standin' over close to the side of the staircase, weren't you? In fact, you had your back to it. Right. And up came the Major here, and Ted Latimer, and Joseph a little way behind them. So? Tell me: what was the floor made of?"

"The floor? Stone. Stone or brick; stone, I think."

"Uh-huh. But I mean the part you were standin' on then, at the back of the hall where the old flooring hadn't been taken up? Heavy boards, hey? Pretty loose; made the staircase rattle?"

"Yes," I said. "I remember how they squeaked when Masters took a step."

"And the landing of the staircase was just over young Halliday's head, hey? And there was a handrail? Quite, quite. It's the old Anne Robinson trick. Haven't you ever noticed, in an old hall with a shaky stair, how if you accidentally tread on the right board connected with the staircase, the stair will shake, and the handrail of a landing will tremble? Now if a heavy weight had been balanced across that handrail so that a hair-line shake would turn its equilibrium——?"

After a silence he went on:

"Ted and the Major, son, were ahead of you; they'd gone on. Joseph was following a few paces behind. And he didn't tread on the right board by accident. . . .

"The more you sort of scrutinize old Joseph, the less he begins to look like an unfortunate marionette dancin' on wires without knowing what goes on. Look at him! There he is, very skinny and not tall for a young man; in fact, you'd consider him small. There are the fine wrinkles in his neck, his hair cropped short and colored red, his freckles and his snub nose and rather too broad mouth; there's his thin dead voice like a boy's; and above all—I want you to remember this—his loud check suits, always distinguishable at a distance. Very much like a kid, weighing maybe ninety pounds. . . .

"And then there was a curious thing which Masters noticed just before the stone flower-box dropped; any of the rest o' you see it? He was makin' funny motions with his hands, as though he were brushin' and touching his face, and he stopped when they turned a light on him. . . .

"So I thought, 'Look here, is it possible that this is any sort of *disguise?*' You see, he'd just been out in the rain without a hat. And I wondered if he might be afraid. . . ."

"Well?"

"Well, say—that his freckles might wash off," replied H.M. "That was only the basis of an idea, still hazy. But I was sittin' and thinkin', and I remembered that tree in the yard. You know the tree? Masters said that a very agile person could easily have got from the top of the wall to the tree, and from the tree to the little house. And McDonnell pointed out how rotten the tree was, and showed a broken branch where it'd been tested. . . . So it might have broken, under a person of normal weight. I say it might, son, because Masters accepted that statement too. *But there was only one person in the whole house light enough to have climbed that tree without breaking it:* the innocent 'boy', Joseph.

"Now, would Joseph have had the skill and agility to do that; or to shoot straight enough through that window to inflict exactly those wounds? What becomes of this stupid, drug-ridden child now? All I suspect, for the moment, is that he's not what he pretends to be; and pretty definitely there's a disguise of some sort. I ask myself, 'Look here,' I say, 'while that popcorn is rattlin' around in the tin, look at something else. What's this feller's *motive,* if he did kill Darworth? He's working with Darworth to befoozle old Lady Benning and her crowd—why does he depart from the plan and shoot Darworth, which seems rather a fat-headed thing to do? 'Twasn't an accident; those last two bullets were intended to make mutton of the whiskery crook. Why kill the source of his income? The only one who inherits any of Darworth's money is his wife. . . .'

"*Wife!* You'd be surprised what a revelation started to show glimmers in the old man's mind. . . . Let's see, what was Darworth's purpose in staging this show? He might have told a confederate it was to proclaim the truth of occultism to the world; to make his name reverberate . . . but it wasn't. Oh, no. 'By God,' says I to myself, 'he was after the Latimer girl. He was goin' to propose marriage to her. But he's got a wife in Nice—a sharp, hard-headed wench who's frozen him into marriage at just the right time; who knows a deal too much about the past hanky-panky. How is *she* goin' to take all this?'"

H.M.'s pipe described a curious motion in the air, as though he were sleepily tracing out somebody's features.

"Provocative-lookin' gal, by her pictures. Thin, very. Age thirty-odd; time for little wrinkles, but not many. Not tall, but 'ud look tall on high heels. You fellers married? Ever notice how small your wives looked the first time you saw 'em without them heels? Um. Funny, too, how a mass o' black hair changes the expression of a face, or what cosmetics do to it. First I thought, 'Burn me, I'd advise that gal to be awful damn careful. Because why? Because our smilin' Darworth has already disposed of one wife, by poison or throat-cuttin' or whatnot, and if he's got his heart clean set on orange blossoms again—well, if I were the wife, I'd look under beds now and then, and stay away from side-streets after dark.'" H.M. gave a long sniff. Then his eyes fixed on us. "'Unless,' I said to myself, '*I simply beat him to it!*'"

He pointed his pipe at us.

"Did somebody tell you how Glenda Watson started her career at the age of fifteen? In a travelin' circus and side-show; ah, you heard it, did you? I'd be very much surprised to hear that negotiating a wall and a tree, or the use of a middle-caliber firearm, would cause her a great deal of difficulty. . . . A versatile gal, and what a woman! She's got talents, and she's got It, or they wouldn't have fallen for her when Darworth's money wangled her a lead in the actin' company at Nice. She had to destroy the sex-appeal during the months she played Joseph; but she didn't play him long at a time. . . . Pity to keep her hair cut short and dyed; but she had a very luxuriant black wig to replace her real hair when she went out to take the air. Remember the mysterious woman who was seen goin' in and out of Magnolia Cottage? You see, there was one conquest she had to complete as Glenda Darworth, and that——"

"This is all very well!" exploded Major Featherton, "but it doesn't get us farther. Dammit, there's one difficulty, I repeat, you can't get over. She had an alibi; she was directly under the eye of a reliable man all the time she might have been out killing

Darworth in the stone house. . . . You can't get around that solid fact. What's more, we were all in the room just across the hall, in absolute silence—she and the sergeant were over across from us—and we didn't hear a thing. . . ."

"I know you didn't," said H.M. composedly. "That's just it. You didn't hear a single damned whisper out of that room. And that's what made me suspicious.

"Now I want those shrewd minds of yours, all mellowed and primed, to consider a variety of funny coincidences. . . . First, immediately after the murder, a newspaper photographer was allowed to climb up on the roof of the stone house: a thing that should have and could have been stopped, because if there were any traces of the murderer's footprints on that roof, they'd have been messed up. Second, somebody walked round on the wall to test that rotten tree, and would have messed up more footprints. Third, in spite of Masters' efforts, the story of this being a ghost-murder—inexplicable, nothing but a supernatural thing—splashed out into the newspapers. . . ." Halliday got up slowly out of his chair. . . . "Fourth, somebody who was very clever had been assigned to keep an eye on Darworth's movements, and would have had a better chance than we to discover that 'Joseph', living in a house at Brixton, was really the fascinating Mrs. Darworth long before we had an inkling of it.

"Fifth," continued H.M., and his voice grew less sleepy, "fifth, my fatheads, have you forgotten that séance of automatic-writing at Bill Featherton's? Have you forgotten that seance at which 'Joseph' wasn't even present? Have you forgotten that *there* the paper saying 'I know where Elsie Fenwick is buried' had been slipped in among Darworth's other papers, and scared him silly because he realized that somebody *besides his wife*—somebody there—some unseen, deadly person according to Darworth's ideas—knew the secret? Why should he have been frightened merely if 'Joseph' slipped in a paper like that? He knew 'Joseph' knew it, didn't he?" Suddeny H.M. leaned across the table. "And who was, admittedly, the only person who could have palmed the paper off on Darworth; bein', as he himself admitted, an expert at parlor magic?"

In the enormous silence Halliday knocked his fist against his forehead. He said:

"My God, are you telling us that that fellow McDonnell——"

And H.M. went on drowsily:

"Bert McDonnell didn't commit the murder, of course. He was an accessory, but not an important one. He wouldn't have been needed at all by Glenda Darworth if—unexpectedly—*Masters* hadn't shown up at Plague Court. That tore it. McDonnell was watchin' in the yard to see nothing went wrong. When he saw Masters he had to intervene; had to get Joseph away somewhere out of Masters' sight; and he was so nervous (wasn't he?) that he almost bungled it. Who suggested that Masters should go *upstairs* in the house and watch while he questioned Joseph alone? Who deliberately led you in the wrong direction every time you showed a flash of intelligence? Who swore to you that tree in the yard couldn't stand any weight? Who said, for a reason you didn't question, that all it meant was that Louis Playge was buried beneath it?"

H.M. saw the expressions on our faces, and scowled.

"He's not a bad young feller. The woman had simply got him where she wanted him, that's all. . . . He didn't know she was going to murder Ted Latimer, and dress Ted in those glaring loud clothes and shove him into the furnace——"

"*What?*" shouted Halliday.

"Humph. Didn't I tell you that?" H.M. inquired blandly. "Yes. Y'see, Joseph had to disappear. Glenda Darworth didn't mean for there to be any more murders; she was simply goin' to fade out, let the police think what they might, and reappear as Glenda Darworth to claim her two hundred and fifty thousand pounds. But Ted Latimer spotted Joseph when Ted slipped out that night. And so, y'see, Ted had to die."

XXI
THE END OF IT

HALLIDAY GOT up and walked aimlessly about the room. With his back to us, he stared into the fire.

"This," he said, "this will just about kill Marion. . . ."

"Sorry, son," said H.M. gruffly. "I—well, y'see, I couldn't tell you two this afternoon. It might have spoiled my game for tonight. And I sort of thought, 'Well,' I thought, 'they're pretty happy, those two. They've been through hell and blight for some time; they've had a crack-brained hag of an aunt riding 'em as badly as Darworth ever did, and even accusing one of 'em of murder when she saw they were happy; and there's no use darkening one day now.'"

He spread his fingers and inspected them sulkily.

"Yes, the kid's dead. He was a good deal the height and build of 'Joseph', you remember? That's what made it possible. It was very nearly spoiled when that workman Watkins looked through the cellar window and spotted the murderer at work. But, d'ye see, it was the fact that convinced us Joseph was really dead. He saw only the *back* of the person on the floor; he saw those

269

clothes—those bright checked clothes; didn't I tell you to remember them—which he'd seen Joseph wearing every day. And the window-pane was dusty, and only one candle was burnin'; who wouldn't assume it was Joseph? . . . Oh, the woman was clever enough. Pouring kerosene on that body, pushing it in the furnace, wouldn't have been necessary; it was unnecessary brutality; if she hadn't only wanted to make identification impossible. They'd get a charred mass out, with a few shreds of Joseph's clothes and a pair of his shoes, and there you are. It was an opportunity, and she took advantage of it. Why do you think she chloroformed him? Why, to get him bundled into Joseph's clothes *before* she stabbed him with the dagger. That's why they were so long together in the house before he was chucked in the furnace."

Halliday whirled round.

"And this fellow McDonnell?"

"Steady, son. Go easy, now. . . . I saw him tonight; I saw him just before I went to Plague Court. Y'see I knew his father. I knew old Grosbeak very well."

"So—what?"

"He swore to me he didn't know there was goin' to be a murder; he didn't know Darworth was to be killed at all. Maybe I'd better tell you about it.

"I come up to him and said, 'Son, are you off duty now?' and he said, 'Yes.' So I asked him where he lived, and he said a flat in Bloomsbury, and I suggested that he invite me over for a drink. I could tell then he knew something was wrong. When we got there he put the latch on the door, and turned on the light; then he just turned round and said flat-out, 'Well?' So I said, 'McDonnell, I thought a lot of your father, and that's why I'm here. She's only been playing you on the string, and you know it now, don't you?' I said, 'She's the ace of she-bloodsuckers, and she's got certain characteristics of the devil; and, since she burnt poor Latimer out at Magnolia Cottage, you know *that* now too, don't you?'"

"What did he do?"

"Nothing. He just stood there and looked at me, but he turned a funny color. Then he put his hands over his eyes for a second; and sat down, and finally he said, 'Yes, I know it—now.'

"Then we didn't say anything, but I smoked my pipe and watched him, and afterwards I said, 'Why not tell me about it?'" H.M. rubbed his big hand wearily across his forehead. "He asked me why he should, so I said: 'After your friend Glenda killed young Latimer yesterday afternoon she put on her regular woman's clothes and took the night Dover-Calais service over the Channel and got into Paris late last night. She'd cleaned everything out of the house that could incriminate her,' I said. 'She turned up in Paris this morning as Darworth's wife. At my request, Darworth's solicitor cabled her to come to England for the adjustment of financial affairs. She's answered that she will be at Victoria at nine-thirty tonight. It's now a quarter to eight, and there's no way of reaching her. When she gets in, Inspector Masters will meet her at the station and ask her to come to Scotland Yard. At eleven o'clock she'll be escorted to Plague Court to witness a little exhibition of mine.' I said, 'She's done for, son. She'll be arrested tonight.'

"Well, he sat there a long time with his hands over his eyes. He said, 'Do you think you can convict her?' And I said, 'You know damned well I can.' Then he nodded his head a couple of times, and said, 'Well, that finishes both of us. Now I'll tell you the story.' And he did."

Halliday strode up to the desk. "What did you do? Where is he?"

"Better hear what he had to say first," suggested H.M. mildly. "Sit down. I'll sketch it out, if you like. . . .

"Most of it you know. How it was the woman's idea that she and Darworth should set up in this line of mulcting the gullible—although she always swore to McDonnell Darworth forced her into it—and, with long intervals between, they've been hooking various people for about four years. Darworth was to pose as the romantic bachelor, as a bait for the women; she was the dull medium who should arouse no suspicion in Darworth's lady friends. And it all went well until two things happened, (1) Darworth fell for Marion Latimer, and (2) last July McDonnell was sent to get a line on Darworth's activities by the police, and discovered who 'Joseph' was.

"It happened by accident; he stumbled on the 'mysterious lady' leaving Magnolia Cottage in her proper costume, and trailed her. What happened subsequently isn't very clear from what he told me, but I gather she used every one of her own tricks to shut *his* mouth. It seems McDonnell went on a holiday not long afterwards; and spent it with Mrs. Darworth at her villa in Nice. . . . Oh, yes. When the persuasive Glenda put herself out to be fascinating, by God, she *was* fascinating! Incidentally, while McDonnell was telling me this, he kept saying, 'How could you know how beautiful she is? You never saw her except in that make-up!' over and over again. Son, it was a bit o' real ghastliness to hear him pleading that, as though it were an excuse. He even rushed to a drawer and got out a lot of photographs, all the time he was tellin' about murder; and I was readin' between the lines. . . .

"Do you know what I was readin' between the lines, and why good old Glenda took such pains to win him over so he'd do anything she liked? By that time she was beginning to realize Darworth's little game. Darworth purported to be bleeding the

Benning circle, and handling the Plague Court matter for their mutual benefit; but Glenda knew all about the Latimer girl, so she determined to——"

"Beat him to the punch, eh?" said Halliday bitterly. "Nice little girl. Ha. Just in case he tries to shove arsenic in *her* coffee, she'll return the compliment and collect two hundred thousand. . . . Good. Marion should hear all this. It'd please her to think——"

"No offense, old son," said H.M. "But that's about it. Oh, y'see, she pretended to believe Darworth when he told her all this; meantime, she was pourin' out a tale of suffering into McDonnell's ears. Darworth's dominating will had forced her to do all this: why? Because she was afraid of him, because he had murdered his first wife and she was afraid he might murder *her*——"

"And McDonnell believed all that?" snapped Halliday. "Rot!"

"Are you sure," said H.M. quietly, "you haven't believed even rawer things in the last six months? . . . Steady. Let me go on. Well, meantime, there was a real danger that Darworth might take it into his head to do just that: dispose of his second wife as he disposed of the first, by smothering her with a pillow and burying the remains. Glenda never could tell. Those two were playing a gentle, polite, murderous game against each other; and, if Marion Latimer had given Darworth more encouragement, he might have had a shot at it. That worried Glenda. She didn't want any hanky-panky until she could get her knife into *him*. Darworth never anticipated any physical attack from her; he thought the most she'd do was threaten to expose him.

"So, when Darworth got his idea of a ghost-attack at Plague Court, Glenda must have danced the saraband. 'Mine enemy is delivered,' said Glenda, 'into—' and the rest of it. Meantime, she twines herself round Darworth and says, 'You'd never want to hurt me, would you?' And Darworth, who had rosy visions of seein' her tucked away underground with a dose of cyanide in her stomach, pats her head and says, 'Of course not.' 'Good,' says Glenda, twistin' his coat-button lovingly; 'because if you did, sweetheart, it would be just too bad.'

"'Come, come,' says Darworth gently; 'refrain from such language, my dear. Forget that you were brought up in a circus, and that the only Shakespearean parts you ever understood were Doll Tearsheet and Petruchio's wife. Why so?' 'Because,' says she, turning up those eyes of hers—and they're damn' attractive eyes—'there may be somebody besides myself who knows you killed Elsie Fenwick. . . . And if anything ever happens to me——?'

"You get the idea?" demanded H.M. "She was goin' to scare Darworth properly, in case he should try any funny business. Probably he didn't believe her when she told him that, but he was worried. If somebody else did know it, down would come all his plans on La Latimer—excuse me, son—down would come everything; and if his confounded wife had been indiscreet, he might find himself had up on a murder charge over a dozen years old. . . ."

"I say!" growled Major Featherton, who had been pulling hard at his mustache. "Then at my house—at *my* house, blast it—she has this chap McDonnell slide that message into his papers? Eh?"

"You got it," nodded H.M. "At a place, d'ye see, where Joseph wasn't even present! Burn me, do you wonder he was scared green? Because it would seem that one of this very circle—one of these people his plans were directed at—knew all about him, and was sardonically chuckling! It must have hit him straight across the back of the neck: one of those devoted acolytes of his was as bland and dangerous a hypocrite as himself. His immediate reaction was, 'I've got to put this Plague Court hoax through as quickly as I can.' Because why? Because somebody seemed out to queer his pitch, and he wanted to make his final smash to impress the Latimer girl; but, good God, which one of 'em had put that note in? Then he had time to reflect that there was a stranger, and it was probably the stranger ... yet, when he questioned Ted Latimer about McDonnell, he got only the reply that it was a harmless old school friend. He suspected, but what could he do? I needn't tell you that McDonnell's apparently accidental falling in with Ted, his wangling of an invitation to Featherton's, was no more an accident than Darworth's death. . . .

"And he walked straight into the trap he'd created for himself, Darworth did. You know what happened. McDonnell swears he didn't know Glenda intended to kill him. He says she told him Darworth had promised her that, if she aided him in this last piece of fraud, he would let her go. And so, night before last, there's the delirious McDonnell waitin' in the yard—not needed, not in the plot, but just in case! And you know how he *was* needed: ayagh, didn't it give him a shock when he saw Masters there? You'll admit he thought fast; he had to account for his presence there—which wasn't natural—so he gave rather a distorted version of the truth. You remember how *he* was the one, as I told you, who insisted 'Joseph' was only a pawn for Darworth?"

"But why say Joseph was a drug-addict?" demanded Halliday.

"Those, my lad, were his instructions from Glenda," said H.M. dryly, "in case anybody questioned him. *He* didn't understand 'em then—but he understood 'em later on. . . .

"His account of the thing to me tonight—I wish I could reproduce it. He tells how he was nearly at his wits' end to get Masters out of the room. He wanted to urge Glenda, now that the police were there, to abandon the crazy design of the fraudulent attack. She wouldn't. In fact—d'you remember, from what

Masters said?—she nearly blew the gaff herself. While Masters was there, she had the nerve to go over and make sure the boards were loose on the window of the room where she and McDonnell had been put. . . ."

"The boards on the window?" interrupted Halliday.

"Sure. Have you forgotten that the wall round Plague Court runs within three feet of the windows in the house? And that they're high windows, from which a good jumper could get to the top of the wall with one swing? That was how she walked round to the back of the house without leaving a footprint; she went on top of the wall. And you know what she did. She left McDonnell there while Masters was prowlin' upstairs—the whole shooting would take only three or four minutes. She and Darworth had prepared the whole scene the night before; you, Halliday, blundered in on them in your travels, and I don't know how they played ghost on you, but it seems they succeeded. . . .

"Meantime, somebody meshed more gears, and caused trouble for us. Ted Latimer got up and sneaked out of the other room. What happened is probably this. Instead of goin' straight through the house—he could see *your* light, Ken, in the kitchen where you were lookin' over that manuscript—he thought he'd escape observation if he went outside and round the house. Well, he'd no sooner got out on the steps than it entered that queer brain of his that he might be funking his duty if he didn't walk straight through the evil influences of the house, and defy them. Yah! So he turns round and goes back through the hall; and he leaves the front door unlatched.

"Now, the probable fact is that Ken didn't hear him when he passed the door of the kitchen going towards the outside. And, no sooner had he got to the door at the rear of the house—the one givin' on the yard—then he saw . . . well, what?

"We'll never know precisely that; the boy's dead, and Glenda never told McDonnell. It's most probable that he saw 'Joseph', in the light of the fire in the window, climbing down from the roof on the window with the gun and silencer in his hand. A silencer, you know, isn't altogether silent; it makes a noise as though you cupped the palms of your hands and brought them together quickly. Now Ted was in a state to see evil spirits; he may even have tried to convince himself that that's what he did see; but it wouldn't quite wash. . . .

"He'd keep quiet, and determine his line. But Glenda saw him in the doorway, and he was marked from that minute. She wasn't sure he'd seen *her*, but it must have been a horrible moment.

"In the interval, what has happened? Masters is coming down from upstairs. When he first went up, the wind had moved the front door, and he had closed it on the latch. Well, down he comes again . . . and sees the front door open as Ted had left it. Son, if he'd gone in the room where 'Joseph' and McDonnell were supposed to have been sitting—well, it would've been all up. But he sees that open door and he charges out like a maniac: to find, of course, no footprints going round the side of the house. He comes round the side of the house as 'Joseph,' the work finished, is returning on the other side. He hears Darworth's moans . . . y'know, I don't really believe Darworth knew his confederate had finished him, even then, or he'd have sung out boldly.

"But young Latimer, standin' in the doorway just outside the house, heard Masters come tearin' round the side of the house; he'd heard those moans of Darworth's also. He still ain't sure what they mean—he still ain't sure of anything. But he hears Masters come chargin' round the side of the house, and he realizes that, if there's really been any dirty work, his position might be embarrassin'. He ducked back to the front room, and arrived not a second before Darworth pulled the bell-cord.

"Meantime, Glenda was back. She'd shoved the gun and silencer under a floorboard that she and Darworth had prepared in that room the night before. And McDonnell's description to me of that woman when she came in and faced him—he was laying out cards in that alleged Rummy game—is fairly revealing. He said she was flushed, and her eyes were shining. She rolled up the sleeve of her coat and (to his own stupefaction) very calmly went about her morphine alibi. 'My dear,' she said to him, 'I believe I've made a mistake. I believe I've really killed the——after all.' And she smiled.

"Do you wonder he was nearly insane when he rushed out? Masters tells me he never saw a man look like McDonnell when he saw him first after that, holdin' a handful of cards like a crazy man.

"I think you know the rest. The doubtful point was: what would Ted say? You know what he did; he kept quiet, and yelled at you that it really was a ghost-murder after all. It had taken possession of him that a fake ghost-murder was better publicity than a common shooting; and he was still puzzled about it anyway, because you all swore Darworth was murdered *with a dagger*. . . . By the way, wasn't that his first question to you? 'With Louis Playge's dagger? With what?' And then he kept quiet until he announced his belief in a supernatural killing.

"The rest of it will always be pure speculation, because the only two people who could tell us how Ted Latimer was lured out to Brixton are both dead. . . . Obviously Glenda had to work very, very rapidly. Ted might change his rather volatile mind at any minute, and decide to talk. One suggestion as to what 'Joseph' had been up to, and Glenda might be done for. If necessary, she was prepared to follow that boy home and close his mouth. So she got Masters to send her home—'Joseph' was very sleepy, much more sleepy than the amount of morphine she'd taken would warrant. But she didn't go home. . . .

"And then she got the brilliant idea of her life. You know what it was. 'Joseph' had planned to disappear; but what if 'Joseph' were supposed to have been murdered? . . . The essential thing was for her to get to Ted *immediately,* and spin some story that would keep his mouth closed until she lured him out to Magnolia Cottage.

"So she waited for him to go home—probably close to Plague Court. The trouble was that, although he was the second witness examined, he refused to go home afterwards; and didn't go until the crowd of them had that row, and broke up.

"But, delayed in that way, Glenda had stayed until the police subordinates themselves had gone; she was working out, even then, the details of that rather neat idea, and, while all you people were engrossed in the kitchen, there was a remarkable opportunity to pinch that dagger. . . .

"Which is why, d'ye see, she lost Ted at the moment; he'd stalked off in a tearin' rage. But, burn me, that woman *would not* be beaten. That's the damnable, amazing thing about her. She relied on her wits and her powers of inventiveness to catch him alone, in his own room—in the house where she'd of course been many times as 'Joseph'—to catch him when his mind was befogged and his reasonin' not up to par—and convince him that he must meet her next day. If she delayed, if he didn't have something to convince him before the very next morning, he might think better of his resolution to keep quiet. Y'see, the police were suspicious of him; and, under press of suspicion, he'd probably have told what he knew when he came to reflect on it."

"And what do you think she did tell him?" inquired Halliday.

"God knows. By the note he left for his sister next morning, saying he was 'investigating', it seems likely that 'Joseph' didn't pretend to him it was a ghost-murder; but said that if he'd come out to Magnolia Cottage he would be furnished with proof. That 'You never suspected it, did you?' seems to indicate, too, that 'Joseph' accused a member of the group; and maintained that he (Joseph) was trying to save Darworth when Ted got that unfortunate look out the back door. After all, when a man's been found stabbed, Joseph mightn't have found it difficult to persuade Ted that Joseph was innocent—because 'he' obviously hadn't been in the room of the stabbing. 'A pistol? What nonsense! Your eyes were deceiving you; I was keeping watch over my patron, who was foully murdered by . . . who?' Lady Benning; I'll lay you a fiver that's the one Glenda picked. 'I was at the window; I saw it done.'

"I say, you get your masculines and feminines considerably tangled in talkin' about Joseph or Glenda; but bear with me, lads. . . .

"What was I sayin'? Oh, yes. Now, obviously, considerable care had to be taken in spiriting away Ted. Because why? Because it must never be known that Ted's disappearance had any connection with Magnolia Cottage. If a suspicious body were found unrecognizably burned in the furnace, and inquiry showed Ted had been messin' about there, people's suspicious minds might say, 'Hey, look here! *Is* that body in the furnace really Joseph's?'

"And there is where my hat remains suspended over my head in admiration of Glenda. She was canny. She didn't rush Ted out to Brixton and kill him then and there. With her knowledge of the Latimer family, she laid a really remarkable false trail. The very subtle and very neat scheme was delicately to hint that Ted had done a bunk for Scotland. He's got a mother up there; a mother not quite right in the head; if the mother says he *didn't* come up there, and that she's *not* shieldin' him, ten to one the police will believe he did and she is. And the purpose? To shift suspicion away from Magnolia Cottage until the body to be found there is accepted as Joseph's; then they can hunt for Ted until they're convinced he's skipped the country—and will believe he's guilty.

"Result—a faked phone-call, not from anywhere near Euston Station—in deliberately vague terms. If the fake Ted said straight out he was going to Edinburgh, it might be discovered too quickly he hadn't; that woman trusted to the way we'd think . . . ayagh, but she did! And the ironical part of the business was that *McDonnell* was taken in by it: he sent a telegram to Ted's mother, and that lady replied to Marion that Ted wasn't there, but she would shield him if he did arrive.

"At five o'clock Glenda, who had been keeping Ted in the background, was ready to go through with the scheme. Mrs. Sweeney was out. . . ."

"By the way," I suggested, "just how does Mrs. Sweeney figure in this business? Did she know what was going on?"

H.M. pinched at his under-lip.

"She'll always say that she didn't. It's like this. She was telling the absolute truth when she said Darworth brought 'Joseph' to her. Mrs. Sweeney is a former medium; Masters has looked her up, and has pretty well decided that Darworth saved her from goin' to prison once, and had a tight hold over her in a good deal the same way as Glenda had over him. He wanted a figurehead for that house in Brixton; between them, he and Joseph scared La Sweeney to death. At first they probably tried to put over on her that 'Joseph' was a boy—but you can't live in a house like that for four years and not get pretty suspicious. She likely became suspicious right off, and Glenda said to her, 'Look here, my friend. You're already mixed up in some very shady business; one word from my friend Roger Darworth, and you'll land in prison. If you should happen to see anything: forget it. Do you understand?' We shan't know the whole truth until Sweeney tells; but, as Glenda's dead now. . . . You see, Darworth wanted somebody always living in that house in Brixton, for a very good reason, and a woman he held and could hold a threat over would make an admirable housekeeper."

"Do you think she knew Glenda had murdered Ted, and substituted the body?"

"I'm damn certain of it! Otherwise she might have been prevailed on to tell us. Don't you remember what she said: 'I'm afraid!' And, son, she was. I shouldn't be at all surprised if it hadn't been good old Glenda's plan to wait for her to return from her day out, after Ted was disposed of, and eliminate Mrs. Sweeney. Fortunately, she was scared off by that workman looking in at the window; and Sweeney didn't get home until past six. . . ."

Big Ben, loud in the silent streets, struck four. H.M. saw that the last of the punch was cold and his pipe had gone out. Disconsolately he shivered a little in the chill room. He got up, lumbered over to the fire, and stared into it.

"I'm tired. Burn me, I could sleep a week. And I think that's all the story. . . . I arranged my little show tonight. A friend of mine I referred to as 'Shrimp', a good little feller who says he's makin' an honest living now, helped me out. He's an arms expert, and light enough to scale that tree at Plague Court. It was all arranged. I'd had him go over the house, and he found Glenda's gun and silencer under the floor-boards in the room she used at Plague Court. We were goin' to use another, a duplicate, if we couldn't find 'em. At shortly after eleven o'clock Masters and his

crowd gravely—without sayin' anything—persuaded Glenda to
go to Plague Court. She couldn't refuse; anyway, she came very
gamely. First they went into the front room and Masters resur-
rected the gun from under the floor. She didn't say anything, and
neither did Masters. They walked just as gravely out to the back
yard. Shrimp took the gun, and, in sight of Glenda, climbed up
on the roof of the stone house. . . .

"I wonder what that woman thought when she saw him firin' those bullets? You know what she did. They were fools not
to search her beforehand. She might 'a' hurt somebody besides
herself."

Stale smoke hung about the lamp. I felt unutterably weary.

"You haven't yet said," Halliday told him harshly, "what you
did about McDonnell. 'His innocence!' Damned rot! I'll bet he
was as guilty as she was. . . . Look here, you didn't let him get
away?"

H.M. stared down into the dying fire. His back jerked a little,
and he blinked round uncomprehendingly.

"Let him—? Son, didn't you know?"

"Know what?"

"No, of course," said H.M. dully. "We didn't stay in that infernal yard—you didn't see. . . .

"Let him get away? Not exactly. I said, 'Son, I'm goin' out of
this room—' this was when we were at his flat. I said, 'You've got a
service revolver, haven't you?' And he said, 'Yes.' And I said, 'Well,
I'm goin' now. If I thought you had a chance to escape hangin', I
shouldn't advise it.' And he said, 'Thank you.'"

"You mean he shot himself?"

"I thought he was goin' to; the way he looked then. . . . I said,
'You couldn't tell a court what you've told me, could you? It would
only look like hidin'.' Well, he saw that.

"But she must have been an amazin' woman, Glenda. What did that young fool do? He joined the party that arrested Glenda, but he couldn't get close enough for a word, Masters tells me. Masters didn't know about him then. We came out with them to Plague Court. *Don't you understand the meanin' of those shots, man?* Shrimp had no sooner done his demonstration, and the crowd of 'em were standin' in the yard, than McDonnell walks out in front of 'em with a gun and says, 'There's a taxi around the corner, Glenda. I've had it waiting. Make a bolt for it. I'll hold these chaps till you can make it.' The God blasted young fool!—his last gesture, y'see, cool as ice, holdin' up the whole crowd. . . ."

"Then those two shots—McDonnell fired——?"

"No, son. Glenda looked at him. She took out her own weapon as she got out from Masters' men. She said, 'Thanks' to Mc-Donnell. Then she fired two bullets into his head just before she ran.

"She died in the right place, son. She and Louis Playge—they both belong there."

THE END

DISCUSSION QUESTIONS

- Were you able to predict any part of the solution to the case?

- After learning the solution, were there any clues you realized you had missed?

- Did any aspects of the plot date the story? If so, which ones?

- Would the story be different if it were set in the present day? If so, how?

- Did the social context of the time play a role in the narrative? If so, how?

- If you were one of the main characters, would you have acted differently at any point in the story?

- Did this novel remind you of any contemporary authors today?

- Did this novel remind you of other titles in the American Mystery Classics series?

- What kind of detective is Sir Henry Merrivale?

- If you've read others of Carr's works, how did this book compare?

AMERICAN MYSTERY CLASSICS

from

*Available now
in hardcover and paperback:*

AMERICAN MYSTERY CLASSICS

from

PENZLER PUBLISHERS

*Available now
in hardcover and paperback:*

And More! Turn the page to learn about some recent releases...

Visit penzlerpublishers.com, email info@penzlerpublishers.com for
more information, or find us on social media at @penzlerpub

John Dickson Carr
The Crooked Hinge

Introduction by Charles Todd

*An inheritance hangs in the balance in a case of
stolen identities, imposters, and murder*

Banished from the idyllic English countryside he once called home, Sir
John Farnleigh, black sheep of the wealthy Farnleigh clan, nearly perished
in the sinking of the Titanic. Though he survived the catastrophe, his ties
with his family did not, and he never returned to England until now, nearly 25 years later, when he comes to claim his inheritance. But another "Sir
John" soon follows, an unexpected man who insists he has absolute proof
of his identity and of his claim to the estate. Before the case can be settled, however, one of the two men is murdered, and Dr. Gideon Fell finds
himself facing one of the most challenging cases of his career. He'll soon
confront a series of bizarre and chilling phenomena, diving deep into the
realm of the occult to solve a seemingly impossible crime.

JOHN DICKSON CARR (1906-1977) was one of the greatest writers of the
American Golden Age mystery, and the only American author to be included in England's legendary Detection Club during his lifetime. Under
his own name and various pseudonyms, he wrote more than seventy novels
and numerous short stories, and is best known today for his locked-room
mysteries.

"An all-time classic by an author scrupulous about playing fair with his readers"
—*Publishers Weekly* (Starred Review)

Paperback, $15.95 / ISBN 978-1-61316-130-2
Hardcover, $25.95 / ISBN 978-1-61316-129-6

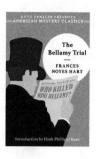

Frances Noyes Hart
The Bellamy Trial

Introduction by
Hank Phillippi Ryan

A murder trial scandalizes the upper echelons of Long Island society, and the reader is on the jury…

The trial of Stephen Bellamy and Susan Ives, accused of murdering Bellamy's wife Madeleine, lasts eight days. That's eight days of witnesses (some reliable, some not), eight days of examination and cross-examination, and eight days of sensational courtroom theatrics lively enough to rouse the judge into frenzied calls for order. Ex-fiancés, houseworkers, and assorted family members are brought to the stand—a cross-section of this wealthy Long Island town—and each one only adds to the mystery of the case in all its sordid detail. A trial that seems straightforward at its outset grows increasingly confounding as it proceeds, and surprises abound; by the time the closing arguments are made, however, the reader, like the jury, is provided with all the evidence needed to pass judgement on the two defendants. Still, only the most astute among them will not be shocked by the verdict announced at the end.

FRANCES NOYES HART (1890-1943) was an American writer whose stories were published in *Scribner's*, *The Saturday Evening Post*, where *The Bellamy Trial* was first serialized, and *The Ladies' Home Journal*.

"An enthralling story."—*New York Times*

Paperback, $15.95 / ISBN 978-1-61316-144-9
Hardcover, $25.95 / ISBN 978-1-61316-143-2

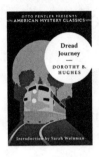

Dorothy B. Hughes
Dread Journey

Introduction by
Sarah Weinman

A movie star fears for her life on a train journey from Los Angeles to New York…

Hollywood big-shot Vivien Spender has waited ages to produce the work that will be his masterpiece: a film adaptation of Thomas Mann's The Magic Mountain. He's spent years grooming young starlets for the lead role, only to discard each one when a newer, fresher face enters his view. Afterwards, these rejected women all immediately fall from grace; excised from the world of pictures, they end up in rehab, or jail, or worse. But Kitten Agnew, the most recent to encounter this impending doom, won't be gotten rid of so easily—her contract simply doesn't allow for it. Accompanied by Mr. Spender on a train journey from Los Angeles to Chicago, she begins to fear that the producer might be considering a deadly alternative. Either way, it's clear that something is going to happen before they reach their destination, and as the train barrels through America's heartland, the tension accelerates towards an inescapable finale.

DOROTHY B. HUGHES (1904–1993) was a mystery author and literary critic famous for her taut thrillers, many of which were made into films. While best known for the noir classic *In a Lonely Place*, Hughes' writing successfully spanned a range of styles including espionage and domestic suspense.

"The perfect in-flight read. The only thing that's dated is the long-distance train."—*Kirkus*

Paperback, $15.95 / ISBN 978-1-61316-146-3
Hardcover, $25.95 / ISBN 978-1-61316-145-6

Ellery Queen
The Siamese Twin Mystery

Introduction by Otto Penzler

Ellery Queen takes refuge from a wildfire at a remote mountain house — and arrives just before the owner is murdered...

When Ellery Queen and his father encounter a raging forest fire during a mountain drive, the only direction to go is up a winding dirt road that leads to an isolated hillside manor, inhabited by a secretive surgeon and his diverse cast of guests. Trapped by the fire, the Queens settle into the uneasy atmosphere of their surroundings. Then, the following morning, the doctor is discovered dead, apparently shot down while playing solitaire the night before.

The only clue is a torn six of spades. The suspects include a society beauty, a suspicious valet, and a pair of conjoined twins. When another murder follows, the killer inside the house becomes as threatening as the mortal flames outside its walls. Can Queen solve this whodunnit before the fire devours its subjects?

ELLERY QUEEN was a pen name created and shared by two cousins, Frederic Dannay (1905-1982) and Manfred B. Lee (1905-1971), as well as the name of their most famous detective.

> "Queen at his best ... a classic of brilliant deduction under extreme circumstances."
> —*Publishers Weekly* (Starred Review)

Paperback, $15.95 / ISBN 978-1-61316-155-5
Hardcover, $25.95 / ISBN 978-1-61316-154-8

Patrick Quentin
A Puzzle for Fools

Introduction by Otto Penzler

A wave of murders rocks an asylum—and it's up to the patients to stop them

Broadway producer Peter Duluth sought solace in a bottle after his wife's death; now, two years later and desperate to dry out, he enters a sanitarium, hoping to break his dependence on drink—but the institution doesn't quite offer the rest and relaxation he expected. Strange, malevolent occurrences plague the hospital; and among other inexplicable events, Peter hears his own voice with an ominous warning: "There will be murder." It soon becomes clear that a homicidal maniac is on the loose, and, with a staff every bit as erratic as its idiosyncratic patients, it seems everyone is a suspect—even Duluth's new romantic interest, Iris Pattison. Charged by the baffled head of the ward with solving the crimes, it's up to Peter to clear her name before the killer strikes again.

PATRICK QUENTIN is one of the pseudonyms of Hugh Callingham Wheeler (1912-1987), who collaborated with several other authors on the books written as by Q. Patrick and Jonathan Stagge. Wheeler was born in London but moved to the United States in 1934 and became a U.S. citizen, as did one of his writing partners, Richard Wilson Webb; he also collaborated with Martha (Patsy) Mott Kelly.

"Another absolute gem unearthed by Otto Penzler
and included in his American Mystery
Classics series. . . . What a find!"
—*Booklist* (Starred Review)

Paperback, $15.95 / ISBN 978-1-61316-125-8
Hardcover, $25.95 / ISBN 978-1-61316-124-1

Clayton Rawson
Death from a Top Hat

Introduction by Otto Penzler

*A detective steeped in the art of magic solves the
mystifying murder of two occultists.*

Now retired from the tour circuit on which he made his name, master
magician The Great Merlini spends his days running a magic shop in
New York's Times Square and his nights moonlighting as a consultant
for the NYPD. The cops call him when faced with crimes so impossible that they can only be comprehended by a magician's mind.

In the most recent case, two occultists are discovered dead in locked
rooms, one spread out on a pentagram, both appearing to have been
murdered under similar circumstances. The list of suspects includes an
escape artist, a professional medium, and a ventriloquist, so it's clear
that the crimes took place in a realm that Merlini knows well. But
in the end it will take his logical skills, and not his magical ones, to
apprehend the killer.

CLAYTON RAWSON (1906–1971) was a novelist, editor, and magician. He
is best known for creating the Great Merlini, an illusionist and amateur
sleuth introduced in *Death from a Top Hat* (1938).

> "One of the all-time greatest
> impossible murder mysteries."
> —*Publishers Weekly* (Starred Review)

Paperback, $15.95 / ISBN 978-1-61316-101-2
Hardcover, $25.95 / ISBN 978-1-61316-109-8